TAKING DETECTIVE STORIE

TAKING DETECTIVE STORIES SERIOUSLY

The Collected Crime Reviews of
DOROTHY L. SAYERS

Foreword by
Simon Brett, OBE

Edited, with an Introduction and Commentary, by
Martin Edwards

TIPPERMUIR
· BOOKS LIMITED ·

TAKING DETECTIVE STORIES SERIOUSLY:
THE COLLECTED CRIME REVIEWS OF DOROTHY L. SAYERS
by Dorothy L. Sayers
Copyright © 2017. All rights reserved.
The right of Dorothy L. Sayers to be identified as the author of the Work has been
asserted by her in accordance with the Copyright, Designs and Patents Act 1988.

This printed edition published and copyright 2017 by
Tippermuir Books Ltd, Perth, Scotland.
tippermuirbooks@blueyonder.co.uk
with permission of David Higham Associates Ltd
(representing the Dorothy L. Sayers Estate).

Foreword by Simon Brett, Copyright © 2017. All rights reserved.
Introduction and Commentary by Martin Edwards, Copyright © 2017. All rights reserved.
The rights of Simon Brett to be identified as the author of the Foreword and
Martin Edwards to be identified as the author of the Introduction and Commentary
have been asserted by them in accordance with the Copyright, Designs and Patents Act 1988.

ISBN 978-0-9563374-9-8
A CIP catalogue record for this book is available from the British Library.

Text styling and artwork by Bernard Chandler, Glastonbury, England.
www.graffik.co.uk
Text set in 10^1/$_2$ pt Times with Gill Sans titling.

Cover design by Roben Antoniewicz.
Production support by Ajay Close and Rob Hands.
Project coordination by Dr Paul S. Philippou.

Printed and bound in Great Britain by CPI Group (UK) Ltd, Croydon CR0 4YY

CONTENTS

FOR

JILL PATON WALSH, CBE

President,
Dorothy L. Sayers Society

ACKNOWLEDGEMENTS

I should like to add my thanks to those expressed by Martin Edwards to the members of the committee who have helped to support this endeavour and to express my admiration as well as thanks to Sarah MacIntosh for her unfailingly accurate work in transcribing the reviews.

The Society owes a real debt of gratitude to Martin Edwards for his dedicated commitment to this project through the Introduction and Commentary which accompany the reviews. We hope this book will bring the reviews to the attention of a much wider audience, particularly those with a real interest in the "Golden Age" of crime fiction.

Lastly thanks to Paul Philippou at Tippermuir Books: it is a real pleasure to work with Paul, who is a person of high standards and enthusiasm, a splendid combination.

SEONA FORD
Chair, Dorothy L. Sayers Society

FOREWORD

by Simon Brett

I OWE A CONSIDERABLE professional debt to Dorothy L. Sayers, because it was her books that got me into the business of crime writing. In the 1970s, as a young BBC radio producer, I was given the task of developing a series of adaptations of the Lord Peter Wimsey books. Ian Carmichael had made a success of the character on television and there was a desire for him to reprise the role on radio.

At that time, I was the author of four very properly unpublished novels, but I'd never tried my hand at crime fiction. I enjoyed reading it, but was rather frightened by the idea of actually writing the stuff. I didn't think I had the kind of brain that could work out devious plots. However, working closely with Chris Miller, the writer who was adapting the Wimsey books, I found that, though Sayers' plots were skilful and intricate, they were only one element in the success of her books. Character and dialogue were at least as important. Encouraged by this discovery, I had a go at writing a crime novel of my own. It became *Cast, in Order of Disappearance*, the first in a series about the actor detective Charles Paris and my first published book.

My admiration for Dorothy L. Sayers grew when I became President of the Detection Club, a role I held from 2001 to 2015, and discovered what a large part she had played in the setting up of that estimable organisation. I also appreciated her organizational input into the Detection Club's first collaborative novel, *The Floating Admiral* – particularly when I took over the editing, eighty-five years on, of its sequel, *The Sinking Admiral*.

Dorothy L. Sayers was not only an expert practitioner of crime writing, she was also a witty and astute commentator on the developing genre. I am therefore delighted that her book reviews are once again available to be read in this splendid volume.

SIMON BRETT, OBE

1

INTRODUCTION

by Martin Edwards

DOROTHY L. SAYERS carved for herself an enviable reputation in three distinct fields: as a translator of Dante, as a writer on religious subjects, and above all, as a detective novelist. Beyond that, she wrote with insight about real life crimes, was a pioneering historian and anthologist of crime fiction, and established herself as the most incisive reviewer of detective novels at the height of the genre's "Golden Age".

Sayers reviewed detective fiction for the *Sunday Times* for just over two years. Her reviews demonstrate a remarkable breadth of reading, and an extraordinary capacity for hard work, but more than that they display flair and forthright, sometimes controversial, views about crime writing, and a good deal else. Throughout that period, she explored the work of others in some detail, whilst at the same time reaching fresh heights in her own literary career.

Taken together, Sayers' reviews provide fascinating insight into her attitudes and opinions; some remain highly pertinent, others have failed the test the time, but all of them cast light on a remarkable woman. The reviews are also historically important, painting a vivid picture of the evolving nature of detective fiction in the Thirties. Although Sayers felt under acute pressure to earn money from her writing, she took great care over her work, and it is significant that, compared to some of the mass producers whom she discussed, she published only a dozen novels. The time and trouble she devoted to writing her reviews means that they provide entertaining reading to this day, even though many of the authors and books she discussed are now long forgotten.

Sayers' detective stories remain popular, and the Dorothy L. Sayers Society, formed almost twenty years after her death, is flourishing. The Society's many achievements include making available a number of Sayers' publications. Most notable of these is *Les Origines du Roman Policier*, the text of a talk intended to strengthen Anglo-French relations at the start of the Second World War, and discussing the key Victorian crime writers: Poe, Gaboriau, Collins, and Conan Doyle.

The Society holds over 1,200 Sayers-related items, including copies of her reviews. Until now, however, the reviews have not been readily accessible by detective fiction enthusiasts and scholars, and although quotes from them surface on copies of reissued Golden Age novels from time to time, they have not been extensively discussed. The only detailed articles about them with which I am familiar are "Reviewing the Reviewer: Dorothy L. Sayers as crime critic, 1933-5" by Mike Ripley, himself a crime writer and reviewer, and the lengthier "Dorothy L. Sayers: Critic of Detective Fiction" by Ralph E. Hone, one of Sayers' biographers.

The reviews deserve to be better known. They cast light not only on Sayers' likes and dislikes as regards crime fiction and English prose writing, but also on her unforgettable personality. More than that, they tell us a great deal about Golden Age crime fiction, and its remarkable evolution during the time Sayers was writing. Today some of these books, and their authors, are forgotten. Despite a lifelong hunt for obscure Golden Age novels, I have failed to uncover the novels of Kaye Sunderland and Hilda Willett, and A. B. Leonard and Sherry King, never mind such titles as *The Flaming Hut Murder*, *Ebenezer Investigates*, and *The Eel-Pie Mystery*. My search continues but, given Sayers' acerbic comments on some particularly inferior books, readers will not be tempted to track them down. However, the praise she heaps on rare novels such as E. C. R. Lorac's *The Organ Speaks* and Catherine Meadows' *Henbane* (neither of which were available for sale on the internet anywhere in the world at the time of writing) will make many readers determined to get hold of them.

The Society felt, as I did, that it was high time that the reviews were gathered together, and made available to readers interested in Sayers, or the Golden Age, or both. In addition to the reviews of novels, we have included a handful of reviews of non-fiction books originally published at various times. The Sayers estate kindly granted their permission for the reviews to be published, and this book is the result. My brief, as a present-day crime novelist and author of *The Golden Age of Murder*, in which Sayers features prominently, was to set the reviews in context, and add a commentary.

Reading these reviews gave me enormous pleasure and deepened my understanding of both Sayers and the Golden Age. My admiration for Sayers was enhanced, not least because of her belief that popular fiction can achieve high literary standards, although occasionally I found myself questioning her judgments, and, even when she made a good case, wincing at her blunt and self-confident certainties. Her robust personality shines through her reviews; although essentially good-natured, she did not pull her punches, and she was unafraid to criticise books written by her friends. One may agree or disagree with her on a host of topics, but her intelligence and articulacy command respect, even when she is at her most provocative.

Above all, I found it fascinating to learn about those books Sayers admired. I dare to hope that the appearance of this book makes it more likely that some of these hidden gems will soon see the light of day again. Happily, the last few years have seen seismic changes in publishing, as technological developments have made small print runs feasible, print-on-demand editions readily available, and ebooks ubiquitous. As a result, many Golden Age novels that have long been highly sought-after but only obtainable by purchasers with deep pockets have now become easy to find. The remarkable success of the British Library's Crime Classics series has also proved that there is an eager and extensive readership for conventionally published Golden Age fiction, if it is attractively presented and not unduly expensive.

In the weeks leading up to Christmas 2014, the British Library's new edition of J. Jefferson Farjeon's *Mystery in White* hit the headlines as an unexpected "runaway bestseller" in the UK, topping the fiction list of the national book chain Waterstones. Its massive sales startled almost everyone – but perhaps they would not have come as such a surprise to Sayers, or anyone familiar with her reviews. In a discussion of *Sinister Inn*, she pronounced that "Mr. Farjeon is quite unsurpassed for creepy skill in mysterious adventures, and he can be glamorous, and even sentimental, without being mawkish – a rare gift."

This collection of reviews would not have been possible without the support and efforts of a good many people, above all Seona Ford, chair of the Dorothy L. Sayers Society, her colleagues on the committee, and Sarah MacIntosh, a member of the Society, whose hard work in transcribing the reviews into a publishable form, and preparing an index, was utterly indispensable. The Sayers estate and their agent, Georgia Glover, also deserve warm thanks for their support of this venture. I am truly grateful to have had the opportunity to become involved with a project that has proved as enjoyable as it is, I believe, worthwhile.

MARTIN EDWARDS

* * *

COMMENTARY

by Martin Edwards

The background

Dorothy L. Sayers began reviewing for the *Sunday Times* in June 1933, the month in which she reached the age of forty. Her creative energies were reaching a peak, and she had at last achieved public recognition of her literary gifts on a scale of which she could scarcely have dreamed a decade earlier, when *Whose Body?*, her first novel, was published.

Her friend and biographer Barbara Reynolds made the point that her "output since 1931 (to go no further back) had been amazing". She had published two highly successful novels, *Have His Carcase* and *Murder Must Advertise*, and a collection of short stories, *Hangman's Holiday*; compiled and introduced an anthology of crime and horror short stories; and made a major contribution to two round-robin detective novels produced by members of the Detection Club, *The Floating Admiral* and *Ask a Policeman*. The "Golden Age of detective fiction" was nearing its high point, even though that term had yet to be coined.

The Detection Club played a significant part in her life. Founded by Anthony Berkeley Cox, who wrote detective stories as Anthony Berkeley, and novels exploring criminal psychology as Francis Iles, the Club came into existence in 1930, although formal rules and a constitution were not adopted until 1932. Sayers was a founder member, and quickly became, with Berkeley, a leading light in the Club. G. K. Chesterton was the first President, and Sayers would become the third President in 1949, succeeding her friend and Chesterton's, E. C. Bentley, author of the hugely influential *Trent's Last Case* (1913).

The Rules of the Detection Club made clear that it was established "for the association of writers of detective novels and for promoting and continuing a mutual fellowship between them." The suitability of each candidate for membership was to be "fully and carefully examined" to make sure that he or she had written "at least two detective novels of admitted merit or (in exceptional cases) one such novel; it being understood that the term 'detective novel' does not include adventure stories or 'thrillers' or stories in which the detection is not the main interest, and that it is a demerit in a detective novel if the author does not 'play fair' with the reader." Key elements of these stern criteria resonate in Sayers' critical judgments for the *Sunday Times*.

She enjoyed thrillers, and she was well aware that the difference between a detective novel and a thriller was: "mainly one of emphasis. Agitating events occur in both, but in the thriller our cry is 'What comes next?' – in the detective story, 'What came first?' The one we cannot guess; the other we can, if the author gives us a chance."

The trouble was that many thrillers were shoddily written: "People sometimes complain that I am harsh and high-hat about thrillers… I give you my word that when I meet the least touch of real originality, or creepy-crawlery, or glamour, or humour, or sheer rollicking cut-and-thrust-and-have-at-'em combativeness in a thriller I hail it with cries of joy. But 99 times out of 100 I find only bad English, cliché, balderdash, and boredom."

These remarks in August 1934 preceded reviews of four thrillers. She appreciated Harry Stephen Keeler's *The Travelling Skull*, despite its preposterous nature, but the other three gave her "nothing but a pain in the neck, though it is only fair to say that they are no worse than many others and better than some." In stark contrast, she was impressed by *Wax*, written by Britain's leading exponent of "woman in jeopardy" novels, Ethel Lina White: "it is the quality that decides, for me, whether a thriller is to be kept upon the bookshelf or cast out when I have finished with it for the purposes of this column. The terror and pity are genuinely human and not mechanical. In short, this is a good novel on a thriller theme."

Golden Age detective stories characteristically gave rise to a game played between author and reader. The challenge, sometimes explicitly stated, was to solve the mystery with the benefit of the clues supplied before all was revealed by the detective. Playing the game entailed playing fairly, by honouring the rules of the game. Towards the end of the Twenties, Ronald Knox came up with a 'Decalogue', ten commandments for detective story writers, some tongue-in-cheek ("No Chinaman may figure in the story"), some quite sensible ("No hitherto undiscovered poisons should be used, nor any appliance which needs a long scientific explanation at the end.") These 'commandments' were regularly broken, sometimes mocked, and frequently misunderstood, but playing the detective amused countless readers during years of economic misery and political uncertainty. Sayers entered wholeheartedly into the game-playing spirit of the time, and in her very first reviews, which included an assessment of Knox's *The Body in the Silo*, she included a jokey reference to the Decalogue.

Yet she was acutely conscious of the limitations of any form of literature that aspires to be no more than a game. As time passed, and her confidence – and that of her contemporaries – grew, so did her ambitions for the genre. Her long essay introducing the first volume of *Great Short Stories of Detection, Mystery and Horror* in 1928 frowned on "love interest" in detective fiction, but she soon changed her mind. Lord Peter Wimsey fell for Harriet Vane in *Strong Poison* (1930) and, seven years later, the sub-title of *Busman's Honeymoon*, "a love story with detective interruptions", showed how far she had travelled as an author.

The Documents in the Case was also published in 1930, and appeared under Sayers' name along with that of her scientific collaborator Robert Eustace. The book was an experiment in marrying a storyline involving a mystery with a serious narrative theme and despite its flaws, it remains an intriguing and underestimated example of the epistolary novel. In *The Nine Tailors* and *Gaudy Night*, she came closer than in any of her other books, and closer than any of her British crime-writing contemporaries, to writing a detective novel of manners. And in her reviews she keeps returning to the question of the future of the detective story, a subject which preoccupied both her and Anthony Berkeley.

––––––––––

Sayers' approach to reviewing

Sayers' reviews offer a multitude of pleasures – they are well-written, detailed, and thought-provoking. They are also witty. From time to time she indulges in unsubtle puns ("*Week-end Murder* is a murder with a weak end") but her writing brims with exuberant humour, even (especially) when she is making a serious point: "What in the name of Chaos and

Old Night possessed Mr. Vivian to call his humorous, well-written, well-characterised and altogether delightful and sensible story by such a slip-slop, sob-stuff, rotten-ripe, rat-riddled title as *Girl in the Dark*?"

Warming to this theme, she insisted that: "There should also be a prohibitive tax on such titles as 'The Murder at — ,' 'The — Affair, Case or Crime,' 'The Body, or Corpse, in the — ,' and 'The Mystery of the —'. Publishers often imagine that the words case, mystery, corpse, death, murder, and so forth are needed in the title, to inform the public that the book really is a crime story and not a tale of passion or an analytical study of neurotic psychology – but the public is not really so stupid as all that."

From the very start of her reviewing career, Sayers' waspish way with words is in evidence, as is her desire to blend demanding standards with an innate kindness that is sometimes obscured by the forthright nature of her judgments. Reviewing *Inquest* by Henrietta Clandon, she says: "I find it a little hard to believe that even a French country doctor would have been quite so stupid about the company director's death as Miss Clandon makes out. But if we overlook a little clumsiness here and elsewhere, and a certain dampness about the denouement... this is an attractive and promising piece of puzzle-making. The book is very well written, the dialogue being quite exceptionally fresh and well-managed, and the characterisation good. This appears to be Miss Henrietta Clandon's first detective story; I hope we shall soon hear from her again."

In fact, the Clandon pseudonym concealed the identity of Belfast-born John George Hazlett Vahey, who had already published a string of novels under an assortment of names: John Haslette, Anthony Lang, John Mowbray, Walter Proudfoot, John Varney, and (most notably) Vernon Loder. According to one biographical note, "He once wrote a novel in twenty days on a boarding-house table, and had it serialised in U. S. A. and England under another name... He works very quickly and thinks two hours a day in the morning quite enough for anyone. He composes direct on a machine and does not re-write."

Had Sayers known this, it is unlikely that she would have been impressed. She was convinced that over-productivity tended to result in weaker books, or at least in carelessness, even in the case of an author whom she rated highly: "a stray slip or two may be due to the fact that this book has followed rather hard upon the heels of Mr. Punshon's last."

Sayers was no stranger to financial hardship, and her work ethic was unwavering, but she had the wisdom to recognise the risks of writing too much fiction too quickly: "There are many reasons which may prompt an author to produce books at this rate, ranging from hyper-activity of the thyroid to the grim menace of rates and taxes. The greatest genius is usually attended by a considerable fertility, but, as a rule, it is too much to expect a fresh masterpiece every four months. With the detective story the temptation to over-production is especially dangerous: first, because it is only too easy to shake up the old pieces of the kaleidoscope into what looks something like a new plot, and, secondly, because the public (and this means You!) is still too indulgent to hasty and mechanical writing where mysteries are concerned."

Sayers took too much care over her work for there to be any danger that her fiction would become repetitive or stale. While some of her peers (including her friends Anthony Gilbert, John Rhode, and John Dickson Carr) needed to adopt pseudonyms simply to avoid flooding the market with books under a single name, Sayers published a mere seven full-length novels during the 1930s, and one of those, *Busman's Honeymoon*, was based on a play that she had written in collaboration.

The most significant point about her review of *Inquest*, however, is that if she had contented herself with the easy option of praising an apparent newcomer, readers would not have benefited from learning of her reservations. Sayers' reviews, even of crime novels written by good friends, were sometimes much more severe than is fashionable nowadays. She consistently showed a readiness to praise unknown writers, when their work merited it, and a robust determination to criticise leading lights whose books, in her judgment, fell below standard.

The prolific, veteran writer J. S. Fletcher, for instance, had enjoyed much success in the years since his *The Middle Temple Murder* was praised by an American President, but Sayers was never one to bow and scrape: "Mr. Fletcher can write very well when he likes, but this reads rather like dull parody." Turning to a novel written by a much less renowned author, *A Killer and His Star*, she says that it concerns "a singularly clumsy and uninteresting murder". As for the man responsible, the wretched H. M. Stephenson, he "has brought platitudinous dullness to the pitch of a fine art. Light dies before his uncreating word."

This determination to make exacting judgments lifts her critical commentaries out of the ruck, and makes them valuable to readers confronted with too many books and too little time in which to read them all. Of course, it is possible to go too far in this direction. Julian Symons, a crime novelist of a later generation was a successor to Sayers in several respects: as President of the Detection Club, as crime critic of *The Sunday Times*, and as the most brilliant and perceptive reviewer of his generation. Yet his views were sometimes so acerbic that they caused deep distress to his colleagues, notably John Creasey (who at one time argued that Symons should be drummed out of the Crime Writers' Association for his unhelpfulness towards fellow writers) and a gifted writer of whodunits in the Golden Age manner, Christianna Brand.

Sayers was acutely aware of the difficulty of combining the roles of author and reviewer: "It is sometimes reasonably argued that no novelist ought also to be a reviewer, because of the difficulty of discounting personal prejudice." This argument has as much force today as ever, and there are plenty of examples of critics with axes to grind and scores to settle. The challenge for the reviewer and commentator, I suggest, is to blend honesty, intellectual rigour and generosity with an attempt to understand the writer's aims and intention.

On the whole, Sayers avoids the traps that abound for the unwary critic, but she revelled in being a woman of strong opinions – so much so that, in 1947, she published a book of twenty-one essays provocatively titled *Unpopular Opinions*. A desire for intellectual rigour and candour is all very well, but the wise critic remembers that his or her judgments, however intelligently conceived and expressed, remain no more than subjective opinions. It is also surely appropriate to keep in mind the maxim "Do unto others as you would have them do unto you."

Sayers liked to give the appearance of indifference to what others thought of her – it was part of a carefully-constructed, protective facade – but on occasion she felt bruised when people whose good opinion she valued expressed criticism of her own fiction. There must have been occasions when her refusal to pull her punches offended not only those thriller writers whom she was unlikely to encounter in person because she and Berkeley insisted upon their exclusion from eligibility to join the Detection Club, but her friends and colleagues in the Detection Club too. Yet there is no malice in her rebukes (or at least, not as far as I can tell) and for anyone not on the receiving end, her jibes are usually entertaining as well as incisive. An example is her remark about her friend Henry Wade's *Mist on the Saltings*: "when it comes to depicting sexual passion, he plans a seduction like Napoleon – and executes it like the famous Duke of York."

A long-forgotten book called *Death in Darkness* exemplified the sort of writing that earned her disfavour: "Mr Charles Barry continually disappoints me. He is fertile in ingenious ideas, but his villain will always take such shocking risks... Also, Mr Barry is rather secretive about his clues. And he writes horrid slipshod English. It is a pity, because he has bits so good that I feel he could do better if he liked." After taking such a pummelling, it is scant consolation for the wretched author that Sayers concludes with the faintest of praise: "you might choose worse than this for a railway journey."

Sayers' remarks about *Crime de Luxe* in her very first column hint at a theme to which she will return many times in the reviews: "The line between the detective story and the thriller." She acknowledges that this line "is sometimes rather fine-drawn", but although the author Elizabeth Gill crosses it, she "writes far better and with much more humour than the average thrill-merchant". Many other thriller writers suffer a mauling in later reviews, above all because of the poor quality of their writing.

Of Ronald Knox's *The Body in the Silo*, Sayers says in the same column: "I hope Father Knox has satisfied himself that his murder-method is physically possible, for some of the details are rather staggering." This gentle rap on the knuckles supplies the first clue that Sayers will not show undue favour to colleagues in the Detection Club, even though the Club's members regarded themselves as members of a crime-writing elite.

As well as teasing Henry Wade, she attacked the tendency of friends such as Milward Kennedy and Anthony Berkeley to focus on the portrayal of "hateful" characters. And she flayed several books written by the husband-and-wife team of G. D. H. and Margaret Cole, prominent socialists whose work in the genre was once well-regarded. She had no time for their *The Affair at Aliquid*, saying: "The mirth is coarse and common-place, the satire clumsy and brutal."

Turning to *Big Business Murder*, she compared the Coles' under-standing of the working classes unfavourably with Agatha Christie's: "Take the servile subordinate who 'plucks up his courage' to say how-do-you-do to his lordship... 'What I've always 'ad is a great respect for the nobility, my mother 'avin' been her ladyship's personal maid.' That is how the conscientious Socialist thinks the 'servant class' ought to talk. But Mrs. Christie knows how they do talk... 'And I was so surprised, sir, at the master speaking like that – quite unlike his usual self – that I didn't know what to say.' There speaks the true voice of the domestic critic, scandalised by the taking of unseemly liberties."

Christie's *Three-Act Tragedy* boasted "an excellent plot, a clever mystery, and an exciting story", but those were not the only respects in which she out-did the Coles: "her chief strength lies in this power to compel belief in her characters. In the lack of this power we find the chief weakness of Mr. and Mrs. Cole." Again, it is hard to think of a much more scathing criticism, but Sayers had a point. What is more, the snippet of dialogue that she quotes also serves as an important, yet subtly concealed, clue to the murder plot. The Coles were no match for Christie as detective novelists, and the adverse comparison was all the more wounding because it was justified.

Even when Sayers enjoyed one of the Coles' books, such as their *Death in the Quarry*, there was a sting in the tail, as she added: "It is free from those errors of taste which sometimes mar their work, and the social problems involved are handled with better tact and truth." It is to the Coles' credit that, as far as I know, they did not harbour a grudge against her because of her biting criticism of their work. This may, however, have been because they cared much less about their detective fiction than their work in the field of politics and economics. Sayers, in contrast, was incapable of not caring about what she wrote, and this helps to explain why her fiction deserved, and achieved longevity, while the Coles' did not.

Such candour must have meant that Detection Club dinners were lively affairs, but I have found no evidence that any relationships between members were seriously damaged by frankness in reviewing; Sayers and her contemporaries were, after all, a generation of survivors, men and women who had come through the war in one piece, if not necessarily unscathed. And Sayers was neither as blunt nor as abrasive as Berkeley, another prolific reviewer, who was far from wholly admiring of (for example) *Gaudy Night*. Perhaps tensions were lessened by the fact that many of the Club's members – certainly including the Coles – regarded their detective fiction as insignificant compared to their more 'serious' writing. Ironically, in the case of the majority of the Club's members, including Sayers, it is their detective fiction for which they are today best remembered.

An eye for accuracy

Sayers set out her credo in her column of 23 December 1934: "Each story has an author, and each author had an aim in writing it. I believe it to be the critic's function to discover that aim and then, and then only, to pronounce whether the aim has been well or ill achieved. But if the aim is trivial, as in the 'pure thriller' it must be, what can one say about it? One can only say: 'This book is a thriller; it is well-written and exciting,or ill-written but exciting, or ill-written and dull,' as the case may be."

Her exasperation with ill-written thrillers is frequently evident, but she was aware of the limitations of subjectivity: "In this column I can only express my personal reactions (blessed word!) to a book, and, frankly, I found Mr. Philmore a little dull. But I am told that a number of people with excellent literary judgment found the book so enthralling that they could not lay it down." It may well be that one of those people was Victor Gollancz, who published Sayers as well as Philmore.

Two linked and recurrent themes in the reviews are the importance of accuracy in matters of detail and the need for authors to write in "good English". Carelessness on the novelist's part lessens the reader's enjoyment, so credibility matters. Thus Sayers says of David Sharp's indifferent *Marriage and Murder*: "The author's pet affectation of writing the word 'hotel' with a circumflex accent should not be intruded into the detective-inspector's notes – nobody is going to believe *that*! A small point, but destructive of probability."

15

Some mistakes are more important than others, but the reviews reveal Sayers' sharp eye for minutiae. Thus she notes of A. B. Leonard's *The Judson Murder Case*: "the nomenclature in the map, by the way, does not agree at every point with the text, which is a little confusing." Even a classic of the genre, which she much admired, does not entirely escape censure. After heaping praise on Agatha Christie's *Murder on the Orient Express*, she adds: "I have only one slight quarrel with his [Poirot's] reasoning: the presence of a pipe-cleaner does not necessarily involve that of a pipe-smoker; I keep a bundle of them myself for my cigarette-holder."

Factual errors in a detective novel can be more damaging than in some other forms of fiction because so much detective work depends on the precise analysis of evidence, and so many plots hinge on questions of detail. Of William C. Harvey's *Death's Treasure Hunt*, she comments: "the word 'nephew' in a will, by the way, would not include a nephew of illegitimate birth." Incidents depending on split-second timing require special care. Although she enjoyed *Death at Broadcasting House* by Val Gielgud and Holt Marvell (the latter name concealed the identity of BBC producer and occasional songwriter Eric Maschwitz), she had one reservation: "it could hardly have taken a person 45 seconds to cross a passage and enter a room (a second is a much longer interval than one thinks, and in 45 seconds I can walk down 20 stairs, out through the back door, shutting it after me, and half-way down the garden.)" One does not doubt that she timed herself with scrupulous accuracy before writing that.

Again, in her critique of Roger East's *Candidate for Lilies*, she comments: "You cannot... obtain from Somerset House information about the testamentary intentions of living persons, and I think Mr. East has confused two allied species of poisonous plant." Yet Sayers readily concedes that these particular points are "trifles" which do not spoil the story, and on occasion she displayed a surprising tolerance. Of *Family Matters* by Anthony Rolls (C. E. Vulliamy) she said: "I have no idea whether the medical details about aluminium poisoning are correct, but I am quite ready to accept anything that is told me by so convincing an author."

The difficulty with being a know-all is that nobody can know everything. Every writer makes mistakes, and Sayers was honest enough to admit that she was no exception: "I, personally, have just been sternly upbraided by a Procurator-Fiscal (no less!), because I ought to have known that in bonny Scotland it is no criminal offence at all to assist a murderer to dispose of the corpse provided one was not previously privy to the killing. *Mea culpa!* It had never occurred to me that any country could provide such facilities for murderers. But I ought to have looked it up."

Good English

The errors in Theodore Hyde's *After the Execution* dismayed Sayers, but she emphasised that "the book's inexcusable fault is nearly 300 pages of excessively dull, bad writing – the one sin which can and should never find forgiveness." For Sayers, "while it is true that the standard of detective fiction has improved greatly of late years, I am still appalled by the amount of sloppy, slovenly, shiftless writing. Mystery stories are not of such great rarity as to excuse readers for snatching, like famished men, at any ill-concocted mess that offers to satisfy their thwarted appetite for blood. Far from it. There is plenty of choice, and they ought to be sufficiently fastidious to reject rank false concord and bad syntax."

Thrillers often roused her ire. *The Ince Murder Case*, by E. J. Pond, for instance, was "written entirely in clichés. Even the most penetrating detective work, even the most agonising excitement (if it had them) could not carry such a load of battered coinage." T. C. H. Jacobs' *Sinister Quest* fared no better: "Plenty of thrills and assaults, you see; plenty of clichés; a fair amount of bosh. Also a mass-murderer, known to Scotland Yard as 'the Ear Hound' from his amiable way with his victims (if you have ears, prepare to shed them now!). Also, wicked Chinamen. And all that."

Traditional detective stories which were poorly written came in for similar punishment. Thus she mocked the slapdash prose of A. Fielding's *The Paper Chase*: "This sentence defeats me altogether. If I tried with both hands for a fortnight I could make nothing of it. And I say it is a shame that any writer should so mishandle the richest, most flexible, most highly civilised language in Christendom."

She was equally severe on Brian Flynn, author of *The Case of the Purple Calf*: "at the close of a stirring tale about inexplicable motor accidents, [he] introduces us to a horrid apparatus of torture and death.

There was no need for him to inflict on us the additional torture of an exasperating style. He wallows in polysyllables, used either absurdly... or with a dreadful facetiousness."

This exasperation with poor writing led Sayers to feature "The Week's Worst English" in her column of 3 February 1935, and this became a regular feature, with one digression into "The Week's Worst Latin". At least when Sayers did lapse into pedantry about grammar she usually managed to do so with a light touch: "The writing is free from the hysteria to which the 'highbrow' American mystery writers so easily fall victims, and, except for an occasional split infinitive and maltreated gerund, is reasonably correct. (I have almost given up hope of rescue for the gerund, poor thing!)"

The best crime writers, however, did more than merely write in "good English" – in her view, they wrote in a style with a marked individuality. On 12 September 1933, she set a little test for readers of her column, inviting them to identify the authors of six short passages, "picked out almost at random. They are not star passages in any way. The only interesting quality that they have in common is individuality. Each is characteristic of its author, and could not possibly have been written by anybody else." The next week, she supplied the answers: the quotations came from Poe, Conan Doyle, Wilkie Collins, Austin Freeman, H. C. Bailey, and G. K. Chesterton. She would, no doubt, be shocked by how far Bailey's reputation has fallen since then – perhaps he is due for a revival.

Fair play

The requirement to "play fair" with the reader presents tricky problems for an author who wants to come up with a surprise solution at the end of the book. A central dilemma, Sayers argues, is: "at what point must we release our vital clue so as to be fair to the reader without exploding the secret prematurely?" She felt that in *The Crossword Mystery*, E. R. Punshon erred a little on the side of generosity, but she was a Punshon fan, and readily forgave him.

Another challenge for the author is how to distract readers from asking themselves that fatal question: "'If this character is not here for the purpose of committing the crime, why is it here at all?' To prevent the reader – and to prevent him by fair means – from ever asking that question is one of the mystery-monger's most exacting technical jobs." Freeman Wills Crofts fell into this trap in *Crime at Guildford*: "It was the secret of the murder that I penetrated out of due time... That Mr. Crofts has in this book failed to stall off the question is the one blot upon a story which is in other respects an excellent piece of construction."

In common with many detective fiction aficionados, Sayers took a masochistic pleasure in having the wool pulled over her eyes, provided the author had not cheated her: "Mr. John Rhode is one of those kind, thoughtful writers who patiently explain all the technical points of the narrative in words that a child could understand... That is why I am so indignant at the perfectly heartless manner in which he led my innocence up the garden path to be *Shot At Dawn*. Fair? Yes, of course it was perfectly fair: that is what makes it so galling. If I had had the gumption of a weevil in a biscuit, I should never have allowed myself – But there!"

The Man in Button Boots, by Anthony Gilbert, likewise boasted "double-crossing ingenuity... It is so immensely complicated that at the end we feel obliged to go back and check up on it to see whether all the complication is really necessary. But it is; and the author is to be congratulated on giving an original and baffling twist to a story which, in its bare outlines, is fairly familiar."

Conversely, she felt disappointed when a talented writer failed to hoodwink her. From the start of Anthony Rolls' *Scarweather* "I knew perfectly well... where the missing man had gone to and who put him there, even if the publisher had not saved me the trouble of guessing by blowing the gaff in a helpful picture on the jacket. Mr. Rolls can write... but the keeping of a secret is not his strong point."

Despite her genuine admiration for Arthur Conan Doyle, and her love of Sherlock Holmes, Sayers regretted the failure of the Holmes stories to play fair: "Mr. R. A. J. Walling is an extremely skilful maker of plots and surprises, and in this book he has also created some excellent and amusing characters... His detective has one bad habit, which I am afraid he acquired from the late Mr. Sherlock Holmes. He occasionally observes some small object or action without communicating his observations to the reader, and is thus able to bring out a set of startling deductions which nobody else has had a chance to make."

Less skilled authors who erred on the side of unfairness were scolded: "Mr. Clive Ryland in *The Murders at the Manor* starts out well with a disagreeable baronet shot dead in a secluded pavilion, five minutes' walk from a houseful of people thirsting for his blood. And then – just as we are getting on splendidly with the timetables and the alibis – he goes and commits the unforgivable sin! Deliberately, unblushingly, and without the least excuse, he conceals the vital clue. The reader has no chance to guess it – even the detective does not guess it – it comes out casually in a conversation about something else. It is all very wrong."

Authors who prided themselves on playing fair sometimes set out an explicit "challenge to the reader" once they had supplied all the clues to the puzzle. This was a method closely associated with Ellery Queen, although other writers adopted it as well. Some authors were even more confident that they had bamboozled their readers, and offered proof of their cleverness.

A prime example was another ingenious American, C. Daly King. Sayers admired his *Obelists at Sea*: "Taken by itself, the detective portion of the book is intricate and ingenious enough to satisfy the demands of the most exacting solver. The clues are most fairly set forth and are, indeed, tabulated at the end for our benefit in a 'clue-finder'. This is scarcely an 'innovation', as the publisher claims, for Mr. Freeman Wills Crofts introduced it, in a slightly different form, in *The Hog's Back Mystery*. Nor is it really necessary as a proof of the author's integrity, though it is certainly a challenge to that of the reader." Sayers was, however, herself mistaken; there is, for instance, a form of "clue-finder" in J. J. Connington's *The Eye in the Museum*, which pre-dates *The Hog's Back Mystery*.

She warmed to the "clue-finder", saying of Ronald Knox's *Still Dead*: "The clues are marshalled with great care, and the solution is provided with a set of cross-references by which we can check their fairness for ourselves. This is an excellent method, arguing courage and candour in the author, and saving the reader much turning of pages." Perhaps the most elaborate of all "cluefinder novels" is C. Daly King's *Obelists*

Fly High, which again earned Sayers' admiration: "If the scope of the satire were just a little wider, this would be a true Peacockian detective story, a new and excellent thing. Caviare to the general, perhaps, but authentic caviare."

A tried and tested technique for directing the reader's attention away from the crucial clues is to introduce interesting but misleading information into the story. But this method had to be used sensibly. As Sayers said of Anthony Weymouth's *The Doctors are Doubtful*: "where the murder is so clearly committed by somebody with medical knowledge, it is foolish to waste time in building up an elaborate case against somebody with special knowledge and no plausible means of access to the apparatus employed. A red herring is good – but it is necessary to provide it with a genuinely ancient and fish-like smell if the reader is to follow its false trail."

More than once, Sayers touched on a theme that preoccupied her: "Nowadays it is accepted that the author must play fair; but there is still an idea going about that the 'Who?' book is the only legitimate variety of the species. Yet, if we demand any sort of likeness to real life, the 'How?' book is much nearer to the facts; for in nine real cases out of ten the difficulty that confronts the police is not to spot the criminal but to bring the charge home to him." Her own novels were often "howdunits" rather than "whodunits", but a recurrent difficulty with the ingenious "howdunit" is that their authors often fail to play *entirely* fair with their readers, who are likely to lack the specialised knowledge needed to enable them to deduce the solution. It is unsurprising that the "whodunit", associated above all in the public mind with Agatha Christie, was and remains more popular.

Readers trying to solve the puzzles confronting them needed to compete with detectives such as Ellery Queen. Sayers' reviews of the Queen books express reservations about their literary excesses, but of the character's sleuthing skill there was no doubt: "He is always picturesque and always ingenious. His characters take after him in this respect, and one sometimes feels that they are fortunate beyond all reasonable expectation in finding a detective clever enough to interpret the ingenious and picturesque false clues and dying messages they leave behind them."

Tropes of the genre

Those dying message clues, found in many detective stories before and since the Golden Age, were a particular speciality of Ellery Queen. Other writers, including another popular American, Stuart Palmer, did not deploy the dying message device with sufficient finesse to persuade Sayers to suspend her disbelief: "The incident which gives *Murder on the Blackboard* its title is the weakest in the book. Why do these foolish victims of murder leave their last messages to the world in a form so cryptic that no ordinary person could be expected to make head or tail of them?"

Some of the tropes of Golden Age detective fiction tested Sayers' patience, as she made clear in discussing *The Case of the Three Strange Faces* by Christopher Bush: "if there is one plot I am thoroughly tired of, it is the one about the murdered man who is made to speak after he is dead, by means of a dictaphone, gramophone, loud-speaker, or other device... it has been worked to death. It is dead. This week it has turned up again, and, like Mark Twain, I want a fresher corpse."

Warming to her theme, she soon expanded on her list of corpses ripe for removal: "The Twins Formula has put in some good, hard work since the detective story was first invented, and really ought, I feel, to retire on a pension, together with the Gramophone Record Formula and the Formula of the Corpse with the Battered Face."

Yet in skilled hands, even the most hackneyed plot device could give rise to a tale of the unexpected. She said of John Rhode's *The Robthorne Mystery*: "I was a little alarmed at first when it was made clear that the new story was to be a variation on the twin brother theme. Was it possible that in this worked-out mine there was a vein still unexplored? Yes, it was really so – a nugget of good gold yet remained for Mr. Rhode to find." The twin brother, by the way, is honourably produced in all his twinnishness in chapter II, and not treacherously sprung upon us to force a surprise ending. The similarity of the brothers is the hypothesis from which we set out, so that everything is scrupulously fair."

Impersonation was a recurrent feature of Golden Age novels, but she felt that the most striking feature of Herbert Adams' *Fate Laughs* was "the extreme slow-wittedness of the hero... It might happen to anybody, I suppose, to encounter his own double in a railway carriage and, being on his uppers, to agree (for a consideration) to impersonate the double for an hour or so. But the successive shocks of losing his heart to a lady and immediately falling heir to a large fortune must have had a stunning effect on our hero's brain; otherwise, when he learned that the husband of his double's former fiancée had been murdered during the hour of the impersonation, he ought surely to have realised, before page 220, that there might be a connection between the one thing and the other."

Locked-room puzzles and stories about other seemingly impossible crimes present comparable difficulties. Commenting on *The Plague Court Murders*, written by John Dickson Carr under the name Carter Dickson, Sayers fretted: "Like all 'sealed-chamber' mysteries, this one has a solution that takes a good deal of swallowing and demands a good deal of long-winded explanation at the end: that is the drawback to all plots of this type." Yet she was willing to suspend her disbelief because of the quality of the writing, and she also enjoyed the same author's *The White Priory Murders*, which was "built up on the fine old theme of the lonely corpse surrounded by an area of snow, virgin except for the tracks of the person who discovers the body. We all know that (excluding suicide and the universally despised secret passage) this problem admits of only three legitimate solutions: the time was wrong, the place was wrong, or the corpse was not alone." She admired the author's skill in "using scrupulous fairness in deduction and concealing the identity of his criminal with considerable cunning."

To this day, Carr is remembered as the master of the locked room mystery, whereas the name of Anthony Wynne (in real life, a well-known doctor, Robert McNair Wilson) was forgotten for many years by all but a handful of connoisseurs. Yet Sayers reviewed Wynne positively, saying of *Death of a Banker* that he excelled "in the solution of apparently insoluble problems. This time it is a huntsman who, under the gaze of 14 people, jumps his horse over a five-barred gate and falls dead in the middle of a wide, bare field with a knife in his back. (No – neither of the two explanations that come first to your mind is correct.) The puzzle is ingeniously solved; and if you think the solution far-fetched, go to a first-class conjuring entertainment and then ask yourself whether the evidence of the human eye is always to be trusted."

Wynne did, however, sometimes seem to Sayers to undermine the credentials of his Great Detective in order to increase the excitement: "I wish Dr. Hailey did not create so many difficulties for himself by a heedlessness and failure to think ahead more suitable to a 'first walking gentleman' than to a man with so many famous cases behind him."

Golden Age stories in which one character impersonated another were commonplace: "Three plots this week turn upon impersonation," Sayers announced on 4 August 1935. Thespian talents came in handy, and she observed that: "If a character in a detective story is or has been an actor, we are intended to understand by that that he can (oddly enough) act almost anything, and will do so before the end of the book. The murder-game seems indeed to hold out unlimited opportunity to those comedians who, under modern stage conditions, are hampered by their own versatility; it will be a sad day for crime-novelists when the character-actor follows the pterodactyl into extinction, and they have to rely entirely upon amateur talent."

'Murder games' were frequently, if unwisely, played by characters in Golden Age detective stories. In *Seventeen Cards* by E. Charles Vivian, Sayers noted wryly that the game had "the usual result". The question in a book which employed a well-worn device was whether it would be handled with a spark of originality as well as with a touch of literary quality. In this case, Sayers was enthusiastic. The basic situation was "thrillerish and not very new; but the vigour of the narrative and the fine sense of strain and tension produced by the interplay of nearly 20 characters, who all suspect one another, make the telling anything but commonplace."

"We are weary of murders in film studios, and particularly weary of the victim who is shot dead in mid-scene just as the blank ammunition is being fired off," Sayers said of *Death as an Extra* by Val Gielgud and Holt Marvell. The authors "sought to enliven the story by introducing – for a motive preposterously inadequate – a bunch of the most tedious American gangsters who ever bumped their victims off." She was equally dismissive of Alan Melville's *Quick Curtain*: "The plot is the one about the actor shot on the stage which we have had so many times lately."

Yet she responded warmly to those capable of an interesting and original variation on this old theme, as her review of *Murder in Public* illustrates: "Mr. John Crozier, who is a new author, tells us the old, old story of the actress who has to be murdered on the stage, and, lo and behold! she is murdered. But there is a great deal more to the story than that; it is a very closely woven and complicated piece of crime and detection, of quite remarkable merit for a first novel...The private detective is a North American Indian (for a change), and this endows him with an exceptionally keen sense of smell and a useful knack of stealthy movement."

Often a detective novelist favours a particular plot ingredient. With Carr and Wynne, it was the apparently impossible crime, and with Freeman Wills Crofts it was the seemingly impregnable alibi, whereas, Sayers noted: "When a young man sets out to hike through one of Mr. Jefferson Farjeon's stories he is certain of meeting (a) a girl and (b) a corpse." She was an admirer of Farjeon's, saying he was "quite unsurpassed for creepy skill in mysterious adventures."

As for Miles Burton (a pseudonym for Cecil John Street, best known as John Rhode), his books featured a friendly rivalry between a Scotland Yard man and a gifted amateur sleuth which followed an all too predictable course: "I think Inspector Arnold might have learned by now that his gifted amateur friend, Mr. Merrion, is Always Right; it would speed his cases up enormously."

Recognising distinction

Sayers was as generous to writers whose books she admired as she was blisteringly dismissive of those who fell far short of her standards. Some of her favourites were well-known authors, such as G. K. Chesterton, first President of the Detection Club, and founder members of the Club including R. Austin Freeman, Freeman Wills Crofts, John Rhode, J. J. Connington, and H. C. Bailey. Bailey was much admired during the Twenties and Thirties, and Sayers liked his series detective, Reggie Fortune: "We all know Mr. Fortune – or, if we do not, it is our misfortune, which should be remedied without delay – and we know that beneath his surface flippancies there are a mind and a heart sensitive to the sins and sufferings of humanity."

Georgette Heyer is now better remembered as an author of historical romances than as a detective novelist, but Sayers found her characters and dialogue "an abiding delight". Similarly, C. H. B. Kitchin was a mainstream novelist who occasionally dipped a toe into criminous waters with books such as *Crime at Christmas.* Sayers enthused over: "Mr. Kitchin's shrewd and sensitive psychology, his excellent English style, and the neatness of his plot, which is complicated by a second death of an obviously murderous kind. And if you want to argue with the author – he has set out all your arguments for you in a final chapter, with the answers to them."

One might expect that Sayers would reserve her most lavish and recurrent praise for giants of the genre, yet this was not the case. A fascinating aspect of the reviews is the acclaim Sayers gives to authors whose names have long been forgotten, even by crime enthusiasts, and whose books are now often extremely difficult to find. Harriet Rutland is an example, and so are Catherine Meadows, James Quince, and Laurence Kirk.

Kirk's *Whispering Tongues* was hailed as: "so natural, graceful, witty, and charming that criticism can do little more than hang it about with a garland of grateful adjectives." Laurence Kirk was the pen-name of Eric Andrew Simson, who later dabbled in science fiction and stories with a supernatural element, but in the long run failed to develop a literary career as enduring as the quality of his writing perhaps deserved.

The author whose books Sayers most frequently extols is E. R. Punshon, a prolific writer in his early sixties whose competence and diligence were not in doubt, but who would not find his way into most people's list of leading Golden Age novelists. She said he had "written a number of detective stories so excellent that it is astonishing they are not much better known. You will love his pair of detectives: the melancholy Sergeant Bell, who does all the work, and the pompous Inspector Carter, who takes all the credit. Everything Mr. Punshon writes is good."

When Punshon ditched Carter and Bell in favour of a new detective, young Bobby Owen, Sayers was even more impressed. "What is distinction – that quality whose name is so often taken in vain by the advertiser? Which is so hard to define and so instantly recognisable when seen?" she demanded, when reviewing *Information Received.* "It is missed by scores of competent mystery-writers who can construct impeccable plots.

The few who achieve it step – plot or no plot – unquestioned into the first rank...and in the works of Mr. E. R. Punshon we salute it every time...all his books have that elusive something which makes them count as literature...Good writing and good characterisation – the secret, I suppose, lies there and in Mr. Punshon's all-pervading and sub-acid wit, whose subtle austerity gives dignity to the vintage."

Many writers and publishers would kill for such a quote from such an eminent judge, and Victor Gollancz kept her encomium on Punshon's dust jackets for years to come. Gollancz happened to be Sayers' publishers – Punshon had, like her, made the move from Ernest Benn, for whom Gollancz had previously worked – but she had too much integrity for this to have infuenced her. Indeed, her reviews of Milward Kennedy's books published by Gollancz were comparatively lukewarm, despite the fact that Kennedy was a fellow member of the Detection Club with whom she was on good terms.

Even when Punshon produced relatively poor books, such as the tedious *Death among the Sunbathers* and the wildly uneven *Crossword Mystery*, Sayers expressed no more than mild disappointment. When he returned to form in *Mystery Villa*, Sayers was ecstatic: "The balance of tone in this book seems to me to be quite perfect, and if here and there the details of the plot seem to be rather lightly sketched in, that is of small consequence in so grotesque a pattern of fantastical light and shade." *Death of a Beauty Queen* was equally to her taste: "a fine and interesting novel, where the emotional discords are resolved in a strain of genuine pathos and of what I can best call nobility."

Punshon was a capable writer whose best work is unusual and interesting and deserves to be remembered. Even in his lifetime, however, he did not command a large readership, and his novels frequently failed to achieve publication in the United States. Perhaps because of the inconsistency of his books, very few commentators have rated him as highly as did Sayers. But her persistent advocacy of the merits of his books reflects her determination to make up her own mind.

Several novelists who emerged during the Thirties wrote with an intelligence and zest of which Sayers approved. Among them was another now-forgotten writer, R. C. Woodthorpe. She regarded his debut,

The Public School Murder, as "the most brilliant and humorous detective story of its season", and was equally impressed by *A Dagger in Fleet Street*: ("dazzling and delicately cynical comedy") and by "the excellence of the writing and the skill with which the atmosphere is conveyed" in *Death in a Little Town*.

Woodthorpe, like Punshon, was quickly recruited into the Detection Club, and so was Nicholas Blake (in real life, the future Poet Laureate Cecil Day-Lewis). She was quick to applaud Blake's debut, *A Question of Proof*: "Mr. Blake's dialogue has an exquisite rightness...The plot is perhaps not the strongest point of the book, but it is adequate and coherent, and the solution is, I think, psychologically reasonable. For a first book, this is an admirable achievement."

Christopher St John Sprigg was another young writer whose books she lauded. She enjoyed *The Perfect Alibi* ("The characters in this book have a way of making acute and entertaining observations, and that is the most attractive feature of a very attractive piece of work") and also *Death of an Airman* ("a most ingenious and exciting plot, full of good puzzles and discoveries and worked out among a varied cast of entertaining characters...his buoyant and vigorous style carries us blithely through all the complications of the intrigue"). *Death of a Queen* was an "extravaganza; with enough gentle humour to make the absurdities of his one-horse kingdom entertaining, and enough romantic glamour to keep the murders in key." Sprigg was pleased with Sayers' reaction to his work, and they entered into a brief correspondence, but the question of his joining the Detection Club did not arise. He was claimed by Marxism, and left Britain to fight in the Spanish Civil War. Sprigg was killed before reaching the age of thirty, yet had already published seven accomplished detective novels.

A young American who was elected to membership of the Detection Club shortly after Sayers ceased reviewing would become a good friend of hers. This was John Dickson Carr, who also wrote as Carter Dickson, and who specialised in coming up with ingenious solutions to apparently impossible crimes. But his books had more to offer than mere cleverness, as she said of *The Mad Hatter Mystery*, "He can create atmosphere with an adjective, and make a picture from a wet iron railing, a dusty table, a gas-lamp blurred by the fog. He can alarm with an illusion or delight with a rollicking absurdity...every sentence gives a thrill of positive pleasure."

Occasionally, she took Carr to task, as when she complained that *The Eight of Swords* "suffers from a kind of general looseness and unevenness", but *The Blind Barber* earned a rave review: "The story has all its author's usual happy touch of the grotesque, with less of the horrible and more of the farcical about it, and all his usual merits of style. In fact, I call it a gorgeous book, and if anybody doesn't like it, I pities 'em." In 1949, she wrote a lengthy review of Carr's biography of Sir Arthur Conan Doyle, included in this book not only for completeness, but also because it is characteristically perceptive.

American detective fiction

John Dickson Carr was an Anglophile who spent many years living in Britain, but he learned his craft in his native country. As an American enthusiast for the classic whodunit, he was by no means alone. It is a mistake, commonly made, to think that Golden Age detective fiction was overwhelmingly the preserve of British writers. At precisely the same time that Dashiell Hammett and other writers of tough private eye fiction were writing for the pulp magazines, a host of novelists who prized ingenious plot above all else were at work in the United States. S. S. Van Dine, creator of Philo Vance, was for some years the best-known and most successful, but Sayers enthused about the cleverness of several of his compatriots, such as Ellery Queen.

When discussing *The Siamese Twin Mystery*, Sayers said: "What saves Mr. Queen is the basis of really acute and ingenious detective work on which he founds his plot, so that one forgives his extravagance for the sake of his fundamental brain-work...He penetrates the workings of the reader's mind with uncanny intuition. If only he would master the 'art of sinking' in prose, he would take the rank to which his intellect entitles him, as one of the supreme masters of the detective story."

In the same vein, she said of *The American Gun Mystery*, "if the reader can stomach these intolerable affectations, most of which, thank goodness, disappear when the author gets into his stride, he will be rewarded by a rattling good yarn with a well-constructed mystery. As to the mystery, I frankly confess that I only guessed about half of it, and on due and sour consideration I am reluctantly compelled to admit that the author was quite honourable and that the stupidity was mine."

Ellery Queen was the pen-name of two cousins, Frederic Dannay and Manfred Lee, who also wrote four novels as Barnaby Ross. Sayers said that Ross's *Drury Lane's Last Case* "stimulates in a different way. He challenges attention with queerness and splashes of (literally) strong colour... Admitting all this, however, there is, with all the extravagance, an element of the unusual which takes us out of the beaten track. The mysterious events have a real atmosphere of oddity, and there is some ingenious detective work which does produce the proper reaction on the reader – the 'I-ought-to-have-realised-that' feeling which it is every mystery writer's ambition to evoke." With a typical flourish, she concluded: "I recommend the book, with the caution that you may find it an irritant."

She also relished two books written by Richard Webb and Mary Louise White Aswell under the name Q. Patrick. *S. S. Murder* was "a most enjoyable tale, breezily and naturally written in a pleasant, individual style; full of thrills, but with a neat little detective problem at the heart of the mystery and at least one good red-herring." *Darker Grows the Valley*, also known as *The Grindle Nightmare,* was an especially dark and powerful novel, arguably well ahead of its time, and although Sayers had reservations about the climax, she acknowledged that the story was "well handled and the writing is good."

Asey Mayo, the central character in a long series of novels by Phoebe Atwood Taylor, was "a detective for whose personality and New England dialect" she had "a great affection and esteem", and she felt that "the characterisation and general atmosphere" of *The Mystery of the Cape Cod Tavern* were excellent.

The vitality of Carleton Kendrake's writing appealed to her, even causing this reflection: "Every so often I get the feeling that we English detective writers are growing rather old and staid and that even the newest and youngest of us have been born old. There is a kind of tired efficiency

about our approach to a problem, as of a Government department ploughing its way through a mass of official reports."

Sayers was not afraid to admit that the literary style of American
detective fiction tended to be more vibrant than that of its British counterpart. She enjoyed Rex Stout's *Fer De Lance*, described his style as
"good in the colloquial American kind", while Means Davis' style, "jerky
and full of American vernacular, is arresting, the sense of character and
actuality strong, and the suspense powerful enough to grip the reader's
attention almost in spite of himself." Erle Stanley Gardner also produced
"very lively reading", although she lamented that "Perry Mason's methods
of cross-examination would hardly go down well at the Old Bailey."

But not all American detective novelists passed muster. Irvin S. Cobb's
Murder Day by Day contained "some ingenious work in the final chapter,
but will annoy the English reader by its eccentricities of style, which may
be divided into (a) Americanisms, (b) bad Americanisms, (c) bad English,
and (d) pretentious monstrosities, such as: 'I baldly am putting down the
triple-crowned climax, but putting it down hind part before.' Some lively
passages of American vernacular show that Mr. Cobb could write, if only
he would not try so hard to be a writer."

Pushing at the boundaries of the genre

As the years passed, Sayers became increasingly dissatisfied with crime
novels that amounted to nothing more than puzzles. She yearned for the
complexity she associated with favourite Victorian novelists such as
Wilkie Collins and Sheridan Le Fanu: "One striking difference between
the mystery novel of to-day and that of the last century is more easily felt
than described, but may be roughly defined as a lack of spaciousness.
When we open *The Woman in White* or *Wylder's Hand*, we step into a
world of people having their roots in time and space and a life which
extends beyond the limits of the immediate problem. Larger issues are
at stake than the precise method by which the arsenic is administered,
and the strings are pulled by a more awful puppet-master than a Chief
Inspector of Scotland Yard."

Formulaic writing was commonplace, and Sayers was dismissive of

Gerald Fairlie's *Copper at Sea*; it was "quite a well-managed specimen of its class. But I wonder a little why writer and reader should remain contented with this tired and mechanical filling up of a set outline. Only angelic qualities of style can make these dry bones live, and angelic visitations are, as we know, few and far between."

Equally unambitious was the crime writing of F. A. M. Webster, better remembered today as a pioneering athletics coach than as a detective novelist. Although he was the creator of Old Ebbie Entwhistle, boldly described in one book title as "Detective Up-to-Date", his work seemed to Sayers to represent the past. *The Gathering Storm* took a heavy pounding for "the stale re-hashing of old material – the evil Egyptian with a formula for exterminating mankind, the idiotic female who lets herself be lured away by the bogus policeman, the languid villain who keeps tame cobras in surroundings of more-than-Oriental splendour, and the final appearance (by aeroplane) of the whole male and female cast on a lonely island, like the last chorus in a pantomime." Sayers scarcely softened the blow by saying that "Detective-Inspector Oaf…is an authentic lamb, who seems to have strayed from some much better book."

The limitations of detective fiction that prioritised the puzzle above all else were made clear in Sayers' remarks about a novel written by the industrious A. Fielding: "The plot is extremely intricate and full of red herrings, and the solution is kept a dark secret up to the last moment. The weakness of *The Cautley Conundrum* is that the people never really come alive." Perhaps more tantalising than her novels is the mystery surrounding Fielding's identity. Even today, industrious researchers have been able to discover relatively little about her, other than that her real name appears to have been Dorothy Feilding; a pleasing suggestion that she was really Agatha Christie working under an alias is sadly unsubstantiated.

The hackneyed nature of much popular fiction of the day encouraged writers of ambition to try something more adventurous and appealing. Achieving originality is, however, easier said than done. Sayers recognised this: "It is, of course, every mystery writer's desire to achieve the "detective story that is different." In spite of the reiterated assurances of blurb-writers, this ideal is seldom attained."

Daring and ambition were not confined to well-known innovators such as Anthony Berkeley and Sayers herself. Of the now forgotten *The Manuscript Murders*, she said: "Mr. Lewis Robinson has made a praiseworthy effort to get away from the whole stereotyped business of clues and interrogatories." She added that: "The final turn is neat and the book is interesting in its construction, besides containing some clever characterisation and a good deal of quiet wit." Nevertheless, Robinson remains best remembered (if at all) for an earlier, more conventional locked-room mystery, *The Medbury Fort Murder*, written under the alias of George Limnelius.

Literary experiments are fraught with risks. Sayers had been disappointed that she failed (in her opinion) in *The Documents in the Case* to execute satisfactorily the ambitious concept at the heart of the novel. Similarly, she regarded *An International Affair*, by Bruce Graeme, a prolific and competent but less gifted author, as a misfire: "One man relates the story... to another, and, by way of making it the more confusing, does so in the manner of a jigsaw puzzle, first displaying a number of piecemeal incidents and gradually fitting them together to make a connected picture. One sees the idea, but the result is rather dull and the writing is definitely bad. Only extreme brilliance of style and treatment could get away with so difficult a convention, and, interesting as the experiment is, we must regretfully confess that it does not come off."

The boldness of Charles Barry's *The Wrong Murder Mystery* lay not in any tricky structural device, but in a central theme touching on a dilemma of ethics: "Would it be justifiable to legalise euthanasia for persons suffering from painful and incurable disease? Mr. Barry thinks not, but he postulates a doctor who sincerely advocates such a measure, and who is in consequence suspected of polishing off certain of his patients (mostly Roman Catholics) who publicly oppose him on this point." Sayers' praise was qualified in part because of the author's carelessness: "The details are not altogether convincing or satisfactory, but the book does represent a real effort to turn the detective story to larger and more serious ends, and the attempt is interesting. If, however, religion is to be brought into it, let us have the facts right. An 'Evangelistic' aunt would not refer to Morning Prayer as 'Mattins,' nor could a boy who attended that service regularly grow up entirely ignorant of the New Testament."

Sayers' devotion to the academic led her to pronounce that: "It is always a healthy sign when we encounter a central intellectual idea in a detective story – something 'meatier' than a mere fresh dodge for faking footprints." But as she kept emphasising, the finished product needed to match the quality of the concept. In Anthony Gilbert's *The Musical Comedy Crime*: "the theme is announced a little too late to be fully effective, nor is the plot constructed so as to exploit that theme in all its logical implications."

Sayers judged *Murder among Friends* by "Simon" much more brutally, confessing: "I do not know which leaves me most bewildered – his medical science, his psycho-analysis, or his incredible tropes and metaphors. I think this is an endeavour to write a detective story in Freudian symbols, but I am really not sure. It may be the height of brilliance, but it sounds to me perilously like bottomless depths of nonsense...I fear there is here only a determination to be different at all costs...I have certainly never read anything like it."

At the same time as she was reading and reviewing the books of her fellow authors, Sayers was hard at work on the two novels that, for many, represent the pinnacle of her achievement. *The Nine Tailors* and *Gaudy Night* reflect the credo that she expressed in the *Sunday Times*: "To combine the novel of mystery with the novel of manners was the great achievement of English writers in the past, and is increasingly their ambition to-day."

She was alive to the scale of the challenge: "After the divorce of plot from psychology had been made absolute in the first quarter of the century, attempts at reconciliation began to be made from both sides, but the difficulties were, and still are, acute. Both parties to the union had become set in their habits, and the detective story in particular had perfected a polished and heartless mechanism upon which all genuine feeling was a mere intrusion. Either the reality of the passions made the detective business look cheap, or the austerity of the detective interest made the passions look tawdry. No one has as yet perfectly resolved the problem. The far-fetched surprise ending is impossible where motive and character are taken seriously."

Henry Wade, another of Sayers' friends, had originally written books reflecting the influence of Freeman Wills Crofts, but even his debut,

The Verdict of You All (1926) showed a range and ambition uncommon in detective novels of the time. Wade was not, unlike some of his contemporaries, under any financial pressure to write, or over-produce, and his novels became increasingly daring. Despite her reservations about Wade's ability to describe a love affair, Sayers regarded *Mist on the Saltings* as: "an interesting experiment which, with a little more firmness in the handling, might have been a memorable book."

Wade continued to develop as a writer, and Sayers considered that *Constable, Guard Thyself!* "might serve as a model of the classical detective story, complete within its own sphere." Crucially, she felt that: "it preserves from beginning to end a perfect unity of tone and action; neither reaching out to the larger and looser universe of the straight novel, nor shrivelling to the dry and restricted two-dimensional circle of the mathematical puzzle. It is excellently constructed, the exposition in particular being worthy of all praise, and the characterisation is of the exact right kind to awaken 'human interest' without swamping the plot in a flood of emotional excitement."

The question of unity of tone also arose in relation to Punshon's *Crossword Mystery*: "In his final chapter Mr. Punshon lifts the story rather abruptly from the level of polite comedy to that of heroic drama, and, being unprepared, we fail to adjust our minds before the curtain falls on the hideous scene. It is, of course, a compliment... that criticism should focus itself on such points. Only when a high level of artistic accomplishment has been reached do we begin to talk severely about values and tone-balance."

Douglas G. Browne, who was elected to membership of the Detection Club in 1949, was another author not content simply to churn out commonplace mysteries. Sayers approved of *The Looking Glass Murder*: "So far we have, what is common to many detective stories, a colourful and slightly whimsical setting for the crimes, which amuses and engages the attention. Many writers go no further than this. Mr. Browne, however, has made the 'looking-glass' *idea* integral to the structure of the book, thus achieving an artistic unity of a very satisfactory kind. However entertaining the background of a story may be, yet, if the same story might equally well have been worked out against another background, then the setting is exterior to the structure, and the book, as a work of art, is incomplete. But here the setting is significant, because the theme of the action is also the theme of the book, and this is artistically right."

Another to earn high praise was Newton Gayle, author of *Death Follows a Formula*: "Mr. Newton Gayle appears to be a newcomer to the world of detective fiction; he deserves a cordial welcome, for his first book is lively, well-constructed, and important. I mean by 'important' that it has the largeness of scope and solidity of treatment typical of the writer who has plenty to say and intends to say it seriously."

Sayers' one reservation was that: "The character who tells the story is an English Foreign Office official who has spent some time in America; this may account for the fact that the author writes sometimes in educated English and sometimes in educated American." The explanation for the inconsistency was that the name of Newton Gayle concealed two identities; one belonged to the American poet Muna Lee and the other to a British oil executive Maurice Guinness. The pair collaborated on five novels in all. Sayers may not have known this at the time of writing the review, but would have discovered the truth soon afterwards, since Newton Gayle was elected to membership of the Detection Club in 1937. In practice, no doubt it was Guinness (much later the author of three thrillers under the name Mike Brewer) who attended meetings, although it seems likely that his main contribution to the partnership concerned plotting, while Lee did the bulk of the writing.

Newton Gayle's name would fade from view all too soon, but the reputation of Margery Allingham remains high half a century after her death. Sayers lauded Allingham's *Death of a Ghost* as "a remarkable book in many ways. Its theme is extremely original, its characterisation is outstandingly good, and it contains one scene which, for genuine pathetic feeling, stands almost alone in detective fiction. The ending, too, strikes a fine note of horror – not violently imposed for the sake of startling, but foreshadowed and inevitable."

Sayers' personal faith, as well as her intellectual interest in religion, underpinned her long-standing admiration for G. K. Chesterton, and she greeted *The Scandal of Father Brown* with enthusiasm. In her view, Chesterton "was the first man of our time to introduce the great name of

God into a detective story without either irrelevance or irreverence...If we wipe out God from the problem we are in very great danger of wiping out man as well. Unless we are prepared to bring our murderers to the bar of Eternity, we may construct admirable jig-saw puzzles, but we shall certainly never write a *Hamlet*. And we owe Mr. Chesterton a heavy debt in that, with very great courage in a poor and materialistic period, he planted his steps firmly upon the more difficult path, and showed us how to enlarge the boundaries of the detective story by making it deal with real death and real wickedness and real, that is to say, divine judgment."

Characterisation

Writers who wanted to do more than concentrate on puzzles needed to portray their characters in some depth, but the conventions of the traditional whodunit complicated the task. Victims were often unsympathetic individuals (rich financiers, elderly misers, unscrupulous blackmailers, and so on) who supplied various suspects with motives for murder. But if the suspects were to be credible killers, how best to characterise them?

Milward Kennedy, whose *Corpse on the Mat* had won the approval of Lord Peter Wimsey, no less, in *The Five Red Herrings*, touched on this question in his foreword to *Poison in the Parish*. As Sayers paraphrased it, the dilemma was: "how to avoid filling his book with vicious and unsympathetic characters and yet avoid the improbability of focusing suspicion upon such agreeable persons as...are obviously not apt to meddle with sharp instruments and poisons. In this story he outlines a set of circumstances in which the amiable innocent might reasonably come to be suspected."

Kennedy was, perhaps, influenced in his approach by Sayers' severe criticism of a previous book: "in *Death to the Rescue* the hatefulness of his human beings reached the point of being actively repellent." She took a more benevolent view of *Corpse in Cold Storage*, where the protagonists are Sir George Bull and his wife, a pair of appealing rogues, although the book suffered from a superfluity of nondescript suspects: "I rather wish that Mr. Kennedy had not presented us with a list of 16 suspects, scarcely differentiated except by their names; it makes Sir George Bull's line of reasoning a little hard to follow." *Poison in the Parish* fared better in this regard – "All the characters are washed in with a neat and accurate touch, in a low key and without extravagance of pose or gesture" – although one observation ("I should think it must be the primmest and quietest murder tale ever written") may have caused Kennedy to conclude that he simply could not win.

Kennedy was influenced by the pioneering work of Anthony Berkeley, a writer whose ingenuity Agatha Christie and Sayers both admired, and whose *Jumping Jenny* prompted Sayers to say that he deserved "gratitude for his energetic efforts to escape from the thraldom of formula." But Berkeley, as Sayers found increasingly in their personal dealings during the mid-Thirties, was a complex, troubled, and often difficult man, and his characters often reflected his own nature.

Sayers gave a decidedly mixed reaction to *Panic Party*, a typically innovative Berkeley novel with a scenario which to an extent anticipates that of *Lord of the Flies*: "The book is consistently exciting and consistently clever; but the author's sneering hatred of his own puppets provides abundant justification for the editor who looked askance at it. Sloppy sentiment is not wanted, on desert islands or anywhere else; but there is a point at which ruthless realism becomes, not merely too unpleasant for popularity, but a little too bad for belief."

———

Motive

For all the tensions that developed between them as the years passed, Sayers and Berkeley were both among the earliest detective novelists to recognise the potential of the genre for explorations of human behaviour, and the reasons why a person may be driven to kill. As she wittily expressed it: "the readers and writers of mystery fiction should hasten to join some Society for the Preservation of Marriage and the Family, since without these institutions the motives for murder would be sadly reduced, and little would be left to us but the Elimination of Financiers by their business rivals and Political Assassination – which, of course, is murder only by courtesy."

Gladys Mitchell, Sayers said, "specialises in deduction by psycho-analytical methods, and I am assured by persons who understand the subject that her technique is impeccable. She believes that the majority of us are capable of committing murder for what may look like very inadequate motives, and here I think she is quite right. It is only because murder 'comes so natural' that we hasten to surround it with so inhibitive a gallows atmosphere."

Discussing Alan Brock's *Further Evidence*, which like much of Brock's fiction drew on real-life cases, Sayers pronounced: "of all motives for crime, respectability – the least emphasised in fiction – is one of the most powerful in fact, and is the root cause of a long series of irregularities, ranging from murder itself to the queerest and most eccentric misdemeanours." What none of her readers knew, and what she never revealed to the end of her life, was that respectability was the reason why she felt she could not acknowledge that she had given birth to an illegitimate child.

When the Wicked Man, by J. F. W. Hannay, a Briton who emigrated to the United States to pursue a career in cotton broking, was "told from the criminal's point of view, and offers a motive for murder unusual in fiction... The blameless and ascetic clergyman of Mr. Hannay's story allowed himself to be victimised by the doglike affection of a well-meaning and insensitive incubus till one evening his boredom and irritation turned to frenzy, and he snatched up the poker and hammered the poor man to death." It takes a daring writer to build a novel, rather than a short story, out of a murder motivated by boredom and irritation, but Sayers approved: "an interesting book, more powerful, perhaps, in conception than in execution, but with passages of fine psychological insight and an ironical twist at the end of the story."

Criminal's viewpoint and inverted stories

A fundamental question for a writer deciding how to structure a novel concerns the choice of viewpoint from which to tell the story. Conventionally, a crime story will follow the detective as he or she investigates, but Sayers was interested in examining the potential of other approaches. The influence of Wilkie Collins' *The Moonstone* can be seen in *The Documents in the Case,* her only full-length detective story in which Lord Peter Wimsey does not put in an appearance. Another attractive option was "the story that is told from the murderer's viewpoint. We see the crime committed and watch, through his eyes, with painful anxiety, while the evidence is piled up against him. Isabel Ostrander's *Ashes to Ashes*, Francis Iles' *Malice Aforethought* and C.S. Forester's *Payment Deferred* are distinguished examples." Francis Iles was another pseudonym of Anthony Berkeley Cox, and the second Iles book, *Before the Fact*, included a witty portrait of a female crime writer evidently based on Sayers.

Irony was Francis Iles' trademark, and several capable crime novelists were inspired by his success. Among them was Richard Hull, the pen-name used by an accountant called Richard Henry Sampson, who made a splash with his first novel, *The Murder of My Aunt*. Sayers loved it, even though "It is not a detective story; it is the story of how one of the most unpleasant youths in fiction kept on trying to get rid of the aunt on whom he was reluctantly and resentfully dependent... It is a study of unbalanced reactions to delight the heart of the psychologist; but the admirable lightness of the style, and the entire absence of pompous comment and medical jargon, keep it essentially a novel, with nothing of the treatise about it. The insensitive might even find it as funny as it appears to be on the surface, the sensitive will find it painful, but continuously interesting and exciting."

Another option was to write an 'inverted story', which "shows us first the crime from the murderer's point of view and then the detection from the point of view of the detective. Dr. R. Austin Freeman used this method in *The Singing Bone*, and now comes Miss Anne Meredith, with less emphasis on clues and more on character." Meredith was a pen-name of Lucy Malleson, whose other pseudonyms included Anthony Gilbert. Sayers found *Portrait of a Murderer* "powerful and impressive, and there is a fine inevitability to the plot-structure which gives it true tragic quality." In a memoir published under the Meredith name, Lucy Malleson described her delight at the review, and at her invitation to join the elite membership of the Detection Club.

Experimenting with viewpoint was attractive to established writers who wanted to try something different. Freeman Wills Crofts was the crime novelist who, according to Sayers, "first made police routine fascinating and distilled romance from the pages of Bradshaw. He is our cunningest fitter of jigsaws, our Time-table King and Master of the Alibi...But he himself has lately shown signs of a certain restlessness" and this led him to write *12.30 From Croydon*, an 'inverted' story which she judged "an excellent book, though here and there the practised hand betrays a little unsureness in working on the unaccustomed material."

Shortly afterwards, he produced a variant on the 'inverted story' theme in *Mystery on Southampton Water*. Again, Sayers' reaction was largely favourable: "Mr. Crofts has combined the two formulae in one tale. Two crimes are committed. In the first we are made privy to every detail up to the point where Scotland Yard is called in. Then, when our old friend Mr. French...is on the point of breaking down the carefully manufactured defence of the criminals, a new crime occurs to disconcert him. This time we are not officially let into the secret, and have to follow the mind of the chief inspector in unmasking the culprit. The use of the two methods in one book provides a welcome variety of interest, and, but for one blemish, the story would have been one of Mr. Crofts' best pieces of work."

Writing from the criminal's viewpoint inevitably meant that authors had to focus on criminal psychology, and the results were mixed. Sayers mused that: "To plot murder is easy and entertaining; most of us must from time to time have idly planned out attractive ways of removing obnoxious persons. Most of us go no further. How does the murderer come to cross the dreadful Rubicon that lies between dreaming and doing? And what does he think about it afterwards? History seldom tells us, and the novelist can only imagine."

At the time that Sayers was reviewing, 'Eurocrime' was virtually non-existent as far as British readers and reviewers were concerned, because even though Continental authors such as S. A. Steeman and Pierre Boileau were writing detective novels of considerable merit, hardly any of them were translated. However, one book Sayers covered was "a free adaptation" by the Americans Virginia and Frank Vernon of a French original, *Aux Abois*, by Tristan Bernard, whose real name was Paul Bernard.

The Diary of a Murderer struck Sayers as "an interesting, vivid, and (I should imagine) extremely truthful study."

Mary D. Bickel's *The Trial of Linda Stuart* earned Sayers' approval for originality if not for strength of characterisation: "The construction of the book is ingenious: Each chapter begins with a passage of cross-examination, deadly in its effect; then follows the true story of the facts underlying the prisoner's damning answers. It is a powerful book; but whether we can accept the central situation as a true tragic conflict depends on how far we are able to sympathise with the obstinate stupidity of the heroine."

True crime

Authors interested in the psychology of the criminal will inevitably be interested in real-life crimes, and one approach popular since the days of Edgar Allan Poe has been to fictionalise actual cases, or at least to take elements from them in concocting a mystery. But the author who fails to take care should beware. As Sayers warned: "The usual fault of novels 'based on' real life cases is a curious baldness of style, hovering between the two-dimensional outlines of a police-court report and the child-like brightness of one of Mr. Punch's 'Simple Stories.'"

Sayers acknowledged that her portrayal of Margaret Harrison, in *The Documents in the Case* was informed by her perception of Edith Thompson, hanged for murder seven years before the book was published. Sayers, like many of her contemporaries, was fascinated by "true crime", and wrote a superb long essay about the famous Wallace case, which appeared in the Detection Club book *The Anatomy of Murder*.

Winifred Duke's *Skin for Skin* drew heavily on the Wallace case, making the (now widely, though not universally, discredited) assumption that Wallace was guilty of killing his wife. Sayers was impressed: "Even for a guilty man, she arouses our painful sympathy: if the real man was innocent, then the situation scarcely bears thinking about. Miss Duke has handled her material brilliantly, her skill in dialogue being exceptional and her presentation of the complicated nexus of evidence remarkably clear and skilful."

The Jury Disagree, by George Goodchild and C. Bechofer Roberts, was also based, "obviously and openly, upon the actual facts of the Wallace murder. It is not, however, a re-interpretation of the case...for the incidents have been altered and fresh material added, so as to produce an entirely different situation. In this respect it more closely resembles Mr. D. Erskine Muir's handling of the Oscar Slater material in *Five to Five*." Sayers was taken with the authors' focus on events in the jury room, which anticipated the approach of better known books written subsequently, Richard Hull's *Excellent Intentions*, and Raymond Postgate's *Verdict of Twelve*: "the solution is unimportant compared with the vivacious to-and-fro of the argument...and the characterisation of the jurors – all so well-meaning, all so much biased, consciously or unconsciously, by personal prejudice and experience, all acting and reacting so curiously upon one another."

Catherine Meadows' approach in *Henbane* was different. She adhered very closely to the facts known about Dr. Crippen, whose psychology intrigued Sayers: she had "spoken to more than one person who had met Hawley Harvey Crippen after his arrest, and they all say the same thing: 'He was a *nice* little man.' And, indeed, I believe he really was. He murdered only under overwhelming stress of circumstances; he chose a most merciful poison, killing at once and without pain; and his devotion to the girl he loved approached the heroic."

Meadows' novel had Sayers in raptures: "She has succeeded in subduing the raw material of fact to the processes of art, and the book would be equally interesting and enthralling if one had never heard of Crippen...the book is not merely a costume-piece, still less a study of morbid psychology; it is a fine novel of human passion and suffering, neither more nor less convincing because it happens to be a transcript of actual facts. I recommend it strongly."

Alan Brock's *After the Fact* was based on the Luard murder of 1908: "This problem was never publicly solved, and although the unhappy husband came under suspicion at the time and took his own life, it is generally held today that he was perfectly innocent. Mr. Brock reproduces the circumstances of the actual murder – the shooting of the wife in a summer house upon a neighbouring estate, the theft of her rings, and the partial establishment of the husband's alibi – but he provides a solution of his own, quite extraneous to the facts of the real case and not intended to elucidate them."

Sayers did not, however, consider that *After the Fact* was comparable in quality with the books by Winifred Duke and Catherine Meadows. Similarly, she had reservations about another collaborative effort from Goodchild and Roberts, *The Dear Old Gentleman*, which drew on the M'Lachlan case: "They have... brought the story up to date, and I cannot help feeling that it loses a little in the process; for when we read the report of the actual case what strikes us most forcibly is the queer, vivid spotlight that it throws upon lower middle-class life in Scotland of the sixties."

She did, however, enjoy Alan Brock's *Further Evidence*, the inspiration for which came from several cases "more or less conforming to a single type, where, though the jury's conclusion was the obvious and probably the true one, an alternative explanation might be made to cover all the known facts. It has interested him, as he says, 'to construct a case on similar lines and to fill in all the gaps.' The result is an exceedingly interesting and well-written book which hovers rather curiously between the detective story and the psychological crime study."

A recurrent theme in Golden Age fiction, evident in books as different as Berkeley's *Trial and Error* and Christie's *And Then There Were None*, was the nature of justice, and the shortcomings of the legal system in ensuring that true justice is done. The legal profession fascinated Sayers, who said in relation to Elizabeth Nisot's *Shortly Before Midnight*: "Everybody enjoys reading the report of a criminal trial, and a book written in this form seldom fails to be interesting when convincingly done."

Sayers was a conservative, and a believer in the status quo, but her views did not blind her to the reality that any system of justice administered by human beings is fallible: "Of the dreadful heart-searchings that follow a miscarriage, or possible miscarriage, of justice, the case of Sacco and Vanzetti provides an example. In *The Untried Case*, Mr. Ehrmann, who was one of the counsel for the defence of these unhappy men, offers his alternative theory of the crime."

However, inferior novelists who tackled the failings of the legal system in their books sometimes succumbed unwisely to the temptation to preach. Leonard Blackledge made clear in *Behind the Evidence* that he was "much concerned about the administration of justice in English courts", but Sayers felt that, for all his sincerity, he voiced his doubts "a trifle naïvely". For good measure, she picked him up on a significant error: "he must not blame 'an English judge and jury' for the Oscar Slater affair: Scotland must take the onus of that."

Occasionally, Sayers reviewed a non-fiction book. An example was *Cornish of the "Yard": His Reminiscences and Cases* by Ex-Superintendent G. W. Cornish, over which she enthused. Shortly afterwards, Cornish agreed to collaborate with Sayers and other members of the Detection Club on an innovative collection of stories about supposedly 'perfect crimes', *Six against the Yard*.

The future of the detective story

Sayers regularly found herself ruminating about what the future held for the detective novel. Authors continued to play games with their readers, and she noted that J. S. Fletcher's *Murder of the Only Witness* had been republished "at 3s. 6d., with the addition of an extra clue in the shape of a jigsaw puzzle, housed in a neat wallet at the back. It is a nice little jigsaw, remarkably well fitting, considering that, like the Knave of Hearts, it is made entirely of cardboard, and should provide good entertainment for the family circle." But game-playing was not enough to keep the genre thriving.

She mused about the possible fate of detectives in long-running series: "Are they to remain the Peter Pans of fiction, unwithered by age and unstaled by custom in the infinite variety of their case-hardening experience? Or shall they, suffering the vicissitudes of love and sorrow like other men, grow old along with us, till detective, author and reader totter querulously into the grave together? Or shall we ruthlessly hurl them over the Reichenbach Falls (at the risk, to be sure, of having to haul them painfully up again later) and let younger rivals step into their shoes?" This was no doubt a subject debated long into the night at the Detection Club. John Rhode came up with an interesting answer to the problem in *Hendon's First Case* (the title refers to the then recently established police college) which Sayers approved: "Three ways of tackling a detective problem are fruitfully contrasted: the way of experience, the way of imagination, and the way of the scientific inquirer."

Sayers told the story of how she gave a talk expressing enthusiasm for books which attempted "to give the detective story a more reasonable psychology than it used to have", and which prompted a member of the audience to ask if she wasn't "taking detective stories rather too seriously". For good measure, he added: "I have noted the tendency you mention. I regret it very much. I like a detective story to be just a puzzle and no more. Do you really think that kind of story is dying out?"

The short answer was yes: "No author who takes the writing of English seriously will be content to spin ropes of sand for ever. One day he will want to put some passion into his work, and if he may not put it into his detective stories, he will go away and write some other kind of thing. Then we shall again have all the detective stories badly written and all the good writing elsewhere. It may be that the heady liquor of ambition will find the detective story too narrow a bottle and burst it altogether... But I believe the future to be with those writers who can contrive to strike the note of sincerity and to persuade us that violence really hurts."

As she said in another review: "Plot is not everything; style is not everything; only by combining them can we get a detective story that is also good literature." History has proved her right. Consider, merely by way of example, the enduring success of the work of P. D. James, a distinguished crime novelist of a later generation, and a fervent admirer of Sayers' work, as well as the acclaim that has greeted the recent ventures into detective fiction of another Sayers fan, J. K. Rowling.

The changing times

Sayers was writing her reviews at a time of rapidly-growing international tension. Woodthorpe and Punshon were among those authors who tackled the menace of Fascism and Nazism in their novels, but the book which addressed Hitler's rise to power most directly and impressively was *The Talking Sparrow Murders* by an American crime writer, Darwin L. Teilhet.

The book's setting in Germany immediately after Hitler's rise to power gave it "a strong topical interest. Periods of political revolution and reform are usually confused and puzzling periods, and the book faithfully reflects this aspect of its setting. Murders occur, and the solution of the problem is made more difficult and embarrassing for the police owing to the fact that the names of prominent Nazis are involved... There are sinister hints of hidden intrigue, lurid flashes of light on the persecution of the Jews, grim little scenes of blood and squalor mingled with the glitter of night-club life, and over it all hangs that atmosphere of suspicion and insecurity which is bound to accompany national upheavals." Sayers' focus was on whether the book succeeded or failed as a detective novel rather than as a slice of history-in-the-making, and concluded, positively but rather anti-climactically, that it was "an interesting book, which may be recommended to those who like something a little out of the common."

The Talking Sparrow Murder has occasionally been reprinted over the years, but *The Death Riders* by Cornelius Corfyn is scarcely remembered. Apparently a debut novel, it was in fact the solitary collaboration between Hilary Aidan St George Saunders (who was one half of the duo who wrote successful thrillers and detective novels under the name Francis Beeding) and John de Vere Loder (a former colleague of Saunders' at the League of Nations who later became Baron Wakehurst, and the last British governor of New South Wales.) Sayers gave the book a mixed review, but noted that the "first part is well written and full of thrills; and though the tone of its references to the German people and their present governors is ill calculated to promote international good feeling, the description of the escape from Germany carries conviction with it." Again, she steers well clear of expressing personal criticism of the Nazis, but this is unsurprising; she avoided discussing politics altogether in the reviews and, even with the benefit of hindsight, most readers are likely to conclude that the reviews are the better for it.

Sayers' workload remained heavy, and the demands on her time were no doubt the main reason why she decided to stop reviewing detective novels. She may, however, also have concluded that there was not much she could usefully add to the observations she had made about the genre and what it took to make a good detective novel.

Her last reviews of detective fiction (a discussion of a "true crime" book by William Roughead appeared in 1937) were printed on 18 August 1935. Unfortunately, neither novel (whose authors, Richard Wormser and H. M. Stephenson, soon faded from view) appealed much to Sayers. As a critic, she had run out of steam, and it is clear that she feared the same was true of the traditional detective novel.

Yet she remained optimistic, feeling that "the detective story is passing, in these days, through an extraordinarily interesting stage of development. It has succeeded in establishing for itself a standard of technical achievement which is recognised by a considerable body of writers, critics, and readers. It is now, for example, generally accepted that the author should play fair, avoid coincidence, tuck in his loose ends, and get his poisons from the chemist instead of distilling them out of his own fantasy. A technique is not perfected all in a moment; it has taken some hard work to reach this point, and we are to be congratulated on having got so far. But now comes the moment when, having made our rules and got them by heart, we can begin to experiment and play about with them. And this will bring us face to face with a whole set of new problems..."

Four years later, Britain was plunged into another global conflict, one which changed everything. As Sayers' friend Michael Gilbert, a crime writer and Detection Club member of a younger generation, once said: "The detective story proper...reached its full flowering in England in the thirties...only to be swept away, along with other less creditable extras, on the rough tide of war."

Sayers wrote very little detective fiction after she stopped reviewing. Her interests shifted elsewhere, although her devotion to the Detection Club remained undimmed. Soon Berkeley, Woodthorpe, and other colleagues followed her in abandoning the genre, although Berkeley continued as a reviewer, under the Francis Iles name, until the end of his life. Milward Kennedy took over at the *Sunday Times*, but he too lost heart as a detective novelist, confining himself to the occasional production of a thriller.

The cerebral and playful novels that we associate with "the Golden Age of detective fiction" represented a form of escapism after one world war, but were increasingly overshadowed by anxieties about the possibility of another. For more than half a century, the quality of the best fiction of the Golden Age of Murder has been undervalued and misunderstood. Today, at a time when Golden Age detective fiction is enjoying a revival of popularity, Sayers' reviews remain as entertaining and informative as when they were first published. What is more, they are written in pretty good English! It is a pleasure to introduce them to a new generation of crime fiction lovers.

MARTIN EDWARDS

* * *

THE COLLECTED CRIME REVIEWS

of

DOROTHY L. SAYERS

––––––––

1933

––––––––

25 June 1933
DETECTIVE STORIES OF THE WEEK
The Whole Scale of Toughness

Inquest. By Henrietta Clandon. (Bles. 7s. 6d.)
The Body in the Silo. By Ronald A. Knox. (Hodder and Stoughton. 7s. 6d.)
Death in Darkness. By Charles Barry. (Hurst and Blackett. 7s. 6d.)
Crime de Luxe. By Elizabeth Gill. (Cassell. 7s. 6d.)

While every detective story is a blend of thrill and puzzle, there is a great deal of variation in the toughness of the amalgam. Some readers prefer to be thrilled by the puzzle, and others to be puzzled by the thrills. This week's assortment ranges over the whole scale of toughness. The first two titles will appeal most to the puzzle-fans.

"INQUEST" deals with one of those embarrassing house-parties – commoner, I hope, in detective fiction than in fact – of which "Shall We Join the Ladies?" provides the classic example. A company director has accidentally (?) perished in France of a complication of toadstool poisoning and a broken neck, and his widow invites to her house in England all the mutually suspect and hostile persons who were present at the time of his death. At the informal inquest which results a thoroughly uneasy time is had by all. And you may not be surprised to learn that, while the guests are engaged in throwing out nasty hints about one another, something particularly unpleasant happens to one of them.

I find it a little hard to believe that even a French country doctor would have been quite so stupid about the company director's death as Miss Clandon makes out. But if we overlook a little clumsiness here and elsewhere, and a certain dampness about the dénouement, which somehow doesn't explode in our face as it should, this is an attractive and promising piece of puzzle-making. The book is very well written, the dialogue being quite exceptionally fresh and well-managed, and the characterisation good. This appears to be Miss Henrietta Clandon's first detective story; I hope we shall soon hear from her again.

Father Knox Again

"THE BODY IN THE SILO" is also concerned with a sinister house-party, and presents the serious solver with a very handsome and meaty problem, which will exercise all his brain power.

I hope Father Knox has satisfied himself that his murder-method is physically possible, for some of the details are rather staggering. (And he will understand me when I say that *some things* are even more regrettable than Chinamen!) However, all the clues are honourably offered for inspection by our old friend Mr. Bredon, of the "Indescribable", while the publisher has (rather treacherously) thrown in a little extra help on the jacket.

To say that the book is beautifully written would be mere impertinence; we expect no less from one of the most brilliant of living stylists. Perhaps, like Meredith, Father Knox is too apt to make all his characters as witty as himself, but wit is not so plentiful in detective fiction that we can afford to quarrel with it. As usual, the follies of the modern world are shrewdly castigated – and, in fact, this book is full of hard Knox.

Mr. Charles Barry continually disappoints me. He is fertile in ingenious ideas, but his villain will always take such shocking risks. In "The Corpse on the Bridge" he ignored the noticeable difference in weight between a corpse and a stuffed dummy. In "DEATH IN DARKNESS" he forgets that a sharp lateral pull – very probable in the circumstances – would have blown his little plot sky-high. (I cannot be more precise without giving it away myself.) Also, Mr. Barry is rather secretive about his clues. And he writes horrid slipshod English.

It is a pity, because he has bits so good that I feel he could do better if he liked. In the meantime, here are plenty of encounters and hot pursuits and shots going off at midnight in the coal-cellar, and you might choose worse than this for a railway journey.

The line between the detective story and the thriller is sometimes rather fine-drawn, but when we find the passengers in a luxury liner plotting to slay one another for the possession of a chemical formula; when that formula concerns the composition of a "Universal Fertiliser" which makes grass shoot up overnight, like Jack's beanstalk; and when the detective is ready to compound three brutal murders in order to secure the Fertiliser for the League of Nations, we feel that the frontier has been definitely crossed. Miss Elizabeth Gill writes far better and with much more humour than the average thrill-merchant, and if you can bear with the Fertiliser, you will get a good deal of entertainment out of "CRIME DE LUXE".

2 July 1933
DETECTIVE STORIES OF THE WEEK
An American Nut Worth Cracking

The American Gun Mystery. By Ellery Queen. (Gollancz. 7s. 6d.)
Death in Fancy Dress. By Anthony Gilbert. (Crime Club. Collins. 7s. 6d.)
Murder Rehearsal. By Roger East. (Crime Club. Collins. 7s. 6d.)

Mr. Ellery Queen is determined to be literary or die. Here are a few choice specimens of herbage and verbiage from the opening pages of "THE AMERICAN GUN MYSTERY": "A puff of the cosmic effluvium" – "sharp effluvium of dung and sweat and breath" – "this might be Pegasus, this arch-necked stallion, naked and sleek as the day he was foaled" – "horses the warp and woof of the outdoors" – "his alabaster bosom" (it is only a white shirtfront) – "he slid, almost slithered over the rug. He was like a cat on his feet" (do cats slide over rugs?) – "he was in a chair, his incredible bulk quiescent as poured steel."

Nevertheless, if the reader can stomach these intolerable affectations, most of which, thank goodness, disappear when the author gets into his stride, he will be rewarded by a rattling good yarn with a well-constructed mystery. The setting is novel and exciting – a Wild West Rodeo show staged on Broadway – with a murder pulled off before twenty thousand spectators.

You get all the cowboy picturesqueness, combined with the fun of night-clubs, news-reels, "tabloid" reporters (who make Fleet Street men look like a Girls' Friendly Society), and a gorgeous broadcast running commentary on a heavy-weight fight. As to the mystery, I frankly confess that I only guessed about half of it, and on due and sour consideration I am reluctantly compelled to admit that the author was quite honourable and that the stupidity was mine. "The American Gun Mystery" is, I think, a harder nut to crack than "The Roman Hat", "The French Powder", or "The Dutch Shoe" (all of which I did solve), and less mannered and exasperating than "The Greek Coffin", or "The Egyptian Cross", though Ellery Queen (the detective, not the author – how confusing it is when the bard is the hero of the story!) "sure does", in his father's words, "talk like a Kentucky mountaineer with the mumps."

Read and enjoy without skipping, or you may easily over-run the trail.

Genuine Excitement

"DEATH IN FANCY DRESS" has at least one uncommon merit. It contrives to persuade us that something really serious and unpleasant is taking place at Feltham Abbey. So often in a detective story trivial irregularities like blackmail and murder seem scarcely to ruffle the placid current of domestic affairs, and the only person who displays any genuine excitement is the detective. Here, the atmosphere of suspense and uneasiness really does pervade the household. Setting aside the obvious 'bad-hat' of the family, who is earmarked for trouble in any case, we are invited to select a murderer and society blackmailer from among a remarkably well-drawn and sympathetic cast of characters. The choice is difficult (perhaps the blackmailer is made a little too sympathetic for absolute fairness), and the cleverest thing in the book is the way in which the heroine's two lovers are played off against one another to the confusion of the reader's critical judgment. The writing is, on the whole, so good that I am inclined to lay the one or two syntactical howlers to the charge of the printer.

Mr. Roger East has hit on an original idea for "MURDER REHEARSAL".

His three murders are not in themselves very outstanding, being of types common enough in mystery fiction. The originality lies in the way in which the threefold plot is traced to the brain that first conceived it. A detective-novelist plays a prominent part in the story, and here Mr. East displays, alas! a too, too penetrating insight into the workings of the mystery-monger's mind, and of the reader's also. "Have you ever realised", asks his novelist, "that the reader doesn't really follow the clues, or rather that the clues he follows are not the ones the author intended? The real clues are ... the way the author introduced his characters ... the inflections of the style, the balance and the proportion."

Let authors look to their mannerisms, for there never was a truer word spoken. There is here no very hard problem for the reader, and the style is not specially distinguished, but the book is out of the common rut, and the Crime Club are justified in making it the selection from their July list.

9 July 1933
TIPSTERS OF CRIME STORIES
Selections to Follow

Murder in the Square. By Johnston Smith. (Archer. 7s. 6d.)
The Monkhurst Murder. By Francis D. Grierson. (Collins. Crime Club. 7s. 6d.)
Mystery on the Centre Court. By Hilda Willett. (Stanley Paul. 7s. 6d.)
The Pepper-Pot Problem. By Olive Cecil. (John Long. 7s. 6d.)
The Return of Arsène Lupin. By Maurice Leblanc. (Skeffington. 7s. 6d.)
The White Glove. By William Le Queux. (Eldon Press. 7s. 6d.)

Publishers, these days, seem to be taking a leaf out of the Government's book and referring all their decisions to committees of experts. Crime Club publications, for example, are chosen by a Headmaster and his team of connoisseurs; Messrs. Stanley Paul and Skeffington rely on the guidance of the Crime Book Society, commanded by an eminent surgeon-admiral; while Mr. Archer goes one better, and presents his candidates under the aegis of a mysterious gentleman called "Enigma", who may be the Prime Minister or Professor Einstein, but whom, judging by the advice on the wrapper to "follow the Enigma's selections", I, personally, suspect of being attached to racing circles. Well, and why not? Entering into the spirit of the thing, let us see if we cannot make up a book or so with the assistance of these sportsmen.

"MURDER IN THE SQUARE" (magenta jacket) is Enigma's nap for the Detection Stakes, run over a very sporting course in the neighbourhood of West Kensington. This stylish-looking youngster is not yet a finished racer, but he takes my fancy immensely. He is thoroughbred, coming of the fine King's English strain, by Humour out of Deduction, and I shall look for some first-class performances in classic events from the same stables in the near future.

Easy Action

The colt is well put together, with good solid understandings and plenty of character, moving with a nice, easy action, and getting away smartly from the gate. A little skittishness from time to time may cause his friends uneasiness, and he has a tendency to fly his fences, which a little more training will correct. His jockey, Johnston Smith, is, I believe, a newcomer. He needs to keep his mount a trifle more closely in hand and to pay better attention to his stops. He should also remember that the use of the Zeugma is now barred in the best writing schools. Nevertheless, he writes cleverly, lying back deceptively for nine-tenths of the course, and keeping something in hand for the finish.

"THE MONKHURST MURDER" (green jacket, green-and-maroon band) is tipped by "Headmaster" for a place, and this estimate is pretty correct. A good, honest nag, a bit showy, but sound, and guided by an experienced rider, he may be relied on to bring your money home.

He has no unexpected tricks, but keeps going and maintains a steady turn of speed from start to finish. He does not seem to me to answer to the whip very well in the final spurt; still, his performance is creditable and will not disappoint. The course is laid across country, from the Battered Head to the Coroner's Court.

A Ding-Dong Finish

"Surgeon-Admiral" selects "MYSTERY ON THE CENTRE COURT" (yellow and green jacket, black-and-maroon band) for a steeplechase from Wimbledon to Thames Valley, via Paris. There are no surprises in this filly. At every point the shrewd student of form will accurately predict her behaviour, as, from a brisk start at the Vanishing Man, she takes Plunders Bank and Blackmail Deep in her stride, floundering a little in the sticky going about Lovers' Chase, rapping her heels all round at the big Coincidence Double, steadily negotiating the familiar turn at Traitor's Tryst and the old blind trap at Lone House Corner, to end with a ding-dong, hammer-and-tongs tussle up the straight at Thriller's Finish. Though not the class of animal I personally fancy, she will undoubtedly find backers.

A little lady who pleases me better is "THE PEPPER-POT PROBLEM" (picture jacket), sired by Wodehouse Nights out of Ruritania, and capably handled by Olive Cecil. I would not recommend her as a stayer in heavy country, but she is well-mannered and light in hand, and will spin along merrily over five furlongs to win in a canter. Well worth a flutter on a holiday afternoon.

The French horse, "THE RETURN OF ARSENE LUPIN" (yellow-and-black jacket, cherry caption, black-and-maroon band), is another of "Surgeon-Admiral's" selections. This latest scion of the illustrious Lupin stock runs as gallantly as any of his forebears. Maurice Leblanc is a seasoned jockey, who has written many favourites to victory.

William Le Queux's new mount is "THE WHITE GLOVE" (rainbow jacket). True to form.

16 July 1933
A FORMULA FOR THE CRIME BOOK
Murders and Humour

Sleep No More. By Florence Ryerson and Colin Clements. (Grayson. 7s. 6d.)
The White Cockatoo. By Mignon G. Eberhart. (Falcon Books: Bodley Head. 7s. 6d.)
The Mantle of Ishmael. By J. S. Fletcher. (Jenkins. 3s. 6d.)
The Almost Perfect Murder. By Hulbert Footner. (Crime Club: Collins. 7s. 6d.)

You will know "SLEEP NO MORE" for a proper detective story at once. It has a map, two plans, and a genealogical table, and conforms very closely to the excellent formula laid down by one of its own characters: "Detective stories must have plenty of blood, chills, and humour. All clues must be plainly stated; all murders must be committed by one character, and that character must have an established place in the story." It has a plot of the 'closed circle' type, in which all the persons of the drama are marooned in a confined area (in this case an old house on an island at the mouth of an American river), so that one or other of them must have done the deed.

This is very cosy and agreeable, though I wish that so many of the suspects were not successively eliminated by coming to sticky ends themselves. This means that by the time you reach the last chapter the choice is not a very wide one, and you ought to have very little difficulty in spotting the culprit. All the same, you will need to have your wits about you to pick up all the clues.

A sound, well-constructed story, pleasantly written and scrupulously fair. I can safely recommend it.

"THE WHITE COCKATOO" hovers on the line between the detective story and the thriller, with a pronounced leaning towards the thriller. Its strong point is its atmosphere. Its action all takes place in a French country-town hotel, in the dead waste and middle of the winter. Its opening chapters, with their picture of the windy courtyard, chequered with bleak light and wavering shadows, the dim old-fashioned corridors and musty rooms filled with furniture of inappropriate splendour, the cramped little slow-moving lift, the melancholy lounge dotted with wicker chairs and desiccated palms, the whole barren dinginess of the abominable place, through which the few visitors and the skeleton staff flit like lone survivors from a catastrophe – these chapters convey more real eeriness and discomfort than you could get from gallons of blood, dozens of sheeted spectres, or scores of conspiratorial gangs in Chinese opium dens.

Not that the author has stinted us of blood and conspiracies – far from it. There are three corpses, three impersonations, an abduction or two, a murderous assault, and a beautiful heroine to keep things lively. The dénouement is a trifle confused and tumultuous. It is the writing that lifts the book right out of the ordinary blood-and-thunder class. The portrait of the little hotel porter is, in its small way, a gem, and the tale is, altogether, exceptionally attractive of its kind.

In "THE MANTLE OF ISHMAEL" Mr. J. S. Fletcher takes us back to the year of Signorinetta's Derby, the period of the hansom cab and the picture hat, when noblemen said, "Off'ly pleased, I'm shaw. Mons'ous bad business, yah know, begad!" There is a villainous mad doctor with hypnotic eyes, a house full of trap doors and secret rooms, an infernal machine which blows up everything except the virtuous characters, a kidnapping on an armoured yacht, and a poisoning – in short the whole bag of tricks.

Mr. Fletcher can write very well when he likes, but this reads rather like dull parody.

"THE ALMOST PERFECT MURDER" contains four stories about that glamorous woman-sleuth, Mme. Storey. The last is, I think, the best, in

spite of the surprising kind of justice meted out summarily at the end
by the District Attorney. (After all, there is worse morality in Act V of
"Measure for Measure"). Mr. Hulbert Footner can always push a crook
yarn vigorously along in a brisk style with no frills on it, and these four
stories are well up to standard in the matter of entertainment.

23 July 1933
A SLEUTH WHO WAS TOO CLEVER
The Case of Berkely v. Sheringham

Jumping Jenny. By Anthony Berkeley. (Hodder and Stoughton. 7s. 6d.)
The Bank Vault Mystery. By Louis F. Booth. (Hutchinson. 7s. 6d.)
The Murders at the Manor. By Clive Ryland. (Grayson. 7s. 6d.)
The Roof. By David Whitelaw. (Bles. 7s. 6d.)

The greatest peril that besets the detective story is that of over-mechanisation.
We have trodden the weary mile so often – the corpse, the constable, the
interrogations, the false clues, the infallible sleuth, the criminal's anxiety to
cover his tracks, the slip, the true clue, the deductions, the dramatic exposé,
and the revolver shots in the final chapter. Mr. Anthony Berkeley deserves
all gratitude for his energetic efforts to escape from the thraldom of formula.

In "JUMPING JENNY" he has kicked over the traces with glee and
gusto. No infallible sleuth or cast-iron deductions for him. He has often
made it plain to us that his own detective, Mr. Roger Sheringham, is an
irritating, conceited jumper to erroneous conclusions, but this time he
treats the poor man with downright savagery. Cocksure and officious,
Mr. Sheringham rushes in to confound confusion, fakes evidence, makes
all the murderer's mistakes for him, nearly lands himself in gaol, stam-
pedes his friends into unnecessary perjuries, falls into every conceivable
fallacy, and exhibits himself in every posture of absurdity. And in order
that no detail of these antics may be lost upon us, Mr. Berkeley reveals
nine-tenths of the solution at the start. He is an adept at showing how,
from a single set of premises, the over-ingenious mind may construct endless

theories, all plausible and all wrong, and it is immensely entertaining to watch the unhappy Sheringham light upon the truth, elaborately prove it to be impossible, and then proceed, with enormous self-importance, to demonstrate the convincing truth of what never happened at all.

If you are hard-boiled and disillusioned about detectives, you will find this tale very refreshing. It reminds me in some ways of "The Poisoned Chocolates Case" and I am not sure that it is not the cleverest thing Mr. Berkeley has done since that very clever book.

The characterisation is lively, though subdued, so as to let the ineffable Mr. Sheringham prance and gambol unpartnered in the spotlight. (Mr. Berkeley should, however, note that it takes more than the interjection "Ach!" and the facetious use of the epithet "wee" to make a Scotsman.) The plot is about a perfectly hateful lady who gets hanged at one of those 'murder parties', and, needless to say, Mr. Berkeley has kept a cunning twist up his sleeve for the last page.

––––––––––

Mr. Booth, on the other hand, keeps to the conventional path. There are two kinds of American detective story. The one reads like a Bedlam nightmare; in the other, police inquiries proceed in as orderly and sensible a fashion as in the works of Mr. Freeman Wills Crofts. "THE BANK VAULT MYSTERY" is of the second kind, and will appeal to English taste. It is a well-constructed, agreeably written yarn about stolen bank-notes and murder, and the action develops sanely and soberly to a logical and satisfactory conclusion.

There are no gangsters, no graft, no Bowery-flowery language, and no stunts of any kind. Except for a difference of procedure in the case of persons arrested on suspicion and a passing allusion to the third degree, the background might be London instead of New York. A workmanlike job, with one or two nice touches.

––––––––––

Mr. Clive Ryland in "THE MURDERS AT THE MANOR" starts out well with a disagreeable baronet shot dead in a secluded pavilion, five minutes' walk from a houseful of people thirsting for his blood. And then

– just as we are getting on splendidly with the timetables and the alibis – he goes and commits the unforgivable sin! Deliberately, unblushingly, and without the least excuse, he conceals the vital clue. The reader has no chance to guess it – even the detective does not guess it – it comes out casually in a conversation about something else. It is all very wrong. A white sheet and a candle for Mr. Ryland, please! He writes so pleasantly that we must hope for his repentance and amendment.

———————

There was a body on "THE ROOF", of course. This is more an adventure story than a detective story, because we are given the criminal's side of the business, instead of being left to guess. But it is exciting and written with some pretensions to style, and it certainly holds our interest from first to last.

30 July 1933
SHACKLES ON CRIME STORIES
No chance for a new Sherlock Holmes?

Policeman's Lot. By Henry Wade. (Constable. 7s. 6d.)
Follow the Blue Car. By R. A. J. Walling. (Hodder and Stoughton. 7s. 6d.)
Murder Comes Home. By Nellise Child. (Collins: Crime Club. 7s. 6d.)

I want to talk this week about short stories. You, gentle reader, are said to have a prejudice against them. Yet the world's greatest reputation in detective fiction was built up on the short story. There are only four full-length Sherlock Holmes novels; the rest of that enormous fame is a short-story achievement.

This week we have an excellent volume of short stories by Henry Wade, who is one of our best and soundest detective writers. His plots are ingenious, his tales well written; taken as a whole, they offer better problems than many of the Holmes series. They lack only one quality:

that touch of glamour which makes such things memorable. The same might be said of almost all detective short stories written to-day.

Why is this? There are still writers who can put this quality into the detective novel. There are, I think, two major causes for its absence from the modern "short". One is, quite brutally and simply, that the magazine editors who publish the tales in the first instance impose a limit of 6,000 words or so. Every word extraneous to the plot has to be ruthlessly cut out. All those fascinating prologues – the most characteristic and best-remembered parts of the Holmes stories – all the fun with Watson's boots, the intriguing allusions to the unrecorded cases, the little disquisitions on "My methods, Watson", the monographs on tobacco-ash and the Polyphonic motets of Lassus, the quaint glimpses of the Baker Street household – all these beloved side-issues which make the personality would have been lost to the world under the 6,000-word rule.

Insistence on Murder

Only three writers have succeeded in establishing a memorable personal-ity under the new conditions: Austin Freeman, by specialising in a very restricted type of plot; H. C. Bailey, by appealing to a rather restricted circle of readers; and G. K. Chesterton, by firmly washing out all the technical complications we have come to expect in a detective story.

This brings us to the second cause of trouble: the determination of writers to write, and readers to read, no detective story that is not concerned with murder. The investigation of a murder has become so full of technical complications in these days that the details clutter the story. Now, out of the twelve "Adventures" of Sherlock Holmes, only four have to do with murder, yet the remaining eight are just as entertaining and memorable as the four. And room has thus been made to exploit the personality of the detective.

Reader, writer, and editor must share the blame for fastening the shackles on the detective short story, but the reader has the whip-hand of the other two. If he will take the short story seriously, and demand from the editor more elasticity and less bloodshed, then the writer will be happy to oblige.

In the meantime, "POLICEMAN'S LOT" is as good a collection of detective yarns as can be looked for under the present conditions – a hundred times better worth reading than many a tale that has been blown up artificially to novel length in an effort to circumvent the prejudice against short stories.

———————

R. A. J. Walling has written several novels which are good entertainment, while falling short of the first class. "FOLLOW THE BLUE CAR" has plenty of excitement in it, though I do not like it as well as "The Stroke of One". Tolefree, the detective, has moments when he almost achieves that elusive glamour, and the plot is sufficiently complex without being too bewildering.

———————

Don't be too much put off "MURDER COMES HOME" by the fact that the hero wears a pale pink shirt and strawberry cravat, with a tobacco-brown suit and a brown hat tipped over one ear. It is good fun of its kind – the plot is the one about the threatened man and the sinister family, with setting near Los Angeles – and there are gruesome corpses in plenty.

6 August 1933
CRIME PUZZLES FOR HOLIDAYMAKERS
Mysteries that may have been missed

This is the season when publishers more or less cease from publishing, and when the holiday-making reader sometimes falls back for entertainment upon reprints and the resources of the local library. And here, tucked away upon an unpromising-looking shelf, among the shockers and the love-romances, one sometimes comes across a surprisingly jolly detective yarn which, somehow or other, one missed on its first appearance. So this week I have overhauled my note-books for a few old titles which merit having the dust blown off them. Setting aside the "regulars" of the mystery profession, whose names (as the advertisers say) are "a guarantee of quality", I shall confine myself to less well-known people who have written one or two books worth reading.

For instance: "THE SQUARE MARK", by Grace M. White and H. L. Deakin, about a murder at a girls' school (Methuen); and "THE MURDER IN THE LABORATORY", by T. L. Davidson (Methuen). Both books have been out some years, and I know of no other works by these authors, but they are very good indeed – sound, well written, fair to the reader, with everything handsome about them. These two books, together with the Methuen prize-book, "THE INCONSISTENT VILLAINS", by N. A. Temple-Ellis, and "THE SECRET OF BOGEY HOUSE", by Herbert Adams, are to be had very cheaply in a fat "omnibus" of "MYSTERY STORIES" (Book I) issued by Newnes at 3s. 6d. – amazing value, though rather closely printed. "MYSTERY STORIES" (Book II) also contains four full-length novels, of which one at least, Thomas Kindon's "MURDER IN THE MOOR" (originally published by Methuen), is quite first-rate.

That Little Extra Something

Of course you read R. C. Woodthorpe's "THE PUBLIC SCHOOL MURDER" (Ivor Nicholson and Watson) last year. If not, do try to get hold of it. The gorgeous picture of life in the masters' common room made it the most brilliant and humorous detective story of its season. It is rather the same type of thing as Dermot Morrah's "THE MUMMY CASE", published by Faber and Faber this year, and is, I think, funnier. Then there was Rufus King's "MURDER BY LATITUDE" (Heinemann), which, with one or two technical faults, possessed that distinction – that little extra something – which the others, alas! so often haven't got. That came out about two years ago.

I now come to two good Benn authors. E. R. Punshon has written a number of detective stories so excellent that it is astonishing they are not much better known. You will love his pair of detectives: the melancholy Sergeant Bell, who does all the work, and the pompous Inspector Carter, who takes all the credit. Everything Mr. Punshon writes is good; you might start on "PROOF COUNTER-PROOF" or "THE COTTAGE MURDER". Both these stories appear in "The Carter and Bell Detective Omnibus" published this year at 7s. 6d. The other author, Nigel Orde-Powlett, is a newcomer. His first book, "THE CAST TO DEATH", was one of last year's good things, and has a special appeal to trout-fishers (technical details audited and found correct). His new one, "DRIVEN DEATH", is also good and deals with grouse shooting.

Woman Doctor-Detective

One of my unexpected "finds" last year was Sidney Fairway's "THE YELLOW VIPER" (Stanley Paul). It has thrillerish bits, but the part about the woman doctor who does the detecting is admirable, and obviously written from inside knowledge. Make a note also of two titles with an ecclesiastical flavour: Kenneth Ashley's "DEATH OF A CURATE" (John Lane) and T. F. W. Hickey's "THE CORPSE IN THE CHURCH" (Methuen). Both authors write very pleasantly, and Mr. Ashley in particular is original in his handling and good on local colour.

Local colour is also the strong point of Harold Best's "THE FLAM-ING HUT MURDER" (Cassell), which has a West African background. Finally, here are two brief honourable mentions: Adele Leaman's "THE GREEN BAG" (Skeffington) and Dorothy Johnson's "DEATH OF A SPINSTER" (Longmans).

All these books are genuine detective stories, good for an hour or so of pleasant puzzlement at holiday-time.

* * *

13 August 1933
OLD STYLE AND NEW IN THRILLERS
A change from "Crossword" crimes

Murder of the Only Witness. By J. S. Fletcher. (Harrap. 7s. 6d.)
Death Whispers. By Joseph B. Carr. (Cassell. 7s. 6d.)
The Haunted Light. By Evadne Price. (Long. 7s. 6d.)

To quote a pronouncement from a book which I must not review till next week, "the really successful detective is the man who sits in his office waiting for people to come and tell him things". Mr. Fletcher's detectives are of that kind. Not that they pass all their time in the office. They run about the country quite a lot, and one of them is actually rash enough to go off all by himself to that dear old lonely house we know so well, where the beautiful woman has been imprisoned by the Gang. But there! If detectives did not sometimes do these things, what would become of the story?

Mr. Fletcher, in fact, does not write detective stories in the modern sense of the phrase – those stories in which detective and reader pant side by side through a labyrinth of clues to a solution which Sherlock Holmes's "ideal reasoner" ought to have deduced from the broken boot-lace on page 25. He writes mystery stories of the old straightforward sort, in which things happen in quick succession, and people (very sensibly and properly) come forward with voluntary statements, until the trouble is cleared up in a brief and bloodstained dénouement. For those who are weary of the "cross-word" type of detective fiction, this is often a relief, and Mr. Fletcher has the knack of writing briskly and holding the attention.

The opening chapters of "MURDER OF THE ONLY WITNESS", which deals with the loss of the Ellingshurst diamonds and the mutual accusations of Lord Ellingshurst, his wife, and his wife's friend, are written in the manner of the best drawing-room comedy, and I was rather sorry when the murders started, and people began to fall over stray corpses in secret passages. The book may be recommended to those who like being puzzled, but do not want to sit down to a mystery story as though it were an examination paper.

We have Mr. Carr's word for it that "DEATH WHISPERS". ("Do you call *that* a whisper?" cried the poor King. "It went through and through my head like an earthquake!") A nurse arrives at a sinister old house to look after a man who has been murderously assaulted. A grim-looking individual lurks in the drawing-room, with a pistol bulging through his jacket. An old mad-woman in antique costume calls the cook a creature of Satan. The butler is seen pointing a gun at the patient. A face peers through the rain-streaked window. A staccato fusillade of shots splits the air. A woman faints. Two detectives burst in with a bedraggled prisoner. The sick man's daughter tampers with the nurse's hypodermic. Another shot goes off and the patient is found dead. That ends chapter three.

If this is Death's idea of a whisper, one wonders what would happen if he made up his mind to shout good and hearty.

———————

Another thriller, and a much better one, is "THE HAUNTED LIGHT" – alarms and excursions in a lighthouse, always a good setting for a grim life-and-death tussle. I found this really exciting, and the cockney hero displays a pretty turn of Mark Tapley humour.

20 August 1933
A CRIME WRITER OF DISTINCTION
Salute to Mr. Punshon

Information Received. By E. R. Punshon. (Benn. 7s. 6d.)
Cross Marks the Spot. By James Ronald. (Hodder and Stoughton. 7s. 6d.)
The Mystery of Villa Aurelia. By Burton E. Stevenson.
(Rich and Cowan. 7s. 6d.)

What is distinction – that quality whose name is so often taken in vain by the advertiser? Which is so hard to define and so instantly recognisable when seen? It is missed by scores of competent mystery-writers who can construct impeccable plots. The few who achieve it step – plot or no plot

– unquestioned into the first rank. We recognised it in "Sherlock Holmes" and in "Trent's Last Case", in "The Mystery at the Villa Rose" and in the "Father Brown" stories, and in the works of Mr. E. R. Punshon we salute it every time. In the mere mechanics of puzzle-making, Mr. Punshon has his masters, but all his books have that elusive something which makes them count as literature, so that we do not gulp them furiously down to get to the murderer lurking at the bottom, but roll them slowly and deliciously upon the tongue like old wine.

Good writing and good characterisation – the secret, I suppose, lies there and in Mr. Punshon's all-pervading and sub-acid wit, whose subtle austerity gives dignity to the vintage. In his entrancing portraits of Scotland Yard officials, this wit displays itself to perfection. His Scotland Yard is a creation peculiarly his own. It is not realism in the dull and pedestrian sense of the word. His policemen are just a little brighter and more beautiful than any earthly policemen. They have that enhanced and glorified reality which is the highest art.

In "INFORMATION RECEIVED" we miss, indeed, that blest pair of sirens, Superintendent Carter and Detective-Sergeant Bell. In exchange we have young Bobby Owen, "university man turned policeman", who is delightful, though a little too good to be true, and also – and triumphantly – the suave and cynical Superintendent Mitchell, who is quite superb for humour and truth. The plot is, perhaps, not one of Mr. Punshon's best, and he has yielded to his besetting sin of letting the criminal explain matters in a long-winded and emotional confession.

It does not matter. This is a real book, not assembled by a journeyman, but written, as a book ought to be, by a man who is a writer first and foremost.

———————

"CROSS MARKS THE SPOT", on the other hand, is just a jolly mystery yarn – and a very jolly one too. Julian Mendoza is a detective who will appeal to every woman's heart, as he does to that of his nice Scotch landlady. He is shabby and lame and occasionally takes one over the eight, but he is exceedingly lovable, and, moreover, does his detecting efficiently. Beginning with the shooting of a film magnate in an actress's flat, the tale leads on, through sentiment and sensation, to the oft-told but always effective episode of the actor who is really killed in a stage fight. It is humorously and agreeably written, with good light entertainment on every page.

It is many years now since Mr. Burton E. Stevenson first thrilled me with the mystery of that "Boule Cabinet" which had once belonged to a Borgia. Well do I remember the sinister charm of its brass-and-tortoiseshell inlay and that of its still more beautiful tortoiseshell-and-brass counterpart.

"THE MYSTERY OF VILLA AURELIA" has not quite the same individuality. The author calls it "a Riviera interlude", and we feel that the dark-eyed lady, the Italian crook, the American millionaire, and the designing secretary have played many similar interludes on the same stage before. It is thoroughly enjoyable for all that – a very pleasant thriller.

27 August 1933
CRIME PLOT THAT HAS HAD ITS DAY
When the dead speak

The Case of the Three Strange Faces. By Christopher Bush. (Cassell. 7s. 6d.)
The Second Case of Mr. Paul Savoy. By Jackson Gregory. (Hodder and Stoughton. 7s. 6d.)
The Jade Hat-Pin. By Maurice G. Kiddy. (Hutchinson. 7s. 6d.)

As Mr. Fitzwilliam Darcy remarked upon a famous occasion: "In vain have I struggled. It will not do. My feelings will not be repressed. You must allow me to tell you"– that, if there is one plot I am thoroughly tired of, it is the one about the murdered man who is made to speak after he is dead, by means of a dictaphone, gramophone, "loud-speaker, or other device". Since Mrs. Christie first used the method in "Roger Ackroyd", it has been worked to death. It is dead. This week it has turned up again, and, like Mark Twain, I want a fresher corpse. A lingering kindness of heart restrains me from saying exactly where it has turned up, but if I meet it again in the course of the year I shall deal very harshly with it. It has done well in its time, but now, definitely, it will not do. We know too much about it.

Having thus relieved my feelings, I can turn more composedly to the week's list. First, we have Mr. Christopher Bush, who is always workmanlike and pleasant to read. He starts off well in "THE CASE OF THE THREE STRANGE FACES" with some very queer occurrences in a railway compartment on a night journey between Toulon and Paris. There were six passengers, but only four lived to complete the course. One of these was our friend Mr. Ludovic Travers, of Durangos, Ltd., and it was fortunate that he happened to be there, taking notes in his usual competent way of the odd behaviour of the man with the dyed face, the man with the spotty face, and the man whose face turned red in the night – not to mention the young man with the weak chin and the woman with the hat-pins, or the meek valet and the two suspicious-looking gentlemen who haunted the corridor.

The tale is exciting and well worked out, the clues are fairly given, and altogether "The Case of the Three Strange Faces" provides very good hunting.

––––––––––

Mr. Paul Savoy is one of those detectives with a superiority complex. He is subtle and theoretical, gets his inspirations by gazing in an affected manner at his sapphire ring, and treats his admiring follower, the bull-headed but energetic Detective Gateway, with a condescension which "would be intolerable from Almighty God to a black-beetle". He concludes his investigations (on the subject of a naked corpse which someone has inconsiderately left in a taxi) by gathering all his suspects together and unmasking the criminal in a dramatic scene. (I wonder how often this kind of thing happens in real life.) Looking like a young god of vengeance, he leaps to his feet, and delivers his denunciation in a voice which not only electrifies his hearers, but splits all the infinitives within earshot.

I cannot really love Mr. Paul Savoy. However, the mystery is a good mystery and the villain very villainous – though in strict fairness we should have been given a few more facts about him beforehand.

The characters in "THE JADE HAT-PIN" seldom see, hear, or touch anything. They "sense" things, and when they have "sensed" them, they "tense". I did not tense very much over this story, because I sensed the solution from the word go. The victim is murdered in – you would never guess – the library; and the detective is Stonewall Stevens. Sound enough, but conventional.

3 September 1933
ONE OF THE FEW REAL DETECTIVES
Re-enter Hercule Poirot

Lord Edgware Dies. By Agatha Christie. (Collins: Crime Club. 7s. 6d.)
Dead Man's Heath. By Jefferson Farjeon. (Collins: Crime Club. 7s. 6d.)
Hot Ice. By Robert J. Casey. (Elkin Mathews. 7s. 6d.)

It is always a delight to meet Hercule Poirot again. Age cannot wither him – if, indeed, we can associate any thought of age with his abounding vitality. He is one of the few real detectives, and, like most charmers, is the complete egotist. But with his enormous vanity he combines that complete freedom from self-consciousness which the British male cannot attain, and would not if he could.

> "Poirot", I said, as he remained wrapt in thought. "Hadn't we better go on? Everyone is staring at us."
>
> "Eh? Well, perhaps you are right. Though it does not incommode me that people should stare. It does not interfere in the least with my train of thought."

"People were beginning to laugh", I murmured.

"That has no importance."

Captain Hastings, whose egotism is of another kind, does not quite agree. But M. Poirot continues to exercise the detective's gift of distinguishing the important from the unimportant.

———————

"LORD EDGWARE DIES" is a very good Poirot adventure. Mrs. Christie's touch seems to me to become firmer and her style mellower as she adds book to book. There are still occasional lapses – "She was one of those actresses who had left the stage on *her* marriage" – but, on the whole, her writing is far above the average, and in the management of dialogue she excels. In this story we have none of her unrivalled studies of village life and gossip (as, for example, in "Murder at the Vicarage"); still, we must not be greedy for good things. The plot leads one up the garden-path very skilfully – a sort of 'Looking-Glass' garden-path. I give it full marks.

———————

"DEAD MAN'S HEATH" begins, as so many of them do, with the benighted wayfarer who stumbles upon the Lonely Cottage containing a Beautiful Girl and a Corpse. It is lively all through, and I congratulate the hero on for once doing his job properly in the final scene, and entrapping his villain without having his revolver picked out of his pocket, or getting himself locked up in a gas-filled cellar, or anything exasperating of that kind.

There is a pleasant ex-thief, who assists quite amusingly with the detection, and the tale is agreeable, if a little stereotyped.

———————

As a thorough change from the gentlemanly tradition of the English detective story try "HOT ICE". The publishers have done their worst for it by tagging it "A Story of Diamonds and Death", and putting it into a frightful glazed jacket, adorned with three columns of ill-conceived blurb and a design which would dazzle a blind man in a dark room.

But it is really a very sound, though rather brutal, tale of detection, as, I fear, it is really carried on, not by arm-chair deduction, but by the hauling-up and grilling of stool-pigeons, crooks and their "frails", among whom the honour of thieves is non-existent. There is a lot of American thieves' slang, but otherwise it is written in straightforward English, and the plot – a rather "bluggy" one – is ingenious.

10 September 1933
LOST HEIRS AND MISSING WILLS

John Brand's Will. By Herbert Adams. (Methuen. 7s. 6d.)

In the good old days of Miss Braddon and Mrs. Henry Wood, an enormous amount of very readable mystery centred about the Lost Heir and the Missing Will. In these old fashioned tales, the Wrongful Heirs were usually thorough-paced villains of the most satisfying kind, and here the author's instinct was probably sound. A country solicitor once told me that, in his experience, the mere smell of a legacy brought out the most evil passions in the most respectable citizens, and that the abominable cruelties practised on helpless old people by relatives eager to secure their poor little bits of money made him feel positively sick. Eccentric wills, forged wills, disputed and irregular wills have provided and still provide the most prolonged and embittered litigation.

Of late, detective novelists have, I think, rather neglected the subject of wills. The laws of inheritance are complicated, and without the legal mind and training of a Wilkie Collins it is difficult to avoid the dropping of bricks, especially now that the public has become so well-informed and so critical. But if the last drops of juice are to be squeezed from the testamentary orange, authors will have to hurry up, for our legislators are busy restricting the possibilities. The Act which came into force in 1926 has already worked havoc with the expectations of the next-of-kin under an intestacy. The Wicked Eldest Son can no longer snaffle the whole estate by destroying the will in favour of the Virtuous Cadet. At best, he will have to go shares: while the Wicked Widow comes off even worse. Marriage (or so I am informed) no longer necessarily and automatically invalidates a previous testamentary disposition. The rights of adopted children and children legitimised after marriage are being progressively safeguarded, to the great benefit of the State and the confusion of the plot-maker.

A Tip for Novelists

Fascinating old local survivals like Gavelkind and the fairy-tale law of "youngest best" have been ruthlessly abolished, and we are periodically threatened with legislation to prevent the testator from disinheriting his wife and family – which will be jam for the wife and family, but Dead Sea fruit for the mystery writer! The moral is that authors should make their hay while the sun shines.

Mr. Herbert Adams has been working energetically in the old field, and it is curious to see how, with an old-world plot, he has adopted an old-world manner. John Brand's adopted daughter Susan has been cut off from her promised inheritance by a will which, though apparently quite regular, is oddly at variance with all that is known of John Brand's character and expressed intentions. The Wicked Next-of-Kin turn her out of the house with the very accents and gesture of the old Adelphi drama. "'So this is Susan Heriot,' she said, looking at me as though I was some common thing, not fit to be touched. 'You had better tell her, Mrs. Heath, that she is no longer mistress here. She is not even an invited guest.'"

In spite of this quaintly unreal atmosphere, the story is well constructed, entertaining and passably exciting. (Indeed, it is almost impossible to write a dull story about a will.) The plot is not quite new – I met it some years ago at the Little Theatre, during their season of Grand Guignol – but it is a good plot, and an incidental murder provides an intriguing situation.

————

Thrillers Received: HARLEQUIN OF DEATH, by Sidney Horler (John Long); THE CAPITAL CITY MYSTERY, by J. H. Wallis (Jarrolds); TWISTED EVIDENCE, by Maurice B. Dix (Ward Lock); LATE HARVEST, by Kaye Sunderland (Stanley Paul). Also OUR MR. RICHARDS, by Jane-Eliza Hasted (Eldon Press): a Ruritanian romance. All 7s. 6d.

17 September 1933
AMERICA WITHOUT SLANG
An old farce re-written

Murder Is Easy. By Armstrong Livingston. (Skeffington. 7s. 6d.)
Death on the Oxford Road. By E. C. R. Lorac. (Sampson Low. 7s. 6d.)
The Affair at Aliquid. By G. D. H. and M. Cole. (Collins: Crime Club.
7s. 6d.)

If, while trekking through the American wilds amid hordes of howling
gangsters, you should catch the accents of a cultivated voice talking perfectly good English, you may courteously raise your topee and exclaim:
"Mr. Livingston, I presume!" "MURDER IS EASY" is at any rate easy
to read, and explodes the prevalent notion that American detective writers
can only be read with the aid of a slang dictionary.

The story opens with a familiar gambit. The old millionaire invites
all his next-of-kin to his house with a view to selecting his heir, and, as a
natural consequence, there is soon "blood – blood on the library desk!"
(I am confirmed in the opinion that no millionaire should ever enter a
library). But the developments are original and exciting. The characters
are likeable and well-drawn, and easily distinguishable from one another.
The police and the amateur detectives are nicely played off against one
another. A quiet and pleasant humour pervades the whole. Indeed, if
Mr. Livingston does not please you, you are very hard to please.

"DEATH ON THE OXFORD ROAD" seems to me less successful.
I found it confusing – partly, I think, because so many of the people in
it begin with an H. There is a Hayward, a Hanton, a Harrison, and a
Harrington, as well as a gentleman who is usually referred to by his
Christian names of Henry Hubert.

Apart from this thoughtless complication, the book left no marked
impression on my mind at all, and I cannot help feeling that this is a fault
rather too common with detective stories nowadays. Competent? Yes.

Reasonably well-written? Yes. Soundly constructed and fairly presented? Yes. But individual, striking, memorable? No. Mr. Lorac's book is no better and no worse than many others, and with the best will in the world I can find no more to say about it.

In "THE AFFAIR AT ALIQUID", Mr. and Mrs. Cole have been perilously inspired to re-write an old farce – the one about the seedy adventurer who masquerades as a parson. Now, to write that story and get away with it is an infinitely more difficult and delicate task than the construction of sociological outlines, because the smallest error of taste is fatal. Charlie Chaplin himself did not succeed perfectly. There is only one man living who can do this kind of thing without tedium and without offence, and that is Mr. P. G. Wodehouse. His exquisite rapier is a more formidable weapon than the bow of Ulysses, and to challenge him on his own ground is to invite disaster.

Here we have a Wodehousian comedy of errors about crooks in a ducal mansion, but without the heaven-born gifts of tact and style. The mirth is coarse and commonplace, the satire clumsy and brutal. One must both know and love these bishops, butlers, and noblemen if one's caricature of their foibles is to be anything more than an ill-bred grin through a horse-collar. The Coles have given us some first-class mystery stories, but this is not one of them, and has, indeed, no proper business in the Crime Club list. It is just one of those unfortunate mistakes. "They should have wiped it up," said my Uncle Toby, "and said no more about it."

24 September 1933
MYSTERY OUT OF THE ORDINARY

The Mad Hatter Mystery. By John Dickson Carr. (Hamilton. 7s. 6d.)
Behind the Headlines. By William Sutherland. (Arrowsmith. 7s. 6d.)

* * *

"Is Mr. Carr Edgar Wallace's successor?" inquires Mr. Carr's publisher, wistfully. The answer is, "Don't ask silly questions." From the very first paragraph of "THE MAD HATTER MYSTERY" it is abundantly clear that Mr. Carr has nothing in common with Edgar Wallace:–

> It began, like most of Dr. Fell's adventures, in a bar. It dealt with the reason why a man was found dead on the steps of Traitors' Gate, at the Tower of London, and with the odd headgear of this man in the golf suit. That was the worst part of it. The whole case threatened for a time to become a nightmare of hats.

If that is like anybody, it is like Mr. G. K. Chesterton. And in the portrait of Dr. Fell himself one may perhaps, without being too personal, trace a certain Chestertonian exuberance of outline.

> All the old genial days, all the beer-drinking and fiery moods and table-pounding conversation, beamed back at Rampole in the person of Dr. Fell ... There was the doctor, bigger and stouter than ever. He wheezed. His red face shone, and his small eyes twinkled over eyeglasses on a broad black ribbon. There was a grin under his bandit's moustache, and chuckling upheavals animated his several chins. On his head was the inevitable black shovel-hat; his paunch projected from a voluminous black cloak. Filling the stairs in grandeur, he leaned upon an ash-cane with one hand and flourished an umbrella with the other. It was like meeting Father Christmas or Old King Cole.

Chestertonian also are the touches of extravagance in character and plot, and the sensitiveness to symbolism, to historical association, to the shapes and colours of material things, to the crazy terror of the incongruous. Mr. Carr can lead us away from the small, artificial, brightly-lit stage of the ordinary detective plot into the menace of outer darkness. He can create atmosphere with an adjective, and make a picture from a wet iron railing, a dusty table, a gas-lamp blurred by the fog. He can alarm with an illusion or delight with a rollicking absurdity. He can invent a passage from a lost work of Edgar Allan Poe which sounds like the real thing. In short, he can write – not merely in the negative sense of observing the rules of syntax, but in the sense that every sentence gives a thrill of positive pleasure. This is the most attractive mystery I have read for a long time.

Either American authors have got a craze for English surroundings or English authors have got a craze for American speech. In "BEHIND THE HEADLINES", also, the scene is laid in England, and it was with a sense of shock that I encountered two "gottens" in one paragraph. This is a pleasant, straightforward story, but the conclusion is disappointing, owing to the use of an old device which makes things too easy for the murderer – and the author!

1 October 1933
GRAND MANNER IN CRIME STORIES
Recapturing the art of Victorians

The Album. By Mary Roberts Rinehart. (Cassell. 7s. 6d.)
Aldringham's Last Chance. By Arthur J. Rees. (Lane. 7s. 6d.)
The Clueless Trail. By Percy Walsh. (Eldon Press. 7s. 6d.)

One striking difference between the mystery novel of to-day and that of the last century is more easily felt than described, but may be roughly defined as a lack of spaciousness. When we open "The Woman in White" or "Wylder's Hand", we step into a world of people having their roots in time and space and a life which extends beyond the limits of the immediate problem. Larger issues are at stake than the precise method by which the arsenic is administered, and the strings are pulled by a more awful puppet-master than a Chief Inspector of Scotland Yard.

Mary Roberts Rinehart recaptures something of this old, grand manner of telling a story. The horrid series of tragedies that make up the plot of

"THE ALBUM" are intimately related to the curious, repressed life lived by the five families isolated in the old-fashioned "Crescent"; we are shown not merely the solution of a riddle but the fall of a dynasty. This is not the first time that the theories of modern psychology have been used to provide a motive for crime, but they have seldom been used so well. Each warped and thwarted personality among the thirteen major characters stands out individual and distinct, acting and reacting upon the rest.

It is no small achievement to handle so large a cast of persons and characterise them so clearly that we never have to turn back the page to remind ourselves who they are or what their previous history has been. Nor, though the plot is extremely complicated, are we ever for one moment at a loss to follow it out. To the criticism that the crimes are too ferocious for their perpetrator the author has provided her own answer, by pointing to the frightful business of the Borden murders, perhaps the most ghastly of all historical murders.

There is, perhaps, occasional over-elaboration, but what true mystery-lover really objects to a little "torture and entoilment"? The book is so largely conceived that its outlines retain their massive purity in spite of their load of detail.

Two other books this week remind us, though in a very different way, of the Victorian masters of sensation. They are constructed upon the "chessboard" system beloved of Wilkie Collins, where move and counter-move of villain and pursuer are openly and alternately shown. This method has its own charm, though it does not, of course, make for purely detective interest.

Mr. Rees is hampered by a thin and old-fashioned style, and by a sentimentality which suggests a weaker and more watery "Raffles". Nor are his details always convincing. Why excite suspicion in a criminal by paying him in "marked" Bank of England notes, when banknotes are readily identifiable by their numbers?

Mr. Walsh has done better with a full-blooded thriller. Here, too, there is some waddling sentiment, and his "hero" is a singularly inefficient detective; but the portrait of the evil Voegamo is as truthful as it is disgusting, and the account of his fight and death reaches an unparalleled pitch of horror and excitement. A very good thriller, but not for queasy stomachs.

8 October 1933
AN IDEA FROM THE LAWYERS
The criminal's best defence

The Musical Comedy Crime. By Anthony Gilbert. (Collins: Crime Club. 7s. 6d.)
Night in Glengyle. By John Ferguson. (Collins: Crime Club. 7s. 6d.)
The Clock Ticks On. By Valentine Williams. (Hodder and Stoughton. 7s. 6d.)

It is not until we reach p. 244 of "THE MUSICAL COMEDY CRIME" that we discover the thesis underlying the plot. "There are three defences", says Bruce, K.C., to Scott Egerton, "that are, roughly speaking, safe. I don't know. I can't remember. Everything was a blank." In other words, criminals fail through over-ingenuity, and the best defence is to say nothing in particular. Lawyers know that this is true. The criminal who seeks to establish a false trail or an elaborate alibi is, in fact, assuming that *onus probandi* which is properly the affair of the prosecution, and if he breaks down on a single point he is lost; while the man who commits himself to nothing may easily be acquitted for lack of proof.

It is always a healthy sign when we encounter a central intellectual idea in a detective story – something "meatier" than a mere fresh dodge for faking footprints. In this book, however, the theme is announced a little too late to be fully effective, nor is the plot constructed so as to exploit that theme in all its logical implications. We might have been shown the defence being successfully employed in court, or, on the other hand, there might have been a dénouement in which the murderer's tactics were made to recoil upon himself in some surprising but inevitable manner. Either ending would have produced an Aristotelian unity of action.

As it is, the necessary proof is obtained by a simple extension of ordinary detective methods, and the catastrophe bears no very close structural relation to the theme. Indeed, the conclusion is somewhat hurried and condensed, as though the idea had been fitted into the plot by an afterthought. Ceasing, however, to be highbrow, we shall find the story, as a story, both interesting and entertaining as it stands, in spite of one or two bits of nasty, sloppy syntax. "She forgot ... that her only son had to be boarded out in a hostel for the children of actors, and whose weekly fifteen shillings wasn't paid any too regularly, with a husband who ... was little better than a labouring man." Detective writers who, like Anthony Gilbert, desire to be taken seriously, are particularly bound to honour the King's English, if only to live down their evil reputation in the past.

"NIGHT IN GLENGYLE" is the Crime Club "selection" for the month. The detection in it is nil, but it is a good, galloping tale of adventure about stealing secret papers for patriotic ends. The action takes place in Scotland, and goes with a whizz – so much so that in the excitement of the chase your reviewer quite forgot to be cunning and was properly taken aback by the surprise-packet at the end.

Though packed with alarums and excursion the plot keeps within reasonable bounds, without any irritating superfluity of shots, explosions, deathtraps, or feats of herculean strength, while the hero does his stealing discreetly, with only a suitable number of set-backs at the hands of the villains.

The hero of "THE CLOCK TICKS ON" rather disappointed me. Having detected with great energy and resource for many pages, he walked blindfold into the spider's parlour towards the end and swallowed the doped cocktail with childlike innocence – and he a Scotland Yard man, too! Love, of course, had addled his wits. But what verve! what gusto! what conviction there is in Mr. William's thrillers! Nobody can tell a crook story as he can. He combines the vigour of a Wallace with the glamour of an Oppenheim, and writes better than either of them.

* * *

15 October 1933
CRIME CONFUSION
Titles that have been done to death

Girl in the Dark. By E. Charles Vivian. (Ward Lock. 7s. 6d.)
Raffles After Dark. By Barry Perowne. (Cassell. 7s. 6d.)
A Killer at Scotland Yard. By G. Davison. (Jenkins. 7s. 6d.)

What in the name of Chaos and Old Night possessed Mr. Vivian to call his humorous, well-written, well-characterised and altogether delightful and sensible story by such a slip-slop, sob-stuff, rotten-ripe, rat-riddled title as "GIRL IN THE DARK"? And anyhow, this business of titles needs overhauling. It is becoming impossible to keep tabs on detective fiction. I can recall straight away "The Man in the Dark", "The Hand in the Dark", "Hide in the Dark", "Death in Darkness", and "Death in the Dusk", to say nothing of "Death in the Dark" of recent and unhappy notoriety.

"RAFFLES AFTER DARK" confronts us in this week's list, and I have no doubt that somebody has written, or will shortly write, the Shot, Stab, Blow, Corpse, Body, Cry, Shriek, Scream, Crime, Murder and Affair in the Dusk, Dark or Darkness. The brain reels, and Memory throws down her tablets in despair. There should also be a prohibitive tax on such titles as "The Murder at — ", "The — Affair, Case or Crime", "The Body, or Corpse, in the — ", and "The Mystery of the — ". Publishers often imagine that the words case, mystery, corpse, death, murder, and so forth are needed in the title, to inform the public that the book really is a crime story and not a tale of passion or an analytical study of neurotic psychology – but the public is not really so stupid as all that. Could anybody doubt that, for instance, "Proof Counter-Proof", "The Footsteps at the Lock", "The King Against Anne Bickerton", "Malice Aforethought", "Police at the Funeral", "The Verdict of You All", or "Crowner's Quest" was a crime story, though not one of these titles contains any of the sacred words? Could anybody forget these titles, once seen? Very well, then.

Apart from the title, I have no grouse against "Girl in the Dark". It is an excellent detective story, though not, perhaps, of the more exacting and crack-brain type, and it is full of really first-class dialogue between amusing and credible people. There is a judicious touch of sentiment (far better done than usual), and its thrills are human and not merely mechanical. I particularly commend Inspector Byrne on the poetry of dustbins, and Mr. Tananeni's dignified epistolary protest against being called a "mahogany-coloured mountebank". Passages like these do much to cheer the reader on as he plods with his nose to the trail.

It is always dangerous to resurrect the slain. Even Sherlock Holmes was "never quite the same man again" after his adventure at the Reichenbach Falls. And if resurrecting one's own detective is perilous, to resurrect someone else's is infinitely more so. Mr. Perowne has recalled Raffles to life "by permission", but we must regretfully confess that this is not that great Achilles whom we knew. The Amateur Cracksman is not at home among the professional gunmen of the Black Bat gang, and we can only enjoy the racket by forgetting that the hero of it is called A. J. Raffles.

———————

"A KILLER AT SCOTLAND YARD" is this sort of thing:–

> Deep down behind it all, lurking unseen and unknown and un-suspected, was Someone. Some fiend, whose grisly tentacles were for ever reaching out and grasping his helpless victims in deathly embrace. It was horrible! Beastly! Terrifying!

Too true, too true! It was and it is.

* * *

DETECTIVE STORIES
Another first-class "Thorndyke"

Dr. Thorndyke Intervenes. By R. Austin Freeman. (Hodder and Stoughton. 7s. 6d.)
The Manuscript Murder. By Lewis Robinson. (Barker. 7s. 6d.)
Death Fugue. By Paul McGuire. (Skeffington. 7s. 6d.)

Dr. Freeman occupies a unique position in the history of detective fiction. He has done more than any single writer to destroy the old, casual, anything-will-do-in-a-thriller tradition. He has taught the reader to be critical and the author to be careful. It is not too much to say that it is the ambition of every serious mystery-writer to do his scientific stuff so that Dr. Freeman might approve it. And in taking the scientific stuff seriously, Dr. Freeman opened up a new field of interest which nobody has ever explored so thoroughly as he. He can get as much excitement out of the melting-point of platinum as a lesser man can get out of a whole bushel of death-rays – with the additional advantage that we do believe in platinum, whereas we seldom believe in the death-rays.

In "DR. THORNDYKE INTERVENES", he has taken as a basis the famous historical case of the Druce claim to the Portland title, which so astonished the 'nineties, and has worked out this theme with many intriguing twists and ramifications. Into it, as by a jigsaw, he has fitted a second ingenious and complicated problem.

The juxtaposition of the two plots is due to a coincidence, but the coincidence is reasonably accounted for. (The minor coincidence by which the parties to the two problems are dramatically brought together at the start is less legitimate, but does not affect the story.) The love-element (always the weakest part of a Freeman novel) has been properly tucked away into a corner where it does nobody any harm, and provides a modest but necessary link in the action. In short, this is a first-class "Thorndyke", and one cannot give it higher praise. Nobody can touch the great Doctor for the callous charm with which he handles a corpse, nor for the cool self-possession with which he leaves criminals to tumble into scientific traps of their own setting. He is becoming, perhaps, a little too much addicted to the analysis of dust and the examination of dene-holes, but there is always some fresh cloud of witnesses arising from the dust, and some grisly and anything-but-fresh body of evidence to come grinning up over the edge of the dene-hole. Have at it, my masters! You may be baffled by the platinum, but you will kick yourselves if you don't guess right about the coffin screws!

―――――――

In "THE MANUSCRIPT MURDER" Mr. Lewis Robinson has made a praiseworthy effort to get away from the whole stereotyped business of clues and interrogatories. A man is found murdered. One of his friends, himself a mystery-writer, offers an imaginative reconstruction of the crime, based on his personal knowledge of the dead man and his circle. This forms the bulk of the book. Another friend then adds a chapter or so to the tale. By a comparison of the two narratives the police arrive at the truth and trap the real murderer. That is all. The final turn is neat and the book is interesting in its construction, besides containing some clever characterisation and a good deal of quiet wit.

―――――――

"DEATH FUGUE" is more conventional. We have the well-worn opening of the belated traveller and the lonely house with a corpse in it. An organ plays mysteriously, doors are locked and unlocked, and there are queer goings-on in the passages. The investigation proceeds competently under the guidance of Superintendent Fillinger (rather a lamb) and a gentleman called Hupper, though the final surprise does not surprise quite enough and the details are left a little vague. The treatment is not particularly fugal, and if John Sebastian Bach could see the remarkable "Fugue" attributed to him by the jacket-artist, he would be whizzing round in his grave like an egg-whisk. But one can't blame the author for that.

* * *

29 October 1933
THE CRIMINAL'S VIEWPOINT
True tragic quality

Portrait of a Murderer. By Anne Meredith. (Gollancz. 7s. 6d.)
Week-end Murder. By Nicholas Brady. (Bles. 7s. 6d.)
The Eel-Pie Mystery. By David Frome. (Longmans. 7s. 6d.)
Mr. Clerihew, Wine Merchant. By H. Warner Allen. (Methuen. 7s. 6d.)

In the "straight" spot-the-villain kind of detective story, the murderer is apt to be the most unreal character in the book. This defect is inevitable, since we must never be let into the inner secrets of his murderous mind – if we did, we should know him for what he is and there would be no story. His motives, his hesitations, the dreadful spiritual convulsion that precipitates him from dreaming into doing – all must be taken on trust, and frequently we remain, after all, unconvinced.

As a counterpart to this, we have the story that is told from the murderer's viewpoint. We see the crime committed and watch, through his eyes, with painful anxiety, while the evidence is piled up against him. Isabel Ostrander's "Ashes to Ashes", Francis Iles's "Malice Aforethought", and C. S. Forester's "Payment Deferred" are distinguished examples. A third method shows us first the crime from the murderer's point of view and then the detection from the point of view of the detective. Dr. R. Austin Freeman used this method in "The Singing Bone", and now comes Miss Anne Meredith, with less emphasis on clues and more on character.

Frustrated Artist
Her sympathies in "PORTRAIT OF A MURDERER" are with the murderer, though she has not allowed them to affect her judgment. She has chosen her man well and dissected him with a firm hand. He is a frustrated artist, with that hard core of egotism which underlies all the surface fluidity of the genuine artistic temperament. It is an egotism more for his work than for himself, and possesses a sort of brutal grandeur which is almost its own justification. He knows his own genius to be better worth

preserving than the lives of his disagreeable relatives, and, after killing his contemptible old father in a fit of passion, sets deliberately to work to get his scoundrelly brother-in-law hanged in his place.

Because he is what he is, we can understand that callous determination, just as we understand his final act of superb self-betrayal. He combines meanness and magnanimity, both in a heroic degree.

Certain technicalities may worry the hardened clue-hunter. Why, for instance, did not the police immediately discover the discrepancy in the finger-prints, instead of leaving it to be pointed out by somebody else? Only, one fears, because the murderer had to be given time for his farewell gesture. But the detection is throughout subordinated to the psychology, and where so much is good, carping is ungenerous. The book is powerful and impressive, and there is a fine inevitability to the plot-structure which gives it true tragic quality.

"WEEK-END MURDER" is a murder with a weak end, for an essential clue is concealed till after the murderer's arrest. I find the Rev. Ebenezer Buckle's fierce zest in the pursuit and questioning of criminals a little unbecoming in a priest; we never feel, as with Father Brown, that the soul of a murderer is precious in his eyes. But the horrible collection of human specimens inhabiting the seaside bungaloid growth known as "Immorality Corner" is unforgettable. Nothing more squalidly dreadful could be imagined, and the book is worth reading, if only for that hateful picture.

I like Mr. David Frome's work, and "THE EEL-PIE MYSTERY" is an excellent specimen of it. It is not about the "spickit and sparkit" variety of eel-pie that did away with Lord Rendal in the ballad, but about a young woman found drowned in her pyjamas at Eel-Pie Island, and our old friends Inspector Ball and romantic little Mr. Pinkerton do some good, solid investigation among a well-drawn group of characters.

Mr. Warner Allen had a grand opportunity when he thought of placing his unrivalled knowledge of vintage wines at the service of detection. But it is disappointing of him in "MR. CLERIHEW, WINE MERCHANT", to have tied it all up with a lost ruby and a Ruritanian revolution and one of those marvellously glamorous ladies. All this gunning and love-making is sheer waste – it is the sound, technical stuff that gets the reader every time – and Mr. Allen should have had more faith in himself and given us more of his own specialities.

5 November 1933
FLESH AND BLOOD IN CRIME STORIES
Problem not yet solved

Mist on the Saltings. By Henry Wade. (Constable. 7s. 6d.)
Death of the Home Secretary. By Alan Thomas. (Benn. 7s. 6d.)
Hearken to the Evidence. By H. Russell Wakefield. (Bles. 7s. 6d.)
The Broken Vase Mystery. By Mary Plum. (Eyre and Spottiswoode. 7s. 6d.)

To combine the novel of mystery with the novel of manners was the great achievement of English writers in the past, and is increasingly their ambition to-day. After the divorce of plot from psychology had been made absolute in the first quarter of the century, attempts at reconciliation began to be made from both sides, but the difficulties were, and still are, acute.

Both parties to the union had become set in their habits, and the detective story in particular had perfected a polished and heartless mechanism upon which all genuine feeling was a mere intrusion. Either the reality of the passions made the detective business look cheap, or the austerity of the detective interest made the passions look tawdry. No one has as yet perfectly resolved the problem.

In "MIST ON THE SALTINGS", Mr. Henry Wade has made the attempt. In the first half, he deals with the social strains and stresses that bring a crime about; in the second, he detects the criminal.

The purely detective part of such a book is necessarily simpler and more restricted in range than in the tale that is all puzzle. The far-fetched surprise ending is impossible where motive and character are taken seriously. Into the solution of the problem, as thus limited, Mr. Wade has put all the interest and suspense of which it is capable. Where he is less happy is in his presentation of the emotional elements in the mixture. He is too essentially amiable to handle his gang of warped and unpleasant personalities, and at times he over-tunes their brutalities to howling-pitch. And when it comes to depicting sexual passion, he plans a seduction like Napoleon – and executes it like the famous Duke of York.

These incongruous pruderies land him in bathos and weaken the book. Yet where he has not tried to force the note, his characterisation is quite excellent: the sullen matrimonial rages of the artist-husband are convincingly true to life, and his incidental sketches of policemen and rustics are outlined with all his usual quiet charm of style: the fog-laden dreariness of the Saltings is conveyed with a finely subdued richness of colour. This is an interesting experiment which, with a little more firmness in the handling, might have been a memorable book.

———————

"DEATH OF THE HOME SECRETARY" also makes us sigh for the might-have-been. Mr. Alan Thomas has wavered between the emotional and the detective treatment, and ended by making a passably good detective story out of what should have been a grand emotional melodrama, rich in dramatic irony. He has kept a surprise for the last chapter – but if only he had let the surprise go hang, and exploited his situation to the full, what a thing he might have made of it!

He has chosen, however, to do otherwise, and offers a plain problem of a Home Secretary strangled after his refusal to reprieve a murderess: a Communist agitator, the murderess's lover and the victim's own step-son being among the suspects. Mr. Thomas can draw living people (except butlers) and put together a workable plot, but I shall be surprised if, having read his story, the connoisseur does not itch to rewrite it on different lines.

———————

Like "The Bellamy Trial" and "The King Against Anne Bickerton", "HEARKEN TO THE EVIDENCE" is built up round a trial, which is, on the whole, well done. The style is jerky, cliché-ridden and sometimes pretentious, but there is some exceedingly shrewd analysis of motive and character. The author deals out a good many whacks at British justice, and the ugly scene in which a police superintendent connives at the use of third-degree methods is bound to give offence, but the book has merits and a good deal of crude power.

"THE BROKEN VASE MYSTERY" is a thriller – lively enough.

12 November 1933
"MYSTERY" TEST FOR CONNOISSEURS
Identify the author

The Empty House. By Francis D. Grierson. (Thornton Butterworth. 7s. 6d.)
The Circle of Death. By Charles J. Dutton. (Hurst and Blackett. 7s. 6d.)
The Belfry Murder. By Moray Dalton. (Sampson Low. 7s. 6d.)

Here is a little examination paper for mystery fans – no prizes offered. In whose works do the following passages occur?

(a) At the first dawn of the morning we closed all the massy shutters of our old building; lighting a couple of tapers which, strongly perfumed, threw out only the ghastliest and feeblest of rays. (b) "Interesting, though elementary," said he. (c) Was this resolution solely inspired by my interest in Lucilla? Or had my own curiosity been all the time working under the surface, and influencing the course of my reflections unknown to myself? I went to bed without inquiring. I recommend you to go to bed without inquiring too. (d) "Is it possible that there are medico-legal possibilities even in a marine worm?" (e) "My dear fellow! Oh, my dear fellow," he protested. "Comfort is what we need." (f) When they saw it [the church] from below, it sprang like a fountain at the stars; and when they saw it, as now, from above, it poured like a cataract into a voiceless pit.

These passages have been picked out almost at random. They are not star passages in any way. The only interesting quality that they have in common is individuality. Each is characteristic of its author, and could not possibly have been written by anybody else.

I wish I could find that individual quality in any of the books on this week's list. There are so many competent mystery stories, each with a plot as good as any other, but no better; with characters human enough, but easily forgotten; written in English reasonably grammatical, but perfectly featureless and flat. We echo the plaintive cry of Mr. Auberon Quin, and, failing "authentic goodness" in a book, desire a "rich badness".

Well, none of these books is bad. Any one of them will while away the time with a pleasant succession of thrills and problems. Mr. Grierson starts "THE EMPTY HOUSE" with that engaging adventure which we must all, in our idler moments, have hoped would some time or other befall us. A gentleman opens a cupboard door and a corpse falls out at his feet. Nothing could possibly be jollier than that. Inspector Barry Blyth, however, was not amused. He feared he had come up against the Perfect Crime, so he called in the amateur expert, Dr. Marrible. He could not have done a wiser thing. Between them they make an exciting chase of it, working up rather subtly to a surprise ending.

In "THE CIRCLE OF DEATH", the head of an American insurance company dies mysteriously. His death is heralded by sinister telephone calls to the Chief of Police. Then his son is slain by a cloth-yard shaft from a long-bow – a very attractive weapon. There is an unusual motive for the crimes, and the detectives – amateur and professional – are nice people. The story moves briskly up to the last few chapters, which are rather too long-drawn-out. The practised reader should, by that time, have detected both method and murderer, and will be a little impatient of the brilliant amateur's unnecessary mystifications.

———————

"THE BELFRY MURDER" is stuffed with thrills about drugs and Russian crown-jewels and murders and gangs. The identity of the chief villain is closely concealed, and I do not think one is really given much opportunity of guessing it. But the story keeps going very merrily, and if you want any extra problems you will find them in the picture on the jacket. How on earth was that enormous church-bell attached to its stock (by sheer will-power?) – how could the stock turn on the beam without gudgeons? – how could they ring without a wheel and with a rope that is attached to nothing? What was the height of the tower, and why did the two gentlemen gesticulating below come into church with their hats on? It is all very mysterious. But the book itself is quite good fun.

19 November 1933
MURDER ON BOARD SHIP
Enjoyable yarns

S. S. Murder. By Q. Patrick. (Cassell. 7s. 6d.)
The Judson Murder Case. By A. B. Leonard. (Thornton Butterworth. 7s. 6d.)
The Resurrection Murder Case. By S. Hart Page. (Stanley Paul. 7s. 6d.)
Murder at the Club. By Luke Allan. (Arrowsmith. 7s. 6d.)

This week let us look at a few imports from America. The first comes, appropriately enough, aboard "S. S. MURDER", and is distinctly worth its passage-money. I hope nobody will reject it on sight because it is written in the first person. I once heard a library subscriber refuse a book so written on the odd ground that "it made it seem too real – as though it was all happening to one's self". Mystery readers are, I think, made of sterner stuff. They will like to feel that they, themselves, sat down to that sinister game of contract with the Passenger Who Was Not, and saw Mr. Lambert drop to the floor with a ghastly grin, and stood alone in the dark cabin with the corpse, and felt a hand clutch theirs. And if they are attentive and observant, they will spot the tiny, all-important word which is so dexterously slipped in near the beginning of the story.

This is a most enjoyable tale, breezily and naturally written in a pleasant, individual style; full of thrills, but with a neat little detective problem at the heart of the mystery and at least one good red-herring.

"THE JUDSON MURDER CASE" is nice, plain detecting on a rather familiar plan. The millionaire is murdered in the library (what death-traps these places are!), and by one of those remarkable accidents to which detective stories are prone, the library was simply swarming with potential murderers during the fifteen minutes allotted for the commission of the crime.

They kept popping in and out of the french windows (as Mr. Wodehouse would say) like rabbits, and all had very good reasons for telling lies about it. The investigation proceeds normally by the examination of physical clues – footprints, fingerprints, and so on – and but for shrewd little Dr. Blair, the police might have overlooked the really vital bit of evidence; though I do not think the reader will miss it. This is a sound, sober piece of work, without extravagance or absurdity, though without any very outstanding features.

The nomenclature in the map, by the way, does not agree at every point with the text, which is a little confusing.

I have seldom read a story in which things happen as fast as they do in "THE RESURRECTION MURDER CASE" – except, of course, in those completely unintelligible books which resemble the hasty synopses of mad movies, and are not proper books at all. This book is perfectly intelligible, but its pace is terrific. Starting mildly with the stabbed man, we hurtle through a succession of strange incidents to the thing in the cellar and the thing in the wood, not forgetting the concealed packets, the cry in the swamp, and the horror seen at the window.

The detective, Christopher Hand, is a bustling fellow, autocratic as a Sherlock and brimming with brisk devices, which carry him bravely through to the dramatic climax foreshadowed in the title. Mr. Hart Page's zest and energy earn forgiveness for some passages of stilted dialogue and cumbersome humour, together with the concealment of clues and the presence of an unnecessary girl. We pant eagerly from corpse to corpse, enjoying every minute of the scramble.

The club where "MURDER AT THE CLUB" took place was "run on English lines", the proof being that they called the "club clerk" a "commissionaire", which was thought rather "law-de-daw" of them. This functionary combined the offices of commissionaire, hall-porter and page, and was always running round the club instead of looking after the door, so that when a young woman rang the visitor's bell and was stabbed in the waiting-room, it was difficult to tell who had been in the lobby.

All this is not so English; but it was a horrid club, anyhow, where blackmail flourished like a bay-tree. Rather a dull effort, not much enlivened by an irrepressible press-man called Tiger Lillie.

The quotations last week were from (a) E. A. Poe, (b) Conan Doyle, (c) Wilkie Collins, (d) Austin Freeman, (e) H. C. Bailey, (f) G. K. Chesterton.

26 November 1933
NEW DETECTIVE STORIES
Mr. Fortune again

Mr. Fortune Wonders. By H. C. Bailey. (Ward Lock. 7s. 6d.)
Epilogue. By Bruce Graeme. (Hutchinson. 7s. 6d.)
House-Party Murder. By Colin Ward. (Collins: Crime Club. 7s. 6d.)

Mr. H. C. Bailey is one of the best living exponents of the short detective story. Quite apart from anything else, his distinction of style would set him at once in the star class and make a new book of his an event of the first importance to those mystery lovers who demand that their favourite reading should bear some relation to literature.

But he has also more specialised virtues. His Mr. Fortune's strongly marked mannerisms are not mere identification tags; they are the outward signs of a strongly and consistently conceived character, which determines the whole approach to the problem. This approach is always psychological and intuitional. He marches straight upon the centre of spiritual conflict, gathering up the external evidence by the way. Mr. Bailey has an uncomfortable knack of indicating, without tediously analysing, the interactions of abnormal minds; his hatred of mental cruelty is sincere and profound. When "MR. FORTUNE WONDERS" the reader wonders rather uneasily, too, and even where all ends merrily, as in "The Love-Bird", is left echoing the detective's usual comment, "Not a nice case; no – not nice."

Confound Mr. Bruce Graeme! He has stirred up again that infernal controversy about Edwin Drood, in which I have sworn that I will never, never, never, engage.

In "EPILOGUE" he sends two of his C. I. D. men back into the past to unravel the mystery by modern methods. They are a little bothered by their surroundings, particularly by an absence of telephones and the knowledge that it is useless to present finger-print evidence to a jury of 1857; still, they contrive to bring a substantial case against John Jasper. Mr. Graeme has most wisely refrained from any attempt to write like Charles Dickens, and has skilfully woven his testimony together, using actual quotation where necessary. He has added very little new action, except that, finding Datchery (whom he identifies with Bazzard) in the way of his detectives, he briskly gets rid of him at an early stage. Tartar does not appear at all.

With the disappearance of these enigmatic characters, the problem becomes rather simpler; the indications as to the ring, the crypt, and the quicklime are followed out in conformity with Dickens's revelations to Forster; one or two new evidential points are made. The trial of Jasper (for the prosecution, Sergeant Ballantine; for the defence, Mr. Henry Hawkins) is cleverly handled, Durdles being rather roughly dealt with in cross-examination, and Deputy playing a decisive part (with a little surprise at the end of it). The connection between Jasper and the Princess Puffer is worked out along the lines suggested by Mr. Cuming Walters, and Jasper's addiction to opium is used to show that he drugged both Neville Landless and Durdles as part of his murder plan. This, I think, is fully justified by the text. I feel sure, however, that Dickens intended more emphasis to be laid upon – but no! I will *not* put my finger into this pie. Let all Dickensians read Mr. Graeme for themselves and fight it out between them.

"HOUSE-PARTY MURDER" is, we are told, the first novel of a master at one of our famous public schools. Mr. Colin Ward has not, however, made use of a public school background, but has chosen the more usual settings of a ship at sea and a subsequent house-party. He begins with a mysterious disappearance, going on to an apparently quite unrelated murder and theft. He trails a very pretty red herring, and possesses an excellent sense of construction, together with a nice feeling for character and considerable humour. I feel, however, that he just stops short of brilliance, so we will make his work ++, with every encouragement to proceed.

3 December 1933
CONUNDRUMS OF CRIME
Off the well-worn track

The Cotfold Conundrums. By Douglas G. Browne. (Methuen. 7s. 6d.)
Drury Lane's Last Case. By Barnaby Ross. (Cassell. 7s. 6d.)
The Case of the Gold Coins. By Anthony Wynne. (Hutchinson. 7s. 6d.)

I took an immediate fancy to Mr. Browne's book when I read, on p.5, this imbecile bit of talk:–

> "I got a book from the library the other week – 'The Long Arm of Nemisis' it was called."
> "What's 'Nemisis?'"
> "One of them Egyptian goddesses."

That is so exactly like the average semi-literate Briton – sense and spelling at the mercy of a misty mental association. "Nemesis" would have been mere snobbery; "Nemisis" is psychology. I at once expected to find "THE COTFOLD CONUNDRUMS" mellow with the humanities – and so it is. It is so charmingly written that it almost disarms technical criticism. One realises, perhaps, after turning the last page, that it contains more incident than detection, that the evidence about the nature of the "sharp instrument" is rather sketchily presented, that the murderer's identity is a little obvious, and that the young couple who so pleasantly wander through the inquiry are quite reckless about wandering into traps. But these things do not spoil the book while one is reading it, simply because it is so delightfully written.

The motive for the crimes is good and unhackneyed, the descriptions vivid and full of atmosphere, and the characters brilliantly drawn. Above all, there is a zest and freshness about the whole thing, immensely stimulating to the jaded spirit. It is certainly a tale to be quietly savoured and rejoiced in.

———————

Mr. Barnaby Ross's "DRURY LANE'S LAST CASE" stimulates in a different way. He challenges attention with queerness and splashes of (literally) strong colour, starting off with the surprising apparition of the man with the blue-and-green beard. His crime is all mixed up with Shakespeare and bibliophily; and this is the weakest part of the book. I do not believe that any Shakespearean enthusiast would be driven to murder by *that* particular motive (though I can imagine another motive which would fill the bill and be quite convincing). Mr. Ross does not seem to me quite to know his Shakespeareans. Also, he has some odd transatlantic ideas about the English. His central mystification has been used too often before, and his plot depends on such an astounding series of freakish coincidences that one is inclined to lose patience.

Admitting all this, however, there is, with all the extravagance, an element of the unusual which takes us out of the beaten track. The mysterious events have a real atmosphere of oddity, and there is some ingenious detective work which does produce the proper reaction on the reader – the "I-ought-to-have-realised-that" feeling which it is every mystery writer's ambition to evoke.

I recommend the book, with the caution that you may find it an irritant.

"THE CASE OF THE GOLD COINS" is a "Dr. Hailey" adventure, with the faults and qualities that we expect from Dr. Hailey. Its strong point is its satisfactory solution of that age-old problem: the dead man on the stretch of smooth sand, clear of all foot-prints, who yet had been stabbed and died where he lay. Good, also, are the exciting life-and-death struggles by land and sea. I wish Dr. Hailey did not create so many difficulties for himself by a heedlessness and failure to think ahead more suitable to a "first walking gentleman" than to a man with so many famous cases behind him.

The criminal is always one jump ahead of him, and it is only through outside intervention that he and his are saved from final catastrophe. Still, one cannot help liking the man and getting some good thrills from the book.

10 December 1933
TWO STYLES OF CRIME STORY
American and English

The Siamese Twin Mystery. By Ellery Queen. (Gollancz. 7s. 6d.)
Death at the Cross-Roads. By Miles Burton. (Collins: Crime Club. 7s. 6d.)
The Silent Bell. By Elaine Hamilton. (Stanley Paul. 7s. 6d.)

There could scarcely be a greater contrast in style and method of presentation than is displayed by Mr. Queen and Mr. Burton. Each author is typical of his national way with detective fiction. Mr. Queen is fantastic, involute, supersubtle, concerned with abnormal psychology and physiology, exaggerative, baroque; Mr. Burton, practical, dovetailed, materialist, balanced, restrained, classical. Yet the result in each case is the same: a uniformity of tone which tends to monotony.

Mr. Burton paves the ground so carefully for his murders and discoveries, and announces them in a key so subdued, that they almost fail to startle or horrify. Mr. Queen starts and continues on a note so shrill that by the time anything really desperate does happen no further crescendo is possible, and neither he nor his reader has any reserves of emotion left.

"DEATH AT THE CROSS-ROADS" opens with a motor-smash near a quiet English village. We hear the comments of the local publican, the routine inquiries of the village constables. A C.I.D. man then takes charge, assisted by his friend, the distinguished amateur of convention. The surroundings are those of the placid English countryside; the motives of the persons concerned are straightforward and realistic. Pleasant and unforced dialogue and a neat solution, dependent on simple mechanical ingenuity, combine to make up a sound, interesting, reasonable book, carried out in the best gentlemanly tradition of the English detective story. Mr. Queen would probably find it a little dull.

The whole action of "THE SIAMESE TWIN MYSTERY" takes place in a strange house on a mountain top, ringed by a raging forest fire and peopled with a collection of oddities all tottering on the verge of hysteria.

An oppressive atmosphere of heat and haste pervades it. At every moment the skin prickles, the flesh crawls, the brain turns blank, the breath comes in hoarse gasps, the voice cracks. There is a lady whose eyes are in continual agitation: within a few pages they are washed cherries about to pop out, their smoke and fire are quenched, they are hot, rich black again; they are blazing pits, or, glazedly black, roll over. The methods of the criminal are extremely tortuous, and the false clues so obscure that only a detective of almost unearthly intelligence could grasp them sufficiently to be deceived by them. All this Mr. Burton would probably consider not only grotesque but indecent. What saves Mr. Queen is the basis of really acute and ingenious detective work on which he founds his plot, so that one forgives his extravagance for the sake of his fundamental brain-work. His memory is a storehouse of observed detail; he is consciously aware of all those habitual reactions which remain for most of us unconscious and automatic; he takes "things we have seen perhaps a hundred times nor cared to see" and welds them into a chain of evidence that holds us because every link, once seen, is recognised as familiar.

He penetrates the workings of the reader's mind with uncanny intuition. If only he would master the "art of sinking" in prose, he would take the rank to which his intellect entitles him, as one of the supreme masters of the detective story.

Miss Elaine Hamilton in "THE SILENT BELL" has moments when one feels she is going to be really good, but it never quite comes off. Glimpses of a turn for characterisation and humour tantalise us from time to time amid a welter of confused or confusing incident, diversified by the appalling archness of a young woman called Mimi of Montmartre. In the complications of the story we lose the thread of the action, and we are left with the same feeling of vague indigestion that must have attended the horrible meal ordered in a night club by one of the characters – "Kippers and a bottle of the Widow"!

* * *

17 December 1933
ORIGINALITY IN CRIME
Turning to serious issues

The Wrong Murder Mystery. By Charles Barry. (Hurst and Blackett. 7s. 6d.)
The Kidnapper. By Sir Basil Thomson. (Eldon Press. 7s. 6d.)
Murder Among Friends. By "Simon". (Wishart. 7s. 6d.)
Death's Treasure Hunt. By William C. Harvey. (Eldon Press. 7s. 6d.)

It is, of course, every mystery writer's desire to achieve the "detective story that is different". In spite of the reiterated assurances of blurb-writers, this ideal is seldom attained. The limits of the genre are so closely defined and the technique so straitened by tradition that any really startling "difference" can only be produced by sheer genius, or by a *tour de force* often more disconcerting than satisfactory. Three out of our four authors this week have made strenuous efforts to be "different". None of them, alas! possesses genius, but they have the merit of striving to be out of the ordinary.

In "THE WRONG MURDER MYSTERY" Mr. Charles Barry differentiates himself from the majority of his fellow-writers, as also from his own previous work, by centring his plot about an ethical problem concerning which he apparently holds strong views himself. Would it be justifiable to legalise euthanasia for persons suffering from painful and incurable disease? Mr. Barry thinks not, but he postulates a doctor who sincerely advocates such a measure, and who is in consequence suspected of polishing off certain of his patients (mostly Roman Catholics) who publicly oppose him on this point. A complicated murder plot is unravelled by our old friend Inspector Gilmartin, and the problem is eventually thrashed out on moral grounds, with a victory for the Catholic party.

The details are not altogether convincing or satisfactory, but the book does represent a real effort to turn the detective story to larger and more serious ends, and the attempt is interesting. If, however, religion is to be brought into it, let us have the facts right. An "Evangelistic" aunt would not refer to Morning Prayer as "Mattins", nor could a boy who attended that service regularly grow up entirely ignorant of the New Testament. And I do wish Mr. Barry would consult a dictionary for the meaning of the word "protagonist".

Sir Basil Thomson's "THE KIDNAPPER" is "different" because it is not so much a detective story as a sprightly fantasia upon a detective theme. He writes good English very amusingly, and some of his characters have real charm. The egregious Mr. Pepper flits elusively through the pages, but we see next to nothing of him – which is a pity, for Mr. Pepper was great fun in the old days. For light entertainment, this imbroglio of a kidnapped boy, a 'lost' Gospel of St. Peter, and an American lady with a Buddha-cult and a tame Swami may be recommended.

"Simon's" bid for originality is the noisiest and most unnerving. I do not know which leaves me most bewildered – his medical science, his psycho-analysis, or his incredible tropes and metaphors. I think this is an endeavour to write a detective story in Freudian symbols, but I am really not sure. It may be the height of brilliance, but it sounds to me perilously like bottomless depths of nonsense. "Horror and anxiety twisted like heraldic snakes round his heart", "The train curved into the station, and it looked like a rattling scimitar. Oh! God! the Turkish Empire!" I fear there is here only a determination to be different at all costs, but if you like that kind of thing you will like "MURDER AMONG FRIENDS". I have certainly never read anything like it.

"DEATH'S TREASURE HUNT", though ill-written and in no way remarkable, is rather a relief after this riot. It makes no great pretensions, but offers plenty of bloodshed and excitement as the sequel to an eccentric will. (The word "nephew" in a will, by the way, would not include a nephew of illegitimate birth.) It ought, I think, to go into the thriller class, but has a more intelligible plot than the majority.

24 December 1933
WHAT TO DO WITH OUR VILLAINS
Crime writers' big problem

The Clue of the Dead Goldfish. By Victor MacClure. (Harrap. 7s. 6d.)
Murder Up the Glen. By Colin Campbell. (Rich and Cowan. 7s. 6d.)
Gathering Storm. By F. A. M. Webster. (Wright and Brown. 7s. 6d.)

A certain acute and experienced critic – was it Mr. Chesterton or Father
Knox? – has observed with great truth that one of the major difficulties
in concocting a detective story is finding a suitable job of work for the
villain. When this necessary nuisance is not actually occupied in crime
he has a tiresome habit of idling about the book with his hands in his
pockets, trying to look ordinary. "Hullo!" says the intelligent reader, in
his nasty, suspicious way, "what is this fellow doing here? Loitering with
intent, I'll be bound." And has him taped.

Mr. Victor MacClure has fallen into this little trap, and it is the only
serious blot upon an unusually agreeable and well-written story. I believe
I am correct in saying that Mr. MacClure, though otherwise a practised
writer, has written comparatively little detective fiction, so that the
regrettable transparency of his villain may be attributed to lack of
experience in a highly specialised technique. Nor are the clues and
the sequence of events always quite so lucidly tabulated as we are
accustomed to expect. Against these defects we may place a clear and distinguished manner of writing and that ability to handle character which
is the mark of the "real novelist" in contrast to the mere maker of plots.
"THE CLUE OF THE DEAD GOLDFISH" will undoubtedly please all
to whom villain-spotting is not the be-all and end-all of detective fiction.

––––––––––

Mr. Colin Campbell has faced this villain difficulty by turning his back
on it (Irish bull). Having brought things to the point where reader, detective, and remaining characters are all quite confident of the murderer's

identity, he coolly remarks that there is, after all, a good deal of doubt about the matter, and leaves us to fish it out for ourselves. This is scarcely cricket. But, then, Mr. Campbell is a militant Scot who deprecates the cricket, and every other English standard. Scotland, he thinks, is a fine country, and more Scotsmen ought to live in it. (Many Englishmen will agree with him about this.) He starts by making an English soldier and gentleman witness a murder in a lonely glen and then run away in a fright and tell a lot of silly fibs to the police. This is strangely unlike the behaviour of most English gentlemen, who are, as a class, chummy with policemen.

However, Mr. Campbell makes up for his unkindness by marrying the Englishman to the heroine and settling him down (in the teeth of his own Scottish-Nationalist prejudices) in the enjoyment of a Scottish estate. So he is not really so vindictive. And his book is thoroughly enjoyable. The Highland scenery of loch and glen, the quaint and delightful Gaelic characters, with their odd humours and racy speech, and the eerie atmosphere that clings about every stick and stone in that haunted land of Hy-Brasil all combine to convince us that Scotland is indeed a place of mysterious loveliness and lovely mystery.

Read "MURDER UP THE GLEN" by the glow of the Yule-log, surrendering to the enchantment, and not worrying too much about who the Black Walker from the Watch really was, or what became of the body.

Mr. F. A. M. Webster cannot plead inexperience for his crimes, since he has written many mystery tales. His fault is the stale re-hashing of old material – the evil Egyptian with a formula for exterminating mankind, the idiotic female who lets herself be lured away by the bogus policeman, the languid villain who keeps tame cobras in surroundings of more-than-Oriental splendour, and the final appearance (by aeroplane) of the whole male and female cast on a lonely island, like the last chorus in a pantomime. But there is one really brilliant spot among all the tinsel – the character of Detective-Inspector Oaf. He is an authentic lamb, who seems to have strayed from some much better book to be caught in this "GATHERING STORM".

* * *

31 December 1933
GRIM AND GAY CRIME STORIES
Death of an Ancient Mariner

End of an Ancient Mariner. By G. D. H. & M. Cole. (Collins: Crime Club. 7s. 6d.)
Old Man Mystery. By J. Jefferson Farjeon. (Collins: Crime Club. 7s. 6d.)
Watch the Wall. By Laurence W. Meynell. (Harrap. 7s. 6d.)
The Snapshot Mystery. By Ben Bolt. (Ward Lock. 7s. 6d.)

The fault of the original Ancient Mariner, as we very well know, was talking too much. The Wedding Guest on that occasion exercised commendable self-restraint and committed no violence, otherwise than by beating his own blameless breast. When, however, a whiskery old seafaring man turned up at Philip Blakeway's house with the obvious intention of talking to some purpose unless bribed to silence, he ended up in the coroner's court with a bullet through the brain. And serve him right.

Unfortunately, this Ancient Mariner, true to type, went on telling tales after he was dead. By a coincidence which nobody could have prevented or foreseen contact was established between his family and the family of Philip Blakeway and all kinds of things began to pop up out of the past, in a manner very disconcerting to all parties. Mr. and Mrs. Cole have not attempted to weave any very impenetrable mystery about the "END OF AN ANCIENT MARINER"; it is fairly clear from the start who killed him and how and why; the interest of the action lies in the relentless march of events towards the conclusion that murder will out. The crime was well planned, having the great merit of entire simplicity, and one can only say that the murderer had exceedingly bad luck.

───────────

Mr. Farjeon is in holiday mood with "OLD MAN MYSTERY". His opening idea is delightful. Two aged clubmen, weary of waiting for death day after day in their comfortable armchairs, suddenly determine to have a final fling of adventure and set forth to investigate a kidnapping. I think their epic would have been more effective if the element of farce had been less lavishly introduced. The old gentlemen (who, after all, are only 70 and 71 – mere children in these days) are alternately excessively senior and excessively acrobatic; a little moderation would have made their heroism at once more moving and more credible. The criminal lunatic whom they track down is, on the other hand, most convincingly portrayed, and the story gathers strength as it goes on, ending in a really thrilling scene in which the cleverer of the two old boys outwits the kidnapper. This is hilarious entertainment touched with grimness, and there are some good, creepy moments in a fog on Dartmoor.

We have had so many startling revelations lately about wickedness in high places that I hesitate to assert that the central character in "WATCH THE WALL" is impossible; but he is, thank goodness, highly improbable, and the story, starting off brightly with a beautiful woman, declines into something much fishier than Horace ever dreamed of. A house agent, a man, and a girl go to look over an empty house; three go in, but only two come out again. This is appetite-whetting. After that there is perhaps rather too much secret passage and dopery. The excitement runs along on thriller lines, and there is nothing much for the reader to guess.

Thrillerish also is "THE SNAPSHOT MYSTERY". The only real mystery about it is how the dickens the heroes contrive to pick out one unknown young woman from London's teeming millions and identify her at once from a small photograph. This mystery is never cleared up. However, since this is one of those stories about the good young man who has a double among the crooks, and about the three different sets of people tumbling over one another in pursuit of the same girl and the same mysterious papers, a few bits of supernatural luck one way and another are only to be expected. The good characters behave with more sense than good characters usually do; the English is good (though the French is rotten), and, altogether, it is quite a jolly thriller.

* * *

THE COLLECTED CRIME REVIEWS

of

DOROTHY L. SAYERS

1934

---

7 January 1934
TRAIN DRAMA IN A SNOWSTORM
Crime on Classical Lines

Murder on the Orient Express. By Agatha Christie. (Collins: Crime Club. 7s. 6d.)
The Robthorne Mystery. By John Rhode. (Collins: Crime Club. 7s. 6d.)
Marriage and Murder. By David Sharp. (Benn. 7s. 6d.)
The Ellery Queen Omnibus. (Gollancz. 7s. 6d.)

Writing last week, with a mind dulled, no doubt, by the influence of turkey and plum-pudding, I forgot to utter those pious hopes for twelve packed months of clotted crime which would have been appropriate to New Year's Eve. It is, however, not too late, especially as Mrs. Agatha Christie has given a noble start to 1934 with a murder mystery conceived and carried out on the purest classical lines. "MURDER ON THE ORIENT EXPRESS" is divided into three parts: in the first, we are given the facts; in the second, the evidence; in the third, Hector Poirot sits back and thinks and produces the solution from his little grey cells.

Moreover, the problem is of the perfect "closed circle" type, the entire action being confined within the limits of a single coach on the "Orient Express", with a snowdrift to cut out interference from the outside world, so that we are spared all the stereotyped police inquiries and uncatalogued suspects and allowed to concentrate upon the matter in hand. Those who like to use their wits for the weighing of evidence will find the problem attractive and the solution satisfactory, while those who love Poirot will rejoice in the rich manifestations of his personality and in his shrewd observations of national character. I have only one slight quarrel with his reasoning: the presence of a pipe-cleaner does not necessarily involve that of a pipe-smoker; I keep a bundle of them myself for my cigarette-holder.

Mr. John Rhode has followed "The Claverton Mystery" by "THE ROB-THORNE MYSTERY". I hope he will not make a practice of using this kind of title. Nothing is more difficult to remember than a series of personal or geographical names with nothing distinctive about them.

One always embarks on a John Rhode book with a great feeling of security. One knows that there will be a sound plot, a well-knit process of reasoning, and a solidly satisfying solution with no loose ends or careless errors of fact. I was a little alarmed at first when it was made clear that the new story was to be a variation on the twin brother theme. Was it possible that in this worked-out mine there was a vein still unexplored? Yes, it was really so – a nugget of good gold yet remained for Mr. Rhode to find. The reader will probably guess confidently and guess wrong, and have the fun of kicking himself all round the field.

The twin brother, by the way, is honourably produced in all his twinnishness in chapter II, and not treacherously sprung upon us to force a surprise ending. The similarity of the brothers is the hypothesis from which we set out, so that everything is scrupulously fair.

"MARRIAGE AND MURDER" is a very different kind of story. I do not care for it very much, but this may be mere personal prejudice. It annoys me when the hero makes all his own difficulties by acting the goat instead of telling a plain story to the police. The absurdity of the situations gives a touch of farce to the whole treatment, and the book is a parody of a detective story rather than a detective problem. But probably a little mockery is good for us, and the ridiculous troubles into which the egregious Mr. Fielding lands himself are handled lightly in reasonably good and readable English. The author's pet affectation of writing the word "hotel" with a circumflex accent should not be intruded into the detective-inspector's notes – nobody is going to believe *that*! A small point, but destructive of probability.

The word "Omnibus", originally applied to a vehicle intended "for everybody", and by transference to a book including a great number of miscellaneous stories, is now used for the publication of three full-length novels under one cover. (The only vehicle which normally carries three full-grown persons and no more is the bike-and-sidecar, a title unsuited for use on a jacket.) The Ellery Queen Combination contains three of this author's best-known novels: "THE FRENCH POWDER MYSTERY", "THE DUTCH SHOE MYSTERY", and "THE GREEK COFFIN MYSTERY", and is published at 7s. 6d. The excellently clear print and well-chosen paper make the volume much lighter and pleasanter to read than the majority of "Omnibus" volumes.

14 January 1934
A FLEET STREET COMEDY
Crime in a newspaper office

A Dagger in Fleet Street. By R. C. Woodthorpe. (Ivor Nicholson and Watson. 7s. 6d.)
The One Sane Man. By Francis Beeding. (Hodder and Stoughton. 7s. 6d.)
The Campden Ruby Murder. By Adam Bliss. (Rich and Cowan. 7s. 6d.)

When Mr. Woodthorpe's first novel appeared I wrote in my notebook *Brilliant!* and experienced that sort of gratitude which has been defined as "a lively sense of favours to come". Its successor, "London is a Fine Town", was charming and amusing, but not a detective story, and I began to be afraid that (like "Trent's Last Case" and "The Red House Mystery") "The Public School Murder" might remain as its author's solitary excursion into the field of mystery fiction. "A DAGGER IN FLEET STREET" has now appeared to relieve my anxiety, and I am happy to record that Mr. Woodthorpe is every bit as good about journalists as he was about schoolmasters.

Mr. Woodthorpe's touch is always light; he is aware of the heartbreaks and broken fortunes which form the darkest blots upon the "Street of Ink", but he turns them into dazzling and delicately cynical comedy. Every character in the long hierarchy from proprietor and editor through "sub", special correspondent, and secretary, to door-keeper and office-boy, is a living portrait, true to type, and yet much more than a mere type.

Struggles of a Humorist

The good things are beyond counting; the hero's struggles to get his "humorous column" passed by an essentially humourless editor; the superbly ridiculous scene in which the same young gentleman gradually and inevitably, but with unquenchable courtesy, succumbs to the influence of old brandy; the difficulty of deciding whether a dietarian's championship of white bread versus brown will please the general public or merely alienate the vegetarians; the tragic comedy of the "crime expert", who can only get his "story" by standing (and consuming) more drinks than either he or his expenses allowance can conveniently carry; the absent proprietor's Northcliffian bulletins to his staff – every page is full of joyful entertainment, even if the reader cares nothing for daggers or detection.

The detection is indeed the least impressive part of the book, though it provides that valuable stiffening to the construction which was, I think, the one thing lacking in "London is a Fine Town". Mr. Woodthorpe has diligently trailed a number of red herrings, but we are not really deceived into following any of them, and the discovery of the murderer is made so casually as to fail of its effect. The central idea is sound and even subtle, and with a little trouble spent on tightening up the joints would have presented a more solid front to technical criticism. But the story, as it stands, is a glad gift to a dull world, and I hope Mr. Woodthorpe will go on and do it again. Detective fiction can do with more writers of his calibre.

"THE ONE SANE MAN" is a good specimen of the more fantastic kind of secret service novel. Personally, I am just a little tired of the mysterious man with a scientific secret who kidnaps people into an organisation for reforming the world by force. Also, I cannot help feeling that the standardised internationalism advocated by the One Sane Man would make life rather dull for the average ass like you and me. Mr. Beeding does not seem quite sure about it himself, and his Colonel Granby, attracted to the new regime, but doggedly loyal to the old, typifies that inner conflict which every thinking man must feel when he looks at the world as it is.

The plot runs on familiar lines, and, but for the fact that Mr. Beeding can write English, would be very like a Secret Service novel by Mr. X or Mr. Y. An air of authenticity is lent by the presentation of the action in a series of official documents, of which the best is the disagreeable "grilling" of a witness by the French police.

"THE CAMPDEN RUBY MURDER" is plain, old-fashioned American mystery stuff about a jewel that kills all its wearers. It moves vigorously and is capably put together, though I must say I guessed the solution from the start. There is a good deal of loose, careless writing, but one at least of the characters – that of the "companion" – is well drawn.

21 January 1934
ANOTHER MYSTERY MONSTER
Dragon in a bathing pool

The Dragon Murder Case. By S. S. Van Dine. (Cassell. 7s. 6d.)
Shadow on the House. By E. Charles Vivian. (Ward Lock. 7s. 6d.)
Shortly Before Midnight. By Elizabeth Nisot. (Stanley Paul. 7s. 6d.)

> "What does any man know of what goes on under the water? ... Can he say that no monsters dwell in those depths?" "There before us, in the shallow mud, was the unmistakable imprint of what seemed to be a great hoof ..."

Is this the latest report from Our Special Correspondent at Loch Ness? No, it is Mr. Van Dine, who, at a moment when monsters are in fashion, presents us with a monstrous and scaly horror of claws and devilment, bringing about mysterious disappearances in the haunted waters of a swimming-pool. Even the imperturbable Philo Vance is a little unnerved by the sinister problem of "THE DRAGON MURDER CASE" and is rather less rude and superior to his friends than is his wont; though by chapter 14 he has sufficiently recovered his old form to reel off eight pages of erudition about dragon-myths of Naga-Min and Galon, the Burmese dragon, and Bilu, who fed on human flesh and never cast a shadow, of Thang Long and Visvarupa and Srvra and Aziz and Azdahak and many monsters more. The man is a monument of learning, and it always amazes me that he should have picked up his English accent among the huntin', fishin', and shootin' aristocracy of the shires rather than at the universities – and who was it taught him the expression "a nice gel"? But his pronunciation, like his scholarship, is eclectic.

In the end, he tracks the dragon to its lair after an exciting chase, with "much of madness and more of sin, and horror the soul of the plot". It is quite a plausible dragon, though most unpleasant in its habits, and those who are puzzled by the various and contradictory sets of footprints left by our Scottish amphibian may find that Mr. Van Dine suggests a solution of the problem.

"SHADOW ON THE HOUSE" is a "How" mystery, not a "Who" mystery, and is none the worse for that. When the distinguished inventor of chemical dyes tells his secretary to answer the telephone and the poor girl is instantly blown to pieces by a terrific explosion, it is easy to guess who staged the crime and why, but the precise details of the method are extremely ingenious, and it will tax the reader's wits to get them exactly right. I am sorry that my old friend Inspector Byrne has so little to do in this book. Inspector Head has not nearly so much personality, but I like the large, fierce, and friendly Superintendent Wadden.

Mr. Vivian believes in a strong love-interest, which he exploits with very pretty sentiment; he must take care not to let himself become mawkish, nor to abuse the old-fashioned novelist's privilege of letting judgments fall upon the head of inconvenient characters who obstruct the course of true love. Still, in these hard-boiled days, it is pleasant to meet a real hero and heroine behaving in the true story-book way, bless their hearts! A touch of romance does us all good now and again.

Everybody enjoys reading the report of a criminal trial, and a book written in this form seldom fails to be interesting when convincingly done. Miss Elizabeth Nisot gives freshness to the formula by placing the scene in France, and handles the unfamiliar legal procedure familiarly and well. A rich old invalid dies suddenly "SHORTLY BEFORE MIDNIGHT" when on the point of altering his will in favour of the heroine, who is promptly arrested and charged with his murder. The examination of the various witnesses by the *procureur general*, the president of the Court, and the defending counsel is excellently handled, providing much skilful argument and some admirable character sketches.

The form of the book debars the reader from doing very much detective work for himself, and he has to wait for the solution until, in the horrid language on the jacket, "an unexpected happening changes the course of events". Miss Nisot, who is a daughter of Mr. Joseph Hocking, writes good, straightforward English, and keeps the action vigorously moving.

On the whole, a good week for the mystery-lover.

28 January 1934
DETECTIVE STORIES AND A THRILLER
Crime, Colour, and Humour

Candidate for Lilies. By Roger East. (Collins: Crime Club. 7s. 6d.)
The Murder at the Flower Show. By Mark Beckett. (Eldon Press. 7s. 6d.)
Disappearance. By Joan Cowdroy. (Hutchinson. 7s. 6d.)
The Gallows of Chance. By E. Phillips Oppenheim. (Hodder and Stoughton. 7s. 6d.)

The difference between thriller and detective story is mainly one of emphasis. Agitating events occur in both, but in the thriller our cry is "What comes next?" – in the detective story, "What came first?" The one we cannot guess; the other we can, if the author gives us a chance. Here, then, are three detective stories and a thriller.

Mr. Roger East gives us plenty of chance to guess – too much, perhaps, for those readers who like to be stunned by a blinding revelation on the last page but one. He is too honest in the drawing of character to disguise the innocence of his innocent people. That does not really matter, because he makes all his people so interesting that we are eager to follow out the story to the end. "CANDIDATE FOR LILIES" is less original in its central idea than his earlier "Murder Rehearsal", but it is much more even in texture and richer in its handling. The murderee is a puckish nonagenarian who gives his guests boiling-hot canteloupe for dinner – which you may consider to be in itself a crime worthy of death. When preparing to alter his will, he is shot in the – dear me! yes – in the library; his heirs, naturally, share the suspicion among them.

The minor problem of what to do with the criminal when discovered is solved in an unusual and impressive way. One or two points call for comment: You cannot, for instance, obtain from Somerset House information about the testamentary intentions of living persons, and I think Mr. East has confused two allied species of poisonous plant. These, however, are trifles, and the book is more than readable.

Coming as I do of ecclesiastical stock, I have attended many village flower shows, but never had the luck to walk into a corpse at any of them. Major Burton was more fortunate. I like Major Burton and I like Inspector Loxley, and they liked each other, and so were able to work harmoniously together in the matter of "THE MURDER AT THE FLOWER SHOW". The major was an expert in firearms, and, with the aid of his knowledge and a surprising piece of luck, they were able to prove conclusively what the reader must guess rather more tentatively. The writing is pleasant, and the sketches of local character lively and amusing. Mr. Beckett has made a good start with his first detective story.

Father Knox once said in his haste that a mystery could not be good if it contained a Chinaman. Apparently this only holds good of wicked Chinamen; virtuous Chinese detectives are excellent: witness Charlie Chan and Miss Cowdroy's Mr. Moh. The charming Mr. Moh is not much in evidence except at the beginning and end of "DISAPPEARANCE", but all that there is of him is admirable, and the rest of the book is even better.

The story is about the kidnapping of a little girl, and the murder does not come till quite near the end. All the action centres about the village green at Little Chitterings, and the local people with their doings and gossipings are delightfully done. There is humour and vivid colour, ingled with a really horrible kind of horror.

Apart from an occasional clumsiness of phrase, Miss Cowdroy writes extremely well, and the only serious fault I have to find with her work is a carelessness in punctuation.

"THE GALLOWS OF CHANCE" starts off with a kidnapping too, but how different! A kidnapping as sane and as preposterous as the other is demented and dreadfully possible. The black villainy of the gang who spirited away the Home Secretary is cheerful as daylight compared with the spiritual darkness that hung over Little Chitterings. But I do hand it do Mr. Oppenheim! He is a grand man for a situation. It is unconvincing – it is ridiculous – but we read on and on, enthralled. Why that grisly gallows? What became of the lady? Why did Sir Humphrye walk out of his house and vanish? What was in the mysterious box? We *must* find out what happens, and under the spell we are almost ready to believe that in some braver, brighter world such things do happen to Home Secretaries. Yes – I hand it to Mr. Oppenheim, every time.

4 February 1934
A DEVELOPMENT IN THE CRIME NOVEL
"Obelists en route"

Obelists En Route. By C. Daly King. (Collins: Crime Club. 7s. 6d.)
Death at Broadcasting House. By Val Gielgud and Holt Marvell.
(Rich and Cowan. 7s. 6d.)
The Crime of Peter Ropner. By Harold Heslop. (Fortune Press. 7s. 6d.)

Those who remember Mr. Daly King's "Obelists at Sea" will remember also that he is a highbrow of the highbrows; others will gather as much from the wrapper of "OBELISTS EN ROUTE", which tells us that his more serious publications include "Integrative Psychology", "The Psychology of Consciousness", and other impressive titles.

Once again in his new book we find a bunch of psychologists – Dr. Iva Poppas the "purposive", Dr. Gottlieb Irrtum the "gestaltist", Dr. Mabon Raquette, and our old friend Dr. Rees Pons – travelling together, this time from New York to San Francisco upon a super-luxury transcontinental express, which also carries with it the banker, Sabot Hodges, with his daughter and suite, a publicity man, a physician, the detective Michael Lord, whom we have met before under the alias of Mr. Younghusband, and various other people of importance. On the second day out, Hodges is found dead in the marble swimming-pool which occupies one of the coaches of this resplendent train, and a little later a second mysterious tragedy occurs.

The rival psychologists all trot out their theoretical hobby-horses, but by the time journey's end is reached, Lord has solved the problem by a rule-of-thumb method of his own, for which Dr. Pons obligingly provides a suitable scientific nomenclature. In the course of the inquiry, many questions of economics and psychology have been ardently debated by the experts.

Challenge to the Reader

Taken by itself, the detective portion of the book is intricate and ingenious enough to satisfy the demands of the most exacting solver. The clues are most fairly set forth and are, indeed, tabulated at the end for our benefit in a "clue-finder". This is scarcely an "innovation", as the publisher claims, for Mr. Freeman Wills Crofts introduced it, in a slightly different form, in "The Hogsback Mystery". Nor is it really necessary as a proof of the author's integrity, though it is certainly a challenge to that of the reader. I am proud to say that I got the correct answer without any illegitimate peeping, rudely as Mr. King shook my self-confidence by a tricky jerk in the last few pages.

But apart from any such odds and ends of technical ingenuity, Mr. King has made an important contribution to the development of the mystery novel. The extravagant dialogue and pungent footnotes in which he castigates the follies of current psychological fashion recall an earlier satirist, and Dr. Rees Pons and his colleagues might well have consumed lobster and buttered muffins at Crotchet Castle or strolled about the grounds of Headlong Hall with Mr. Panscope and the beautiful Cephalis without finding themselves in any way out of their element. If the scope of the satire were just a little wider, this would be a true Peacockian detective story, a new and excellent thing. Caviare to the general, perhaps, but authentic caviare.

"DEATH AT BROADCASTING HOUSE" may be called middlebrow. An actor is murdered in the middle of a broadcast *(O si sic omnes!)* and millions of listeners hear him die. But he was alone in the studio at the time, and – well, there you are! No one could help finding this tale enjoyable, first, because it is excellently well written; secondly, because it has an exciting plot neatly put together; thirdly, because to listen-in on other people's "shop" is the most entertaining thing in the world, and the authors have made full use of the technical details of the Dramatic Control Panel and the inner organisation of the B.B.C. in staging their drama.

Except that it could hardly have taken a person 45 seconds to cross a passage and enter a room (a second is a much longer interval than one thinks, and in 45 seconds I can walk down 20 stairs, out through the back door, shutting it after me, and half-way down the garden), I have no fault to find with the mechanism of the plot, and all clues are scrupulously given. This is not caviare, but a light and savoury omelette, cooked to a turn and served piping hot.

"THE CRIME OF PETER ROPNER", on the other hand, is strong meat, and will not suit every stomach. Here is no mystery – only the straight-forward brutality of crime and its punishment. It is as well that we murder-fans should occasionally be reminded that in real life a murder is not a pretty piece of pattern-making, but an ugly mess of lust, greed, violence, and spiritual disintegration.

A foolish and egotistical woman betrays her husband and kills herself; the husband, a weak and fretful womaniser, throws her lover into the Thames, turns for consolation to the housemaid, is convicted of murder and reprieved, and becomes a monomaniac. The book is so ill-written in parts as to read like a bad translation, and is further marred by unnecessary tendenciousness, but it has a crude and sordid power that leaves its mark, and the characters of the housemaid and her stepmother are strongly and finely conceived.

11 February 1934
THREE HORRID HOUSEHOLDS
Mass poisoners who made a mistake

Family Matters. By Anthony Rolls. (Bles. 7s. 6d.)
The Cautley Conundrum. By A. Fielding. (Collins: Crime Club. 7s. 6d.)
Death by Misadventure. By Barbara Malim. (John Murray. 7s. 6d.)

"FAMILY MATTERS", in every sense, occupy a leading place in this week's crime list. Indeed, the readers and writers of mystery fiction should hasten to join some Society for the Preservation of Marriage and the Family, since without these institutions the motives for murder would be sadly reduced, and little would be left to us but the Elimination of Financiers by their business rivals and Political Assassination – which, of course, is murder only by courtesy.

Mr. Anthony Rolls has exploited to the full this well-known tendency of families to expunge their less desirable members, and has produced one of the best books of its kind that have appeared for some time. Mr. Rolls, it seems, is really Mr. Somebody Else, well known in other fields of literature. I can easily believe it, for he handles his characters like a "real" novelist and the English language like a "real" writer – merits which are still, unhappily, rarer than they should be in the ranks of the murder specialists.

His book is a crime story in the Illes-Forester tradition, and not a detective story, though a small element of mystery is left at the end. It concerns the efforts of various members and friends of the Kewdingham family to get rid by poison of one of the most futile and exasperating men who ever, by his character and habits, asked to be murdered. Oddly enough, the poisons they select counteract one another, and this leads to a most original and grimly farcical situation, and an ironic surprise-ending, pregnant with poetical injustice.

The characters are quite extraordinarily living, and the atmosphere of the horrid household creeps over one like a miasma. I have no idea whether the medical details about aluminium poisoning are correct, but I am quite ready to accept anything that is told me by so convincing an author.

A Puzzle – and No More

The Cautley family were rather tiresome, too, especially Fabian, who had lived in the East and dressed like a bare-footed friar, and had an inconvenient habit of going off into trances and becoming perfectly stiff (like Mr. Traddles's dearest girl's sister Sarah – the one who had something the matter with her spine), and (again like her) subsisting for two days on nothing but toast-and-water, or such trifles. The nicest Cautley got murdered early in the book, and any of the others might well have done the deed, for from time to time a cruel look came into their faces, which was part of the Cautley inheritance.

The plot is extremely intricate and full of red herrings, and the solution is kept a dark secret up to the last moment. The weakness of "THE CAUTLEY CONUNDRUM" is that the people never really come alive. Though every effort is made to characterise them, they persist in remaining mechanical figures, with attributes fastened to them like labels. Those who like a puzzle to be a puzzle and no more will find the mystery intriguing enough.

In "DEATH BY MISADVENTURE", one of those rude, tiresome men who never would be missed sets out for home by a cliff path at night – and the next thing is the discovery of the corpse. His wife, naturally enough, is suspected of the murder, so are his niece and cousin; then there is a gentleman who was engaged with him in some shady business far away and long ago; also a person who had been wronged in the shady business; also a deferential butler; and there is also Professor Izzard, very active and ubiquitous – suspiciously so. The murderer certainly is the Most Unlikely Person, though I cannot say I think the motive altogether convincing.

The writing is agreeable and the characters are adequately presented, without the strained emphasis of "The Cautley Conundrum", though equally without the deadly reality of "Family Matters".

18 February 1934
THREE TYPES OF CRIME
Poisons and thrills

The Poison Duel. By Peter Dingwall. (Methuen. 7s. 6d.)
Murder at Bayside. By Raymond Robins. (Hutchinson. 7s. 6d.)
The Grinning Avenger. By Edgar Jepson. (Jenkins. 7s. 6d.)

Here we have typical examples of the three chief forms which the tale of murder can take: the crime story without mystery, the detective story proper, and the pure thriller.

"THE POISON DUEL" centres about the figure of a poisoner. This looks like a glimpse of the obvious; I mean, not a casual poisoner, but one of those people who, having used poison once and got away with it, begin to look upon it as the natural and proper instrument to use in the regulation of their worldly affairs. Though all poisoners cannot boast the amazing record of Gesina Gottfried, who, in the early years of the last century, rid herself by arsenic of her first husband, her father, her mother, her two children, her second husband, her brother, two or three lovers, and the wife and entire family of her employer, besides other miscellaneous victims, it appears to be a fact that once a poisoner, always a poisoner.

Palmer, Pritchard, Neill Cream, and Catherine Wilson, among others, were poisoners of this habitual type, and Mr. Dingwall's heroine, Rosaline Dimelow, was in a fair way to model herself on their pattern. Having successfully poisoned one husband in order to marry a second, she incautiously confided the details of her criminal and amatory irregularities to a diary. (Thomas Wainewright is said to have done likewise.) When Husband No. 2 began to suspect her of infidelity, he succeeded in decoding the cipher in which the diary was written, and when she discovered that he was playing the amateur detective, Rosaline promptly decided that he had better go the way of No. 1.

The husband was none too strictly virtuous himself, and the progress of this couple's extra-matrimonial love-affairs is related perhaps at rather too great length, but the discoveries and counter-discoveries, the mutual spying, the hesitations and apprehensions on both sides leading up to the "poison duel" which forms the dénouement, are full of interest and excitement. A book full of unpleasing and small-natured people, of cheap intrigue in all its vulgarity, of crime as it is, without glamour or touch of the heroic, "The Poison Duel" is well constructed and well written, and may be recommended to all those who do not view murder through rose-coloured spectacles.

———————

"MURDER AT BAYSIDE" is straight detection, and a sound specimen of its class. In its central theme it bears some affinity to Mr. John Rhode's "The Davidson Case", but the method is so different that even those who remember all they read will not resent my "giving away" as much as this allusion implies, while they may derive some entertainment from comparing the technique of the two writers. I have submitted Mr. Robins's solution to a reader more qualified than I am to pronounce on the details of a murder by shooting, and am informed that everything is quite plausible. This author is an American, and this is his first novel.

A certain poverty and flatness of style rob it of any pretension to first-class rank, but it is a pretty puzzle, worked out along orthodox lines to a simple and satisfying conclusion.

———————

Mr. Edgar Jepson has gone all gangster in "THE GRINNING AVENGER". It is a story of one racketeer's revenge on another kindred spirit seven times worse than himself, and is packed full of thrills and bloodshed without presenting any mystery for solution. Mr. Jepson writes in a light-hearted, galumphing mood, with so much ferocious enjoyment of the victim's humiliations as almost to alienate our sympathy from the Avenger.

There are some regrettable errors of taste, and at least two passages of bad and careless English, which suggest that the book was written at a top speed suitable to its subject. Still, thrills are thrills, and this is an exciting chase from the first to the last shot.

25 February 1934
DETECTIVE AUTHORS' TROUBLES
A new Wills Crofts experiment

12.30 From Croydon. By Freeman Wills Crofts. (Hodder and Stoughton. 7s. 6d.)
The Windmill Mystery. By J. Jefferson Farjeon. (Collins: Crime Club. 7s. 6d.)
The Baddington Horror. By Walter S. Masterman. (Jarrolds. 7s. 6d.)

Among the major temptations that assail the detective author (and others) is that of writing the same book over and over again. Publishers and public encourage him to do so, because they like to know what to expect. Then, quite suddenly, they turn on the poor man and rend him, complaining that his books are all alike and that he has written himself out. The author, who is probably as heartily weary of the book as they are, but has been too timid to abandon a vein which has hitherto paid very well, is then faced with the task of starting all over again, under a heavy handicap.

When Mr. Freeman Wills Crofts wrote "The Cask" in 1920 he devised a formula and became thereby the only begetter of a numerous and distinguished detective progeny. As the other great Freeman stands for precision of scientific statement, so he stands for accuracy of practical method. He first made police routine fascinating and distilled romance from the pages of Bradshaw. He is our cunningest fitter of jigsaws, our Time-table King and Master of the Alibi, and no one has ever yet wearied of his skill. But he himself has lately shown signs of a certain restlessness: in "Sudden Death" he was groping after a new formula, and though in "Death on the Way" and "The Hog's Back Mystery" he returned to his own beaten track, in "12.30 FROM CROYDON" he has made a deliberate right-about-face and marched bravely away along the path of the psychological crime-story. Having unloaded the dead body of the victim from an Imperial Airliner, he flashes us back to the beginning of the drama and thereafter shows us the crime through the eyes of the criminal.

An Elaborate Alibi

The result is an excellent book, though here and there the practised hand betrays a little unsureness in working on the unaccustomed material. There are small incidental awkwardnesses, and the murderer does not perhaps show quite as much subtlety in working out his plans as we are accustomed to find in a Crofts villain. He constructs his alibi with immense elaboration, and it is only by sheer bad luck that he happens to be spotted at the crucial moment by a blackmailer, and is thus forced to commit a second crime in order, as he fondly supposes, to conceal the first. But he has made the elementary error of overlooking the obvious: the second murder is as futile as it is clumsy; police routine has taken all his ingeniously erected defences in its stride. Long before he set out to silence the direct evidence of the blackmailer circumstantial evidence has damned him, and the case is complete.

The first few chapters move a trifle slowly, but afterwards the action grips and holds to the end. The murderer's nervous self-consciousness after the crime is well done, and there are some admirable passages of pleading and counter-pleading in the trial scene. One might wish the various personages to be a little more strongly characterised, but the story, as a story, is highly successful, and Mr. Crofts is to be congratulated upon his experiment.

When a young man sets out to hike through one of Mr. Jefferson Farjeon's stories he is certain of meeting (a) a girl and (b) a corpse. The hero of "THE WINDMILL MYSTERY" encounters a couple of each, and plenty of other strange things as well, in and about the grim old mill in the pelting rain. This is a delightful and light-hearted adventure in the writer's best vein, of which I need only say that every word is entertaining, and one, at least, of the heroines a really charming and sensible girl.

"THE BADDINGTON HORROR" is horrid indeed, as any story must be which turns on people of sadistic tendencies. We start with the murder of a cruel old judge in the secret garden of a queer house, where strange footsteps creep about and mystery is heaped on mystery. It is all, happily, very improbable, but full of excitement, and, despite the improbability, perfectly fair to the solver.

4 March 1934
PAST, PRESENT AND FUTURE CRIMES
A University puzzle of 1937

The Mystery of Vaucluse. By J. H. Wallis. (Jarrolds. 7s. 6d.)
Ebenezer Investigates. By Nicholas Brady. (Geoffrey Bles. 7s. 6d.)
Creaking Gallows. By T. Arthur Plummer. (Stanley Paul. 7s. 6d.)
The Charabanc Mystery. By Miles Burton. (Collins: Crime Club. 7s. 6d.)

Mr. J. H. Wallis writes, as it were, in the future-perfect tense. In 1937, Yale University will have founded the College of Vaucluse, where persons not under 40 may go and take an academic course in any subject they choose, and at the same time enjoy a period of semi-monastic seclusion from the botherations of the outer world.

A delightful idea, and when it materialises I hope I may be able to renew my youth at Yale. But I shall avoid 1937, for I know that in that year "THE MYSTERY OF VAUCLUSE" is doomed to take place and destroy all hopes of a quiet term. In a self-contained wing of the college, consisting of an ancient Abbey building transported stone by stone from the Orkneys (Orcadians, be warned in time and demand a stiff price for your antiquities!), Professor Dart is found mysteriously stabbed when on the verge of perfecting a chemical discovery that will knock the bottom out of the oil market.

One of the 10 students in the Abbey Wing must be the culprit, and Captain Devaney of the New Haven police shrewdly suspects that the truth will be found at the bottom of the oil well. But he has many agitating adventures before he solves the puzzle of the missing formula, the shrivelled finger-prints and the undiscoverable weapon. A very fine weapon it is, too, and was first used by a pair of mystery-writers on this side of the Atlantic. Patriotism compels me to utter this Boost for Britain, but I will conceal the names of the writers, lest you should remember all about it, and so spoil your enjoyment of Mr. Wallis's thrilling and suspense-making yarn.

A Cleric-Criminologist

I like the Rev. Ebenezer Buckle much better in "EBENEZER INVESTI-GATES" than I did in "Week-end Murder". He is still, as he frankly admits, a better criminologist than clergyman, and I do not think that just after Early Service was the seemliest moment to choose for clue-hunting. But there is some excuse this time for his eager pursuit of the murderer, for the victim is a girl in his own parish, and he does show himself a faithful, though rather austere and sardonic, pastor of his flock. His detective work is well thought out, and at one point I, personally, was most successfully led up the garden. Mr. Brady writes well, and if he will remember to exercise tact in his handling of ecclesiastical matters, he should make the character of Ebenezer as generally popular as it is already striking and individual.

Mr. T. Arthur Plummer in "CREAKING GALLOWS" reminds me curiously of Miss M. E. Braddon. There is a flavour of the last century about this melodrama of erring womanhood, about these ill-matched couples who never tell their love till it is too late, about the weak and despicable ne'er-do-well who yet loved his mother and takes an oath upon her memory that he is innocent of murder. But the tale certainly keeps moving, and in its rather old-fashioned and heart-throbbing style provides a sufficiently exciting mystery.

"Wonderful", observes a character in "THE CHARABANC MYSTERY", "how the smell of beer seems to pervade this case". But what else could you expect from an author whose happy name is Burton? This is a good brew, mild and mellow, full of the tattle of country inns and the genial riotings of the village Dart Club, on which the local policeman turns an ox-like and indulgent eye. I think Inspector Arnold might have learned by now that his gifted amateur friend, Mr. Merrion, is Always Right; it would speed his cases up enormously, and this one drags just a little in the closing chapters. Perhaps, though, Mr. Burton is right after all – a leisurely draining of the last few drops is the proper etiquette in a rural inn.

11 March 1934
CRIMINOLOGICAL DOUBT
Mysteries that leave disquiet behind

Insoluble. By Francis Everton. (Collins: Crime Club. 7s. 6d.)
The Case of the 100% Alibis. By Christopher Bush. (Cassell. 7s. 6d.)
Murder on the Blackboard. By Stuart Palmer. (Eldon Press. 7s. 6d.)

The first two mysteries on this list end alike upon a note of doubt. The truth has been told: but was it the whole truth? The more obvious criminal has been tracked down and has chosen the quick way out: but was he merely the scapegoat for a still subtler accomplice?

This may or may not be the most artistic way of winding up a detective story; it is certainly very life-like. At the end even of the most exhaustive criminal trial, we are often left saying to ourselves: "I wonder how much his wife knew." "If you ask me, they were all in it together." "That witness was dashed lucky to get away with it – they ought to have charged them both." And where the case is never brought to trial, speculation may range yet further. The effect of a story so inconclusively concluded is to charge us with that sense of uneasiness which we associate with a good ghost story: the feeling, "it may have been all perfectly rational, but –"

Mr. Everton's story is the more intricate in plan. Its major complication depends upon a coincidence, and some of his expedients are a little strained. It is difficult to criticise in detail without giving everything away, but while I might believe, separately, in the coincidence of time and means, in the connivance of a really nice girl in a minor felony for a praiseworthy motive, in the execution by an unskilled person of a rather delicate mechanical poisoning job, and in the elaborate and unlikely scheme devised by the amateur detectives for confounding the criminal by means of a snapshot taken *ad hoc*, I find it a strain on my credulity to believe all these things at once in the same book.

One of these difficulties might easily have been cleared up by a word of explanation in the closing chapters, which are a little crowded and confused. Allowing, however, as in most mystery stories we must, for a few improbabilities, we shall find "INSOLUBLE" intriguing (though possibly not quite insoluble) and full of life and movement.

Breaking an Alibi

Mr. Christopher Bush, more blandly, more directly, and more convincingly, confronts us with the question: What is a 100 per cent alibi? In a sense, no alibi is unbreakable unless it is true; but it is not enough to show how it might be broken – we must be able to prove the breakage in a court of law.

The alibi constructed by Mr. Bush is so unblushing, so staggering in its simplicity, that even the great Ludovic Travers has to rely partly on accident for breaking it, and even then the very accident which seems to clinch the proof serves also to raise the final, unanswerable doubt. It may be asked whether the chief suspect would really fall into the detective's subtle psychological trap, but the character of that suspect is so neatly adapted to the situation that we are forced to admit that he might. I am rather sorry that the scapegoat (if scapegoat he was) is allowed to commit suicide. We might have had a good trial scene if the author had taken the risk of submitting that alibi to the scrutiny of judge and jury. "THE CASE OF THE 100% ALIBIS" is full of meat for argument, and that in itself is a proof of its high merit.

———————

The incident which gives "MURDER ON THE BLACKBOARD" its title is the weakest in the book. Why do these foolish victims of murder leave their last messages to the world in a form so cryptic that no ordinary person could be expected to make head or tail of them? The scene is a day-school in New York, and the case involves some exciting work with bootlegging in a basement and the use of a poison whose alleged action (supported by a distinguished biological authority) is entirely new to me.

Miss Withers, the middle-aged school-teacher, has appeared in other mysteries by the same author, and is a pleasant improvement on the usual run of female detective.

18 March 1934
ADVENTURE AND DETECTION
From Bayswater to Trinidad

Death of a Ghost. By Margery Allingham. (Heinemann. 7s. 6d.)
Murder in Trinidad. By John W. Vandercook. (Heinemann. 7s. 6d.)
The Chinese Jar Mystery. By John Stephen Strange. (Collins: Crime Club. 7s. 6d.)

Miss Margery Allingham has, as she herself points out in a foreword to her new book, two distinct "manners" in narrating the adventures of that attractive gentleman, Mr. Albert Campion. Sometimes she makes him the hero of a purely adventurous "thriller", sometimes of a "detective" story of the severer kind. I think Miss Allingham gains by this versatility. Her thrillers are the more convincing for the habit of accuracy imposed on her by detective writing, and her more intellectual problems enlivened by the sense of colour and movement that invades them from the thriller side of her mental make-up. This would not happen to anybody but a very good writer, and her writing is, in fact, excellent.

"DEATH OF A GHOST" is a detective story in the manner of "Police at the Funeral". It is a remarkable book in many ways. Its theme is extremely original, its characterisation is outstandingly good, and it contains one scene which, for genuine pathetic feeling, stands almost alone in detective fiction. The ending, too, strikes a fine note of horror – not violently imposed for the sake of startling, but foreshadowed and inevitable.

I am bound to say that there seems to be one weak point in the actual plot – one point at which the murderer's scheme depended more upon almost incredible good luck than it really ought to have done. But the whole conception and handling of the story are so fresh and vivid that this flaw is a trifling matter. The atmosphere of the studios which envelops the little colony of artists in Bayswater is triumphantly realistic. Altogether, this is a book you should not miss.

Crooks in the Tropics

"MURDER IN TRINIDAD" is a blend of detection and adventure. It is concerned with the secret investigations of a League of Nations agent into dope-smuggling as carried on in Trinidad, and there is a hidden lair of crooks in a tropical swamp all set about with mangrove trees, and an old map, and a concealed cave, and even a hint of pirates' treasure.

But there is also an inquiry into a thirteen-year-old murder mystery, with all the proper clues, and the detective really uses his brains for detecting and does not merely tumble into one discovery after another. This is a kind of story which one would like to get more often, for it appeals to the eternal boy in the grown man, while providing him with a little more intellectual stimulus than the plain tale of blood and thunder. Mr. Vandercook writes vigorously and well, and his detective, Bertram Lynch, has an engaging ruthlessness which gives one a high opinion of his efficiency.

In "THE CHINESE JAR MYSTERY" we are introduced to one of those large and involved families, every member of whom is seething with resentment against every other. This makes the opening chapters a little confusing, because of the difficulty of keeping the family tree clear in the mind.

The persevering reader will be rewarded with a good, lively melodrama involving three murders, and centred about the lethal contents of the curse-ridden Chinese jar. Mr. Strange keeps his tale going up to the very end with plenty of ingenuity. His work, though without Miss Allingham's distinguished literary quality, is competent and straightforward in style, and will please you by its sound construction and strong detective interest.

25 March 1934
STYLE IN CRIME STORIES
Why good writing pays

Death Among the Sun Bathers. By E. R. Punshon. (Benn. 7s. 6d.)
The Eight of Swords. By John Dickson Carr. (Hamish Hamilton. 7s. 6d.)
That's Your Man, Inspector. By David Frome. (Longmans. 7s. 6d.)

It is not true, as some people seem to think, that the worse a detective story is written the better it sells. Quite the contrary. No book intended for intelligent readers gains anything by bad writing.

It is, unhappily, true that a kind of wholesale and indiscriminate badness of plot, style, and sentiment alike is relished by that vast illiterate public which cannot and will not think and only asks to be doped into daydreams by its daily dose of talkie, thriller and tabloid news. But that public will not in any case bother itself with a real detective problem demanding concentrated attention, whereas those thoughtful and hand-picked minds that enjoy an intellectual puzzle are merely affronted and repelled by being called on to pick out their pabulum from a mess of sloppy cliché and incoherent syntax.

The most intricate plot ever woven will never carry bad writing; but good writing will often carry a thin plot and really inspired writing will carry almost anything. That is why, in reviewing crime stories for an intelligent paper, I lay what some people may consider an exaggerated emphasis on style. Bad English has not even the excuse of expediency. It is a criminal blunder, and its perpetrators should, and frequently do, commit financial suicide by hanging themselves in their own participles.

English Undefiled

The three writers who offer to entertain us this week have this in common, that they engage in no treason against the King's English, and for this, though their sins were as scarlet, I would willingly whitewash them. Actually, I feel that neither Mr. Punshon nor Mr. Carr has written quite up to his usual form.

With Mr. Punshon, this is due to the layout of his plot, which obliges him to give more space to his criminals and less to those delightful policemen by whom he chiefly wins our love and enthusiasm. What there is of Superintendent Mitchell is excellent, and we long for more; and the establishment at Leadeane where health-seekers chew carrots and sun-bathe clothed only in virtue and their birthday suits, is touched in with caustic by a relentless hand. The plot itself is an able re-handling of an established theme, and is commendably free from long explanations and confessions. If "DEATH AMONG THE SUN BATHERS" disappoints us a little, it is in being less characteristic and less lovable than the author's previous work.

Moments of Brilliance

"THE EIGHT OF SWORDS" suffers from a kind of general looseness and unevenness. There are moments of good detection, moments of brilliant character-drawing, and moments of horror and of the queer suggestiveness in which Mr. Carr excels, but there are too many moments of what I can best call, in the wireless sense of the word, "fading".

We start off with the Bishop sliding exuberantly down the banisters, but the episcopal glory grows dim in the sequel, and the tone of this noble opening is not consistently maintained. Nor does Dr. Gideon Fell ever get quite enough scope for his endearing eccentricities. The curious Mummerzet spoken by the local policeman reminds us that the author is not an Englishman, and, while it is probably no worse than English attempts at rendering American dialect, it helps to make the story stagey and unreal.

The book needs pulling together. It shines, but only by intermittent flashes, and it is by the light of those flashes that it must be read.

An Engaging Tale

Mr. David Frome glows, by contrast, with a clear and steady light. Inspector Lord and his mother-in-law's white peacocks (which were white elephants) set the key for the story, and for their quiet charm we may forgive the blazing idiocy of the young hero who pockets an essential clue in chapter 2 and hugs it in secrecy, only to drop it into the hands of the villains at the most unfortunate moment. "THAT'S YOUR MAN, IN-SPECTOR" is an engaging tale, well worked out and instinct with gentle humour, and though, perhaps, we might have been told a little more, I think the author has given us enough clues to guess with.

I April 1934
CRIME METHODS IN CONTRAST
A light comedy triumph

The Unfinished Clue. By Georgette Heyer. (Longmans. 7s. 6d.)
Smash and Grab. By Clifton Robbins. (Benn. 7s. 6d.)
Death at the Opera. By Gladys Mitchell. (Grayson. 7s. 6d.)

I said last week that good writing would often carry a poor plot, and here is a case in point. Reduced to its main outlines, "THE UNFINISHED CLUE" has the stamp of the stereotype all over it. Here is the same old week-end party: the disagreeable rich man who is stabbed in the study, the down-trodden wife, the rebellious son with the undesirable fiancée, the hard-up nephew, the wife's lover, the husband's potting-partner and *her* husband – all the stock characters, including the mysterious widow out of the victim's past and the gentlemanly detective with a sugary love-affair, together with a solution which had grown whiskers in the sixties and is as preposterous now as it was then.

And yet, simply because it is written in a perfectly delightful light-comedy vein, the book is pure joy from start to finish. Lola, the fiancée, by herself is worth the money, and, indeed, all the characters, from the Chief Constable to the Head Parlourmaid, are people we know intimately and appreciatively, from the first words they utter. Miss Heyer has given us a sparkling conversation-piece, rich in chuckles, and all we ask of the plot is that it should keep us going till the comedy is played out.

Never Comes to Life

Mr. Robbins's "SMASH AND GRAB" is the exact opposite of this. With every ingredient that should make a story thrilling – gangsters, jewels, disguises, pistol-shots, and hairbreadth escapes in profusion – it obstinately remains as stodgy as tapioca pudding.

The mechanical ingenuity of the plot and the laboured humours of Mr. Clay Harrison and his staff do nothing to relieve the utter flatness of style and dialogue through which we toil to reach, after 300 closely printed pages, a conclusion which was obvious from the beginning.

Murder in School

Finally, "DEATH AT THE OPERA". It was obvious also from the beginning that there was bound to be trouble over the School Operatic Society's performance of "The Mikado", since in casting the opera they took everything into consideration except the compass of the performers' voices. "Do you sing, Miss Ferris?" asked the Headmaster of the Assistant Mistress; and with no other assurance from her but a blush, he proceeded to hand her out the big contralto part of Katisha.

However, the audience were spared hearing her rendering "Alone and Yet Alive", for, long before that point was reached, the poor lady was lying alone and quite dead with her head in a wash-basin. The action of Miss Mitchell's story takes place in one of those enlightened co-educational schools, and I note, with a certain unregenerate glee, that its masters, mistresses, and pupils, though possibly free from the common-or-garden inhibitions and repressions which we now take for granted in all segregated societies, all suffer from a most varied set of malignant emotional complications, for which neither marriage, free love, nor free discipline appears to afford the slightest alleviation.

Skill and Lucidity

Miss Mitchell specialises in deduction by psycho-analytical methods, and I am assured by persons who understand the subject that her technique is impeccable. She believes that the majority of us are capable of committing murder for what may look like very inadequate motives, and here I think she is quite right. It is only because murder "comes so natural" that we hasten to surround it with so inhibitive a gallows atmosphere.

If the criminal in "Death at the Opera" seems to us a Most Unlikely Person, let us remember the reply of Thomas Griffiths Wainewright, when asked why he murdered the inoffensive Helen Abercromby. "Upon my soul", said he, "I don't know, unless it was because she had such thick legs." Miss Mitchell has woven together a highly complicated story with remarkable skill and lucidity, and the horse-laugh and crocodile grin of the unscrupulous old Mrs. Bradley are even more engagingly displayed than usual. Moreover, the author plays perfectly fair. She does not shelter herself behind the possibly doubtful interpretations of psychological diagnostic, but presents, in addition, a complete set of material clues for the plain reader to follow.

* * *

8 April 1934
CRIME WITHOUT ROMANCE
Study of an ignoble knight

Corpse in Cold Storage. By Milward Kennedy. (Gollancz. 7s. 6d.)
The Time-Table Murder. By Roger Denbie. (Nicholson and Watson. 7s. 6d.)
Murder from Three Angles. By Vernon Loder. (Collins: Crime Club. 7s. 6d.)
Murder Day by Day. By Irvin S. Cobb. (Cassell. 7s. 6d.)

When Mr. Milward Kennedy first set out to concoct detective fiction as part author of "The Bleston Mystery", he equipped himself with a literary spice-box well supplied with the sweets of romance and the bitter herbs of cynicism. He may have felt the resulting dish to be a trifle too senti-mentally sugared – did we not weep tears of pure rose-water over the sins of that engaging ruffian, Denis Hallam of the rare and charming smile? At any rate, in "The Corpse on the Mat" the proportion of cynicism was stronger, and indeed many of us felt that the perfect blend was then and there attained.

After that, however, Mr. Kennedy's manner became steadily more and more austere, until in "Death to the Rescue" the hatefulness of his human beings reached the point of being actively repellent. To-day the wheel has come full circle. Mean, raffish, drunken, and unprincipled, Sir George Bull, hero of "Bull's Eye", and now again of "CORPSE IN COLD STORAGE", is so openly and unblushingly unheroic that we begin almost to like him, almost to understand why his wife finds pleasure in being his companion and decoy-duck.

A Depressing Island

The scene of the new story is laid on a melancholy near-island somewhere off our flatter and more depressing coasts, tettered over with a horrid eczema of bungalows that were rotten before they were put up, and populated by a dreary band of disappointed down-and-outs – a sort of

English "Eden". Some of the islanders are halt and some are maimed, and all are sick in their souls.

It would not have been surprising if any one of them had murdered the only well-to-do inhabitant of the place and put his body in the ice-cream van. Indeed, I rather wish that Mr. Kennedy had not presented us with a list of 16 suspects, scarcely differentiated except by their names; it makes Sir George Bull's line of reasoning a little hard to follow. But the honours of the day are with Lady Bull, who, being, with all her dubious activities, an essentially womanly woman, asserts her superiority over the male investigators, not in the sphere of "intuition", thank Heaven, but in that of practical affairs – which is as it should be.

The Bulls are well-matched yoke-fellows, and I hope they will plough many a long furrow together before they land themselves in the pound, or the dock, or some other undesirable place.

"THE TIME-TABLE MURDER" is, as one might guess from the title, a straightforward alibi story, with no pretensions to being a novel of manners or character. It is brisk and workmanlike, and, although a murder that takes place on a train between Boston and Washington necessarily involves a considerable number of suspects, these are skilfully sorted out for us, so that we keep them in mind with remarkably little difficulty. An extremely ingenious solution rounds off this excellent specimen of the plain detective story without frills.

From Three Angles

The "three angles" from which Mr. Vernon Loder's story is told are those of the party present at the house where the murder is committed, of the local police, and of the C.I.D. man who is called in to succeed when the others have failed. They are thus not complementary, like the twelve viewpoints in "The Ring and the Book", but merely supplementary to one another.

The problem, that is to say, is not spiritual but material. It centres about the death of a business magnate who has gathered his rivals together for the purpose of forcing them into an amalgamation, the only alternative to which seems to be Carey Street. Here again is a large cast, very ably handled with some good lightning sketches of various types of business man. The atmosphere of the book is refreshingly masculine, with no *cherchez la femme* complications, and I feel that "MURDER FROM THREE ANGLES" is altogether one of the best things Mr. Loder has yet done.

"MURDER DAY BY DAY" contains some ingenious work in the final chapter, but will annoy the English reader by its eccentricities of style, which may be divided into (a) Americanisms, (b) bad Americanisms, (c) bad English, and (d) pretentious monstrosities, such as: "I baldly am putting down the triple-crowned climax, but putting it down hind part before." Some lively passages of American vernacular show that Mr. Cobb could write, if only he would not try so hard to be a writer.

15 April 1934
SKELETON IN THE CRIME CUPBOARD
Every author's plot

Copper at Sea. By Gerard Fairlie. (Hodder and Stoughton. 7s. 6d.)
Author in Distress. By Cecil M. Wills. (Heritage. 7s. 6d.)
Big Ben Strikes Eleven. By David Magarshack. (Constable. 7s. 6d.)

In chapter four we find the chief officer staring down at the dead body.

> "Er – where shall we put it, sir?" he hazarded.
> Captain Yorke swung round and glanced at him coldly.
> "Put him? Why – the usual place, of course."

From this snappy bit of dialogue we readily deduce that the captain has done it before. Also, that he is the master criminal of a gang. And we shall probably guess that the hero (police or secret service – in this case police) will, after a number of shots and/or identities have been exchanged, track the master criminal down, with the assistance of the Lovely Girl, to the Mysterious Headquarters of the Gang. Further, that he will then waste time on some tomfoolery or other, and so fall into the hands of the gang, to be imprisoned (with or without torture), condemned to a sticky death, and rescued at the fifty-ninth minute of the eleventh hour by the Lovely Girl – and so on to the wedding bells.

An Ancient Pastime

In short, Mr. Fairlie has been engaged in the ancient pastime of clothing the Skeleton. I am not giving away his plot – it is everybody's plot; it is the Skeleton in the mysterymonger's closet. We know from the start that it is all going to happen like that, and, while we derive a mild excitement from the working out of detached incidents, the main action of the story never arouses one moment's speculation.

I have no particular quarrel with "COPPER AT SEA", which is quite a well-managed specimen of its class. But I wonder a little why writer and reader should remain contented with this tired and mechanical filling up of a set outline. The Skeleton is obviously a sturdy one, or it would not have kept so much vitality all these years. But now and again we feel it is time that it was decently returned to its closet and had the key turned upon it. Only angelic qualities of style can make these dry bones live, and angelic visitations are, as we know, few and far between.

The Mixture as Before

Mr. Cecil M. Wills, in what is apparently his first detective venture, has been hypnotised by the Skeleton. He is working away nicely at his clues and making his tale quite interesting, despite some crudities of presentation and style, when it suddenly occurs to him that nobody has as yet been kidnapped. So he has the Lovely Girl kidnapped, and the hero, hastening in search of her, lets himself be kidnapped too, and the villain, having tied them up and done a little gloating, is just about to set fire to the place, when, at the 59th minute – and so on, to the wedding bells as before. There is a good opening situation, with an "AUTHOR IN DISTRESS" who admits to firing one shot at a burglar but cannot explain the presence of a second bullet in the burglar's body, and the plot is tidily worked out.

I do not believe that, at this time of day, the entire conduct of a case would be handed over to a young local police-sergeant, and there are other indications that Mr. Wills has not modelled himself upon the best modern examples of detective fiction. But if he will only bury the Skeleton and achieve a maturer style, I believe he will prove to have the root of the matter in him.

An Eccentric Financier

Mr. Magarshack describes "BIG BEN STRIKES ELEVEN" as "a murder story for grown-up people." He means, I suppose, that the motives and behaviour of his characters are such as the adult mind can reasonably accept, and they certainly contrast favourably with the infantile absurdities of the Skeleton. He tells us about a financier whose eccentric habit of transacting all his business in a saloon car leads to his being found murdered in a car instead of in the library – which is a distinction in itself.

This is really a very jolly book, with sound plot, some good characterisation, a number of thrills, and everything handsome about it. I recommend it as the best of the week's bunch.

22 April 1934
MURDER IN THE HEBRIDES
Crime in a castle

The Portcullis Room. By Valentine Williams. (Hodder and Stoughton. 7s. 6d.)
The Case of the Sulky Girl. By Erle Stanley Gardner. (Harrap. 7s. 6d.)
Murder Runs in the Family. By Hulbert Footner. (Collins: Crime Club. 7s. 6d.)

This week is thriller week. We open the programme with Mr. Valentine Williams, in first-class form, staging a murder in the Hebrides. The laird of Toray was poor and proud, and was being blackmailed by an unpleasant crowd, which included a degenerate vicomte. So he determined to sell his castle to Mr. Stephen Garrison, a rich American, who came over on his yacht with his older friend, Philip Verity, and also brought with him Mrs. Dean and her daughter Phyllis. Phyllis was more or less expected to get engaged to Stephen, but when she saw Toray Castle and found that it provided only hip-baths and no face-cream she felt rather like Mary Queen of Scots landing at Leith. "These", said the Queen, "are not like the appointments to which I have been accustomed, but it behoves me to arm myself with patience." Phyllis bore patiently enough with the factor's long-winded tales, and with the family piper, and with the old Gaelic servant who had not the English, but less patiently with Stephen, who objected to her mild flirtations with the vicomte, rightly conjecturing that he and his lot were there for no good.

So Phyllis, to annoy, arranged to go ghost-hunting with the vicomte; but when she reached the haunted room he was there before her, lying dead with the laird's dirk between his shoulder-blades. The castle was cut off from the mainland and from the yacht by a stormy sea, so there were grand opportunities for sleuthing and counter-sleuthing by Stephen's party and the vicomte's gang, all strongly suspecting each other and the laird – not to mention the laird's daughter, who obviously cherished a guilty secret.

Romance and Colour

A tale of the right sort is "THE PORTCULLIS ROOM", full of romance and colour and movement, with the wild water racing through the Flow and the dark castle steeped in blood-stained legend, and no wearisome police with their finger-prints and official interrogatories. Mr. Valentine Williams does this kind of thing just as well as it can be done, giving us lively characters, brisk dialogue, good English, and a vivid local background. I have only one bone to pick with him: I will swear that a West Highland castle, all hip-baths and candle-light, could not possibly provide cracked ice for cocktails. Roc's eggs would be easier.

"THE CASE OF THE SULKY GIRL" is nearer the plain detective story. The girl was only sulky because she was badly frightened. Her foolish father had made a foolish will, giving her uncle large discretionary powers to disinherit her if she did not behave herself. She had not behaved herself – so, as somebody had found this out and was blackmailing her, she went to Perry Mason, the criminal lawyer, to see if he could get round the trustee. At this crucial moment the trustee was spiflicated with a blunt instrument. *Cui bono?* said the police, and put the girl on trial for murder. The trial is excellent fun when once the English reader has reconciled himself to what seems to him the undignified and incomprehensible behaviour of American lawyers and judges. They are so oddly rude and unscrupulous, from our point of view, and Perry Mason's methods of cross-examination would hardly go down well at the Old Bailey. This gives the whole thing a thrillerish flavour, but there is some ingenious detection, and altogether Mr. Gardner's tale makes very lively reading.

Ancient and Modern

Mr. Hulbert Footner starts off full-bloodedly in the style of the old-fashioned "Family Herald" Supplement. "Keep your hands off me, or I'll shoot you down like a dog! ... Keep out of my affairs, or I'll step on you as I would a worm!" He becomes rather more modern as his agitating story proceeds. His hero, getting mixed up in a murder, scorns (of course) to inform the police, gets himself suspected (and no wonder), fights single-handed against the law, on the one hand, and a ferocious bunch of crooks on the other, and wins out in the end after as pretty a rough-and-tumble as any young man could desire. If you want good tough stuff with a thrill on every page, order "MURDER RUNS IN THE FAMILY" from your library or bookseller and begin right now.

* * *

29 April 1934
MURDER AMONG THE DOCTORS
Behind the scenes in a queer hospital

The Hospital Murders. By Means Davis. (Bell. 7s. 6d.)
Death in the Fog. By Mignon G. Eberhart. (Bodley Head. 7s. 6d.)
Strange Witness. By Beryl Symons. (Jenkins. 7s. 6d.)
A Shot in the Night. By Ben Bolt. (Ward Lock. 7s. 6d.)

It is odd that the detective story, which specialises in themes of crime and carnage, should be distinguished from the rest of modern fiction by a prim, almost classical, reticence of handling. Mayhems and slaughters are, indeed, promoted to the front stage, but the unbridled passions which led to their perpetration are, for the most part, banished to the decent obscurity of the *coulisses* and the respectable reports of Messengers. Nor, though the architectural plans which illustrate the action do now show more regard for modern sanitary requirements than was formerly the case, is the lavatory school of fiction at all well represented among detective writers.

"THE HOSPITAL MURDERS", by Means Davis, is in this respect, unusual. With unblushing truth to life, as life is known in hospitals, the meaner necessities of the living body are made to play almost as important a part in the plot as the dead bodies themselves, while the background and antecedents to the crime are filled in with a singularly frank brutality.

Originality of Treatment
If the reader does not mind this, the book is well worth reading for its originality of treatment and its robust, though crude, humour. "Hospitals are noisy places", observes one of the characters, and one does indeed wonder how, with loud-speakers "paging" the doctors every few minutes and a continual skurry of agitated suspects in the corridors, the patients in the "Elijah Wilson" ever got any rest at all. Still, seeing that mysterious murders were occurring almost nightly in Ward B, it was natural that the nursing and medical staff should have become rather erratic and

unreliable; even at their best, they were not a normal bunch of people.

Melodrama rather than pure detection governs the tone of the book, for the final discovery is made by chance, and one or two loose ends are left hanging: we are never told, for instance, how the murderer obtained access to a room whose only key was in another person's possession. But the style, jerky and full of American vernacular, is arresting, the sense of character and actuality strong, and the suspense powerful enough to grip the reader's attention almost in spite of himself.

Atmosphere is Mrs. Eberhart's long suit. In "DEATH IN THE FOG" she makes us feel the fog in our bones, and that with very few words. As we accompany the heroine in her nerve-wracking task of driving a heavy car blindfold over steep and slippery roads, our own feet keep stretching out to imaginary brakes, and, when a black figure looms into the misty gleam of the headlights, the driver's helplessness to avert disaster is our helplessness too. This weird atmosphere persists throughout; all the characters look larger and queerer than life through the distorting fog, and our nerves are kept on the jump.

Here again a few loose ends tantalise us; it is not so easy as all that for the untrained layman to procure deadly drugs and insert them into pills and capsules. On the whole, however, the plot is much more firmly constructed than that of "The White Cockatoo", and marks an advance on that attractive, but uneven, tale. The technique is detective throughout, with no switching over to thrillerism.

And now for two yarns full of honest-to-goodness excitement. "STRANGE WITNESS", by Beryl Symons, employs not only a dream-mechanism, but also one of those Borgia-poisons unknown to the pharmacopoeia, so we must class it as a thriller. And very gash and grim it is, with its nightmare horrors and insanities and its glass goldfish with beady black eyes and its nasty black apparition crawling over the carpet – Booh! Fetch me my smelling-salts, Susan, and hand me Ben Bolt's "A SHOT IN THE NIGHT". That is a cheerful, jolly adventure of masks and man-hunts, with nice, foolish young men grappling with gun runners and talking naturally and pleasantly after the manner of Bertie Wooster. A first-class light entertainment of the brisker sort.

6 May 1934
ACCIDENT, SUICIDE OR MURDER?
Mr. Fortune again

Shadow on the Wall. By H. C. Bailey. (Gollancz. 7s. 6d.)
Stark Naked. By Lawrence R. Bourne. (Muller. 7s. 6d.)
Inspector Higgins Sees It Through. By Cecil Freeman Gregg.
(Methuen. 7s. 6d.)

It seems that the week before last I did Mr. Valentine Williams an injustice over "The Portcullis Room". Ice *can* be obtained in Hebridean castles. It is cut in the winter from mountain loch or tarn and stored underground in a "sinister oubliette" somewhere on the estate. "It is used", adds my informant, "for refrigerating carcases ..." What a grand opening for a mystery! "Donald," says the laird, "hae ye fetched yon carcase of mutton fra' the ice-house?" "Ay, imph'on," says Donald, "I hae fetched the carcase, but I wadna say it was mutton. Na, na – I'm thinkin' 'twill jist be yon puir Sassenach body that went a-missin' last Mairch. Will I bury him or send for the poliss?"...A new lurking place for a corpse is a boon indeed to the hardworked detective writer.

None of this week's corpses, however, is found in any very remarkable spot. Mr. Reginald Fortune, who now appears for the first time in a full-novel-length adventure, encounters several of them, but the deaths are all cunningly arranged to suggest suicide, accident, or natural causes, and so take place in more or less commonplace surroundings. The first two or three might, indeed, have defied suspicion by their calculated ordinariness, if only Mr. Fortune had not had so quick an ear for sinister undertones in garden-party chat, so quick an eye for the shape of a "SHADOW ON THE WALL".

As the investigation proceeds, the criminals become more flustered, the murders more incautiously planned, and the action moves ever more swiftly to a dramatic conclusion.

In the early chapters the characters crowd together rather confusingly, and the clues are conveyed in hints so delicate that it is hard to pick them up. Later, the pattern defines itself more clearly, though I feel that the psychology of the murderers is not quite sufficiently indicated for perfect fairness to the reader. With Mr. Bailey, the mental disease which issues in the lust of cruelty for its own sake is always the mainspring of criminal action ("Anything to give pain", as the gentleman says in "The Wrong Box"), and thus the character of the criminal is an essential clue, which ought not to be left so shadowy and obscure.

Mr. Fortune moans and mumbles even more than usual over this perverse series of villainies, and, on the whole, his eccentricities of manner seem best suited to short-story form, but his swiftness and sureness of psychological deduction carry him triumphantly through the intricacies of the longer plot, and keep the interest well sustained.

Battle of Wits

Mr. Bourne has given us an excellently written and constructed story of the type in which the criminal's identity and manoeuvres are made known to the reader, and the detective interest linked up to them in parallel. The corpse is found on the sea-shore, "STARK NAKED", but in company with a few misleading clues which cast suspicion upon a blameless, though intolerable, Puritan.

Accident, as the author frankly points out, plays a considerable part in the solution – rather more, perhaps, than is common in real life – but not so much as to destroy the interest of the detection, which is ably dealt with by a very agreeable inspector. The character-drawing has the quiet solidity characteristic of the "straight" novel, and the man-hunt in the closing chapters is full of exciting seamanship. I must add a word of praise for the get-up of the book, which is well jacketed, well printed, and bound so as to open flat without springing or cracking.

The corpse in "INSPECTOR HIGGINS SEES IT THROUGH" is found

in a safe, which is not altogether unusual. The circumstances have, however, a touch of originality, and the story abounds in thrilling situations. This is sturdy, homespun police work – a little jumbled here and there, but good, galloping fun. The style is undistinguished, but one perfect passage of dialogue remains in the memory:-

"That kind o' lock, sir, is unintamperable with."
"You took the very words out of my mouth, sergeant."

From which you will see that the book is not without humour.

13 May 1934
CRIME WITH CROSS-REFERENCES
Father Knox's puzzle

Still Dead. By Ronald A. Knox. (Hodder and Stoughton. 7s. 6d.)
A Career for the Gentleman. By David Farrer. (Chatto and Windus. 7s. 6d.)
Death in the Quarry. By G. D. H. and M. Cole. (Collins: Crime Club. 7s. 6d.)

There are coincidences in real life so staggering that the writer of fiction can only gape at them abashed, and one of them is that, after writing my remarks last week about Scottish castles, I should have opened a parcel of new books and taken out Father Knox's "STILL DEAD". I will say no more about that except that it just shows how reckless and inartistic life can be, compared with the careful and conscientious logicality of the sensation-monger.

Father Knox introduces us to a most beautiful and original situation. A Scotsman sees a corpse by the roadside on Monday; by the time he has fetched help there is no corpse there. On Wednesday he finds it again at the same hour and place, and the question is: Did he really see it on the Monday, or was his vision merely the product of that prophetic second sight for which his family is celebrated? The Fiscal, supported by the medical evidence, accepts Wednesday as the date, and accident as the cause of the death, and thus, by a masterly stroke, the whole apparatus of police routine is cleared out of the way and the path left clear for Mr. Bredon, of the "Indescribable", to wrestle with an exceedingly pretty problem of insurance and survivorship.

This is, in my opinion, a better tale than "The Body in the Silo". There are some improbabilities, but they are psychological, not physical, and who shall set any limit to the improbability of human behaviour? All the qualities that delight us in Father Knox's work are present here. He treats us, as usual, to a highly complex pattern of double-crossing, and a delicate exercise in casuistry. "What is truth?" said jesting Pilate, and, if he had stayed, he would have found Father Knox's answer interesting.

The clues are marshalled with great care, and the solution is provided with a set of cross-references by which we can check their fairness for ourselves. This is an excellent method, arguing courage and candour in the author, and saving the reader much turning of pages. An exquisite English style, many entertaining characters, and a wealth of witty comment on life and manners lend the true Knoxian savour to the feast of reason.

Career of Smash-and-Grab

By another of those coincidences of which life is so irrelevantly lavish, Father Knox and Mr. Farrer both start off with a young man who has accidentally slain a fellow-creature by drunken and dangerous driving. In the former case, the matter is hushed up and the driver exonerated, but the hero of "A CAREER FOR THE GENTLEMAN" is more roughly handled by the law. He is sent to gaol for manslaughter, and here, being a youth of feeble character though amiable instincts, he succumbs to the shoddy charm of a slick young crook whom, after their release, he inevitably follows into a career of smash-and-grab.

The final catastrophe is manufactured, but the picture as a whole is painfully convincing, and persuades us that the author knows what he is talking about. An unwholesome sentimentality is seen lying, like a fundamental putrescence, beneath the phosphorescent glitter of the criminal life. Crime, indeed, is obviously no career for any gentleman, and we may ask ourselves whether a penal system which exposes weaklings to so virulent an infection does not still need a good deal of improving.

"DEATH IN THE QUARRY" is the best story we have had for some time from Mr. and Mrs. Cole.

It is free from those errors of taste which sometimes mar their work, and the social problems involved are handled with better tact and truth. The plot is well constructed, and if it was a coincidence that brought Dennis Jordan to the quarry at the moment when a blasting charge exploded and blew the works manager into eternity – well, this week I am in no mood to quarrel with coincidence. Everard Blatchington is here again, irrepressible as ever, with our good friend Superintendent Wilson to give him the ticking-off he so richly deserves for his scandalous interference with valuable evidence.

All three of these books may be recommended to crime-fans.

20 May 1934
SPATE OF MYSTERY STORIES
Too kind to hasty writing

An Old Lady Dies. By Anthony Gilbert. (Collins: Crime Club. 7s. 6d.)
Artifex Intervenes. By Richard Keverne. (Constable. 7s. 6d.)
An International Affair. By Bruce Graeme. (Hutchinson. 7s. 6d.)
Murder of the Only Witness. By J. S. Fletcher. (Harrap. 3s. 6d.)

Here is another new Anthony Gilbert, the third within a year, which is rather good going. There are many reasons which may prompt an author to produce books at this rate, ranging from hyper-activity of the thyroid to the grim menace of rates and taxes. The greatest genius is usually attended by a considerable fertility, but, as a rule, it is too much to expect a fresh masterpiece every four months. With the detective story the temptation to over-production is especially dangerous: first, because it is only too easy to shake up the old pieces of the kaleidoscope into what looks something like a new plot, and, secondly, because the public (and this means You!) is still too indulgent to hasty and mechanical writing where mysteries are concerned. This is not to say that "AN OLD LADY DIES" shows any noticeable falling-off from the author's usual standard; in fact, it is quite up to the average, and is actually better put together than "The Musical Comedy Crime". But I do not feel that there was any strong and compelling reason for writing it.

Coroners in Fiction

We begin with the usual rather complicated family all waiting to step into a dead person's shoes. The "old lady" is a horrid old soul, who has married beneath her apparently for the sheer fun of tormenting and humiliating the husband and relations dependent upon her. Somebody puts poison into her gruel, and, at an inquest presided over by one of the most scandalously ill-conducted coroners in fact or fiction (and that is saying a good deal), a verdict of murder is brought in against the wrong person. The rest of the family rally round in defence of the accused and argue the thing out at considerable length. Our interest, which flags a little at this point, is quickened by the intervention of a private detective, who sleuths round quite amusingly disguised as a photographer, and finally our friend Mrs. Egerton is hauled out of the House of Commons to clear the matter up, and the culprit is forced into confession by an exceedingly ingenious device, which is the best thing in the book. The various characters are quite well distinguished and there are passages of pleasing dialogue, but the book as a whole is a little lacking in zip. As the authors of "1066 and All That" would say, it is not memorable.

The three long-short stories in "ARTIFEX INTERVENES" are, according to the blurb, "full of movement, menace, and thrilling escapes". Two of them deal with smuggling and one with kidnapping. Mr. Keverne's chief asset is a knack of casting a suspicious atmosphere round a character, so as to make us wonder whether he is a villain or a detective in disguise. The second story is the best, but none is very convincing, nor is the writing particularly good. I will mark it "For railway journeys", and leave it at that.

A Jigsaw Puzzle

Mr. Bruce Graeme has chosen a very awkward method of narration. One man relates the story of "AN INTERNATIONAL AFFAIR" to another, and, by way of making it the more confusing, does so in the manner of a jigsaw puzzle, first displaying a number of piecemeal incidents and gradually fitting them together to make a connected picture. One sees the idea, but the result is rather dull and the writing is definitely bad. Only extreme brilliance of style and treatment could get away with so difficult a convention, and, interesting as the experiment is, we must regretfully confess that it does not come off.

Mr. J. S. Fletcher's "MURDER OF THE ONLY WITNESS", which I enjoyed some months ago, is now issued at 3s. 6d., with the addition of an extra clue in the shape of a jigsaw puzzle, housed in a neat wallet at the back. It is a nice little jigsaw, remarkably well fitting, considering that, like the Knave of Hearts, it is made entirely of cardboard, and should provide good entertainment for the family circle.

27 May 1934
A CROSS-WORD MYSTERY
Puzzle gives Key to the Plot

The Cross-Word Mystery. By E. R. Punshon. (Gollancz. 7s. 6d.)
Death in the Dove-Cot. By Q. Patrick. (Cassell. 7s. 6d.)
Murder Underground. By M. Doriel Hay. (Skeffington. 7s. 6d.)
Murder Mask. By Garstin Begbie. (Jenkins. 7s. 6d.)

"THE CROSS-WORD MYSTERY" gives us an opportunity for discussing two of the most awkward of the technical problems that confront the mystery writer. First, at what point must we release our vital clue so as to be fair to the reader without exploding the secret prematurely?

Mr. Punshon has erred a little on the side of generosity. As is obvious from the title, a cross-word is the master-key to the plot, and the puzzle in question is presented complete to the reader for solution at a moment in the action when Detective Owen has himself had no more than a glimpse of it. This fact, together with the title and the map on the fly-leaf, gives us an immense advantage over Owen, and the main lines of the story become obvious to us just a little bit too early for complete enjoyment. The cross-word is supposed to be constructed by an amateur, and is rather unnecessarily amateurish; it would, I think, have been better to place a few more obstacles in our way. We are, as a nation, so exceedingly cross-word-conscious that it is a mistake to underrate our intelligence in that respect.

From Comedy to Drama

The second problem is still more delicate – it is the old, old difficulty of keeping up a unity of tone. In his final chapter Mr. Punshon lifts the story rather abruptly from the level of polite comedy to that of heroic drama, and, being unprepared, we fail to adjust our minds before the curtain falls on the hideous scene.

It is, of course, a compliment to Mr. Punshon's work that criticism should focus itself on such points. Only when a high level of artistic accomplishment has been reached do we begin to talk severely about values and tone-balance. Bobby Owen (B. A., Oxon) makes better use of his University training in this seaside country-house atmosphere than in the melodramatic masquerade of "Death Among the Sun-bathers", and Superintendent Mitchell delights us again with his caustic comments on police officialdom.

The startling phenomenon of the line of light that is heard to vanish on p. 136 does not invalidate the general excellence of the writing; a stray slip or two may be due to the fact that this book has followed rather hard upon the heels of Mr. Punshon's last.

I am glad to welcome another story by Q. Patrick, author of "S. S. Murder". "DEATH IN THE DOVE-COT", like the next book on our list, deals with life in a boarding-house. Both are full of brisk writing and amusing characters. Mr. Patrick introduces us to an all-female cast, except for a stray fiancé or so and the exquisitely named police officer, Manfred Boot. The action is laid in an American "Women's Club", and has an ingenious psychological twist, calculated to lead the reader meekly up the garden, following in the Manfred Boot-prints. Miss Deborah Entwistle, plump and psychic, is an excellent recruit to the body of women detectives, which has been greatly strengthened of late.

Murder at Belsize Park

"MURDER UNDERGROUND" is committed in pleasantly familiar surroundings at Belsize Park Station. The author does not keep the secret quite so well as Mr. Patrick, and is apt to obscure sufficiently complicated intrigue by a continual skipping back and forth in the time-scheme. But this first detective novel is much more than promising. The numerous characters are well differentiated, and include one of the most feckless, exasperating, and life-like young literary men that ever confused a trail by their follies.

Some years ago, a real murderer deposited a corpse in a railway cloak-room and threw away the ticket. This incident of abiding charm provides a lively opening to "MURDER MASK", and a vigorous and entertaining tale follows naturally from it. Supt. Quan and Det. Sergeant Urbrill are an engaging pair of policemen, and their sleuthing goes forward energet-ically to a hearty rough-and-tumble finish. Mr. Begbie writes decent, straightforward English, but should consult a reference book for the meaning of (*sic!*) and the concord of the participle *née*.

* * *

3 June 1934
WHISPERS ABOUT A MURDER
Humane and inhumane studies

Whispering Tongues. By Laurence Kirk. (Heinemann. 7s. 6d.)
Panic Party. By Anthony Berkeley. (Hodder and Stoughton. 7s. 6d.)
The Bravo of London. By Ernest Bramah. (Cassell. 7s. 6d.)

The first two books on this list are not exactly detective stories, though in each there is a murder problem to be solved. Both deal with the repercussions set up in a small community by the knowledge that there is an uncaught murderer in its midst. Otherwise, no two stories could be more unlike.

"WHISPERING TONGUES" is so natural, graceful, witty, and charming that criticism can do little more than hang it about with a garland of grateful adjectives. In a little English village a tiresome, harmless woman has been poisoned; her husband, suspected and accused, is acquitted; his second wife forces him to remain among neighbours who do not know whether to accept the verdict or not: here is a situation rich in possibilities of apprehension and misapprehension.

The villagers, from highest to lowest, are men and women of like passions with us, full of failings and absurdities, some stupid, some spiteful, some merely inconsistent, some even a little cracked, but all with their underlying human dignity and decency. It has been said that "la meilleure comédie est celle qui côtoie sans cesse le tragiqué et n'y tombe jamais", and Mr. Kirk's comedy is of this excellent and pitiful kind.

Murder and madness must always contain the elements of tragedy, but it is the achievement of the comic artist to weave these lurid threads so closely into the stout warp of daily life that the garrulities of small gossip, the fond fancies of young love, the bitter jealousies of thwarted desire, and the distorted fancies of the unbalanced mind, form a texture like shot silk, dark and bright by turns, but all one cloth. I do not want to exaggerate: the work is on a small scale, but it is admirably done, and full of incidental felicities, which I will not spoil by ripping them from their context. I will rather recommend you to enjoy for yourselves this sympathetic specimen of humane letters.

Too Bad to be True

Mr. Anthony Berkeley, in a slightly aggressive epistle dedicatory, claims that in "PANIC PARTY" the only interest is not the detection but "precisely the opposite", whatever the opposite of detection may be. He adds that, in spite of this, the story was once refused by a "leading popular magazine" as "lacking sufficient human interest", and he seems to think that this was a hard judgment.

The fact is that the interest is not human but inhumane. The framework of the story is, unlike that of "Whispering Tongues", highly artificial. A rich cynic maroons an ill-assorted generation of human vipers on a desert island, informs them (just for fun) that one of them is an undetected murderer, and sits back to enjoy their reactions. The first reaction (very rightly) is the murder of the cynic; after which Mr. Roger Sheringham has to grapple with the reactions to that. As the veneer of civilisation wears thin, these accomplish a fine crescendo of nastiness, from furtive intrigue, malice and hysteria to delirium tremens, shooting and lynching, until, by the time rescue arrives, very few of these mean souls have a rag of dignity or decency left to cover their Bedlam nakedness.

The book is consistently exciting and consistently clever; but the author's sneering hatred of his own puppets provides abundant justification for the editor who looked askance at it. Sloppy sentiment is not wanted, on desert islands or anywhere else; but there is a point at which ruthless realism becomes, not merely too unpleasant for popularity, but a little too bad for belief.

Max Carrados Again

If "THE BRAVO OF LONDON" is, on the other hand, a little too good to be true, what does that matter in a tale so stirring and so instinct with literary quality? Max Carrados is Max Carrados still, even when thwarting the extravagant schemes of a monster of wickedness and deformity, who wants to smash the financial machinery of the world by flooding the

Oriental market with forged banknotes.

Enthusiasts like myself who know the Carrados cycle by heart may be disappointed to find the plot of one of the short stories reappearing as the climax of the novel, but this will not trouble new readers; while upon new and old readers alike, Mr. Bramah's style will exercise its usual irresistible charm.

10 June 1934
NAZI OFFICIALS AND A CRIME
Political setting of a queer story

The Talking Sparrow Murders. By Darwin L. Teilhet. (Gollancz. 7s. 6d.)
Poison for One. By John Rhode. (Collins: Crime Club. 7s. 6d.)
Richardson Scores Again! By Sir Basil Thomson. (Eldon Press. 7s. 6d.)
Ten Minute Alibi. By Anthony Armstrong and Herbert Shaw. (Methuen. 7s. 6d.)

"THE TALKING SPARROW MURDERS" comes to us recommended by the Book Society; less, no doubt, on its merits as mystery pure and simple than on its claims to literary quality.

Its background is modern Germany immediately after Hitler's rise to power, and this gives it a strong topical interest. Periods of political revolution and reform are usually confused and puzzling periods, and the book faithfully reflects this aspect of its setting. Murders occur, and the solution of the problem is made more difficult and embarrassing for the police owing to the fact that the names of prominent Nazis are involved.

The German police are shown courteous, efficient, reasonable, but extremely cautious and sensitively aware of the danger of investigating too recklessly in the immediate neighbourhood of a powder-mine. There are sinister hints of hidden intrigue, lurid flashes of light on the persecution of the Jews, grim little scenes of blood and squalor mingled with the glitter of night-club life, and over it all hangs that atmosphere of suspicion and insecurity which is bound to accompany national upheavals.

The opening episode, which gives its name to the story, has a queerness and fancifulness which slightly suggest the work of another American mystery writer, John Dickson Carr; the surprise-solution makes use of a familiar twist, which is always effective when it comes off – in this case it would, I think, have come off better if the problem itself had been rather more clearly set before the reader. One has the sensation of moving in a kind of phantasmagoria in which nothing is really astonishing and nothing really inevitable.

The style combines passages of determinedly "forcible" writing – "the wrinkles in his cheeks, about his eyes and around his triangular mouth splayed back and forth like the pleat of a worn accordion" – with passages which are simply not English at all: "The nose withdrew. Less than it would take time to blow such a monstrous appendage, the door opened." An interesting book, which may be recommended to those who like something a little out of the common.

Disclosures on the Jacket

"POISON FOR ONE" was rather spoilt for me by the jacket, which deliberately gives away one-half of the solution. Chattering friends who reveal the plot of a mystery story before one has read it are merely thoughtless; reviewers who commit this offence are just naughty and lazy (because summarising the plot is the easiest way to write reviews), but the publisher who sanctions a babbling jacket has no excuse at all. Get your bookseller to remove the jacket before you sit down to enjoy Mr. Rhode's latest mystery.

It is, as usual, sound, pleasantly written and entertaining, though the identity of the murderer is not quite so well concealed as usual. The murder-method has an engaging – an almost Heath-Robinson – simplicity, but I feel sure that it would work if Mr. Rhode says so, because I suspect him of being the kind of man who tries everything out on the dog in his own back kitchen (under proper safeguards, of course, for the dog).

Sir Basil Thomson's tales are always good reading, and he has the knack of being accurate about Scotland Yard without being boring. His book is full of agreeable people, and his case is neatly put together.

He makes rather shameless use of coincidence here and there, and there is a green parrot in the story whose guardians wickedly feed it on buttered toast, which is really criminal of them. Tea, brandy, beef, and buttered toast should be withheld from parrots, much as they enjoy these things – the unnatural little demons! But I would not seriously quarrel with anything so amiable as "RICHARDSON SCORES AGAIN!"

"Ten Minute Alibi" as a Novel

"TEN MINUTE ALIBI" is, of course, the book of the play, and, like all books of the play, suffers from that curious, bald kind of writing that suggests a synopsis. Examining the plot away from the glamour of the footlights, one notices the curiously clumsy handling of that business of the door-key. It was ridiculous of Colin Derwent to pretend that his "suicide" first locked and then unlocked the door. He should have left it locked, broken the panel himself, and inserted the key on the inside when he put his hand through to reach the lock.

On the stage, of course, the audience would not have been able to see what he was doing, so common sense had to be sacrificed. In print, the folly of these proceedings stands out a mile. And then there is the question of the clock. Turning the hands back from five minutes past to five minutes to upset the strike – naturally – but it did not upset the quarter-chimes! I should like to meet that clockmaker. And, of course, the first thing a proper detective should have done, when he began to suspect that the clock had been altered, was to test the strike. It served Pember right if he missed his man – had he never read Gaboriau?

---

17 June 1934
ONE OF THE BEST CRIME NOVELS OF THE YEAR

There's Death in the Churchyard. By William Gore. (Harrap. 7s. 6d.)
The Blank Cheque. By Richard Blake Brown. (Fortune Press. 7s. 6d.)
The Horn. By Brian Flynn. (John Long. 7s. 6d.)

Again I am dogged by misfortune. Again a serpent in human form has spoilt my enjoyment by giving away the plot, before I had read it, of one of the jolliest detective novels of the year. It was no friend of mine, nor yet, this time, was it the publisher. It was one of those whom Tennyson, in a metre of Catullus, stigmatises as indolent and irresponsible, and for such the great curse of Ernulphus is inadequate. Nevertheless, "THERE'S DEATH IN THE CHURCHYARD" triumphantly overcame even this heavy handicap.

It is quite delightful. With a right little, tight little plot it combines a gay humour, many pages of vivacious and free-flowing dialogue, and a set of entertaining characters, including a really natural and attractive child. Also, the village-church background has a satisfying rightness, as you realise when you read of the vicar's wife, who, "sincere Christian though she might be, was compelled to attend divine service in a semi-official position...so that her interests had become technical rather than devotional," and, later on, when you are present at the ransacking of the churchyard rubbish-heap.

I give Mr. Gore full marks for atmosphere and entertainment value, with a special distinction for one quaint device which he has worked into his solution.

Not for Simple Minds

Mr. Richard Blake Brown presents us with a kind of thriller-farce for highbrows. "THE BLANK CHEQUE" is about a clever young undergraduate, and has an air of appealing to clever young undergraduates too, with its quotation from "Ouida" on the fly-leaf, and its irritating rough-edged pages which call for the use of a paper-knife. Since I faithfully used the paper-knife, it is clear that I was sufficiently entertained not to skip anything.

This is the story of Gabriel Block, of King's College, who, strangely obtaining possession of a blank cheque which was not meant for him, endorsed it (though it was drawn to Bearer), cashed it, and thus involved himself in a murder and in a tangle of intrigue with a Polish ambassador, an exotic Countess, and the millionaire Baron Purpleheim.

Gabriel, being too clever by half, makes several sorts of romantic fool of himself, and finishes off in a very topsy-turvy situation. It is all rather superior and satirical, and will not appeal to simple and earnest minds; but Mr. Brown writes with great gusto and many touches of poetical fantasy. And of the quality of his writing there is no possible doubt whatever.

Old-Fashioned Melodrama

Mr. Brian Flynn has been browsing in Baker Street. Indeed, he admits as much. "Shades of Stoke Moran and Dr. Rylott!" exclaims his hero, after listening to a story powerfully reminiscent of the bedroom scene in "The Speckled Band".

The opening scene in the detective's consulting room is conceived in the stilted style of the nineties: "Small wonder that a young girl wilts and withers under the agonising strain of it all! Small wonder, Mr. Bathurst, that it saps all her vitality and that she dreads the coming of to-night." And when we come to the mention of the Giant Rat of Sumatra – "a story", as Mr. Sherlock Holmes observed, "for which the world is not prepared" – we can but say, "Well, well!" We must assume that the world's preparation has advanced a good deal, for the theme of "THE HORN" is sadistic. Apart from this, it is plain, old-fashioned melodrama: without life, certainly, but not without movement.

24 June 1934
GOOD WRITING AND SOUND PLOTS
The whole scale of crime

Journey Downstairs. By R. Philmore. (Gollancz. 7s. 6d.)
The Knife. By Herbert Adams. (Collins. 7s. 6d.)
Death Rides the Air Line. By William Sutherland. (Arrowsmith. 7s. 6d.)

I do not quite know what to say about "JOURNEY DOWNSTAIRS". In this column I can only express my personal reactions (blessed word!) to a book, and, frankly, I found Mr. Philmore a little dull. But I am told that a number of people with excellent literary judgment found the book so enthralling that they could not lay it down. They found the dialogue lively and the characters attractive where I found a failure to grip and a number of conscientiously drawn but uninspiring people.

Perhaps I was in an unresponsive mood. One must always remember the late A. D. Godley's lines about the Examiner: "Perchance the Delta on your paper marked Means that his lunch has disagreed with him." I can truly say that the story is excellently written and the plot sound, with a good little piece of observation and deduction to finish up with. I do think, though, that the central idea was a little too slight to carry the weight of a novel. It looks to me like a short-story plot, with a character-intrigue added to bring it up to book length.

But I may be quite wrong. I offer you both sets of opinions, and you can pay your money and take your choice.

Mr. Herbert Adams' Success

"THE KNIFE" starts off in a rather stiff and old-fashioned manner, with a conventional heavy father forbidding a conventional daughter, in the conventional stagey phrases, to marry the conventional unreliable actor, under pain of being cut off with the conventional shilling. But after the first few pages it cheers up, and thrill follows thrill.

Robbery, murder, blackmail, and arson – Mr. Adams has worked them all in and made a very entertaining job of it. There is a good sketch of a jealous and nasty-minded old spinster, and on p. 176 the student of detective technique will find an exceedingly illuminating paragraph on certain difficulties inherent in the writing of murder mysteries.

In "DEATH RIDES THE AIR LINE", Mr. Sutherland has used a formula which makes a pleasant change from the usual mystery-story pattern. Having got his victim stabbed in an air-liner and provided murder-motives for a number of suspects, he flashes back to the past life of each suspect in turn, showing how that motive came into being. In this way he gives the characters a substance and reality which suspects too often have to do without.

Having the motives thus set plainly before him, the reader may take his pick of them; but he is likely to fail unless he asks himself one very simple question, which admits of only one answer. Mr. Sutherland has given his detectives a little more help than he gives the reader, but even without that we ought, I think, to be able to get as far as at any rate asking the question.

1 July 1934
CRIMINALS WHO ARE TOO INGENIOUS
Ellery Queen's three problems

The Chinese Orange Mystery. By Ellery Queen. (Gollancz. 7s. 6d.)
The Berg Case. By John Bentley. (Eldon Press. 7s. 6d.)
The Fleetwood Mansions Mystery. By Maurice B. Dix. (Ward Lock. 7s. 6d.)

There is an engaging essay by Mr. P. G. Wodehouse which describes how the average murderer of fiction would set about swatting a fly. Unhappily, I have not the book by me, and so cannot describe in detail the monstrous engine devised by Mr. Wodehouse's murderer for this purpose; but the essay is a dreadful warning to the over-ingenious, and it is a pity that Mr. Ellery Queen's criminal did not read and take it to heart before setting us the involved problem contained in "THE CHINESE ORANGE MYSTERY". I cannot say too much, for fear of blowing the gaff; but believe me when I say that for perverted ingenuity this murderer takes the absolute bun. Certainly he receives full marks for resourcefulness in an awkward situation; but a little careless simplicity would have served his turn better. But then, of course, we should have lost the grotesque richness of the opening situation, and that would have been a pity.

Back to Front
Figure to yourselves, my friends, a room of which one door is bolted on

the inside and the other under continual supervision from the corridor – a room in which there sits an unknown man waiting for a business interview. And figure to yourselves that when the corridor room is opened there is the stranger sprawled upon the floor with his head bashed in and all his clothes on back to front – and that everything else in the room is back to front also! There is something to get you groggy!

Who killed him? How was the room entered and left again after the murder? And why was everything put back to front? Well – I was completely led up the garden by problem No. 3, but I guessed the other two, just because of the elaboration of the methods employed, so this time I think I was one up on Mr. Queen, the author, and Mr. Queen, the detective. On one score, however, I think Mr. Queen, the author, shows distinct improvement in the direction of simplicity: he has toned down the elaboration of his literary style. Though this is not his best work by a long way, I enjoyed it more than I did the "Siamese Twin Mystery".

––––––––

Over-Elaborate

Mr. John Bentley is also over-elaborate in a rather dull way. He has put together quite a good series of murders, but he and his detective are too slow in getting to the point. They argue everything out so conscientiously that the reader is apt to get ahead of them. Nor is the length of the book compensated for by any distinction of style, for Mr. Bentley has some oddities of syntax and vocabulary which grate on the ear. What, for instance, is "a tone of aggressive raisonnance"? (resonance?) Is "having consort with anyone else" a misprint for "having consorted", or a pretentious variation on "being in consort with"? And the central idea of the plot is a little threadbare. But "THE BERG CASE" has the merit of careful construction and close attention to detail, and is not without promise as a first novel.

––––––––

"THE FLEETWOOD MANSIONS MYSTERY" is written in such a preposterously melodramatic style that the reader may lose patience with it before he gets to the really ingenious parts. There are at least two bright new ideas in the plot, when this can be disentangled from the surface absurdities. It would have been a good story, if written in a more sober manner and with more regard to minor probabilities. (There will, I think, be some moaning at the Bar over the K. C. who permitted his briefs to be marked 6s. 8d.) I wish Mr. Dix had not spoilt his two good ideas like this.

1 July 1934
AUTHENTICITY OF FAMOUS FIRST EDITIONS
Scientific detection

An Enquiry into the Nature of Certain Nineteenth Century Pamphlets. By John Carter and Graham Pollard. (Constable. 15s.)

If this book could be turned into a detective novel, called "The Catalogue Crimes" or "The Clue of the Crook-backed F", it would grace the annals of a Carrados or a Thorndyke; for it chronicles as pretty a piece of investigation as those heroes ever accomplished. Connoisseurs of detective method will find it more fascinating than any fiction; while for the book-collecting world it is obviously of urgent importance.

The authors are responsible persons, well known in bibliographical circles, and their work appears over an imprint of the very highest standing. They boldly claim to have proved that some 40 or 50 book "rarities", accepted as genuine in all standard bibliographies for the last 50 years, are, in fact, an unparalleled series of forgeries.

Negative Evidence
The majority of these "rarities" purport to be privately printed issues in pamphlet form of works by eminent nineteenth century authors, ranging from Wordsworth, Tennyson, the Brownings, Dickens, Thackeray, and so forth to Stevenson and Kipling. They usually pre-date the earliest published edition, thus ranking as "pre-firsts" or "genuine firsts", with a correspondingly enhanced market value. From the late eighties onwards, these items kept appearing at intervals in the salerooms, in little associated groups from "the library of a gentleman", or some other such vague source.

At first, this only suggested that the "rarities" were rather less rare than they claimed to be. But presently, uglier rumours began to centre about the most interesting and valuable of the series, Mrs. Browning's "Sonnets from the Portuguese". Its pedigree, though picturesque, contained suspicious and contradictory features. Worse, it was found in association with two Ruskin items which had already been proved spurious on internal evidence; though the proof, tucked away in a footnote to the standard edition of Ruskin, had for some time escaped notice. The entire series of pamphlets thus became suspect; for a book is known by the company it keeps.

So, say the authors, the investigation began. There was already a good deal of "negative" evidence against the pamphlets. They were Melchizedeks, without beginning or descent; they generally appeared in "mint" condition; unlike most privately printed books, they never bore any presentation inscription; their own authors seemed never to have heard of them, or, in one or two cases, had actually repudiated them.

Analysis of the Paper

Such anomalies might be explained away. Positive evidence was needed. The analyst brought his microscope into play – with startling results. The Browning "Sonnets", dated 1847, turned out to be printed on a wood-pulp paper that was not due to be invented till 1874 at earliest; the paper of Tennyson's "Morte d'Arthur", dated 1842, showed a mixture of wood and esparto 30 years before its time; Ruskin's "Scythian Guest", dated 1849, on an esparto paper of 1861, contented itself with a modest 12-years' anticipation of the future. In all, the authors of this book inform us, some 22 items showed a more or less serious inversion of the time-scheme.

To the later-dated pamphlets, the paper test was inapplicable. Occasionally, as in the two Ruskin items already mentioned, the alleged "pre-firsts" showed revisions unknown to the published "first", and clearly taken from a later edition.

Was there any peculiarity that might serve to date the type? In some items the small "f" was an ugly, crook-backed letter, designed without any "kern" or overhang in the upper portion. Now, about 1880, Richard Clay, the printer, had been inspired to invent a small "f" without the frail, easily broken kern, and the first fount of type containing this kernless "f"– an ill-favoured thing, but his own – had been cast to his special order in 1883. With growing excitement, the investigators counted up 16 pamphlets, all dated between 1842 and 1873, and all displaying Richard Clay's crook-backed, kernless "f" of 1883!

Finally, there was the lucky Clue of the Tilting Question-Mark, whose thrilling history must be read in the book itself. It led straight to the printing works of Messrs. Clay themselves, and convinced the searchers that here, at last, they had found the firm who, in all innocence, had printed the dubious pamphlets. During the nineties, printers were frequently employed to make facsimile reprints, and an order to produce title-pages with old dates and imprints would not have aroused any suspicion.

The firm readily agreed that they must have done the work – but for whom? Here the luck gave out. No ledgers had been preserved previous to 1911. The shadowy quarry went to earth among the cases in Messrs. Clay's composing-room, just as the hunters thought to lay hands on him.

Acute Detective Work

The pamphlets seem to have taken their place unquestioned on the book-shelves and in the bibliographies of all contemporary experts; and if they are in fact forgeries, then more than one established reputation is likely to suffer a rude shock.

To hurl such a challenge as this in the face of authority, the authors must feel very sure of their ground. They claim to have proved forgery beyond a peradventure in at least 25 cases: seven items being condemned on the paper analysis alone, 12 on paper and type, two on type and text, one on the text alone, and three on all three tests. What is the value of this evidence? The analysis of the paper was made by Messrs. Cross and Bevan, who are regarded as the leading authority in this highly specialised subject and whose report must carry great scientific weight. If no way of escape can be found from their conclusions, the evidence of the paper is damning and the pamphlets are forgeries. The internal evidence of the text is the classic test for all documents whose authenticity depends upon date of issue; this, too, if no reasonable explanation can be adduced for the anomalies, is damning. The typographical evidence appears less conclusive only because of the difficulty of proving a universal negative; but if it can be absolutely established that *no* type-fount with a kernless "f" was cast before 1883, then that evidence is damning also. It is at any rate obvious that there is a strong prima-facie case against the pamphlets.

So far as the layman can judge, the book is soundly argued and scrupulously documented. The narrative of the investigation, clearly and agreeably written and illustrated with plates, occupies the first half, and no expert knowledge is needed to enjoy this record of patient and acute detective work. A complete dossier follows for each pamphlet, giving full details of description, auction record, provenance, and bibliographical references. The authority for the crucial paper-test ought to have been set out conspicuously in the text and not banished to a "list of acknowledgments", and the index might have expanded here and there. The work should interest not only bibliophiles, but every reader who likes a good mystery.

8 July 1934
AMUSING DETECTIVE ADVENTURES
Wits and Eccentrics

The Perfect Alibi. By C. St. John Sprigg. (Eldon Press. 7s. 6d.)
Death of a Banker. By Anthony Wynne. (Hutchinson. 7s. 6d.)
The King's Elm Mystery. By John Goodwin. (Herbert Jenkins. 7s. 6d.)

"THE PERFECT ALIBI" did, indeed, seem to be cast-iron, but that, as Mr. Sprigg's detective acutely observes, is "the most dangerous kind of alibi, because it is so brittle". The characters in this book have a way of making acute and entertaining observations, and that is the most attractive feature of a very attractive piece of work. The mystery of the corpse found in a blazing garage on the Fairview Estate is well worked out, and will doubtless, in the publisher's words, "test the wits of the keen detective story reader"; but this particular reader was less moved to test her own wits than to enjoy the pleasant wit of the author and the rather eccentric wits of some of the dwellers on the Fairview Estate.

One would have liked to hear more from Dr. Marabout, who carried a dried alligator and planted garlic in his garden as a protection against werewolves, and who yet spoke so sensibly and feelingly about the illusion of romantic love, and whose placid assertion that he had seen the devil emerge from the garage the day before the murder was so useful to the investigators of the crime. Then there was Lord Overture, whose method was always to do the easiest job first, and who therefore began his scheme for building a new model estate by erecting a children's play-pen, handily converted later into an enclosure for goats. And Mrs. Murples, who trained pugilists, and was suspected by Dr. Marabout of lycanthropic tendencies. And Mr. Filson, the artist, sulky and foolish, but really a very decent creature, and Miss Delfinaye, who was horsey by profession, but a London bohemian at heart, and joined forces with Filson in some delightful and amusing detective adventures.

If you like a book to be charmingly written and full of the sort of people you would like to meet, you will enjoy this.

Not Insoluble

Mr. Anthony Wynne excels in the solution of apparently insoluble problems. This time it is a huntsman who, under the gaze of 14 people, jumps his horse over a five-barred gate and falls dead in the middle of a wide, bare field with a knife in his back. (No – neither of the two explanations that come first to your mind is correct.)

The puzzle is ingeniously solved; and if you think the solution far-fetched, go to a first-class conjuring entertainment and then ask yourself whether the evidence of the human eye is always to be trusted. The plot centres about a Ruritanian revolution, and has the weakness common to its type that it is difficult to take Ruritania seriously. I do not quite know why this is – there are still quite a number of countries in the world where little revolutions are an everyday matter. Probably it is because one never sees the people of Ruritania earning their bread, or marrying or dying, or engaged in any human activity except politics. The true murder-fan likes a cosier and more domestic atmosphere for his crimes. But this fault, if it is a fault, does not detract from the excitement of Dr. Hailey's adventures or the mysteriousness of the "DEATH OF A BANKER".

Saved from the Gallows

The juvenile lead of "THE KING'S ELM MYSTERY" hurled the villain over a railway embankment on to the line; and while, of course, he was eventually saved from the gallows, I do not know why he and his friends should have been so indignant when he was accused of murder, since morally he was as guilty as sin, though acting under great provocation. However, the circumstances turned out to be extremely complicated, the story is filled with excitement, and if conscientious scruples do not worry you, you will rejoice when the young man is exonerated by the energetic detective work of the heroine and a very nice police-sergeant.

15 July 1934
PRETTY SINISTER
"If you have ears pepare to shed them now"

The Mystery of the Cape Cod Players. By P. A. Taylor. (Eyre and Spottiswoode. 7s. 6d.)
Sinister Inn. By J. Jefferson Farjeon. (Collins: Crime Club. 7s. 6d.)
Sinister Quest. By T. C. H. Jacobs. (Stanley Paul. 7s. 6d.)
Sinister House. By Gerald Verner. (Wright and Brown. 3s. 6d.)

If it were not for one blemish, I should give Miss Phoebe Atwood Taylor nearly full marks for "THE MYSTERY OF THE CAPE COD PLAYERS". The fresh, breezy style makes it an ideal companion for a summer holiday, the characters are pleasant and natural, and the quaint local "jack-of-all-trades" who does the detecting talks a rich transatlantic lingo which is racy without being ugly or unintelligible.

The plot, too, would readily pass muster if Miss Taylor had not contrived to overstep the boundary between what is fair and what is not.

The rule is this: the author may bamboozle the reader as much as he likes, provided that any statement he makes on *his own authority* is absolutely true. Thus, if he says that the housekeeper was an old servant in whom her employer placed complete confidence, he may still make the house-keeper a liar, for the employer's confidence may have been misplaced. But if he himself affirms categorically that "the housekeeper was clearly speaking the truth", then she *must* be speaking the truth; for the author has personally vouched for the housekeeper's integrity.

Miss Taylor's transgression is a slight one – nothing more than the use, in one place, of the present tense instead of the past – but it does amount to a mis-statement by the author, and so must be condemned. But this small breach of faith will not spoil the story for any but the purist, and on every other ground the story may be highly commended.

Confusing Titles

The other three titles on the list suggest that mystery-writing is a very sinister business indeed. These all-alike titles are most confusing.

Some months ago, the Society of Authors put out a scheme for registering the titles of forthcoming books, so that authors might find out beforehand what titles had been already "bagged", and so avoid duplications and resemblances. The scheme has fallen through temporarily, but it seems a pity that something of the sort cannot be arranged, for it would save some headaches among writers, publishers, librarians, readers, and reviewers.

However, I will do my best to disentangle the present muddle with the aid of rhyme and reason. Mr. Farjeon's story is far and away the best of the sinister trio. He maroons his heroine and her two attendant swains in a most discomfortable little hostel in Brittany, where the oddest things happen in the creepiest of corridors, all on a foggy evening. The plot is a little fantastic, but not too much so; the writing is, as usual, lively and atmospheric; romance is lightly and dexterously mingled with the thrills; and the nice people are as genuinely nice as the nasty ones are engagingly nasty. Memory-tip: *Good for a win is* "SINISTER INN"!

I am told that, in reviewing, an ounce of quotation is worth a pound of opinion. So here is a quotation to show why *I rather detest* "SINISTER QUEST"!

> Propped upon a couch amid scenes of the wildest disorder, lay a tall man who seemed not to have washed, shaved, nor combed his hair for weeks. A dirty white, bloodstained sheet covered him; otherwise he appeared to be naked. Yet for all that, Trotter recognised a gentleman.

Plenty of thrills and assaults, you see; plenty of clichés; a fair amount of bosh. Also a mass-murderer, known to Scotland Yard as "the Ear Hound" from his amiable way with his victims (if you have ears, prepare to shed them now!). Also, wicked Chinamen. And all that.

Mr. Verner's thriller is really three separate stories with one common hero. Corpses strew the page. Black, shapeless, deformed figures creep through doorways. Talon-like hands clutch. Masked men menace victims with gas-bombs. Beautiful girls are chloroformed and kidnapped. And so on, monotonously. *That is my grouse against* "SINISTER HOUSE"! And I must protest against the disgusting picture of blood and throttling on the jacket. I am fairly hard-boiled, but I do think there are limits.

22 July 1934
"WHO" AND "HOW" IN DETECTIVE STORIES

Desire to Kill. By Alice Campbell. (Collins: Crime Club. 7s. 6d.)
The Charge is Murder. By J. M. Spender. (Eyre and Spottiswoode. 7s. 6d.)
Burn, Witch, Burn! By A. Merritt. (Methuen. 7s. 6d.)

There is a school of criticism which takes it for granted that any detective story which does not conceal the identity of the villain is *ipso facto* a failure. I am afraid that detective writers have only themselves to blame for this. For many years there was a vogue for the kind of story in which the real culprit was kept unguessed at and unguessable until the last chapter, when he frequently turned out to be somebody entirely improbable, of whose motives and previous history nothing had been heard. Nowadays it is accepted that the author must play fair; but there is still an idea going about that the "Who?" book is the only legitimate variety of the species. Yet, if we demand any sort of likeness to real life, the "How?" book is much nearer to the facts; for in nine real cases out of ten the difficulty that confronts the police is not to spot the criminal but to bring the charge home to him.

Crime on Classical Lines

In "DESIRE TO KILL", the reader will doubtless identify the murderer long before the detective does; but from the candour with which the evidence is set forth it is clear that he is meant to do so. From page 132 onwards there is no attempt at concealment; the murderer is known, and all that remains is to break his alibi. The solution follows classical lines and displays no extraordinary originality. The opening situation is dramatic: a number of rather degenerate young people are tricked by the unpleasantest members of the party into swallowing a preparation of hashish and datura; when they recover from the stupefying influence of the drug, one of them is found to be lying, stabbed to death, in their midst. The story, which might well have developed as sheer melodrama, is lifted out of the rut by the soundness of the characterisation and the lively vigour of the writing. The detective is that same Tommy Rostetter who came into Miss Campbell's earlier book, "The Click of the Gate". He is a likable person, and there is a good man-hunt before the murderer is finally overpowered in an exciting fight.

"THE CHARGE IS MURDER" is a "Who?" book. Here the killer is kept hidden till the last, jealously, on the whole successfully, but perhaps not quite honourably; for the reader is given little opportunity to establish the motive for the crime. The style, too, is undistinguished and pedestrian, and the wrongfully suspected hero alienates our sympathy, and that of the police, by pocketing clues and doing his own detecting in the most unnecessary way. The agitations of the final reconstruction scene do not, I feel, compensate for these radical defects.

"BURN, WITCH, BURN!" is pure thriller. The witchcraft is genuine witchcraft, though the materialist may, if he likes, account for it all by hypnotism. Art magic has its rules, like any other art, and I do not pretend to know whether Madam Mandilip's animated dolls (elaborate varieties of the traditional wax "mommet"), her "witches' ladders" of human hair, and all the rest of it, are according to Cocker or not. But I do know that the atmosphere of glamour and sorcery has somehow been caught and made persuasive; and, if you are capable of feeling a "cauld grue", then Mr. Merritt's book ought to give it to you.

29 July 1934
MURDER OF A CHIEF CONSTABLE
Watching the police at work

Constable Guard Thyself! By Henry Wade. (Constable. 7s. 6d.)
Silence of a Purple Shirt. By R. C. Woodthorpe. (Ivor Nicholson and Watson. 7s. 6d.)
Death in Goblin Waters. By Margaret Peterson. (Hutchinson. 7s. 6d.)
Death on the Swim. By "Simon". (Wishart. 7s. 6d.)

The week that brings a new Wade and a new Woodthorpe must be reckoned a gala week for detection-lovers; with Mr. Wade's book, the accent is on the detection, with Mr. Woodthorpe's on the gala.

"CONSTABLE GUARD THYSELF!" might serve as a model of the classical detective story, complete within its own sphere, and it preserves from beginning to end a perfect unity of tone and action; neither reaching out to the larger and looser universe of the straight novel, nor shrivelling to the dry and restricted two-dimensional circle of the mathematical puzzle. It is excellently constructed, the exposition in particular being worthy of all praise, and the characterisation is of the exact right kind to awaken "human interest" without swamping the plot in a flood of emotional excitement.

The scene is laid in the police-station at Brodbury, and Mr. Wade, unlike many of his colleagues, has taken pains to acquaint himself with the precise workings of the complicated police machinery. He understands the functions of the Chief Constable and his headquarters staff, their relations with the county police and the relations of both with the Joint Standing Committee (how many of us know or take the trouble to enquire about the existence of that important authority?), what steps are taken, and by whom to call in the help of Scotland Yard, and how the finance of the whole thing is handled.

Behind the Scenes

This provides the reader with that extra interest and sense of reality which always comes of "seeing the wheels go round", and the ordinary citizen, meekly paying his rates, ought to take a more lively interest in that modest proportion of them allocated to "Police", after reading this fascinating account of the organisation which his 3d. or so in the £ helps to keep going.

The crime is the murder of the chief constable himself; the C.I.D. man is our old friend Inspector Poole; the clues are given with scrupulous – with even generous – fairness to the reader, and a touch of tragedy in the conclusion reminds us, very rightly, that murder is a melancholy business at best. Mr. Wade must be congratulated in general upon a very fine book, and in particular upon introducing and handling a large cast of police officials without ever once confusing us as to their duties and identities.

Purple Shirts

Mr. Woodthorpe has treated himself this time to an excursion into the realms of fantasy. The Purple Shirts are a political organisation with the vague object of Making Britain Free, and the author gets a great deal of light-hearted entertainment from their spectacular, though rather ill-directed enthusiasms. One of the Purple Shirts is found murdered on the Dorset coast, and suspicion falls on a fellow-member of the Movement – a tiresome young doctrinaire whose obstinate refusal to defend himself by breaking his oath of silence betrays a wide strip of the old Public-School-Tie still lurking beneath the Purple Shirt.

His uncle by marriage – a nice old boy – who, urged by a reluctant sense of duty, undertakes to investigate the matter, goes down to Dorset and has some very remarkable experiences in a marvellous inn, which would, indeed, be the inn of every man's desire, were it not populated at the moment by a most extraordinary staff, all of whom seem to have something weighing heavily on their minds. After many adventures, the uncle-by-marriage succeeds, though handicapped by the "SILENCE OF A PURPLE SHIRT", in tracing the murder to a Most Unlikely Person. This is a tale to be read in a holiday spirit. Mr. Woodthorpe's wit and geniality will provoke many chuckles, and there are many delightful characters to fall in love with: my own especial pet is the uncle's confidential clerk, Alfred Hicks, who is a gem of the purest water.

"DEATH IN GOBLIN WATERS" is a rather melodramatic handling of the type of mass-murderer of whom George Joseph Smith was a notorious example in real life. The author, the late Margaret Peterson, is not very sound on dew-ponds or the appointment of chief constables, but in a rather slap-dash way she can draw character and put a touch of genuine grimness into a quickly moving story.

"Simon" has pruned away some of the extravagances of his style since writing "Murder Among Friends", though an ugly jerkiness still remains. "DEATH ON THE SWIM" is about the murder of a Channel swimmer; the murder method, if sound, is ingenious, and the book shows great improvement, both in writing and construction, upon its predecessor.

* * *

5 August 1934
MOTIVES FOR CRIME
"Respectability" as a root cause

Further Evidence. By Alan Brock. (Ivor Nicholson and Watson. 7s. 6d.)
Frozen Death. By Anthony Weymouth. (Arthur Barker. 7s. 6d.)
Poison in Kensington. By Charles Kingston. (Ward Lock. 7s. 6d.)

Mr. Brock, delving among the murder trials of the last half-century, has been struck by a number of cases, more or less conforming to a single type, where, though the jury's conclusion was the obvious and probably the true one, an alternative explanation might be made to cover all the known facts. It has interested him, as he says, "to construct a case on similar lines and to fill in all the gaps".

The result is an exceedingly interesting and well-written book which hovers rather curiously between the detective story and the psychological crime study. It is not a true detective story, because none of that "FURTHER EVIDENCE" which brings about the final solution is placed before the reader until the last chapter; but it is more than a "straight" crime story, because of the presence of a mystery and of a number of possible suspects. The reader will have little difficulty in guessing the identity of the central actor in the plot, merely because most of the suspects are obvious dummies; but whether Mr. Brock's solution is psychologically quite convincing, I am not quite sure. There is this to be said for it: that of all motives for crime, respectability – the least emphasised in fiction – is one of the most powerful in fact, and is the root cause of a long series of irregularities, ranging from murder itself to the queerest and most eccentric misdemeanours. The story is, in any case, extremely readable, and has an especial topical appeal at this moment when headless female bodies in trunks and other packages loom so large in the news.

Manners of the Police
"FROZEN DEATH", on the other hand, is plain detective work by a new

author. The plot is worked out with care, and a conscientious effort has been made to introduce a detective with novel tricks of speech and manner. Perhaps I was in an unresponsive mood when I read it, but the book seemed to me to be rather stiff and dull, as though a malignant emanation from the title had got into the text and frozen it to death. Inspector Treadgold of Scotland Yard ought to be amusing with brusqueness and his apparently irrelevant remarks always introducing a shrewd question or observation; but there is something of a manufactured air about his conversation, and his roughness of manner is not endearing, but merely unbelievable. Any C. I. D. man who spoke as he speaks to the persons he is interrogating would lay himself open to the severest reprimand. A mere inspector does not burst rudely into the Colonial Office and haul the heads of departments out of conferences with the abrupt insolence of a gunman breaking in on a poker party; and if he really said to the local police superintendent (who is his superior officer): "Now get this into your silly fat head!" the superintendent would have something to say about it. Mr. Weymouth would gain a great deal from a study of Mr. Henry Wade's admirable police novel, "Constable Guard Thyself!" which was reviewed in this column last week. His faults are chiefly those of inexperience; he can put a mystery together; and if he will pay a little more attention to the reactions of living people in a credible social framework, he ought to be able to write a good detective story with less of a machine-made air about it. It is a pity that the nicely drawn map is placed on the jacket, where the majority of library subscribers will never see it.

Mr. Kingston has written a romance about a financier who has administered arsenic to a rich old uncle, and a young doctor who, discovering this, blackmails the financier *pour le bon motif*. When the doctor falls in love with the financier's daughter, and when the young couple devote themselves to slum work, we know that everything must end happily and virtuously in spite of all appearances. None the less, the tale in "POISON IN KENSINGTON" is worked out quite entertainingly for those who do not mind taking a good dose of sentiment and melodrama as a substitute for probability.

12 August 1934
WHAT A THRILLER SHOULD BE

The Travelling Skull. By Harry Stephen Keeler. (Ward Lock. 3s. 6d.)
Calling All Cars. By Henry Holt. (Collins: Crime Club. 7s. 6d.)
Death by the Mistletoe. By Angus MacVicar. (Stanley Paul. 7s. 6d.)
The Ince Murder Case. By E. J. Pond. (Heritage. 7s. 6d.)

People sometimes complain that I am harsh and high-hat about thrillers. May not the thriller, they ask, be as excellent in its own way as the most intricate piece of desiccated detection that ever furrowed a brow? It may, indeed – and I give you my word that when I meet the least touch of real originality, or creepy-crawlery, or glamour, or humour, or sheer rollicking cut-and-thrust-and-have-at-'em combativeness in a thriller I hail it with cries of joy. But 99 times out of 100 I find only bad English, cliché, balderdash, and boredom.

This week, Mr. Keeler's thriller, "THE TRAVELLING SKULL", has given me great joy; but the other three give me nothing but a pain in the neck, though it is only fair to say that they are no worse than many others and better than some.

Ever since April I have been trying to read "CALLING ALL CARS", but its dullness defeated me until yesterday, when I made a great effort. It is about a young man and a young woman who spend 250 pages hunting for a master crook called "The Shadow". Their adventures are as stereotyped as the love affairs of the Bloomsbury school. Crooks and cops wander confusedly and indistinguishably through featureless chapters, and in the end not one character, not one episode, not one phrase is memorable.

A Nameless Horror
"DEATH BY THE MISTLETOE" begins with nine clergymen being

murdered in a thunderstorm. This is hopeful; but with sinking hearts we realise that this is (to quote the jacket) "the first hint of a nameless horror which threatens to destroy the peace and safety of the whole of Britain". In short, a gang – a mystical, Celtic-twilight sort of gang, with a pre-Druidical religion, blood-sacrifices, hypnotic powers, and what not. A "semi-official secret society" sets out, guided and encouraged by ancient prophecies, to track down the chief priest of the cult, whose identity is obvious to everybody but themselves. There are caves, and secret passages and rats, and revolving bookcases, and a "sacrifice-scene" at the end which reads like a bad imitation of Mr. John Buchan. (He really *can* do this kind of thing – but then, he knows his black cults inside out, and speaks with the tongue of men and of angels.) Needless to say, no spark of humour lightens the darkness from beginning to end. This is less boring than the crook-and-cop stuff, but it is terrible balderdash.

––––––––

"THE INCE MURDER CASE" is written entirely in clichés. Even the most penetrating detective work, even the most agonising excitement (if it had them) could not carry such a load of battered coinage. "Vision of feminine loveliness – finely chiselled features and athletic frame – clear-cut features and attractive form – a magnificent specimen of manhood – moved with the silence and grace of a panther – some subtle sixth sense warned him of impending tragedy – this gently nurtured girl was capable of plumbing the depths of love or hate – anxiety gnawing at the speaker's heart-strings – the demon of fear has been gnawing at my heart-strings – raging inferno of flame – surging mass of humanity – dogged by the workings of a malign fate – white, set face – white and set face – white set face – white, set face" – dear Heaven! What has the English language done to be served up in this dismal mess of rehashed phrases, like a resurrection-pie? Nobody would endure it in a "straight" novel. Then why should it be supposed that "anything will do" in a thriller?

––––––––

And now for "THE TRAVELLING SKULL", which is, in my opinion, exactly what a thriller should be. Balderdash if you like, but balderdash with a difference. It is extravagant, but with a jolly, humorous, whimsical, unusual, chucklesome extravagance. It dances absurdly along and you follow riotously, wondering where you will end up. The characters are amusing; on no account miss Legga the Human Spider or Sophie Kratzen-schneiderwumpel (the very names, you see, have a tang to them); the writing is crisp; everything is fresh and unexpected; and if the ending seems a little involved, who cares? it was such good fun getting there. From the moment that the hero gets landed with the Barr-Bag with the Billy Bulger Bulge and finds the silver-plated skull stuffed with sonnets – But there! like a good chairman, I will sit down and leave Mr. Keeler to entertain you.

19 August 1934
SURPRISES FOR THE LAW-BREAKER – AND THE READER

Murder on the Cliff. By Clive Ryland. (Grayson. 7s. 6d.)
Eight to Nine. By R. A. J. Walling. (Hodder and Stoughton. 7s. 6d.)
The Case of the Lucky Legs. By Erle Stanley Gardner. (Harrap. 7s. 6d.)
The Bowstring Murders. By Carter Dickson. (Heinemann. 7s. 6d.)

How do you choose a book at the library or bookstall? Do you, after glancing at the title and author, have a look at the first page "to see how it starts"? If so, don't be put off "MURDER ON THE CLIFF" by the rather fourth-form witticisms of its opening conversation. When it gets going, after this preliminary wobble, it is a very pleasing murder-tale, with two good corpses, a bunch of well-spoken and credible characters, and a smart surprise played on the reader – and the criminal – at the end. The scene is an English seaside village, and the action, though full of movement, is worked out in the quiet atmosphere which such a setting implies.

Curious People

In Mr. Walling's "EIGHT TO NINE" we are in London. Here the pace is rather more vigorous and the accent more *sforzando*. The inhabitants of Elford Mansions were a curious set of people, and some of them had had rather unusual pasts; so that when a dead man was discovered in one of the flats, there were a good many suspects for Mr. Tolefree the detective to deal with.

Mr. R. A. J. Walling is an extremely skilful maker of plots and surprises, and in this book he has also created some excellent and amusing characters – particularly Mrs. Louisa Pilling, the caretaker, and the imperturbable Mr. Mason, who took such a detached view of the noisy disturbances that accompanied the murder. His detective has one bad habit, which I am afraid he acquired from the late Mr. Sherlock Holmes. He occasionally observes some small object or action without communicating his observations to the reader, and is thus able to bring out a set of startling deductions which nobody else has had a chance to make.

Thus, the contents of the corpse's pockets should have been *fully* described, and when certain items disappeared, we should have been given a timely hint to that effect, so that we might guess by whom the disappearance had been contrived. The mystification is cleared up before the final solution, but not quite early enough for perfect fairness. With this reservation, the tale is a good one – in fact, one of the best things Mr. Walling has done. But he must watch this besetting sin of his, which was the chief defect of some of his earlier books, particularly "The Strong Room".

Mr. Perry Mason Again

"THE CASE OF THE LUCKY LEGS" takes place in an American town, and the atmosphere is, appropriately, still more agitated. I am beginning to like that odd criminal lawyer, Mr. Perry Mason. He is not content, like our dull English solicitors and barristers, with sitting comfortably in offices and chambers while other people collect evidence for him. He rushes quixotically out and involves himself in the crime, falsifying the facts, whisking away witnesses and suspects from under the noses of the police, making free with other people's luggage, in order to stage dramatic impersonations in hotels, and generally behaving in a manner which keeps him just – but only just – on the windy side of the law.

However, he is a good fellow, and considering the way his own clients behave to him, he is to be excused for a little irregularity of method. The tale is ingenious and exciting and written in straightforward English, and I shall look forward to Mr. Mason's next adventure, which, to judge by the indications on the last page, will be "The Case of the Howling Dog".

"THE BOWSTRING MURDERS" take place, if anywhere, in the Castle of Otranto. There is a mad old baron in a weird old castle, where corpses appear mysteriously in a great old hall filled with suits of armour, and apparitions of armed knights haunt the staircase.

The plot is of the "hermetically sealed chamber" type, and the mysteries all have a plain, physical explanation, but the style is rather Adelphi, and some of the details are not convincing. I have my doubts about the ballistics, and I *know* that a vambrace is not a kind of armour-plated skirt, but a defence for the forearm (*avant-bras*). But there are ingenious touches here and there, and, with better handling, this might have made a good tale of the near-thriller type.

26 August 1934
MR. FREEMAN WILLS CROFTS' DOUBLE MYSTERY

Mystery on Southampton Water. By Freeman Wills Crofts. (Hodder and Stougton. 7s. 6d.)
The Cadaver of Gideon Wyck. By Alexander Laing. (Thornton Butterworth. 7s. 6d.)

A good many years ago now Dr. Austin Freeman, in that excellent volume of stories, "The Singing Bone", introduced us to a new formula for the detective story. In these stories the true solution of the mystery was given first, the actions of the murderer being detailed from the first step in the commission of the crime to the last false clue laid down to baffle the police. In the second part of each story the detective was seen unravelling the problem, separating the false from the true, taking up points which the criminal had missed altogether, and so bringing the investigation to a conclusion which was known to the reader from the beginning. The author, in an introductory note, expressed his belief that stories written to this formula might prove interesting to the reader, in spite of the fact that the usual element of surprise was lacking.

They did, indeed, prove interesting; and it is surprising that the formula should not have been imitated more often. For the intelligent reader the fascination of seeing an apparently water-tight defence laboriously built up and then scientifically picked to pieces again more than counterbalances the loss of the "Who?" problem; the "How?" problem, of course, remains; but is transferred from the murder itself to the detection. But the majority of detective writers have still preferred to retain the conventional surprise element.

Two Crimes – Two Methods

In "MYSTERY ON SOUTHAMPTON WATER" Mr. Crofts has combined the two formulae in one tale. Two crimes are committed. In the first we are made privy to every detail up to the point where Scotland Yard is called in. Then, when our old friend Mr. French (now at length, and deservedly, promoted to chief inspector as a reward for his excellent work on the affair of the "12.30 from Croydon") is on the point of breaking down the carefully manufactured defence of the criminals, a new crime occurs to disconcert him. This time we are not officially let into the secret, and have to follow the mind of the chief inspector in unmasking the culprit.

The use of the two methods in one book provides a welcome variety of interest, and, but for one blemish, the story would have been one of Mr. Crofts' best pieces of work. The plot centres about the invention and theft of a chemical formula for the manufacture of cement, and the care with which the technical details are worked out makes it much more plausible and entertaining than the usual plot of this description. It is unfortunate that, in staging the second crime, Mr. Crofts should have resorted to a device so threadbare that it betrays itself instantly to the reader, thus greatly diminishing the interest and mystery of that part of the story.

Otherwise, the machinery is admirable. The characters, also, of the criminals are particularly well differentiated, that of the weak member of the conspiracy being most naturally and sympathetically treated.

"THE CADAVER OF GIDEON WYCK" is a story that will offend some readers very much, for it deals with a subject that many people feel should not be written about except in medical works. It has to do with the deliberate production, by a semi-mad doctor, of monstrous human births, and this singularly disagreeable theme is handled with a frankness of scientific statement which, in the opinion of some, will make it just decently tolerable, and, in that of others, will only aggravate the offence.

The writing is good, and Mr. Laing's medical knowledge obviously adequate; those who are not disgusted will find the story exciting and mysterious enough in all conscience. It displays much more originality than the ordinary American thriller, but anybody who reads it after this warning will do so at his own risk.

2 September 1934
THE "TWINS" THEME ONCE MORE
AND A NIGHTMARE CRUISE

The Life He Stole. By Sefton Kyle. (Herbert Jenkins. 7s. 6d.)
The Murder of Sigurd Sharon. By H. Ashbrook. (Eldon Press. 7s. 6d.)
Murder Cruise. By Michael Keyes. (Harrap. 7s. 6d.)

Hullo, Twins! Two sets of them this week. The Twins Formula has put in some good, hard work since the detective story was first invented, and really ought, I feel, to retire on a pension, together with the Gramophone Record Formula and the Formula of the Corpse with the Battered Face.

"THE LIFE HE STOLE" runs along familiar lines. A young man with a heart of gold but an irascible temper, returning from Canada (where he is supposed to have died long since) meets his twin brother, quarrels with him, dots him one, and finds that he has killed him. Following the natural impulse of any hero faced with such a situation, he resolves at once to impersonate his brother, thus taking over the family title and estate, the dead man's fiancée, mistress, yacht, racing-stable, and other embarrassments, and also a handsome bunch of sins and wickednesses – for it was the wicked twin who was killed.

After a period of uneasy juggling, the deception becomes obvious to practically everybody – even to the police; the only difficulty being whether the hero is to be arrested for his own murder or the other fellow's. These complications are inevitable from the start, and, since (as I have explained) the hero has a heart of gold, it is also inevitable that there should be a happy ending. But I am willing to swallow all these major improbabilities. What I refuse to believe is that "the best-known artist of the day" delivered a portrait to its purchaser *rolled up* and "loosely tied with a piece of dirty tape". No, no – one must draw the line somewhere!

Between Two Stools

Miss Ashbrook's twins are a very different pair of people. Indeed, stripped to its essentials, the plot of "THE MURDER OF SIGURD SHARON" is a fine one, rich in possibilities both detective and psychological. In the actual working out, the story falls between these two stools. The mystification is not sufficiently well kept up to make a first-class puzzle. The secret of the twins becomes clear to the reader rather too early if surprise is the chief aim and object of the author, and the detective part at the end is too loosely and hastily put together. On the other hand, the psychological interest is weakened by being subordinated to the machinery of mystification; and this is a pity, since, of the two, it is by far the stronger and the more worthy of careful handling.

The book is just good enough to make one feel, regretfully, what a really powerful thing it might have been made in the hands of a master writer.

"MURDER CRUISE" is one of those tales which make you feel that yachting for peace and pleasure is not all it is cracked up to be.

The Princess is a boat in which things keep happening. People disappear in the night, stealthy footsteps pad around the decks, lights are mysteriously extinguished, corpses roll about the state-rooms, stranglers leap upon passengers on the after-deck, pomeranians are impaled and par rots hideously mangled, and you are not surprised that the owner has to be kept behind bars, that the captain seems uncertain where his duty lies, and that the young man who loves the owner's daughter finds that his inquisitiveness makes him unpopular in a good many quarters.

Stirring stuff, my hearties! and one surprise which really is a surprise, if by that time you are not too much bewildered to be surprised at anything. A plain thriller, this, and – though American – written in plain English.

9 September 1934
THREE GOOD CRIME NOVELS
Discord in a mad and bad family

The Murder of My Aunt. By Richard Hull. (Faber and Faber. 7s. 6d.)
Why Didn't They Ask Evans? By Agatha Christie. (Collins: Crime Club. 7s. 6d.)
The Case of the Dead Shepherd. By Christopher Bush. (Cassell. 7s. 6d.)

It may be extravagance to pick out three first-class books and wallow in them in one review, but this week we will give ourselves that treat.

First, for its originality and unlikeness to anything else, I put Mr. Hull's "THE MURDER OF MY AUNT". It is not a detective story; it is the story of how one of the most unpleasant youths in fiction kept on trying to get rid of the aunt on whom he was reluctantly and resentfully depend-ent, and the not wholly unexpected consequence of his blundering borders on the farcical; but it is not long before we realise that the ludicrous antics of the zany are really the ghastly antics of a madman.

Even more skilful than the portrait of the warped and effeminate ego-centric beast of a nephew is that of the aunt herself. She, on the surface blunt, hearty, masculine, and likeable, shows, in the savage humiliations she inflicts upon the wretched specimen of humanity committed to her care, and in her hooting and horrible enjoyment of them, that she has inherited a strong strain of the family insanity. It is a study of unbalanced reactions to delight the heart of the psychologist; but the admirable light-ness of the style, and the entire absence of pompous comment and medical jargon, keep it essentially a novel, with nothing of the treatise about it. The insensitive might even find it as funny as it appears to be on the surface, the sensitive will find it painful, but continuously interesting and exciting. The action takes place in a small Welsh village, and the writing is excellent. Incidentally, the story is a useful warning against endeavouring to put in practice those ingenious and elaborate methods of murder that you read about in detective fiction.

Mrs. Christie's new book is much more comfortable reading. The plot is very elaborate and full of surprises and adventures, but the great merit of "WHY DIDN'T THEY ASK EVANS?" lies in the delightful, easy dialogue and the really charming characters of the two young people who do the detecting. One is, of course, sorry to miss Monsieur Poirot, but the greatest of detectives must take a rest sometimes, and Bobby Jones and Lady Frances ("Frankie") Derwent are a most attractive substitute. With them Mrs. Christie has been much more successful than with her earlier pair of youthful investigators, Tommy and Tuppence, who were a trifle sentimental and tiresome. Bobby and Frankie are really jolly youngsters with a tang to their talk.

The tale starts on a golf course and ends in a madhouse – well, no, not quite there, for there is a comic and quite natural twist in the tail of it, and the actual finish is elsewhere. But the madhouse produces many exciting scenes, though nothing so genuinely mad and bad and dreadful as the madness in "The Murder of My Aunt". This is one of Mrs. Christie's best and liveliest stories, and may be enjoyed without a qualm from cover to cover.

Murder in School

"THE CASE OF THE DEAD SHEPHERD" occurs in a school. For some reason, nearly all school murder stories are good ones – probably because it is so easy to believe that murder could be committed in such a place. I do not mean this statement to be funny or sarcastic: nobody who has not taught in a school can possibly realise the state of nervous tension and mutual irritation that can glow up among the members of the staff at the end of a trying term, or the utter spiritual misery that a bad head can inflict upon his or her subordinates.

Woodgate Hill County School was (we must believe and hope) exceptionally unfortunate in its head, who was a brute without a redeeming feature; and one feels too much sympathy with his slayer to be anything but heartily sorry when Mr. Ludovic Travers detects him. The plot is ingeniously worked out, though it has perhaps one or two rather improbable features, and the characters of the staff are well indicated. I should not place the book on quite the same level as Mr. Bush's "Case of the 100 per Cent Alibis", as it runs on rather more conventional lines, but it is thoroughly engrossing, well written, and full of legitimate puzzlement.

16 September 1934
COMPREHENSIVE CRIME STORIES
The Whole Scale of Villainy

Five to Five. By D. Erskine Muir. (Blackie. 3s. 6d.)
Death at the Pelican. By Cecil M. Wills. (Heritage. 7s. 6d.)
Murder at Lancaster Gate. By Francis D. Grierson. (Thornton Butterworth. 7s. 6d.)

On December 21, 1908, old Miss Marion Gilchrist, of Glasgow, sent her servant out to do some errands. While the girl was away, the ceiling of the flat below was shaken by the thud of a heavy fall. The occupier went up to see what had happened, but found Miss Gilchrist's outer door locked. In a few minutes the maid returned with the keys. She said she thought something must have fallen down in her kitchen, and the two of them entered the flat together. In the hall they were passed by a man coming out. He said nothing to them, nor they to him; according to their evidence later, neither of them recognised him, but supposed him to be some legitimate visitor.

In the dining-room, they found the body of Miss Gilchrist, horribly battered to death, apparently by the legs of a chair which stood near. Nothing appeared to have been taken from the dining-room, or from the bedroom, with the possible exception of a diamond brooch; but some papers which were kept in the spare room had been scattered about.

This was the opening scene of one of the most famous and mysterious of all recent murder cases. Everybody knows the sequel: that a travelling salesman, named Oscar Slater, pawned a diamond brooch and was arrested for the murder; that the brooch was found to be the wrong brooch, but that Slater was nevertheless convicted on the inconclusive and contradictory evidence of various persons who claimed to recognise him; that the sentence was commuted to penal servitude; and that, after many years, the case was reopened, mainly through the devoted efforts of Sir Arthur Conan Doyle, and the sentence quashed, but upon technical grounds which shed no further light upon the central problem of who really did the murder.

No New Solution

Mr. Muir has not attempted to provide a new solution to the Glasgow mystery; but he has used the opening situation as the thesis for an exciting and well-constructed murder story. In his version, the victim is an unpleasant old man, whom many persons might gladly have wished out of the way, and some minor details and incidents are altered and added.

It is surprising that no one has used this particular mystery before as the foundation for a murder novel, for it is rich in possibilities, which are, on the whole, very well exploited in "FIVE TO FIVE". The conduct of the servant (who now becomes a trained nurse) is made more understandable in the book than it was in the actual case; a greater wealth of motives and suspects is provided, and the tale is enriched with a second murder, which helps to guide the detectives to a dramatic and soundly argued conclusion.

Whether the reader is or is not closely acquainted with the ins-and-outs of the Gilchrist tragedy, he will find Mr. Muir's story good and entertaining reading.

―――――――――

All Sorts of Crime

Mr. Cecil M. Wills's new book shows a considerable advance upon "Author in Distress". He is still a little too much inclined to drag in romantic rescues for their own sake, and in two places he has helped on the story by a shameless use of coincidence; but his style has acquired much more freedom and strength, and he shows great fertility in the invention of plots and escapes.

His hero is again Det.-Sergeant Boscobell, now married and transferred to Scotland Yard. This time he is engaged in the pursuit of a gang whose comprehensive criminal activities begin with the theft of gold bullion and proceed to white slavery and the drug traffic. "DEATH AT THE PELICAN" leans, as may be seen, to the thriller side of the business, but contains some good detective work, especially in the first few chapters.

―――――――――

"MURDER AT LANCASTER GATE" has one of those exasperating heroes who give more trouble than all the gangs put together. He is engaged by some crooks to impersonate the long lost son of a dying millionaire; and when the millionaire is so inconsiderate as to go on living and the crooks decide to bump the poor old gentleman off, the silly ass (who possesses secret knowledge which would easily frustrate their knavish tricks) prefers to go on being too clever by half.

The result is that the murder comes off, though by a fortunate accident the victim is the bad butler instead of the good millionaire. And after a lot of fuss it all ends happily – which was more than this egregious young juggins deserved. Mr. Grierson can do better than this.

* * *

23 September 1934
MURDER IN FANCY DRESS
Complicated Crime

Murder in Public. By John Crozier. (Hutchinson. 7s. 6d.)
Masks Off at Midnight. By Valentine Williams. (Hodder and Stoughton. 7s. 6d.)
Fancy Dress Ball. By J. Jefferson Farjeon. (Collins. 7s. 6d.)

All our three books this week are costume pieces.

Mr. John Crozier, who is a new author, tells us the old, old story of the actress who has to be murdered on the stage, and, lo and behold! she is murdered. But there is a great deal more to the story than that; it is a very closely woven and complicated piece of crime and detection, of quite remarkable merit for a first novel. There is a very large cast of characters – the theatre staff by itself occupies a whole page of the book – and in addition we have the detective and his secretary, a police officer, and a number of subsidiary helpers; while the action is concerned with three different varieties of iniquity, many alibis, and a brisk series of alarms and excursions.

It is not a story for the inattentive reader to skim through with his eyes on the page and his ears on the radio; but, all things considered, this vast mass of material is very capably and clearly handled, and the style, though not impeccable, is vigorous and attractive. The private detective is a North American Indian (for a change), and this endows him with an exceptionally keen sense of smell and a useful knack of stealthy movement. He does not, however, exploit his racial origin in any irritating or melodramatic way, and operates quite sensibly and humanly in familiar London surroundings. His American secretary, Miss Mitt, is a treasure in more ways than one, and her passages-of-arms with the Scotland Yard man bring a touch of humour to lighten the heavy work of detection.

Sherlock Holmes (we are incidentally assured) is a real and living person, and the Chief of the C. I. D. wishes he could call him in to solve the problem of "MURDER IN PUBLIC", but, as Holmes has definitely refused to take any more cases, Falcon (the name is not too subtly chosen) is accepted as a reliable second-best. This is modest – but, since Holmes must now be 80 years old, he would probably not have done quite so well as Falcon in the really thrilling shooting drama which takes place in the dark theatre at the end of the story. Mr. Crozier has made an excellent start, and may be strongly encouraged to go on.

The Old, Old Story

Mr. Valentine Williams, on the other hand, is a seasoned craftsman in the production of mysteries, and though his easy and practised skill never fails him, I feel that he was perhaps a trifle jaded when he wrote "MASKS OFF AT MIDNIGHT". He, too, tells the old, old story – this time it is the masked mummer in a sedan chair, who is found to be dead when the chair is opened. The smooth flow of the narrative is there as usual, the natural dialogue, the pleasant charm of the sympathetic characters, the brisk entertainment value; but in its outlines the plot is conventional, and something of Mr. Williams's accustomed zest seems to me to be missing from this latest book.

It is well written and exciting, but not quite Valentine Williams at his best.

Bad Marksmanship

There was once a prolific and excellent writer of serial mysteries who made a point of getting his hero into the most appalling situations at the end of every instalment. Drugged, gagged, and bound, the poor man would be left languishing in a dungeon which was rapidly filling with water from below, while a sinister Chinaman or ferocious tiger guarded the only exit. "How on earth are you going to get him out this time?" the author's friends would ask. "That's simple", was the reply. "I shall just begin the next chapter: 'Quickly throwing off the effects of the drug and exerting all his strength, Algernon broke the ropes which bound him, and made them into a lasso, which he flung dexterously round the neck of the Chinaman (or the tiger).'"

I was forcibly reminded of this author's methods at the point in

"FANCY DRESS BALL" where a good character, lying helplessly trussed up on a bed, is fired at point-blank by the villain. Having mourned his death in an intervening chapter, we discover in the next that the bullet has not only missed his body by an inch, but also obligingly cut his bonds, while the villain has carelessly decamped, without waiting to see the results of his bad marksmanship. This, I feel, is a little thick, so to speak, in volume form, though admirable serial practice. But still, this is only one riotous and reckless episode in a tale which is one reckless and delightful riot from beginning to end. When Mr. Henry Brown saved up his scanty wages to purchase a ticket for the Chelsea Arts Ball, he had no idea what a mad tangle of plot and counterplot he was going to be mixed up in, nor what a really tender and charming romance would be woven into the web of intrigue surrounding him.

Mr. Farjeon is quite unsurpassed for creepy skill in mysterious adventures, and he can be glamorous, and even sentimental, without being mawkish – a rare gift. And though there are two corpses in the book, no official person ever finds them; so that the whole mystery is cleared up without finger-prints, interrogations, or policemen, or any of those worthy but oft-repeated things of which we sometimes – yes, even you and I – grow just a little bit weary.

30 September 1934
ACCIDENT, SUICIDE, OR MURDER?
MR. J. J. Connington's puzzle

The Ha-Ha Case. By J. J. Connington. (Hodder and Stoughton. 7s. 6d.)
Three Went In. By N. A. Temple Ellis. (Hodder and Stoughton. 7s. 6d.)
Murder on the Moors. By Colin Campbell. (Rich and Cowan. 7s. 6d.)

It is far too long since we had a new story from Mr. J. J. Connington. But here it is at last, presenting itself in one of those admirable "map" jackets (cross indicates the body) which not only make an attractive pattern, but which are also very handy for reference.

"Once upon a time there was a king who had three sons." So the fairy tales begin; and in the end it is usually the youngest son who inherits the kingdom, even though he may be something of a simpleton. It has been suggested by folklorists that this is a relic of the ancient custom of "Borough English" (still surviving, or surviving till very recently, in certain parts of the country), by which the heirship passed to the youngest son instead of to the eldest. The estate which caused all the trouble in "THE HA-HA CASE" was entailed according to "Borough English", and the youngest son was, in the traditional manner, but a poor, simple youth, easily led by a cunning master, but exceedingly hard to drive. Here, however, Mr. Connington parts company with fairy tale; for young Johnnie Brandon never succeeds to his heavily encumbered inheritance. Instead, he is found dead while out shooting rabbits with his friends, and the problem is: Accident, Suicide, or Murder? It is all made very complicated by the financial entanglements in which his rapscallion of a father has tied up the estate, and by the fact that a gentlemanly lunatic with large gaps in his memory wanders on to the scene at the crucial moment.

There is no need to say that Mr. Connington has given us a sound and interesting plot, very carefully and ingeniously worked out. In addition, there are the portraits of the three brothers, cleverly and rather subtly characterised, of the eldest brother's young woman, and of Detective-Inspector Hinton, whose admirable qualities are counteracted by that besetting sin of the man who has made his own way: a jealousy of delegating responsibility. Sir Clinton Driffield takes up the reins in the end, to conduct the investigation to its goal and so conclude a work in every way worthy of Mr. Connington's high reputation as a detective writer.

―――――――――

More Ingenuity

Mr. Temple Ellis has in the past been rather too lavish of romance and adventure and unprepared surprise-packets to take rank as a first-class puzzle-maker. "THREE WENT IN" is, however, strictly detective and exceedingly ingenious. His police official and his amateur investigator pit theory against theory in amusing alternation, and each new theory works out in the most disconcerting way: entirely wrong, but leading to some new and startling discovery which starts the hunt off in a new direction. An old and dying man is found stabbed, and a diamond is missing. Three people successively visited the victim round about the time of his death, and two of them ran away afterwards, so that it is very difficult to ascertain which of them, if any, was the thief or the murderer, or which two of them in collaboration with each other and/or the dead man's manservant.

The author shows a persistent determination to the unexpected in the final scene; but the unexpected is quite properly prepared, and the only criticism I can make is that the motive demands a good deal of credulity. But if it amuses you to see how many different webs of theory can be woven from the same evidence, this is the book for you.

All So Simple

Mr. Colin Campbell is rather disappointing. He is so much preoccupied with a tale of young love among the purple hills – all terribly pure and passionate, with people taking all their clothes off with the noblest motives and chivalrously choking down their overmastering emotions – that he makes but a very poor pretence of concealing the identity of the villain who does the murders. It is all so simple: anybody who talks sentimentally to dogs or was anybody's batman in the war is a good character; and anybody who behaves haughtily to an attached old Scottish retainer is a bad character. One grasps these points at the start, and all further camouflage is unavailing. Also, it is an artistic error to tell part of the story in the third person, from the point of view of omniscience, and part in the first person of the supposed narrator; because one immediately wants to know how the supposed narrator became privy to all the intimate details of the love-affair, and the illusion of reality is destroyed. Still, there you have it: a heart-throbbing, palate-tickling, pretty romance pleasantly spiced with villainy, and many readers will ask no better entertainment than "MURDER ON THE MOORS".

* * *

7 October 1934
CRIPPEN AS TRAGIC FIGURE
Fine story based on real life

Henbane. By Catherine Meadows. (Gollancz. 7s. 6d.)
Arsenic in Richmond. By David Frome. (Longmans. 7s. 6d.)
The Divorce Court Murder. By Milton Propper. (Faber and Faber. 7s. 6d.)

I have spoken to more than one person who had met Hawley Harvey Crippen after his arrest, and they all say the same thing: "He was a *nice* little man." And, indeed, I believe he really was. He murdered only under overwhelming stress of circumstances; he chose a most merciful poison, killing at once and without pain; and his devotion to the girl he loved approached the heroic. It is ironical that his name should – owing to his method of disposing of the body – have become a byword for cold-blooded brutality; but the public is sensitive on certain points, and will more readily forgive a man for inflicting the long-drawn agonies of arsenic on the living than for dismembering a senseless corpse. Miss Meadows, who interprets Crippen's tragic history in "HENBANE", has hit on the right word to explain that odd callousness by which he shocked the world so much: he was unimaginative.

The miseries of his wretched married life, the terror and danger that threatened himself and his lover, were things which he could see and feel acutely; but the purely imaginative horror attending the dissection of his own murdered wife does not seem to have troubled him much, and he went about the task with the straightforward efficiency to which a medical training had accustomed him.

Minute Exactness
Miss Meadows says that her book "is based on" the story of Crippen, but "does not claim to be a representation of the persons or events". With the exception of a few minor and incidental portraits, which are fictitious, it nevertheless reproduces all the actual details with a minute exactness. The usual fault of novels "based on" real life cases is a curious baldness of style, hovering between the two-dimensional outlines of a police-court report and

the child-like brightness of one of Mr. Punch's "Simple Stories". This fault Miss Meadows has completely and brilliantly avoided. I cannot give her book higher praise than to say that it reads as though every word of it were fiction.

She has succeeded in subduing the raw material of fact to the processes of art, and the book would be equally interesting and enthralling if one had never heard of Crippen. With the murderer and his mistress she has dealt tenderly and sympathetically, making their poor little sordid and grotesque drama the terrible and inevitable thing it actually was. The character of the wife – noisy, over-vitalised, animal, seductive, and intolerable – is a fine piece of bravura painting.

The background has the authentic feeling of the early years of the century, that tightly-stuffed period of hips and busts and padded hair-dressing and overblown hats, when trimmings ran riot, and the frou-frou of silk petticoats was at once the hall-mark of worldly standing and the siren-song of hidden allurements. But the book is not merely a costume-piece, still less a study of morbid psychology; it is a fine novel of human passion and suffering, neither more nor less convincing because it happens to be a transcript of actual facts. I recommend it strongly.

Family Poison Drama

Mr. David Frome always gives me pleasure. The plot of "ARSENIC IN RICHMOND" is nothing very out of the way – just one of those little family poison-dramas to which we are accustomed, where everybody and anybody might very well be guilty and the person with the least apparent motive turns out to be the criminal. But I do like Inspector Bull and Mr. Pinkerton, and the other amusing characters who pop in and out of the tale. I like the pleasant, easy-flowing style and the brisk conversations. I like the agreeable tone of the whole thing, and the way in which violent tempers and passions, though skilfully indicated, are never forced above the natural pitch of the narrative. One or two details of procedure seem to me a little sketchy, and I do not think it would really be wise to use arsenical weed-killer lavishly on the flower-beds; but, on the whole, I feel cheerful and refreshed after an hour or so in Mr. Frome's company; and that is a good thing to feel.

U.S. Divorce Tangle

One rather gains the impression, from newspapers and movies and what-not, that America takes its divorces light-heartedly. But on this point the States are not united, as in Pennsylvania the divorce laws (thoughtfully summarised for us by Mr. Milton Propper at an early stage of his story) seem to present much the same complication, unreasonableness, and puritanical obduracy as our own. If both parties have been unfaithful, they have got to stay married; so that when the respondent in the Rowland divorce suit brought a witness to prove that the petitioner also had been guilty of adultery, the only way to get the divorce through was to silence that witness by murder. There is one terrific coincidence on which the whole plot turns, and which is really, I think, coming it a little bit too strong – with this reservation, "THE DIVORCE COURT MURDER" is a good, exciting yarn, leading up to an unexpected conclusion.

14 October 1934
CHRISTMAS EVE CRIME AND
A FAMILIAR "DEATH TRAP"

Crime at Christmas. By C. H. B. Kitchin. (Hogarth Press. 7s. 6d.)
The Grouse Moor Mystery. By John Ferguson. (Collins: Crime Club. 7s. 6d.)
When the Wicked Man. By J. F. W. Hannay. (Methuen. 7s. 6d.)

It is far too long since we had a detective story from Mr. Kitchin. He, you remember, wrote that excellent tale "Death Of My Aunt", which is on no account to be confused with that other excellent tale "The Murder of My Aunt", by Richard Hull (something will really have to be done about these titles!). Mr. Malcolm Warren, who lost his aunt so unfortunately in the former book, is again involved in "CRIME AT CHRISTMAS", and his personality once more lends its characteristic savour to the story. It is a savour, like that of caper sauce, difficult to define in words, and not ap-pealing to every palate; but those who do like it like it very much indeed.

Mr. Kitchin calls his book "a study of the behaviour of normal people in abnormal circumstances", and he does not depict that behaviour as being particularly dramatic or heroic. After all, if you and I were members of a house party, and a woman we did not know very well happened to fall out of a window on Christmas Eve and get killed, how should we react?

We should agree that it was very sad indeed, and a very great nuisance – a damper on the festivities, and an annoying interference with our own private arrangements. Our personal anxieties would still predominate in our own minds – our love affairs, our investments, our own petty likes and dislikes would still bulk larger to us than the catastrophe, and the strained and depressing atmosphere of the house would make us nervy, awkward, and quarrelsome. Or so Mr. Kitchin thinks, and I would not for one moment contradict him. Here and there we may find a kind, unselfish person, like the hostess in the story, who can feel genuinely for others, but the majority of normal people do not in fact behave any too appropriately when things go wrong.

But even if you "think nobly of the soul and in no way approve his opinion", you will approve Mr. Kitchin's shrewd and sensitive psychology, his excellent English style, and the neatness of his plot, which is complicated by a second death of an obviously murderous kind. And if you want to argue with the author – he has set out all your arguments for you in a final chapter, with the answers to them, so there, as Humpty-Dumpty said, is glory for you!

Another Corpse in the Library

In the meantime I am getting rather nervous about my library. True, it is on the first floor and has no french windows; moreover, I am not a millionaire financier, and so far I have unearthed no example of a *female* victim's being found murdered in a library; but there is no doubt that these places are fraught with the utmost peril. The young man in "THE GROUSE MOOR MYSTERY" went out with some friends to shoot grouse in a fog, which was foolish of him. He escaped, however, with a charge of No. 6 shot in his left arm. But a day or two later he went into the library to write a letter. From this death-trap there was, naturally, no escape, and he very soon was lying dead with his head in the wastepaper basket.

I like Mr. Ferguson better in the more adventurous mood of "Night in Glengyle". This time he has confined himself to pure detection; but there are loose ends here and there in the story, and somehow it never quite grips. The police are rather too easily hoodwinked by tricks that the reader will readily see through, and the characters of the suspects never become sufficiently alive or distinct, with the result that we do not greatly care which of them was really guilty.

The Criminal's View

"WHEN THE WICKED MAN" is told from the criminal's point of view, and offers a motive for murder unusual in fiction. To be sure, there is the classic instance of the Old Man with a Gong, who (you remember) bumped at it all the day long till they cried out "O lor'! you're a horrid old bore" – so they smashed that Old Man with a Gong. Beneath the surface frivolity of that limerick lies a melancholy truth to human nature. The blameless and ascetic clergyman of Mr. Hannay's story allowed himself to be victimised by the doglike affection of a well-meaning and insensitive incubus till one evening his boredom and irritation turned to frenzy, and he snatched up the poker and hammered the poor man to death.

This is told with impressive conviction – one would gladly seize the poker one's self, so deeply does one sympathise with the exasperated clergyman. Then comes the impulse to confess – the self-deceptions by which conscience is quieted – the concealment of the crime – the suspicion thrown on the innocent – the effect on the clergyman's fiancée, whose violent and possessive passion make her a powerful advocate in the devil's cause – and so to the necessary and proper end to such a spiritual struggle. It makes an interesting book, more powerful, perhaps, in conception than in execution, but with passages of fine psychological insight and an ironical twist at the end of the story.

* * *

21 October 1934
"STRAIGHT" STORIES AND CROOKED PEOPLE

Skin and Bone. By Edwin Greenwood. (Skeffington. 7s. 6d.)
The Crooked Lane. By Frances Noyes Hart. (Heinemann. 7s. 6d.)
Inspector Richardson, C.I.D. By Sir Basil Thomson. (Eldon Press. 7s. 6d.)
Death on the Set. By Victor MacClure. (Harrap. 7s. 6d.)

All our four books this week have readable qualities of one kind or another, though none of them (to quote the words of a certain American editor about some short stories written by your humble servant) makes me want to roll about on the floor and bite the carpet with excitement. But, indeed, few books have that effect on the hardened nerves of British readers.

Mr. Edwin Greenwood has done his best to harrow up our souls in "SKIN AND BONE", which is a straight crime story without detection. Mr. Arthur Machen, in a brief foreword, after mentioning Wilkie Collins, Rider Haggard, and William Shakespeare, claims for the book that it is "compounded on the true and ancient recipe, it mixes mirth and murder with immense spirit and success"; while the publisher asserts that the deadly dowager Lady Eugleton "brings a laugh every time she opens her mouth". Personally, I did not find the story such a riot as all that, but all taste in humour is personal. Rabelais was coarse, and Mr. Greenwood is a trifle coarse; but Rabelais was good-humoured and Mr. Greenwood is not. Jane Austen was malicious and Mr. Greenwood is malicious; but Jane Austen was urbane and Mr. Greenwood is not. I feel that "Skin and Bone" rattles the bones a little hollowly. And I am worried by the plot.

It was all right for Lady Eugleton to persuade her whole family to insure their lives in favour of the impoverished heir to the estate and then to start killing them all off; but when the third unfortunate victim perished from a huge dose of acetate of lead I think there would have been an inquest, not to say a police inquiry, and I am quite sure that the insurance company would have thought twice about paying out the money. Still, if a series of horrid deaths and boisterous humours with a dash of rather lush religious sentiment make a brew to whet your appetite, here you may sup full of horrors.

Bright Young Americans

In "THE CROOKED LANE", everybody is so incredibly rich, luxurious, beautiful, and wicked that it gives one a sensation of having dined rather too lavishly in an overheated restaurant. You simply wouldn't believe how dreadfully these bright young people in American society do go on. Drink, drugs, passion, blackmail, nothing comes amiss to them, and when they are feeling really worked up they play backgammon with their lovers on boards of lapis and malachite with jade and ivory markers.

No wonder that young Karl Sheridan, of the Criminalistic Institute of Vienna, found his heart and brain set all awhirl when the lovely lady with immense eyes of the purest, clearest silver grey, still and shining as the sky just before dawn, as young rain falling and spring twilight and all the rest of it called him in to investigate the death of the exquisite child who looked like a little Persian page from a long-forgotten fairy-tale. It was all rather heartrending, really, and one admires the young man for setting his teeth and going through with it. But it does keep on being thrilling and exciting, and you simply have to go on and find out what happens, and there are moments that make you go all trembly with agitation over the woes of all these poor little rich girls and boys – and the general effect is like drinking a very sweet and very intoxicating cocktail. But it isn't as good as "The Bellamy Trial".

Inspector Richardson Again

In the hands of Sir Basil Thomson things are calmer and (from the gentler British point of view) pleasanter. "INSPECTOR RICHARDSON, C. I. D.", whom we knew and liked in the days when he was a humble police-constable, has to investigate the death of a detective novelist who is found with her head in a gas-oven just after a publisher has accepted her first mystery on favourable terms. Rightly supposing that no one would commit suicide under such circumstances, he puts in some of that excellent, sober, straightforward detective work which he so well knows how to do and follows the clue of a post-mark to the heart of a very plausible and proper mystery. I find him a most agreeable companion after all these feverish shudders.

Mr. MacClure in "DEATH ON THE SET" deals with murder in a film studio, and I think the influence of the talkies has affected his English style. He starts out with a touch of the penny novelette ("the vexed look of hauteur which Lady Blanche gave him"), and later on has a rush of polysyllables to the pen, contriving to work "noctivagous", "maculation", and "steatopygous" all into one page. And the plot is not too new. But I will forgive him a great deal for having created Mr. Rosenbaum, the studio manager. "'Ere's Mr. Morden gone and bin moidid, an' all the stoodio work 'eld up! Pounce and pounce goin' down the drain! … Nobody wants to be 'eartless, but it's pounce and pounce down the drain." I would give pounce and pounce of blue-eyed lovelies for another ounce of Mr. Rosenbaum.

28 October 1934
DR. THORNDYKE COMES AGAIN
Fine entertainment

For the Defence: Dr. Thorndyke. By R. Austin Freeman. (Hodder and Stoughton. 7s. 6d.)
Death Cruises South. By Roger Denbie. (Nicholson and Watson. 7s. 6d.)
Death Strikes from the Rear. By Antony Marsden. (Sampson Low. 7s. 6d.)
Scarweather. By Anthony Rolls. (Bles. 7s. 6d.)

I must say that when one of Dr. Freeman's innocent suspects gets caught in a web of circumstance he does it handsomely. There is no skimble-skamble, trivial ambiguity about his position. Fate remorselessly marks him down with an infernal machine rammed to the muzzle with coincidences, and, lest there should be any doubt about it, the silly idiot plants himself fairly and squarely at the cannon's mouth while he fires the match with his own hand.

But my metaphor seems to have slipped its moorings and run amuck with the bit in its teeth. "Andy," says the wife of the hero, "you have, really and truly, behaved like a perfect old donkey!" And that expresses my meaning fairly enough. If, when Andy found himself the witness to a murder on the King's highway, he had gone to the police and said so, he would have been all right. He would not then have rushed in a panic to have his broken nose mended by a beauty-doctor, so as to make him the twin-image of his rascally cousin who had just been squashed in an accident, and would not have had to impersonate the cousin and so get charged with murdering himself – and so there would have been no need to call "FOR THE DEFENCE: DR. THORNDYKE". Which would have been a pity, because the more we see of Dr. Thorndyke the more we like him. But one cannot help feeling that the situation has been rather violently manipulated to produce a case worthy of the great man's forensic skill. The book must be taken for what it is: an exhibition of virtuosity; and, as such, it is excellent entertainment. None the less so for being handled along the lines of "The Singing Bone", with the solution first and the detection afterwards.

Mr. Roger Denbie, author of "The Time-Table Murder", has produced another good mystery in "DEATH CRUISES SOUTH". The scene is set, for a pleasant change, in the still-vexed Bermoothes, and very much vexed the local police are by the nasty murder which threatens to upset the tourist population of those agreeable islands. The opening chapters need a careful attention to keep the characters and sequence of disjointed incidents clear in the mind, but all the clues are given with perfect fairness, and the only fault I have to find is that the revelation of the murderer's identity does not greatly excite us. Dr. Quentin Pace again does the detective work; he is an efficient researcher with a pleasant personality.

All the Vices

"DEATH STRIKES FROM THE REAR" is about a newspaper magnate, who planned a horrid hoax and was caught in his own trap. He is, of course, a handy epitome of all the vices. Nothing is too mean for him, and very little is too mean for the men on his staff and on the staff of the rival paper he tries to hoax. Newspaper proprietors, like trustees and Chinamen, are always wicked in detective fiction – it is one of the rules; but newspapers, with meek magnanimity, kiss the rod and allow their critics to review these shocking exposures favourably. And, indeed, I was thoroughly entertained by Mr. Marsden, who hoodwinked me most successfully for the greater part of his vivacious and briskly moving tale.

"SCARWEATHER" did not hoodwink me at all. I knew perfectly well from the start where the missing man had gone to and who put him there, even if the publisher had not saved me the trouble of guessing by blowing the gaff in a helpful picture on the jacket. Mr. Rolls can write, as he showed us in "Family Matters", but the keeping of a secret is not his strong point. He ridicules the quarrels of archaeologists amusingly. If, however, you wish to dispose archaeologically of a corpse with modern dentistry and a Potts fracture, I recommend rather the method used in Dr. Freeman's famous masterpiece, "The Eye of Osiris". To unravel *that* mystery really did demand a Thorndyke at the top of his form.

4 November 1934
THE PROFESSIONAL SLEUTH
Scotland Yard in fiction

Mystery Villa. By E. R. Punshon. (Gollancz. 7s. 6d.)
The Execution of Diamond Deutsch. By Cecil Freeman Gregg. (Methuen. 7s. 6d.)
Scotland Yard Takes a Holiday. By Luke Allan. (Arrowsmith. 7s. 6d.)

No amateur sleuths this week – Scotland Yard every time, and every time so different you would hardly believe the authors were all talking about the same place. But, indeed, the Scotland Yard of fiction is an elfin realm, seen by every writer in the beglamoured light of his own poetic fancy. I often wonder what Scotland Yard thinks of itself, if it ever gazes upon its own features in this curious magic mirror.

If Scotland Yard is anything like Mr. Punshon's vision of it, then it is a delightful place indeed. "MYSTERY VILLA" is, if I may say so, a Punshon of the right brew, and I could do with a tun of such genuine matured mild and bitter. As soon as it came into my hands I hastily turned over the pages to see if it contained plenty of Superintendent Mitchell – a gentleman for whom I cherish an uncontrollable passion.

Satisfied on this point, I settled down to enjoy myself and was not disappointed. Mitchell is here at his astringent best, and Bobby Owen, who threatened of late to become a little too big for his constabulary boots, has been made a sergeant and acquired, with his increased responsibilities, a modesty suitable to his station in life; though he can still pull Mitchell's leg with bland impertinence.

The story is about one of those strange old women of whom one reads from time to time in the papers who shut themselves up with the remnants of their riches and live in unspeakably squalid secrecy till one day the groceries are not taken in, and the police break through the rust and dust and cobwebs to find that a more dreadful visitor has been there before them. It is a superb subject for a mystery, and Mr. Punshon has handled it superbly.

The Real Thing

It is inevitable that one should compare his old Master Barton with Miss Havisham of "Great Expectations", but, to my mind, the honours are with Mr. Punshon. Miss Havisham never quite played the game; she was not too mad to interview her man of business and pay the rates; sordid considerations about company's water and gas and firewood were never allowed to intrude on the dignity of her theatrical sorrows. But in "Mystery Villa" we have the real thing – real solitude, real filth, real starvation of mind and body, with a real and ghastly necessity underlying the whole horrible superstructure of unreason. The picture is pathetic and terrible and convincing to the last degree, and the mordant humour with which the detectives and subsidiary characters are treated serves as an acid to bite that picture unforgettably into the mind.

The balance of tone in this book seems to me to be quite perfect, and if here and there the details of the plot seem to be rather lightly sketched in, that is of small consequence in so grotesque a pattern of fantastical light and shade.

Dogged Inspector Higgins

With Mr. Gregg, we come out of the haunted dark of madness and decay into a cheerful sunshine populated by crooks and villains and large, bluff policemen, with revolvers going off, and chases over the roofs and safes being broken open and crimes of a comfortably rational sort perpetrated for comfortably rational ends.

I like Inspector Higgins very much. He is a nice, sensible, hardworking man who gets on well with his fellow-detectives and who, though frequently outwitted by ingenious criminals, gets there in the end by dogged perseverance and personal courage. The situation at the Great Financier's house was a very involved one, because everybody there seemed to be playing a queer little game on his own, and when the masked robbers broke in, it was not very clear who, if anybody, was really on the side of the angels. But after many stirring ins-and-outs and ups-and-downs, everything was cleared up, and "THE EXECUTION OF DIAMOND DEUTSCH" carried out in an efficient, if unorthodox, manner.

Mr. Gregg's Scotland Yard is genial and human, less witty than Mr. Punshon's, but perhaps nearer to the Scotland Yard of prosaic fact.

Two Months' Leave

With Mr. Allan, "SCOTLAND YARD TAKES A HOLIDAY" – a busman's holiday, of course, but also (I feel) a holiday from any pretence to verisimilitude. When Detective-Sergeant Strangway loses track of a suspect through having his attention called away by a pretty girl, it is kind of his chief inspector to send him away for a two months' holiday by way of freeing his mind of the woman-complex that is interfering with his work – very kind, but I do not believe a word of it.

Of course, he goes to see a friend off at Southampton and finds that both the pretty girl and the suspect are travelling by the friend's boat; and, of course, he follows them, and they all behave very oddly, and he falls, first, in love with the girl, and finally into the dear old trap in the lonely house, and so on – but none of it ever comes to life for a moment, and the last chapter is just one laboured explanation after the other. At the end, the good chief-inspector throws an arm round the sergeant's neck and weeps for joy to see him come safe home. Tell *that* to the C.I.D.!

11 November 1934
AN EXTRAVAGANZA OF CRIME
Clues and hilarity

The Blind Barber. By John Dickson Carr. (Hamish Hamilton. 7s. 6d.)
Shot at Dawn. By John Rhode. (Collins: Crime Club. 7s. 6d.)
Murder of My Patient. By Mignon G. Eberhart. (Bodley Head. 7s. 6d.)

I laughed uproariously over "THE BLIND BARBER". But I admit that I am one of the simple-minded people who become weak and ill over the antics of Nervo and Knox, and have to be led away suffering from convulsions. Perhaps it was unrefined of me to be amused when the dignified and choleric skipper of the Queen Victoria was laid out flat by an impulsive but mistaken young investigator armed with a whisky-bottle, and subsequently half-smothered in his own cabin by the uncontrollable blast of the Mermaid Automatic Bug-Powder Gun. But even those who only joke "wi' deeficulty" must spare a chuckle for Captain Valvick, who tells such delightful and irrelevant stories in so persuasive a Dutch accent, and for the other preposterous passengers who roam and wrestle and tumble (not always, alas! with strict sobriety) about the decks of that outraged and respectable liner. Never can a nasty, bluggy murder have been detected to the accompaniment of so much hilarious horseplay. Yet, in all the confusion, the clues are not neglected. Sixteen of them, all magnificently Chestertonian and incomprehensible, are listed by Dr. Gideon

Fell. He, of course, is the god in the Carr who makes majestic descent upon the final hurly-burly to unravel the tangle; *dignus*, I am delighted to say, *vindice nodus*.

The story has all its author's usual happy touch of the grotesque, with less of the horrible and more of the farcical about it, and all his usual merits of style. In fact, I call it a gorgeous book, and if anybody doesn't like it, I pities 'em.

––––––––––

Shot at Dawn

Mr. John Rhode is one of those kind, thoughtful writers who patiently explain all the technical points of the narrative in words that a child could understand. He does not expect his reader to be an authority on ainhum or haemophilia or trajectories or the obscurer barbituric compounds or this, that, and the other, as some people do.

That is why I am so indignant at the perfectly heartless manner in which he led my innocence up the garden path to be "SHOT AT DAWN". Fair? Yes, of course it was perfectly fair: that is what makes it so galling. If I had had the gumption of a weevil in a biscuit, I should never have allowed myself – But there! I did guess who fired the fatal shot, though at a disgracefully late point in the story. The body was found lying on board a motor-boat in an estuary; the body's companion was snoring heavily in the cabin; on the other side of the river, a "good long mile away" was a rifle range. That was the problem with which Superintendent Hanslet had to deal; but it took Dr. Priestley with his little tape measure to act really intelligently on information received.

––––––––––

Mrs. Eberhart's new book again has the red-headed Nurse Keate for its heroine. I would hesitate to say that Nurse Keate neglects her patients, but she does seem to take a good deal of time off, and to spend a surprising amount of it listening behind doors and keeping tabs on the comings and goings of the family. But there was some excuse where the Thatchers were concerned, for, as a family, they did not behave in a way to inspire confidence. "MURDER OF MY PATIENT" is one of those problems in which everybody tells lies from start to finish, and the game is to spot the one essential fact about which no lie is possible. It is very ingeniously put together, and, as usual with this author, the atmosphere of discomfort and suspense is well maintained.

18 November 1934
RE-ENTER PHILO VANCE
More irritating than ever

The Casino Murder Case. By S. S. Van Dine. (Cassell. 7s. 6d.)
The Man in Button Boots. By Anthony Gilbert. (Collins: Crime Club. 7s. 6d.)
The Jury Disagree. By George Goodchild and C. E. Bechhofer Roberts. (Jarrolds. 7s. 6d.)

Just as each new baby ushered into the world is the finest child its nurse ever saw, so every successive crime investigated by Philo Vance is more shocking and unnerving to his attendant Van Dine than any of its predecessors. It is a solemn and affecting thing to see human beauty and human turpitude thus advancing side by side to perfection; but perhaps both the nurse and Mr. Van Dine are apt to exaggerate in the excitement of the moment.

I think myself it is a mistake to insist too loudly in the first chapter of a mystery on the awful revelations to follow; it is an opening that takes a lot of living up to. I doubt whether the reader will be greatly upset by "the terrific and fatal *dénouement* that came so suddenly" – he has met too many *dénouements* of the same kind. He will probably content himself with wondering (not for the first or the twentieth time) why the criminals of fiction should be at so much pains to explain their methods in detail to the detective before proceeding with the job of polishing that inconvenient person off. If any criminal ever does succeed in slaying Mr. Vance, I shall heartily sympathise. He has now begun to model his style on Mr. Reggie Fortune; he says, "My dear Markham – oh, my dear Markham!" and "I could bear to know a few facts" and "same like a shillin' shocker"

– and, dearly as I love the original Reggie, I could not bear to hear every detective talk same like him.

It is, however, sheer natural cussedness that makes Mr. Vance say "in yon *lavatorium*" when he means "in the bathroom"; something lingering with boiling oil in it should be reserved for tormentors of the King's English.

Although nothing in "THE CASINO MURDER CASE" is quite so nerve-racking as its hero's conversation, the problem is a nicely complicated one and the criminal highly ingenious. True, in the actual technique of the murder he does not take quite enough trouble to verify his references, but when he goes about to cast suspicion on the innocent his methods are laudably up to date and show a really self-sacrificing attention to completeness. The theme is poison; the characters belong to America's "Social Register"; the setting is in a private casino of unparalleled luxury.

Immensely Complicated

The plot of "THE MAN IN BUTTON BOOTS" reaches a still higher level of double-crossing ingenuity than that of the Casino case. It is so immensely complicated that at the end we feel obliged to go back and check up on it to see whether all the complication is really necessary. But it is; and the author is to be congratulated on giving an original and baffling twist to a story which, in its bare outlines, is fairly familiar. There are one or two points at which the reader is quite certain to be a good deal cleverer than the detectives, and I think that intuition will lead him to spot the murderer; but, even so, he will have plenty of puzzles on which to exercise his brains. He had better not read the blurb on the fly-leaf, which gives a good deal of information – most of it inaccurate, but, even so, compromising.

Let him rather concentrate on the story itself, which is written in a curiously precise and almost old-fashioned style, not by any means unattractive, and a great improvement upon the slipshod writing which marred the previous two "Anthony Gilberts".

Based on Life

"THE JURY DISAGREE" is based, obviously and openly, upon the actual facts of the Wallace murder. It is not, however, a re-interpretation of the case, as Miss Meadows' "Henbane" was of the Crippen murder, for the incidents have been altered and fresh material added, so as to produce an entirely different situation. In this respect it more closely resembles Mr. D. Erskine Muir's handling of the Oscar Slater material in "Five to Five". It is indeed better to forget Wallace, if possible, while reading it, otherwise the mixture of fact and fiction may cause some mental confusion. Its chief interest lies in showing the immense variety of constructions placed by different people upon the accused man's actions and behaviour; and here it does accurately reproduce the atmosphere of ambiguity that surrounded the real case. In the end, the novelist steps in to provide the one decisive and unambiguous key-incident necessary to the solution of any detective story, though often, alas! lacking in real life.

But the solution is unimportant compared with the vivacious to-and-fro of the argument in the jury-room, and the characterisation of the jurors – all so well-meaning, all so much biased, consciously or unconsciously, by personal prejudice and experience, all acting and reacting so curiously upon one another. A few of the portraits tend slightly to caricature, but on the whole they make up a convincing and representative picture of what learned counsel is accustomed to call "a highly intelligent jury".

25 November 1934
THRILLS WITHOUT FRILLS
Complications at an aero club

Death of an Airman. By C. St. John Sprigg. (Hutchinson. 7s. 6d.)
Give Me Death. By Isabel Briggs Myers. (Gollancz. 7s. 6d.)
Pattern in Black and Red. By Cora Jarrett. (Barker. 7s. 6d.)

These three books all possess that primary quality without which a mystery story is but Dead Sea apples – they maintain their enthusiasm up to the last page. Too often, a fine, fruity corpse appears in the first chapter, only to have its effect spoiled by a dreary and mechanical investigation, as though the author were bored with his own body and would thankfully bury it and be done, were it not for the necessity of grinding out so many thousand words of doubt and difficulty to satisfy the conditions of book publication. And, indeed, poor soul! he very often does feel just like that. But this week all our authors seem to have written eagerly on, and as a result the reader reads on eagerly too.

Mr. St. John Sprigg in "DEATH OF AN AIRMAN" bubbles over with zest and vitality in describing the exceedingly odd goings-on at a rather oddly managed Aero Club. I doubt whether any business concern run on such happy-go-lucky lines could survive for a month – but, of course, when nefarious activities are being carried on under cover of the daily routine, irregularities are bound to arise, and the people concerned have some excuse for seeming a little distrait and careless from time to time.

His Saving Grace

If the Bishop of Cootamundra (who is a darling) had not been on the spot when the aeroplane crashed, there might – owing to the extreme laxity of the medical organisation – have been no proper inquiry into the death of the unfortunate pilot. The Bishop had some smatterings of technical knowledge about *rigor mortis*, which persuaded him that something was wrong. With a trifle more knowledge he might have done better still and saved himself a great deal of needless confusion of mind. Nor is *rigor* the only, or the most certain, indication of the time of death; and there was at least one person present who could have cleared the confusion up if the Bishop, or anybody else, had had the wits to ask him the right questions.

But if we allow that these mistakes could have been made, then we shall find ourselves involved in a most ingenious and exciting plot, full of good puzzles and discoveries and worked out among a varied cast of entertaining characters. The solution depends upon certain flying technicalities which are outside the province of an ignorant critic like myself. Mr. Sprigg certainly gives the impression of being thoroughly at home in the air, and his buoyant and vigorous style carries us blithely through all the complications of the intrigue.

Gloom and Terror

Miss Isabel Briggs Myers writes in a very different mood. "A splendid detective story, red-hot for Christmas," says the publisher's announcement, sardonically. To the question, "What would you like for Christmas, Aunt Maria?" the answer "GIVE ME DEATH" has but an ominous sound; and the matter of the book is about as far removed from Yuletide jollity as anything could very well be. It is a tale of gloom and terror from beginning to end, and the spectre that haunts the Darneil family is no turnip-ghost either. As a rule, when one person after another in a book kills himself or is killed to prevent the betrayal of a horrible secret, the weak point is that the secret, when disclosed, is insufficiently horrible to justify the horrible preliminaries. In this book the secret really does justify the horror; though the mere fact that it does so will seem more horrible to the majority of us than the secret itself. I must not say too much about this for fear of spoiling the mystery.

The story is the more depressing because, if only the family and the detective had faced the secret more resolutely and let the light in upon it at once, and at whatever cost, one, if not two, of the four tragedies would have been averted; and the conclusion, while dramatic to a degree, is anything but a happy one. The writing is good, the personality of the detective pleasing, the plot well put together, and the subject one of genuine interest and importance. Provided that cheerfulness is no object, you will find the book well worth your attention.

Rich Mixture

"PATTERN IN BLACK AND RED" is a detective story of good, rich texture, with plenty of clues, plenty of thrills, and a fine, spectacular dénouement. It is what I should call a highly coloured story, and none the worse for that. All the characters are interesting, from old Professor Ames, who does the detecting, down to the quaint and superstitious negro servants, who play so large a part in the action.

The proportion of deduction to excitement is well balanced, and although there are some conventional features in the plot, the handling is brisk and novel. Miss Jarrett, like Miss Myers, is an American writer, and their books both go to show how much the standard of American detective fiction has improved in recent years.

2 December 1934
PITY THE POOR CRIME WRITER
Errors to be avoided

The Secret of Matchams. By Nigel Barnaby. (Ward Lock. 7s. 6d.)
Quick Curtain. By Alan Melville. (Skeffington. 7s. 6d.)
After the Execution. By Theodore Hyde. (Eyre and Spottiswoode. 7s. 6d.)

The late Sir Arthur Conan Doyle, when told that "Silver Blaze" abounded in errors about racecourse procedure, replied stoutly that he did not care in the least, provided it made a good story.

The modern detective writer picks his way more timorously among the man-traps, spring-guns and pitfalls that beset his difficult path. I, personally, have just been sternly upbraided by a Procurator-Fiscal (no less!), because I ought to have known that in bonny Scotland it is no criminal offence at all to assist a murderer to dispose of the corpse provided one was not previously privy to the killing. *Mea culpa!* It had never occurred to me that any country could provide such facilities for murderers. But I ought to have looked it up. With a deep sense of my own fallibility I shall now proceed to examine the books on any list from the point of view of accuracy in procedure.

Chief-Constables and the C.I.D.
Mr. Barnaby comes out tolerably well by this test. He has remembered the existence and duties of a chief constable, and knows that when a detective-inspector is called in from another county – yea, even from

London – to assist in an investigation, he is under the orders of the local C. C. and may be ticked off by him if necessary. (It is a common superstition among writers that the humblest C. I. D. man takes precedence over the whole county constabulary, but the facts are otherwise.) He also knows that a coroner must be either a doctor or a lawyer, and by choosing a doctor has extracted some good fun out of the coroner's medical wrangles with the police surgeon. He raises, however, an interesting point when he makes his coroner exclude the inhabitants of the village from the jury on the grounds that they know too much about the persons affected by the crime. Unlike the jurors at a trial, a coroner's juries are expected and required by their oath to return their verdict, not merely "according to the evidence", but also "to the best of their skill and knowledge". That is, their acquaintance with local people and conditions is an asset of which they are supposed to make good use.

In practice, they may, perhaps, as they do in this story, reach their decision in accordance with nothing but unreason and local prejudice, all precautions notwithstanding. The whole countryside rejoiced heartily in the sudden taking-off of the unpleasant Mr. Graeme, and would not bring it in murder, not for nobody. The obduracy of the village folk in the face of official inquisitiveness is well and truly rendered in this rural tale, and the characters are in general good and lively portraits. There are, maybe, rather too many of them, and this makes the opening chapters of "THE SECRET OF MATCHAMS" sticky going for all but the most attentive readers. The solution is acceptable, though not altogether unforeseen.

A Leg-Pull

Mr. Alan Melville takes all this detective business as a huge joke. He knows and despises the whole tricky technique of vast and expensive theatrical productions, and gets great enjoyment out of scarifying all the leading lights of the profession, from producer to dramatic critic. His satire tends to be shrill and obvious, and includes several thinly veiled personal attacks.

Having got this off his chest, he blows the solemn structure of the detective novel sky-high. "QUICK CURTAIN" is a leg-pull – and this, no doubt, adequately accounts for the remarkable behaviour of Inspector Wilson, C. I. D. This happy policeman never visits Scotland Yard, never turns in a report, acknowledges no official superiors, bounces into country police stations and bullies the constables without reference to the local authorities, and does all his detecting from his private house with the sole aid of his journalist son. Light entertainment is Mr. Melville's aim, and a fig for procedure! The plot is the one about the actor shot on the stage which we have had so many times lately.

Dean's Dilemma

Mr. Theodore Hyde's notions of procedure strike an outlandish note. "AFTER THE EXECUTION" (carried out by three hangmen pushing a button), a reporter visits what appears to be meant for one of our older universities, and "rings the bell of St. Cuthbert's College". A dubious-looking butler opens the door and admits him to a dark-panelled hall and thence to the Dean's study. Most college deans live in rooms in college, with neither butler nor bell – but St. Cuthbert's seems to have had no buildings other than the dean's residence; or perhaps the dean was not dean of the college (for he seems to have had no disciplinary duties and no undergraduates to discipline), but some other kind of dean. He is referred to as "Dean Hankey", which has an ecclesiastical sound; but I fancy his proper title would be "Dean Hankey-Pankey". Anyway, this hoary nuisance tells a tedious tale about how he got mixed up with the murder; and then dies of taking a mysterious poison; and then there is more rigmarole, including an impossible military coroner, a judge who confuses the Public Prosecutor with Counsel for the Prosecution, and the statement that a death can only be registered by a person who was present at the death (which would be awkward if the deceased had thoughtlessly died without witnesses). But the book's inexcusable fault is nearly 300 pages of excessively dull, bad writing – the one sin which can and should never find forgiveness.

* * *

9 December 1934
SINS OF THE CRIME WRITERS
Murder of the King's English

Daylight Murder. By Paul McGuire. (Skeffington. 7s. 6d.)
The Paper Chase. By A. Fielding. (Collins: Crime Club. 7s. 6d.)
The Case of the Purple Calf. By Brian Flynn. (Methuen. 7s. 6d.)
The One-Minute Murder. By John G. Brandon. (John Long. 7s. 6d.)

"DAYLIGHT MURDER" has a competent and interesting plot, centred about a corpse in a haystack. The characters, most of whom belong to the newspaper world, with a sprinkling of financiers and farmers, are generally speaking reasonable and believable human beings, whose motives are intelligible without being stereotyped and whose conversation is sensible and suited to persons in their respective callings. The guilty person is perhaps a little unlikely, but not more so than is permitted by the detective-story convention. My chief reason, however, for placing Mr. McGuire's book at the head of the list is that it is written in good English. I do not mean that it abounds in passages of great poetical beauty or eloquence; I merely claim for it that all its pages can be read without discomfort and some with mild but positive pleasure.

Better Writing Wanted

Though this may seem but faint praise I only wish I could say as much of every book I review. While it is true that the standard of detective fiction has improved greatly of late years, I am still appalled by the amount of sloppy, slovenly, shiftless writing. Mystery stories are not of such great rarity as to excuse readers for snatching, like famished men, at any ill-concocted mess that offers to satisfy their thwarted appetite for blood. Far from it. There is plenty of choice, and they ought to be sufficiently fastidious to reject rank false concord and bad syntax.

Here, for example, is Mrs. A. Fielding, with 16 books listed to her name on the fly-leaf of "THE PAPER CHASE". This means that she has been writing for some time and has received a certain amount of encouragement. Yet she allows herself a sentence like this:–

> And she swiftly dealt, holding up two fingers and pointed to her diamond brooch which meant two diamonds.

Now that, I swear, means nothing whatever. Study of the context shows that the lady "dealt and, holding up two fingers, pointed..." but why should the reader be obliged to reconstruct the sentence before he can extract any sense from it? That is the writer's job. Here are some more gems:–

> He knew ... that whoever came in had had fairly dry shoes. Not walked any distance that night, that meant; and that the desk, at any rate, had already been thoroughly searched.

The deduction might stagger Sherlock Holmes; but the author does not mean what she says. "A knock came upon the door. It was the enlarged photograph." (Animated photography?) "Pointer held no card (?brief) for blackmailers, but they do punish criminals *which* the law cannot touch." "His lobby was too tiny not to step on the paint when crossing it." (The entrancing vision of the little lobby stepping on its own paint blinds me to the logic of this obscure statement.) "[The story] was related after the safe was opened and the bottle could have been seen, that bottle would interest you." This sentence defeats me altogether. If I tried with both hands for a fortnight I could make nothing of it. And I say it is a shame that any writer should so mishandle the richest, most flexible, most highly civilised language in Christendom.

Affectations

Mr. Brian Flynn, at the close of a stirring tale about inexplicable motor accidents, introduces us to a horrid apparatus of torture and death. There was no need for him to inflict on us the additional torture of an exasperating style. He wallows in polysyllables, used either absurdly ("erosive fear", "grandiloquent bow", "an overturned car is approximate") or with a dreadful facetiousness ("the gentle creature timed her epistolary effort with the matutinal coffee" – i.e., her letter came at breakfast time). He and his characters hate to use an English expression where a Latin or French one will do, and pepper the pages with such rags and tags as *in toto*, the leopard will retain his *maculac, coram publico, verbatim et literatim, j'y suis, j'y reste, in excelsis, quot homines tot sententiae, mea culpa and peccavi*, and, of course, *bête noir*, without the "e". And the heroine says to the hero in the night-club, "Enough of all this. Oh, how you weary me. Take me to the card-room, please. I would gamble." These silly affectations put me out of patience with "THE CASE OF THE PURPLE CALF", which contains, however, some ingenuities.

Unkind to the Police

"THE ONE-MINUTE MURDER" tells us all over again about the actress who is really killed in a stage killing. It has some exciting moments (among the sewer-rats, for instance), but I cannot approve the detective methods of the Hon. A. S. Pennington. Any competent sleuth should get his sleuthing done without braining harmless policemen at every turn. All the same, bashing the constable's skull is better exercise than breaking Priscian's head.

16 December 1934
INSIDE STORY OF A MURDER
An imaginary diary

The Diary of a Murderer. By Virginia and Frank Vernon, after Tristan Bernard. (Cresset Press. 6s.)
The Diamond Ransom Murders. By Nellise Child. (Collins: Crime Club. 7s. 6d.)

* * *

There are obviously two ways of writing a novel about a murder. You may tell the story from the inside or from the outside – that is, you may concentrate either on the murderer's state of mind or on the activities of the detectives. By the one method you get a study of morbid psychology; by the other, a narrative of action. It is generally felt – even by readers who prefer the second kind of novel – that the first is, somehow or other, "better literature". Psychology is more fashionable at the moment than action, and serious-minded writers may tackle it without loss of self-respect. In consequence, the murder-study is very often in fact better written than the detective story. It is not, however, necessarily "more life-like". Many a crime in real life is presented to us in detective-story order: first the corpse; next the clues; last of all (if we are lucky) the murderer's identity; while the murderer's motives and emotions may remain a mystery which he carries with him to the quicklime.

To plot murder is easy and entertaining; most of us must from time to time have idly planned out attractive ways of removing obnoxious persons. Most of us go no further. How does the murderer come to cross the dreadful Rubicon that lies between dreaming and doing? And what does he think about it afterwards? History seldom tells us, and the novelist can only imagine.

Adapted from the French

"THE DIARY OF A MURDERER" is one of these imaginings. I have not read M. Tristan Bernard's "Aux Abois", of which this is offered as a "free adaptation", so that I cannot tell how much of the story is due to him and how much to his two American adapters; the detachment and realism of the handling are, in any case, characteristically French.

The murderer is an ex-insurance agent, who has fallen into financial difficulties and murders an elderly business man to get his money. He deliberately wangles an invitation to go round and see the man with the vague idea that he may negotiate a loan. He realises that he will be in the flat at night, alone with the man and his hoard of cash. Idly he thinks, "How easy to kill him!" Idly he plans the thing out. He will do it with a hammer. He will take such-and-such precautions.

When he goes he takes the hammer and he takes the precautions, saying to himself that it is just a game he is playing with himself. But he is excited. It flashes over him that something is really going to happen. But no – the man opens the door and the feeling vanishes. The interview is innocent, peaceful, ordinary. Then, suddenly, the opportunity presents itself and he strikes – almost automatically. And after the first blow the real madness seizes him and he goes on hitting his victim over and over again. That is how he passes the Rubicon, and it seems to me to be admirably described.

Anxiety – and Arrest

So, too, is what follows. The first reaction is a terrible impatience and anxiety – a false alarm that he has left a trouser-button behind – a nervous waiting for the murder to be discovered. Then follows a period of lethargy. Then comes indecision – stay or fly? He goes to Le Havre. He meets a detective and suffers another false alarm. He talks to the detective – tries to be clever – fears he has been too clever – fears he may make matters worse if he tries to put the slip right. He doesn't know how to knock down time (and excellent touch, this: one is reminded of the interminable hours one puts in waiting to start on a journey). He goes to Monte Carlo and loses some of the stolen money at the tables. He picks up a woman – feeling, as many murderers do, the need of a woman as an outlet for his nervous activity.

More complications arise producing alternations of fretful irritability and do-nothing abandonment. He loses his nerve. When at length he is arrested he confesses at once, and his chief sensation is of fatigued relief. Then follow prison and trial. Here the murderer's sentimental egotism comes to the fore. He takes a violent dislike to his lawyer and an equally violent fancy to the lawyer's clerk. He displays himself in odd attitudes of self-aggrandisement. It is a curious and pathetic picture of a sensitive but essentially inadequate personality at odds with a situation which he has created but cannot control. The book is an interesting, vivid, and (I should imagine) extremely truthful study. The "adaptation" is marred by a few clumsy renderings, but is, on the whole, spirited and readable.

"THE DIAMOND RANSOM MURDERS" is a good, straight "action" story about kidnapping American business men. The plot is rather involved, but moves along rapidly and holds the attention. The writing is free from the hysteria to which the "highbrow" American mystery writers so easily fall victims, and, except for an occasional split infinitive and maltreated gerund, is reasonably correct. (I have almost given up hope of rescue for the gerund, poor thing!) Of these two books the psychological study is admittedly the "better literature", but the other will depress you less.

23 December 1934
DETECTIVE NOVEL PROBLEMS
Are "serious" stories wanted?

The Murder Market. By Charles Rushton. (Herbert Jenkins. 7s. 6d.)
The Five Suspects. By R. A. J. Walling. (Hodder and Stoughton. 7s. 6d.)

"Aren't you taking detective stories rather too seriously?" said a man to me the other day, when I had been making some rather heated observations about professional ethics. A little later, at the SUNDAY TIMES Book Exhibition, I had been expressing approval of the efforts made of late to give the detective story a more reasonable psychology than it used to have and to link it up with problems of less ephemeral interest than the barren ingenuities of murder mechanics. A charming stranger among the audience said to me afterwards: "I have noted the tendency you mention. I regret it very much. I like a detective story to be just a puzzle and no more. Do you really think that kind of story is dying out?"

Every week sees the publication of so many crime stories. Each story has an author, and each author had an aim in writing it. I believe it to be the critic's function to discover that aim and then, and then only, to pronounce whether the aim has been well or ill achieved. But if the aim is trivial, as in the "pure thriller" it must be, what can one say about it? One can only say: "This book is a thriller; it is well-written and exciting, or ill-written but exciting, or ill-written and dull", as the case may be.

Take "THE MURDER MARKET", chosen at random from a pile of thrillers. The English is fairly grammatical, the characters are crooks of various kinds, the psychology is childish, the dialogue rude and violent, the humour crude, the plot complicated and unlikely. But there is a great deal of action and menace and bloodshed, and the story will pass the time for you merrily enough without exercising your wits or rousing any powerful emotions or requiring you to think twice about any ethical problem. And so it goes with many and many a one.

Very Readable

Next comes the story whose aim is to puzzle you. Mr. Walling's "THE FIVE SUSPECTS" will serve as an example. Here criticism can discriminate more exactly between the good and the bad. Since the reader is asked to choose between five suspects, we can ask whether the problem is fairly stated, whether the suspects are properly distinguishable, and whether the puzzle, as a puzzle, is worth the solving. Mr. Walling is always very readable. Here is an old lawyer murdered. Why? Because (like many lawyers) he knew a secret or two. Were they good secrets? Well, one of them was rather a silly secret; it is difficult to understand the uproar made about it at this time of day. The other was, perhaps, good enough to commit murder for, though it was not, like the secret in "Give Me Death" (reviewed the other day), a secret of any large social importance.

The characterisation is adequate, indeed good on the whole. What I quarrel with is the secretiveness of Mr. Tolefree, the detective. He *will* not impart his discoveries to us at the time when they are made. This gives him an unfair advantage over the reader, and spoils the pure puzzlement of the story. But the book is on a very much higher level, both of aim and accomplishment, than the "thriller"; it is, in fact, an average good specimen of the old-fashioned detective story as it was understood before the fair-play rule was formulated.

But there is nothing this week that I can take "seriously" as a contribution to literature. Are you, perhaps, glad to hear it? Do you think the detective story is ruined by trying to touch such ultimate values as real beauty, real problems of conduct, real tragedy of pity and terror? If so, the remedy is in your hands. Stop reading and the authors will stop writing; for they have their bread to earn. But there is this to be said: No author who takes the writing of English seriously will be content to spin ropes of sand for ever. One day he will want to put some passion into his work, and if he may not put it into his detective stories, he will go away and write some other kind of thing. Then we shall again have all the detective stories badly written and all the good writing elsewhere. It may be that the heady liquor of ambition will find the detective story too narrow a bottle and burst it altogether. Nevertheless, I cannot see how we are to avoid making the experiment.

30 December 1934
A RESOLUTION FOR THE NEW YEAR
AND A GLANCE BACK

The Crime at the Quay Inn. By Eric Aldhouse. (Philip Allan. 7s. 6d.)
He Laughed at Murder. By Richard Keverne. (Constable. 7s. 6d.)
First Came a Murder. By John Creasey. (Melrose. 7s. 6d.)

"THE CRIME AT THE QUAY INN" is, according to the blurb, "merely the first of a series of sensational events which", etc., etc. But actually, you know, it is not. That sentence only represents the blurb-writer's idea of what a crime-story ought to be. As a matter of fact, the only thing that really happens after the crime itself is that somebody falls off a ladder and fractures his skull. The rest is pure investigation – the detective story in its most classical form.

That is good; and the book is well written, too – which is better still. There is, however, a fundamental weakness in the solution. It is not merely that the murder-mechanism is elaborate and unreliable: one is always ready to concede a few points to over-ingenious murderers. The trouble is that the scheme depends upon a circumstance, known beforehand to the murderer, though not to us, which, though not perhaps impossible or even too improbable, is entirely unconvincing as related.

It is unconvincing because unprepared. In the final chapter we have, all of a sudden, to take the murderer's word for it, and we are reluctant to do so. This throws an interesting light upon the necessity of the "fair-play" rule. We see that the demand for it is not only ethical but artistic. Without it, the book is thrown off its balance. In this particular case enough clues are given to allow us to guess the murderer's identity, but that is not enough. The sudden intrusion of an unknown factor shocks us, and the moral of that (said the Duchess) is that secrets, like other things, may go bad by keeping. This is the chief flaw in a story which is otherwise lively, intriguing, and agreeable, and free from those thrillerish complications so misleadingly hinted at upon the jacket.

Continuously Exciting

Mr. Aldhouse is a newcomer to the crime-story; Mr. Keverne is an old hand. They have this in common, that they can write English. "HE LAUGHED AT MURDER" is much fuller of thrills and escapades than the affair at the Quay Inn, and it is all the more remarkable that the one excitement that does not occur is murder. Assaults, kidnappings, intrigues, spies, treasure-trove – everything is exploited, down to romantic love; but there is only one death, and that a natural one.

The tale is very complicated – so much so that in the end it is quite difficult to disentangle what really happened at the lonely cottage, and who, out of all the wicked and untruthful characters involved, was the greatest villain and the most unblushing liar. But it is consistently exciting, and the excitements are such as might conceivably take place in a secluded spot where criminals are gathered together. Thrillers of this more restrained type can be enjoyed without entire surrender of the divine faculty of reason.

Nothing Barred

Not so "FIRST CAME A MURDER". Here we have the thriller with all its gorgeous absurdities full-blown. Starting mildly with a hypodermic poisoning in a Piccadilly club, we pass to the attempted squashing by motor-car of a Secret Service agent near the Admiralty Arch, an assault on a heroine by gunmen outside a country pub, revolver-fire and Mills bombs in Clarges Street, a bank robbery with silenced automatics in Lombard Street, machine-guns and arson in a country house, a gas-attack by masked policemen in a block of London flats, bombing from an aeroplane at Barnes, and a final grand free-for-all with guns, gas, and bombs on board a yacht in the Channel, with police force, naval destroyers, private speed boats, and assorted good and bad characters all assisting.

It is characteristic of the *genre* that the son of the dope-sniffing baronet should be an "Hon." and that the English should be of that curious hit-or-miss variety in which, if you cannot think of the right word, anything vaguely approximate in sound will serve, as "endured" for "inured", "limber" for "limbo", "hold his own council" for "keep his own counsel", "passing" for "passably", and "laying" (of course) for "lying".

A Full Year

On this Saturnalian note, in this orgy and triumph of the preposterous, let the Old Year end. It has been a year full of admirable things, ranging over the detective story proper, the psychological crime-study, and the thriller pure and simple. Henry Wade's "Constable, Guard Thyself", E. R. Punshon's "Mystery Villa", Richard Hull's "The Murder of My Aunt", Catherine Meadows' "Henbane", Margery Allingham's "Death of a Ghost", John Dickson Carr's "The Blind Barber", Agatha Christie's "Murder on the Orient Express", William Gore's "There's Death in the Churchyard", Georgette Heyer's "The Unfinished Clue", C. Daly King's "Obelists en Route", R. C. Woodthorpe's "A Dagger in Fleet Street", C. St. John Sprigg's "The Perfect Alibi", Lawrence Kirk's "Whispering Tongues", Harry Stephen Keeler's "The Travelling Skull" – all memorable, together with fine examples of work by Freeman Wills Crofts, Gladys Mitchell, Father Knox, Austin Freeman, Anthony Berkeley, John Rhode, J. J. Connington, Milward Kennedy, and the Coles. Let us wish for 1935 another rich feast of all the crimes in the calendar.

Except one. Here is our New Year's resolution:–

I will not cease from mental fight nor shall my sword sleep in my hand till I have detected and avenged all mayhems and murders done upon the English language against the peace of our Sovereign Lord the King, his Crown, and dignity.

'Tis deeply sworn. Now, sleuth-hounds! Noses to the trail! ...

* * *

THE COLLECTED CRIME REVIEWS

of

DOROTHY L. SAYERS

———

1935

———

6 January 1935
MRS. CHRISTIE AT HER BEST
Reality and crime

Three Act Tragedy. By Agatha Christie. (Collins: Crime Club. 7s. 6d.)
Big Business Murder. By G. D. H. and M. Cole. (Collins: Crime Club. 7s. 6d.)
The Toll-House Murder. By Anthony Wynne. (Hutchinson. 7s. 6d.)

Some time ago this column contained the statement that Hercule Poirot was "one of the few real detectives". It was a well-sounding phrase, and I have no quarrel with it, except that I am not quite clear what it means. What I meant to write and what I thought I had written and what I now propose to write clearly with no mistake about it was and is this: Hercule Poirot is one of the few detectives with real charm. Plenty of authors assure us that their detectives are charming, but that is quite another thing. I don't know that Mrs. Christie has ever said a word about the matter. She merely puts Poirot there, with all his little oddities and weaknesses, and there he is – a really charming person. And it is true, too, that he is "real", in the sense that we never stop to enquire whether his words and actions are suited to his character; they *are* his character, and we accept them as we accept the words and actions of any living person because they are a part of himself. *Le style c'est l'homme.*

Belief in the Characters

Indeed, when Mrs. Christie is writing at the top of her form, as she is in "THREE ACT TRAGEDY", all her characters have this reality. She does not postulate a character – retired actor, West End mannequin, family retainer – and put into its mouth sentiments appropriate to its station in life. She shows us character and behaviour all of a piece. However surprising or enigmatic the behaviour, we believe that everything took place just as she says it did, because we believe in the reality of the people. Poirot is charming, not because anybody says so, but because he *is*, and all her other people exist for us in the same objective manner.

This is the great gift that distinguishes the novelist from the manu-facturer of plots. Mrs. Christie has given us an excellent plot, a clever mystery, and an exciting story, but her chief strength lies in this power to compel belief in her characters. In the lack of this power we find the chief weakness of Mr. and Mrs. Cole.

I do not think that the plot of "BIG BUSINESS MURDER" is quite up to standard. It is true that the police were led away in the beginning by a foolish young man, who insisted on confessing to a crime he could not have committed, and so focusing their attention upon another person who could not have committed it either. All the same, they ought not to have waited till the end of the book before tracing the weapon. The moment they embarked on that very ordinary piece of routine the murder was out.

Manufactured Behaviour

But we are accustomed to the follies of policemen in detective fiction. We may forgive also a couple of inaccurate metaphors and some confidential buttonholing of the reader in the most tiresome manner of Anthony Trol-lope, for these blemishes are confined to the first chapter. What ails the book is a general flatness, due to the fact that throughout the behaviour is manufactured and attributed to the characters instead of being an integral part of them.

Take the servile subordinate who "plucks up his courage" to say how-do-you-do to his lordship… "What I've always 'ad a great respect for the nobility, my mother 'avin' been her ladyship's personal maid." That is how the conscientious Socialist thinks the "servant class" ought to talk. But Mrs. Christie knows how they do talk. "Poor she may be, but you can see she's someone – and so considerate, never giving trouble and always speaking so pleasant." Great respect, certainly, provided the nobility know how to behave and never step out of their place. "And the doctor he laughed and said, 'You're a good fellow, Ellis, and a first-class butler. Eh, Beatrice, what do you think?' And I was so surprised, sir, at the master speaking like that – quite unlike his usual self – that I didn't know what to say." There speaks the true voice of the domestic critic, scandalised by the taking of unseemly liberties.

Without Trace

Mr. Anthony Wynne specialises in a particular kind of problem: the hermetically sealed chamber, the sand without a foot-print, the open field without cover, and a dead man in the midst of it all. In "THE TOLL-HOUSE MURDER" the corpse is alone in a closed car, with every door jammed fast, while round about it "all bloodless lay the untrodden snow". Four or five other murders follow, all committed by one who passes and leaves no trace. These are puzzles indeed, and if the machinery is sometimes a trifle elaborate, if the murderer sometimes enjoys astonishing strokes of luck, still, he will be a lynx-eyed reader who sees the truth before Dr. Hailey.

13 January 1935
TWO DETECTIVE STORIES
Good plots well told

Death in a Little Town. By R. C. Woodthorpe. (Nicholson and Watson. 7s. 6d.)
Seventeen Cards. By E. Charles Vivian. (Ward Lock. 7s. 6d.)

Mr. Woodthorpe is unexpectedly developing a vein of Machiavellian cunning. I do not mean that the vein itself was unsuspected, for the glint of it came to the surface once or twice before; but he was then led away from following it up by the surface attractions of his people and their surroundings. This time he has remembered that he is writing a detective story, and has given unusual care to the underground workings of his slight but adequate plot.

He has begun, very judiciously, by selecting the kind of crime which of all others is most difficult to detect, because it knocks away one of the three legs on which the tripod of detection is accustomed to stand. He has then introduced his innocent person who conceals clues; but, by a most eloquent piece of economy, he has given this person not only a sufficient reason for his behaviour, but also a reason which can be ingeniously turned into a defence against suspicion. It would be improper for me to go into the details of this business; but the handling of it is quite masterly, and will repay very careful attention as an example of technical construction. Incidentally, we are thereby spared the prolonged and boring spectacle of a police chase after somebody we know to be guiltless. Thirdly, Mr. Woodthorpe has planted a major clue directly in view, and drawn attention to it in such loud and unequivocal terms as to deprive us (or, at any rate, me) temporarily of sight and hearing. It is true that later on he permits the criminal to reveal himself, but that, I think, is intentional; the time had come.

On the excellence of the writing and the skill with which the atmosphere surrounding "DEATH IN A LITTLE TOWN" is conveyed, I need not insist: we know what Mr. Woodthorpe can do in this way. I will merely mention the admirable marital relations of the ill-mated Chrystals; the remarkable interview between Mrs. Chrystal and the worthy Sergeant Whalebone; the frightful tea-party at Miss Martindale's; and the old-world charm of Miss Perks's house, where you went up four steps and down four steps to get over the threshold and could only approach the sitting room by way of a bathroom with four doors. The author tells us that the "little town" has a geographical basis in fact: so, I am sure, has Miss Perks's house; for it is too impossible not to be true.

"Murder Game" Excitement

Mr. Vivian's plot is of a closer, a more clotted, consistency. Mr. Houghton wanted to give himself a jolly birthday party, so he invited a number of friends to stay with him in his country house. A bond of union ran through the party, in that its members were nearly all the financial victims, discarded mistresses, or enemies in one way or another of a disagreeable gentleman who was more or less blackmailing the host and paying dishonourable addresses to the host's young woman.

Unfortunately, the disagreeable gentleman invited himself to stay too. To ease this awkward situation they started to play a "murder game" – with the usual result. So far, the situation is thrillerish and not very new; but the vigour of the narrative and the fine sense of strain and tension produced by the interplay of nearly 20 characters, who all suspect one another, make the telling anything but commonplace.

The thrills all spring from the one central situation – there is no reckless adding of blood to blood – and the action is confined to the one place and to a few breathless hours. When the pent-up emotions of the suspects are about to break out into hysteria, our old friend Inspector Head arrives – after heroic struggles with snowdrifts and broken telephone communications – and reads the truth from the "SEVENTEEN CARDS" dealt out to the players in the "murder-game"! I cannot well imagine a pleasanter or more exciting tale to read by the fire of a winter's evening.

13 January 1935
SCOTLAND YARD AT WORK AND
SACCO-VANZETTI THEORIES

Cornish of the "Yard": His Reminiscences and Cases.
By Ex-Superintendent G. W. Cornish. (John Lane: The Bodley Head. 18s.)
The Untried Case: Sacco and Vanzetti and the Morelli Gang.
By Herbert B. Ehrmann. (Hopkinson. 7s. 6d.)

Few men can have had a wider experience of crime and detection than "CORNISH OF THE 'YARD'". He began his career as a constable in 1895, coming straight from his father's farm to a beat in Whitechapel – a tougher Whitechapel in those days; in 1933 he retired, a superintendent with a brilliant reputation, having in those 38 years seen and handled every kind of case, from petty fraud to murder, and watched the technique of detection develop to keep pace with the ever-increasing facilities provided by science for criminal and detective alike.

Famous Crimes of the Past
The mere list of some of his great cases stirs us with the memory of nation-wide sensations: the great Pearl Robbery of 1909, the murder of Lady White by Jacoby, Maltby, the Regent's Park murderer, who kept his

victim in a bath and ate his dinner on the lid, the Charing Cross Trunk Murder, the murders of Norah Upchurch, Vera Page, Dr. Zemenides, and – perhaps most thrilling of all – the case of Samuel James Furnace, with its "Austin Freeman" plot, its great man-hunt (the first occasion, I think, on which we ever heard that sinister call "Wanted for Murder" on the wireless), and the strange suicide of the suspect. But besides these there are other cases, less well known, but with titles that would grace a new volume of "Sherlock Holmes": The Great Turf Fraud, the Case of the One-Day Barmen, the Shooting in Whistling Copse, the Strange Case of the Kidnapped Grandfather, the Welford Travis Baby Case, the Case of the Paddington Horse-Stealers and their bird-shop, and the amazing Maida Vale Murder, where the killer slew and stamped noisily out of the house, banging the door, and was never seen again.

These cases contain every bit as much interesting and exciting detective work as the "star" cases; indeed, we feel that we could spare a few of the pages devoted to reports of famous trials in exchange for some more of the scores of good stories which Mr. Cornish has left unwritten. He modestly says very little about his own part in the work, but we can read between the lines the story of pluck, energy, courage, and industry which lies behind every investigation.

"The Untried Case"

Not all the cases reached solution. Sometimes the detectives were genuinely "baffled"; more often, perhaps, they felt sure of their man, but could not produce the final proof that should convince a jury; sometimes the issue was brought to trial and the jury, being doubtful, acquitted. It is better that a few guilty should go unpunished than that one innocent man should suffer. Of the dreadful heart-searchings that follow a miscarriage, or possible miscarriage, of justice, the case of Sacco and Vanzetti provides an example. In "THE UNTRIED CASE" Mr. Ehrmann, who was one of the counsel for the defence of these unhappy men, offers his alternative theory of the crime.

It will be remembered that Sacco and Vanzetti were two Socialists of humble origin who were accused of a brutal murder and robbery in

Massachusetts in 1921. The time was one of great political unrest in America, and an impression was created that the men had been convicted less on the evidence than because of their opinions. The wretched business dragged on with repeated applications for re-trial till 1927, when the men were sent to the chair, though in the meantime (1926) another man had confessed to the crime.

A Gang Crime?

This man was a condemned murderer named Madeiros. He said that Sacco and Vanzetti were innocent, and that he himself had helped to commit the crime as a member of the Morelli gang. The State said this confession was a lie. Mr. Ehrmann and his colleagues, by a most intricate piece of detective work, sought to prove that it must be true, because not only did it fit all the facts, but it was supported by a host of small corroborative details which could not be guesswork or invention. Their argument is a more elaborate jigsaw of evidence than any Freeman Wills Crofts novel, and appears entirely convincing. There must, of course, have been another side to the story, and the question was complicated by a re-semblance between Sacco and one of the Morellis, as also by the fact that Sacco and Vanzetti told a number of lies on arrest. But certainly the case for the defence seems a strong one and worthy of more attention than it apparently got from the State.

Mr. Ehrmann's book makes bitter reading. In this country we do not allow people to moulder seven years in gaol and then hang them after all; while the smallest suggestion of political interference with the judicature brings the Lord Chief Justice fulminating into the House of Lords in defence of our liberties. Let us, without too much self-righteousness, admit as much and be thankful. In any case, merely from the point of view of detective interest, these two books are as exciting as a dozen "thriller" novels all put together; and both are so agreeably written and clearly arranged as to make their reading a pleasure.

* * *

20 January 1935
IRREGULAR BUT LIKEABLE
Perry Mason again

The Case of the Howling Dog. By Erle Stanley Gardner. (Cassell. 7s. 6d.)
The Strange Boarders of Palace Crescent. By E. Phillips Oppenheim.
(Hodder and Stoughton. 7s. 6d.)
Murder in Make-up. By Charles Ashton. (Nicholson and Watson. 7s. 6d.)

I cannot help it: I always enjoy Mr. Gardner's stories about Perry Mason.
All the time I have an uneasy feeling that I ought not to enjoy them; that
I have no business to admire a criminal lawyer whose methods are so
unorthodox, not to say (in the American tongue) "unethical"; that to forge
documents, impersonate witnesses and suppress evidence are shocking
methods to use in conducting a case; and that with a little patient industry
the same result might have been attained in a soberer manner, and that
I ought to say so; but there it is!

I agree that Mr. Mason ought to be disbarred, and in this country
would be disbarred; but I would not have him disbarred for the world:
I like the man. And as he says himself: "We (the American people) are
not like the English. The English want dignity and order. We want the
dramatic and spectacular. It's a national craving." So let us, with that fine
British feeling for expediency which other nations have called by harsher
names, hold the American temperament responsible for the irregularities
and proceed to take advantage of the results.

Watch the Dog
"THE CASE OF THE HOWLING DOG" has a lovely opening, in the
best Sherlock Holmes tradition. It starts with a queer trifle: a man in a
state of nervous collapse calls to get an injunction against a neighbour
whose dog annoys him by howling. He also makes an odd kind of will.
Then the dog's owner is shot, and his wife disappears with the other man
– only she isn't his wife – ; and the dog is shot, too – and did it really
howl, and if not, why not? – and it all gets deeply involved and dramatic;

but the great thing is, to keep your eye on the dog.

Next comes Mr. Phillips Oppenheim with a tale about a queer boarding-house. There is probably a good deal of queerness always hidden behind the respectable frontages of London boarding-houses; but this one was queerer than most, and even before the Major was murdered, Mr. Roger Ferrison had begun to wonder about the boarders who came in so late, and about the landlady's curious rules concerning door-keys, and one thing and another. I think he fell too easy a victim to the meretricious and too-too-obvious sex-appeal of the lovely lame girl (who, between you and me, is a bit of a bore); but he fortunately contrived to keep his heart, though not always his head, in the face of temptation. The characters of the other "STRANGE BOARDERS OF PALACE CRESCENT" are sketched in a very lively way, and the tale is kept moving with all its author's usual skill, until the dear old lady with the knitting tells what she knows and brings the affair to a happy conclusion.

Murder of an Actor

"MURDER IN MAKE-UP" is a perfectly good mystery about the stabbing of a film actor. A commendable feature of the plot is the neat way in which we are kept hesitating over the motive for the murder; and the alibi also has an ingenious little hoist in it. The detective amateur is one of those casual, silly-ass people who turn out to be somebody important in the Secret Service (not that this is a Secret Service yarn; the murder is purely domestic); and he is quite a pleasant specimen of his kind. Apart from occasional naïveté of style and presentation, this is an agreeably written story, and if it is, as it seems to be, a first novel, it gives considerable promise of good work to come.

* * *

27 January 1935
GLOOM AND GAIETY IN CONTRAST
Studies in morbid psychology

The Trial of Linda Stuart. By Mary D. Bickel. (Hamish Hamilton. 7s. 6d.)
Death Cuts a Caper. By David Magarshack. (Constable. 7s. 6d.)
Frame-Up. By Collin Brooks. (Hutchinson. 7s. 6d.)

"A fascinating study", says the blurb of "THE TRIAL OF LINDA STUART" complacently, "of a mind deliberately bent on subtle, ruthless, disintegrating cruelty." The enjoyable contemplation of cruelty has become rather fashionable of late, particularly if the cruelty is mental and the enjoyment can take cover under the cloak of scientific analysis. We are not, of course, like the spectators at a bullfight, yelling encouragement to the *picador* – far from it. We deprecate the spectacle, while pitifully dissecting the poor, diseased mind that rejoices in the infliction of pain. Thus we add to our stock of knowledge, and, incidentally, have all the fun of the fair.

This is a very civilised and superior way of working off our own cruel impulses, and, when both torturer and victim exist only on paper, is about as good and inexpensive a cathartic as could well be devised.

The gentleman for whose richly deserved and quite unregrettable murder Linda Stuart is tried did, certainly, devise a peculiarly underhand and disagreeable method of torture. Himself the victim of a Hamlet-complex, or a mother-fixation, or whatever the thing is called, he vented his spite on female frailty by enforcing an undesired virginity upon his official fiancée for ten years. He did this by simply letting everyone assume that she was his fiancée, without ever asking her to marry him. She was too proud to let anybody know what the real situation was – and, besides, he was to all intents and purposes keeping her old aunt.

Unpleasant as Clay Carroll was, one feels that a young woman as stupid as this was really asking to be victimised; and perhaps it is true that there can be no intolerable exploitation without the connivance, or at the least the contributory negligence, of the exploited. However, the worm did turn at last in a desperate wriggle of escape; and the end is melodrama. The construction of the book is ingenious: Each chapter begins with a passage of cross-examination, deadly in its effect; then follows the true story of the facts underlying the prisoner's damning answers. It is a powerful book; but whether we can accept the central situation as a true tragic conflict depends on how far we are able to sympathise with the obstinate stupidity of the heroine.

Murder of an Actress

Mr. Magarshack's book also turns upon the disagreeable madness of one of the chief characters. It is an exceedingly well-drawn madness; in fact, all the characters are well drawn, though a nastier lot of people have seldom stumbled through the intricacies of a plot. An actress is murdered in the bedroom of her boarding-house, while the landlord – an ineffectual poet – is giving a party downstairs. There is a complicated time-table of exits and entrances, in which the lavatory forms an important feature. Great stress is laid on the symbolism of the Tarot cards which are found laid out upon the actress's table; this part of the solution seems to me to be forced and clumsy.

On the whole, "DEATH CUTS A CAPER" is less good than the author's "Big Ben Strikes Eleven"; for the creaking of the machinery is not sufficiently compensated by the undoubted cleverness of its morbid psychology.

Excellent Fooling

After these gloomy horrors it is refreshing to come to Mr. Collin Brooks's breezy absurdities. Here again there is, I suppose, "much of madness", since a plot to overthrow the Government by framing accusations of immorality against all its ministers in succession is no product of a sane mind. But what a merry and likeable madness it is! How jolly to have a hero who can disguise himself at a moment's notice as the Prime Minister or the Home Secretary and get away with it at close quarters in any surroundings! What fun to have conspirators interchanging passwords, and corpses falling out of refrigerators, and prominent members of the Cabinet being silenced in their own interests with "knock-out drops"! And to have all this presented in such pleasurably restrained English that it sounds almost plausible!

"FRAME-UP" is an excellent piece of fooling, dedicated by its author to "all those jolly people who read shockers for fun and not as a mental discipline". I beg Mr. Brooks to believe that even the most austere mental disciplinarian is ready to read shockers "for fun", provided that the fun is there and that the shocks do not shatter the grammatical foundations of language. He has done his part in supplying the fun, so let us all be jolly together.

3 February 1935
MYSTERY & BEAUTY IN STORIES OF CRIME

The Organ Speaks. By E. C. R. Lorac. (Sampson Low. 7s. 6d.)
The Puzzle of the Silver Persian. By Stuart Palmer. (Collins: Crime Club. 7s. 6d.)
The Man with Bated Breath. By Joseph B. Carr. (Cassell. 7s. 6d.)

Did you ever read "The Nebuly Coat"? Perhaps not. But here and there, all over the kingdom, a reader will raise reminiscent eyes and say softly to himself: "Yes; *that* was a book; there has never been anything quite like it." It was written over 30 years ago by John Meade Falkner, and the people who love it cherish it in their hearts with a shy and secret passion.

It was a kind of romantic mystery story, unique in its period and remaining for many years without followers or imitators. Now, I believe, the case is altered, and its influence is making itself felt among the new school of mystery writers. The chief character in the story is the great church tower that dominates the whole of the atmosphere and action, and whose fall in the last chapter provides one of the most beautiful and heartrending pieces of writing in romantic fiction. In the course of the story, a young architect comes to the church at night and hears the monotonous muffled booming of the organ on the deep pedal D flat. Going in, he finds the organist lying murdered, with his head holding down the pedal note. It is one of the great discovery-scenes of murder-literature.

The Organ's Din

In "THE ORGAN SPEAKS", Mr. Lorac has struck the same note. The scene is an eighteenth century music pavilion in Regent's Park. A young journalist hears the organ making a strange and hideous cacophony late at night, and, rushing in with the police, finds the organist murdered, sprawled this time across all four manuals.

Readers interested in the nervous psychology of the twentieth century will note with interest that Mr. Lorac feels it necessary to turn on the full organ to produce the same reactions of horror that Mr. Falkner could call up with a single pedal-point. From this episode onwards the plots of the two books bear no resemblance to one another. Mr. Lorac's story is entirely original, highly ingenious, and remarkable for atmospheric writing and convincing development of character.

The "personality" of the music pavilion does, however, permeate the book, and this gives a continuity and aesthetic value to the work which I have not previously observed in this author's writing. Mr. Lorac knows his musical "stuff" inside out, and uses that technical knowledge very skilfully to produce effects of mystery and beauty. I am growing more and more convinced that an infusion of beauty is what the detective story needs to-day if it not to die of desiccation but to remain a living branch of the great tree of English fiction.

In "THE PUZZLE OF THE SILVER PERSIAN", that attractive schoolmistress Miss Hildegarde Withers appears again for our delight. The action begins with the disappearance of a young woman from the deck of a small Atlantic liner; and thereafter the murders follow fast. The scene shifts to London, and Mr. Palmer, who is an American, has some caustic words to say about our cold rooms and tepid cocktails, and the discomfort of our hotels.

The book is diverting and exciting, and contains some well-drawn characters, including the most exasperating demon of an American child that ever wrecked the peace of a happy household. I admit that I did "spot the villain" – with regret, because I rather liked the person – but the author shows great skill in keeping, at every point, just one jump ahead of the reader's anticipation.

"THE MAN WITH BATED BREATH" features the fat and genial Oceola Archer whom we met before in "Death Whispers". This detective's favourite pick-me-up is raw eggs beaten up in port *and iced* – a horror which may be held to avenge the British nation upon U. S. A. complaints against tepid cocktails.

Shock follows shock. Near a house in Georgia a corpse is found lying with the mask of a strange, ruthless face impressed in the mud beside it. Four men are shot and hideously gashed in a lonely attic. The effects of *cannabis americanus* (?americana) are described in colourful detail (the drug is a close relation of our old friend *cannabis indica*, or hashish). The solution – well, no; there, I think, ingenuity has overstepped the bounds and fallen into extravagance; but thrills are here in good measure, and thrills are always fun.

The Week's Worst English: "While placing Noel under arrest, the man swallowed a packet of paper and immediately fell dead." (It was Noel who died, and not the man who arrested him.) Mr. Palmer is the culprit; it is only just to say that this is an isolated instance.

10 February 1935
CONVINCING CRIME STORIES

The "Looking-Glass" Murders. By Douglas G. Browne. (Methuen. 7s. 6d.)
Death Follows a Formula. By Newton Gayle. (Gollancz. 7s. 6d.)
Death Joins the Party. By J. V. Turner. (Geoffrey Bles. 7s. 6d.)

I was glad to see a new book by Mr. Douglas G. Browne, because I felt sure beforehand that the characters would be entertaining, the plot capably put together, and the writing good. "THE 'LOOKING-GLASS' MURDERS" turned out to be all that I had expected in these respects, and it is scarcely necessary to say more to recommend it.

I should like, however, to emphasise one point in its construction which is of importance to the detective story considered as a work of art. As the title suggests, the theme of the book has to do with Lewis Carroll's "Through the Looking-glass". This theme is formally announced in the first scene of the story, where a man who is taking the part of the Red King in an amateur production of an "Alice" play is found dead half-way through the performance. The rest of the action centres about this play, and the theme is pleasantly embellished by the chapter-headings and by various allusions in the text.

So far we have, what is common to many detective stories, a colourful and slightly whimsical setting for the crimes, which amuses and engages the attention. Many writers go no further than this. Mr. Browne, however, has made the 'looking-glass' *idea* integral to the structure of the book, thus achieving an artistic unity of a very satisfactory kind. However entertaining the background of a story may be, yet, if the same story might equally well have been worked out against another background, then the setting is exterior to the structure, and the book, as a work of art, is incomplete. But here the setting is significant, because the theme of the action is also the theme of the book, and this is artistically right.

––––––––––

Mr. Newton Gayle appears to be a newcomer to the world of detective fiction; he deserves a cordial welcome, for his first book is lively, well-constructed, and important. I mean by "important" that it has the largeness of scope and solidity of treatment typical of the writer who has plenty to say and intends to say it seriously.

"DEATH FOLLOWS A FORMULA" deals with the murder of the man who has invented the formula for a petrol substitute. He is killed while leaving the liner on which he has crossed from America to England, and the suspects include various oil-magnates, diplomats, and others with professional or national interests which the formula might affect. The detective is a likeable man with a pleasing hobby, namely, the Rehabilitation of Neglected Positives. The detective work is highly ingenious, and the conclusion particularly fine. The character who tells the story is an English Foreign Office official who has spent some time in America; this may account for the fact that the author writes sometimes in educated English and sometimes in educated American.

If Mr. Gayle could manage to keep his English characters always talking English and his American characters American, he would add the final touch of verisimilitude to an otherwise convincing narrative.

"DEATH JOINS THE PARTY" starts well, but somehow falls to pieces. A horrid gentleman, living in a lonely house in a marsh, invites a number of deadly enemies and sets them at one another's throats, calling in the detective, Amos Petrie, to see fair play. Then come shootings and escapes, during which the horrid gentleman (not unnaturally) suffers the fate which he had hoped might befall somebody else. While the character of Petrie himself is quite attractive, his methods are disagreeable, for he bullies and threatens his witnesses shockingly.

Also, I feel that Mr. J. V. Turner has made a mistake in letting so much of the evidence be disclosed in witnesses' statements and in cablegrams from abroad. The reader is obliged to receive it all passively and cannot take much part in the discovery. This whittles away his interest in the proceedings and reduces the book to the "thriller" class; whereas Petrie is obviously the kind of character who ought to figure in straight detective work.

The Week's Worst English: "The party had been arranged to secure the deaths of both he and his former partner." – Fie, fie, Mr. Turner!

* * *

17 February 1935
DRAMA IN AN AIR LINER
Criminals & cranks

Obelists Fly High. By C. Daly King. (Collins: Crime Club. 7s. 6d.)
The Corpse in the Car. By John Rhode. (Collins: Crime Club. 7s. 6d.)
The Chamois Murder. By Cecil M. Wills. (Heritage. 7s. 6d.)

I do hope that no well-meaning busybody has been urging Mr. C. Daly King to "cut the cackle and come to the 'orses". In "OBELISTS FLY HIGH", his 'orses are indeed a fine, spirited team, driven along at a spanking pace by our old friend Captain Michael Lord of the New York Police. But the caperings of Dr. Rees Pons and the other cranks upon their theoretical hobby-horses have been sadly limited and subdued to the necessities of the plot; and the witty Peacockian footnotes which were wont to delight us have gone altogether.

Nevertheless, this is a fine story, though some of the clues are rather in the nature of "psychic bids". The solution is so shattering to one's feelings that Mr. King will have to write us another book in hot haste to relieve our anxiety for Captain Lord's future. Never has detective hero been left in so perilous a situation!

Needless to say, the psychology, in the hands of this master of psychology, is as convincing as it is unnerving, while the writing is, as usual, excellent. The action takes place in an air-liner, and the incidents of the flight and the landings are described with a wealth of picturesque detail, giving admirable local atmosphere to the story.

Mr. John Rhode has found a grand new way of eliminating people. It is so undetectable that he and his Dr. Priestley would have had very great difficulty in getting the problem solved at all, had not Fate taken a hand in the matter. Happily, the murder-method is one that requires a special set of circumstances to make it feasible: otherwise one might expect to find the countryside peppered with the corpses of tiresome old ladies and gentlemen, now that we know the way to get rid of them.

It is true that I did guess the murderer pretty quickly, but that was as far as I got, and as far, I should think, as anyone would get without highly specialised knowledge. One personal quarrel I have with Mr. Rhode – he does not love cats; I do – though I admit that Lady Misterton's affection for them was demonstrated in a way that I cannot approve, and that, all things considered, she richly deserved to figure as "THE CORPSE IN THE CAR".

Mr. Cecil M. Wills, who promised well in "Death at the Pelican", has rather disappointed me in "THE CHAMOIS MURDER". For one thing, he has been far too hackneyed and obvious. Listen to this, from p. 16:–

> The first notes of the chime were heard on the loud speakers in the [hotel] lounge. ...Geoffrey pulled out his watch and ... remarked ... in surprise: "My watch is three minutes slow."... The London announcer wished everybody his two-fold "good-night". Then the [hotel] manager's voice was heard, giving particulars of a fancy-dress dance.

Now, if you do not know instantly from that who committed the murder, what his alibi was, and how that alibi was produced, you are not the reader I took you for. I am sick and tired of these radio-gramophone alibis. They give themselves away in the first sentence, and, after that, the whole rigmarole of false clues becomes a bore and a nuisance. I think Mr. Wills can do better than this if he tries.

The Week's Worst English. – (1) A man whom my wife told me afterwards was Keinton. (2) Geoffrey turned to Ginesta to inquire whom Madame Scharza might be.

Mr. Rhode and Mr. Wills – partners in crime.

* * *

24 February 1935
TWO CRIME STORIES BASED ON REAL CASES

Skin for Skin. By Winifred Duke. (Gollancz. 7s. 6d.)
After the Fact. By Alan Brock. (Nicholson and Watson. 7s. 6d.)
The Body in the Bunker. By Herbert Adams. (Collins: Crime Club. 7s. 6d.)

A prosecuting counsel is reported to have said one day, in the course of an eloquent peroration: "We have it on the highest authority that, skin for skin, yes, all that a man hath will he give for his life." "Indeed?" remarked the judge, drily; "it is interesting to know, Mr. So-and-so, who it is that you consider to be the highest authority."

Learned counsel might perhaps have replied that the authority, if not exactly the highest, was one of very great experience. And where the Adversary himself conducts the bargain, he often sees to it that the commodity is not worth the price. This is the theme of Miss Winifred Duke's novel, and she has stated her case most convincingly.

"SKIN FOR SKIN" is the second work of fiction which we have had within a few months founded upon the trial of William Herbert Wallace for the murder of his wife; and it keeps very much more closely to the facts of the case than Mr. Bechhofer Roberts's "The Jury Disagree", which I reviewed in November. There are, I think, only two points of fact on which I noted any discrepancy between the novel and the published report of the trial; and the problem is brought to a solution without the aid of any additional or invented circumstances except an imaginary confession by the murderer. Like Mr. Roberts, however, Miss Duke has assumed for the purposes of her narrative that the husband was, in fact, the murderer; though she makes it very clear in her foreword that this assumption must not be held to apply to the actual case. Allowing that the husband was the murderer, then this (she feels) is the kind of man he must have been, and this must have been the manner and motive of the crime.

Why, after 18 years of mutual devotion, should a respectable married couple come to this violent and bloody divorce? The motive put forward is, plainly and simply, the appalling monotony of a peaceful married life.

"Always together. Day and night, week in week out, year after year for 18 years". Or, as the charlady's friend puts it: "O'od be bothered murderin' a married woman except 'er 'usband?" Miss Duke has put the motive across with terrifying conviction. And then, when the trial is over and the husband's conviction quashed on appeal, she has shown, no less terribly, the sick longing of the murderer to have the old, peaceful, wearisome life back again.

The verdict of the Court of Appeal could not (and in fact did not) remove the stigma of guilt from the accused. The neighbourhood still believed him guilty, and the life that had been restored to him was made an intolerable burden. This the author makes shockingly and pitifully clear. Even for a guilty man, she arouses our painful sympathy: if the real man was innocent, then the situation scarcely bears thinking about. Miss Duke has handled her material brilliantly, her skill in dialogue being exceptional and her presentation of the complicated nexus of evidence re-markably clear and skilful.

"AFTER THE FACT" is also based upon a real case – the murder of Mrs. Luard in 1908. This problem was never publicly solved, and although the unhappy husband came under suspicion at the time and took his own life, it is generally held to-day that he was perfectly innocent. Mr. Brock reproduces the circumstances of the actual murder – the shooting of the wife in a summer house upon a neighbouring estate, the theft of her rings, and the partial establishment of the husband's alibi – but he provides a solution of his own, quite extraneous to the facts of the real case and not intended to elucidate them. Compared with Miss Duke's, his handling of a murder problem is theatrical, mechanical, and, worst of all, rather dull. He has written a stereotyped detective story, including all the stereotyped characters: the shoddy adventurer, the roguish spinster of 40, the comic vegetarian, the betrayed wife, the conceited detective and his Watson. The surprise at the end would be a better surprise if we could believe in any of these people: but they never really come to life. Set side by side with the psychological handling of a mystery, "straight detection" cuts here but a poor figure.

Mr. Herbert Adams entertains us with a breezy tale of villainy, whose scene is laid on the golf links. His dialogue is brisk and natural (though I wish his lovers were a trifle less arch), and he keeps the tale moving and conceals his villain very cunningly. I think he overestimates the power of disguise, and I hope it is not so easy as he suggests to obtain access to somebody else's safe deposit. "THE BODY IN THE BUNKER" is the lighter kind of detective fiction, to be welcomed by those who want "a good story" free from portentous psychological seriousness.

The Week's Worst English: "I could see this morning that she is most vindictive towards him." Mr. Brock sins in company with all the daily Press and half the army of contemporary novelists, to whom the proper consecution of tenses has become meaningless; but "is" should be "was" for all that.

3 March 1935
THE ADVENTURES OF A HIGHBROW DETECTIVE

The Adventures of Ellery Queen. By Ellery Queen. (Gollancz. 7s. 6d.)
Behind the Evidence. By Leonard Blackledge. (Hutchinson. 7s. 6d.)
Naked Murder. By Firth Erskine. (Thornton Butterworth. 7s. 6d.)

In his latest volume Mr. Ellery Queen has adventured forth into short-story form. I am not sure that I do not like him better when thus short-circuited; for the mechanical limitations of the medium force him to control his besetting sin of over-writing. He is always picturesque and always ingenious. His characters take after him in this respect, and one sometimes feels that they are fortunate beyond all reasonable expectation in finding a detective clever enough to interpret the ingenious and picturesque false clues and dying messages they leave behind them.

All these strange fantasies of bearded ladies and glass-domed clocks would be wasted on a mere forthright police constable, who would neither interpret nor misinterpret, but probably merely ignore them. But they are sure of obtaining full recognition in the "silvery eyes" of Mr. Queen, and so provide a very high-class, not to say highbrow, collection of detective exploits. Sometimes the necessary compression makes the argument seem rather breathless, but otherwise the peculiar personality and mental characteristics of the hero shine forth undimmed in "THE ADVENTURES OF ELLERY QUEEN".

"BEHIND THE EVIDENCE" is Mr. Leonard Blackledge's first novel, and shows some of the faults of immaturity. He has tackled a curious and difficult psychological study with a "surprise" ending, and I do not feel that he has quite succeeded in making the surprise convincing. It is possible, I suppose, that a person showing so much determination in the outset of an undertaking should bring it to such a lame and impotent conclusion; but somehow Mr. Blackledge fails to persuade us of the central weakness in his poisoner that should make that conclusion inevitable. Nevertheless, the attempt is interesting and makes an interesting book. The style is plain to the point of occasional baldness; but this is no bad fault in a new writer.

Mr. Blackledge is much concerned about the administration of justice in English courts, and voices his doubts a trifle naïvely, though sincerely. (But he must not blame "an English judge and jury" for the Oscar Slater affair: Scotland must take the onus of that.) Some of the evidences given in his court scene would, I fancy, not be admissible in any court in the United Kingdom. All things considered, however, the book shows promise, and is well worth reading.

No other titles are listed to Mr. Firth Erskine's credit on the title-page of "NAKED MURDER"; if this also is a first book it displays a good measure of competence. The identities both of the murderer and of the headless lady found on somebody's roof in New York, are, indeed, fairly clear from the start to the experienced reader; while a whole bunch of little problems is melodramatically cleared up at the end by a "scene in court" that ought never to have been allowed to happen anywhere – not even in America, where so many strange things happen. But for a detective-story on the thriller side of the great divide, this is exciting enough, and the detective, Cyrus K. Mantel, is a pleasant person.

The Week's Worst English. – Well, I do not know. Which do you dislike most – the aged, aged humour of Mr. Erskine's "any one of the masculine *persuasion*" or the pretentious innovation of Mr. Queen's: "An *antiqued* sign sprang whitely into view"? I leave the choice to you.

10 March 1935
TROUBLE IN TURL STREET
Crime among the dons

The Body in the Turl. By David Frome. (Longmans. 7s. 6d.)
A Question of Proof. By Nicholas Blake. (Collins: Crime Club. 7s. 6d.)
The Purple Claw. By Holloway Horn. (Muller. 3s. 6d.)

I have returned from a visit to Oxford in rather a mellow mood. It may have been the college port at St. Jehoshaphat's. Or it may have been some other beautiful influence. At any rate, I am glad that I am not called upon to distribute any sour reprimands to this week's trio of authors. They can all write tunable English: *gratia gratiam parit.*

Mr. David Frome has taken Oxford for the setting of his story. Mr. Pinkerton comes to Oxford, timid and eager, to dine with his friend Mr. Owen Owen of Jesus. Knowing Mr. Pinkerton, we know with what wistful awe his richly romantic soul will thrill to the clamour of the Oxford bells, and quiver at the sight of an Academic gown. Inevitably he misses his dinner, inevitably he finds a corpse cluttering the age-worn stones of Turl Street (with what relish does Mr. Pinkerton learn to speak familiarly of "The Turl", "the High", and "the Broad"!), inevitably he gets himself into sad trouble and has to be rescued by Inspector Bull. And what an evening he has when he actually does dine in Hall and (mellowed by those

Oxford influences which I have mentioned earlier) tells stories in the Junior Common Room!

Well, well! Distressing as the murders are, Mr. Frome has surrounded "THE BODY IN THE TURL" with the true Alma Maternal atmosphere, and has rightly so contrived his Oxford story that it could not very well have happened anywhere but in Oxford. I think he has pulled Mr. Pinkerton's leg a little. He has somewhat exaggerated for his benefit the difficulty and expense of getting into college after Great Tom's "Hundred-and-One" (after midnight is another matter); and while it is Mr. Pinkerton's proud familiarity with Oxford tradition that supplies the central clue to the mystery, I feel that his premise, and therefore Mr. Bull's inference, is a little unsound. I must not say what the clue was – but only last Wednesday I myself saw a Master of Arts trip across the quad accompanied by the Impossible Thing. And did not that eminent and learned man, the Master of Jehoshaphat's, himself admit when I asked him – No matter! Mr. Pinkerton is the thing, and we cannot but love Mr. Pinkerton.

"A QUESTION OF PROOF" is also concerned with an educational establishment. It is a school mystery; why are school mysteries always so convincingly "real"? I suppose it is the poignant suffering undergone by assistant masters that wrings out of them these devastatingly accurate pictures of common-room friction and the tiresomeness of little boys. Mr. Blake's dialogue has an exquisite rightness, and his attitude to school life is balanced and humane. The only really intolerable character is happily murdered at the outset; the headmaster is a pompous nuisance, but a decent creature enough; the frailties of the masters, though they sometimes take disagreeable forms, are handled with sympathy; and the boys are very natural – particularly the two leading members of the Black Spot Gang. The plot is perhaps not the strongest point of the book, but it is adequate and coherent, and the solution is, I think, psychologically reasonable. For a first book, this is an admirable achievement.

"THE PURPLE CLAW" is not (as its title might suggest) a foolish thriller about a gang of crooks. It is a "straight" story, without mystery, about a man who planned a theft and found he had committed a murder. It tells of his hopeless efforts to get away from himself and from the consequences of this disaster, and does so with simplicity and some pathos. It is a slight book, rather melancholy, which does not lay itself out to excite, but it will make its appeal to readers in a quiet mood.

The Week's Worst English. – None, thank Heaven! to worry about. I might heckle Mr. Blake about his cavalier treatment of the gerund – but no! Dash it, the man can write; we'll have no carping.

17 March 1935
CRIME STORIES IN CONTRAST
Horror and quiet argument

The Plague Court Murders. By Carter Dickson. (Heinemann. 7s. 6d.)
The Devereux Court Mystery. By Miles Burton. (Collins: Crime Club. 7s. 6d.)
The Chinese Fish. By Jean Bommart. (Longmans. 7s. 6d.)

The first two titles on our list both contain the word "Court", and the two books which they adorn resemble one another in a certain feature common to their respective plots. In all other respects, the stories are as much unlike one another as two crime-stories could very well be. Even the titles, so much alike, are eloquent of this unlikeness. "Plague Court" – the words are horrid in themselves and suggestive of horrors to come. "Devereux Court" – why? Very naturally and soberly because Devereux Court leads out of Essex Street, and Robert Devereux was Earl of Essex; nothing could be more reasonable or less horrific.

Mr. Carter Dickson belongs to the school of mystery-writers who want to make your flesh creep; Mr. Burton prefers to engage your intelligent interest in a quiet and logical piece of argument. Both do their work well, and each displays the particular advantages and drawbacks of his chosen method.

"THE PLAGUE COURT MURDERS" seems to me to show a very great advance upon Mr. Dickson's previous book, "The Bowstring Murders". It is less jerky and confused; he has got his style under better control. The tale is about a circle of people who have come under the influence of a gentleman who deals in the psychic; and the atmosphere of grotesque horror surrounding this person's murder in a "hermetically sealed chamber" is really well done.

It is the kind of thing to which you must willingly abandon yourself if you are to enjoy it; but if you like being deliciously frightened into fits you can, to quote a tailor's advertisement which once delighted me, "have a fit here". Like all "sealed-chamber" mysteries, this one has a solution that takes a good deal of swallowing and demands a good deal of long-winded explanation at the end: that is the drawback to all plots of this type, except, perhaps, the famous "Mystere de la Chambre Jaune". Mr. Dickson's burly and eccentric Sir Henry Merrivale exudes personality and – positively! – an original charm; and that is no small feat in a world where eccentric detectives are as common as blackbeetles. Also, Mr. Dickson can write; he tends to the violently picturesque, and nine times out of ten he brings it off. Incidentally (while we are fighting about syntax) he has staggered me by producing a perfectly correct gerund: "Something about the servants' hearing things in the house." Burn me! (as Sir Henry Merrivale would say) but I would forgive him more sins than one for that blessed apostrophe!

––––––––––

"THE DEVEREUX COURT MYSTERY", like all Mr. Burton's work, is quietly and engagingly written. It is carefully reasoned, and the clues are neatly and fairly displayed. Almost too fairly, perhaps; for about two-thirds of the way through the identity of the hidden criminal becomes clear beyond all argument. This is the drawback of the too-neat-and-intelligent kind of mystery. For the rest we have at least one very well-drawn character, a good deal of elegant jig-saw with alibis and covering-up work, some industrious and reasonable police detection, and the pleasure of again meeting our old friends Inspector Arnold and Mr. Desmond Merrion.

"THE CHINESE FISH" is not detection, nor even exactly mystery; nor has it anything to do with evil Chinamen. It is a short but entertaining story about how a newspaper man gets mixed up in some Secret Intelligence adventures in the Balkans. The author, M. Jean Bommart, is French, and the book has the French virtues of lucidity and the "nothing-too-much"; the confusing to-and-fro play of political complication is entertainingly conveyed. The translator is Milton Waldman, author of those two entertaining studies of Queen Elizabeth, which if you have read, you will know that his English is delightful. In translation he hits the difficult happy medium; that is, to preserve the Gallic flavour of the original without falling into foreign locutions.

The Week's Worst English. – Shaking him like a dog shakes a rat. We all say it, but not in print, Mr. Burton – not in print!

24 March 1935
A THRILLER OF QUALITY
Night spent among waxworks

Wax. By Ethel Lina White. (Collins. 7s. 6d.)
The Perjured Alibi. By Walter S. Masterman. (Methuen. 7s. 6d.)
The Strange Case of the Antlered Man. By Edwy Searles Brooks. (Harrap. 7s. 6d.)

The case of the thriller is a difficult one for the reviewer. By what standard is it to be judged? I call all three of these books thrillers, because in all of them the elements of horror, suspense and excitement are more prominent than that of logical deduction. But "WAX" has a quality that the other two have not. It is a quality that I and such as I rate highly; it is the quality that decides, for me, whether a thriller is to be kept upon the book-shelf or cast out when I have finished with it for the purposes of this column. But how far this quality affects – even sub-consciously – the reader who wants a good thriller to while away an idle hour I really do not know.

Three quotations, taken almost at random, will illustrate what this quality is. Here is one, from "Wax":–

> She looked at Mrs. Ames, and decided that if her face were lifted and made of wood, it would be a handsome figure-head for a ship. She saw it, wet and magnified, rising and falling triumphantly, through a smother of green sea.

Well, there is a description of somebody; it conveys the suggestion, perhaps, of something a little odd, even a little sinister; but what exactly that suggestion is, we are left to imagine for ourselves. The words deliver their warning by some mysterious power of association; the stroke is oblique and not direct.

———————

Now a line or two from "THE PERJURED ALIBI":–

> The words came in a thin stream of vitriolic abuse from the lawyer's cruel lips. He never raised his voice once, and even the bright sunshine through the latticed windows seemed to grow dark.

The difference is not merely that here the images – "thin stream", "vitriolic", "the sunshine grew dark" – are all stereotyped, whereas the image of the figure-head was a little out of the way; it is that here the suggestion is direct. The reader is not made to feel; he is told what to feel. It is the difference between the fear of the known and the fear of the unknown.

———————

Lastly, a more luscious kind of description from "THE ANTLERED MAN":–

> In spite of the gloom, Andrew could see the lovely oval of her face; he could see her slightly-parted lips – her eyes, deep pools of purity. The perfume of her stole about him, adding to the intoxication of the scented summer's night.

Nobody is going to puzzle over the suggestion conveyed by that passage. There is no suggestion. The thing hits you over the head like a bludgeon. And if the highbrow critic denies to the thriller the name of "literature" it is, I think, chiefly because of its fondness for bludgeoning tactics.

———————

Miss White's story is about a dreary hall of decayed wax-works in a provincial town. The place is made the centre for some very unwholesome intrigues and several murders; and we have – almost of course – the *motif* of the horror and danger of passing a night among the waxworks. Well-worn as the theme is, the horror "gets across", because of the obliquity of the suggestion and the excellent drawing of the characters. The plot is sound, and is very little complicated with mechanical mystery-making. The terror and pity are genuinely human and not mechanical. In short, this is a good novel on a thriller theme.

———————

Mr. Walter S. Masterman has an involved plot of a rather old-fashioned, melodramatic kind, with all the dear old-fashioned melodramatic characters. There is the squire with the mortgaged acres – ruined and drunken and crossed in love, but noble at heart and ear-marked for reform. There is his chivalrous friend, perjuring himself to save him, in spite of his hopeless passion for the squire's young woman. There is the young woman in love with the squire and marrying the wicked murderee to save the squire's acres. And the attached old retainers. And the rascally lawyer. And the whole bag of tricks. These people all act a little hysterically, as is only to be expected. It is all highly exciting, and entirely incredible.

Mr. Brooks is rather incredible, too, and he also has a number of the stock characters – the nice, manly young man, the lovely victimised girl, the hired gang of desperadoes and so on. His villain is a very thorough-going person, who uses all the most elaborate mechanism of the false-wig-and-secret-passage school of thrillerdom. But he enlivens his story with a really pleasing pair of detectives, whose behaviour and conversation are as lifelike and amusing as the rest of it is stereotyped and unconvincing. I should like to meet the Grouser and Detective-sergeant Cavendish again in a less "thick-ear" kind of plot.

The Week's Worst English: I stood on the platform with him, watching his sunburnt, handsome face, keen grey eyes and firm jaw, upright as a dart, a man who stood out above his fellows. – No wonder Mr. Masterman's squire took to drink, with a jaw like that to put it in.

31 March 1935
RESTRAINED AND FANTASTIC
Contrasted methods in crime stories

Poison in the Parish. By Milward Kennedy. (Gollancz. 7s. 6d.)
Death-Watch. By John Dickson Carr. (Hamish Hamilton. 7s. 6d.)
Fer-de-Lance. By Rex Stout. (Cassell. 7s. 6d.)

If anybody were so rash as to suggest that crime stories must of their nature be violent and melodramatic, Mr. Kennedy's latest story would contradict him. It is a story of "POISON IN THE PARISH", told by a middle-aged bachelor; and its atmosphere is parochial and old-bachelorish from first to last. I should think it must be the primmest and quietest murder tale ever written. There is not even any very great mystery about it; for the identity of the criminal is hinted almost at once, and becomes obvious within the first 60 pages, while the murder-method also is simple, straightforward, and made known to us gradually, with little attempt at mystification. All the characters are washed in with a neat and accurate touch, in a low key and without extravagance of pose or gesture.

In a foreword, Mr. Kennedy has touched upon one of the difficulties that always beset the detective writer, namely, how to avoid filling his book with vicious and unsympathetic characters and yet avoid the improbability of focusing suspicion upon such agreeable persons as, being every one *integer vitae*, are obviously not apt to meddle with sharp instruments and poisons. In this story he outlines a set of circumstances in which the amiable innocent might reasonably come to be suspected. The book is not for those who like a gasp on every page and an explosion at the end of every chapter; those who appreciate its reason and tranquillity will appreciate also its minor incidental beauties, such as this, for instance, which sums up its scope in a few words:–

None of your "see five counties", or, for that matter, five continents, for me; give me a stretch of country where every change of light and shadow makes it a different picture; and a ridge of hill with a belt of trees clambering up it, so that you sometimes think that they are slipping back.

In almost ludicrous contrast to Mr. Kennedy comes Mr. John Dickson Carr, with a new adventure of Dr. Gideon Fell. Mr. Carr has the knack of surrounding his plot and characters with a perpetual aura of excitement. Everything about them is fantastic; his people are all a little larger than human; they thrill with a kind of spiritual violence, even when they perform the most ordinary actions. His story may be too complicated, too improbable; his crimes may be performed by means and for motives too far-fetched for belief; but he has the art of the genuine *frisson*. He deals with the thing that is not quite reasonable, with the thing "on the wrong side of the door", and his own love of these things is so infectious that, before your judgment has time to assert itself, he has "coost the glamour ower ye". I do not believe in the man who was stabbed, by so strange a contrivance, amid a household of people so unbalanced, and for so insane a motive; but between the dark and the light I am ready to listen to the voice of the enchanter and to the sinister ticking of the "DEATH-WATCH".

Mr. Carr is an American with a passion (as it seems to me) for England, and especially for the older and more secretive parts of London. (His English diction and atmosphere are very good: only occasionally does a phrase – "rooming-house", "the defence rests" – trip him up.) Mr. Stout is pure American, and his style is good in the colloquial American kind. Indeed, his detective, Nero Wolfe, who for bulk and beer-drinking may be put in the same class with Dr. Gideon Fell, talks really well, and does actually convey by his talk that he has some claim to be called an "eccentric genius". The plot of "FER-DE-LANCE" is more commonplace than those of the other two books, and has more of the thriller about it; but it will serve well enough to carry this quite agreeable and entertaining tale about a man mysteriously poisoned on the golf links.

The Week's Worst Latin: "I was curious about anybody who would have the nerve to turn his name into 'Johannus' in this day and age." – I agree with Mr. Carr; a man with less nerve would have compromised on "Johannes".

7 April 1935
SALUTE TO MR. G. K. CHESTERTON
More Father Brown stories

The Scandal of Father Brown. By G. K. Chesterton. (Cassell. 7s. 6d.)
The Spanish Cape Mystery. By Ellery Queen. (Gollancz. 7s. 6d.)
Red Lilac. By Lord Gorell. (Murray. 7s. 6d.)

If the writers and readers of detective fiction had nothing else for which to thank Mr. G. K. Chesterton, they should surely thank him for this: that he was the first man of our time to introduce the great name of God into a detective story without either irrelevance or irreverence. The fact that by 1911, when the first "Father Brown" story appeared, it had become almost impossible to do any such thing, proves to what extent mystery writers had become ashamed of their own craft. Like the journalist in one of

Mr. Chesterton's novels, whenever that name threatened to intrude upon the narrative they automatically crossed it out and wrote "circumstances".

Their instinct was perfectly sound: for that name is an acid test. If any writer feels that to introduce it into his book (otherwise than as a meaningless expletive) would be, not merely unnecessary, but blasphemous, then he may be pretty sure that neither the characters nor the passions nor the crimes that he is describing bear any fundamental relation to reality. This, of course, is not a fatal defect in a book, but it is a serious limitation. I once said idly to Mr. P. G. Wodehouse that, with his amazing knack of plot-spinning, he ought to be able to write a first-class detective story. His reply was to the effect that he had thought about it, but that to bring such exquisitely artificial creations as Bertie Wooster and Jeeves into contact with real crime and real corpses would be an artistic error and throw the whole thing out of key. He was, of course, perfectly right.

But when we are by hypothesis dealing with crime and corpses, what then? Are the crimes to be real sins, or are they to be the mere gestures of animated puppets? Are we to shed blood or only sawdust? Are we to have love or only love-making as the motive for the *crime passionnel*? And is the detective to figure only as the arm of the law or as the hand of God?

So far as artistic unity goes, it does not matter at all which alternative we choose, provided that we stick to it; but when we look at the whole scope of our work, we shall see that it matters a great deal. If we wipe out God from the problem we are in very real danger of wiping out man as well. Unless we are prepared to bring our murderers to the bar of Eternity, we may construct admirable jig-saw puzzles, but we shall certainly never write a "Hamlet". And we owe Mr. Chesterton a heavy debt in that, with very great courage in a poor and materialistic period, he planted his steps firmly upon the more difficult path, and showed us how to enlarge the boundaries of the detective story by making it deal with real death and real wickedness and real, that is to say, divine judgment.

Having said so much about Mr. Chesterton's general significance in the history of detective fiction, I have left myself little space for a particular estimate of "THE SCANDAL OF FATHER BROWN". Here are eight tales of the true vintage, all instinct with the author's shrewd insight into human error, his mellow charity towards human weakness, and his warm love of all beauty, human and natural. Here and there his material clues may be a little far-fetched; here and there he may even have unrighteously concealed a material clue from our eyes; but his essential clues are in the hearts of men, and in dealing with these, Mr. Chesterton makes no mistakes.

———————

Mr. Ellery Queen seems to me to be sobering down a little. Fantastic he still is, in this story of a dead man found sitting on a terrace, naked except for a hat and a cape, but he is far less extravagant in language and behaviour than in, for example, "The Siamese Twins" or "The American Gun". His manner (I am referring now to the detective, not the author) is suaver and less hysterical, and he has the right way with servants (always a test of breeding). In fact, I am beginning to like the man. I think it is easier to guess the murderer in "THE SPANISH CAPE MYSTERY" than in some of the other books, but even so there is plenty of mystery to grapple with.

———————

In "RED LILAC" Lord Gorell reintroduces Evelyn Temple, who figured in "In the Night". There are a good many detectives called in – or calling themselves in – to deal with the problem of the unpleasant gentleman stabbed in his study, and among them they make a nice hash of it all, and bring the story to a strictly immoral conclusion. Lord Gorell has a nice ear for dialogue, and a light and pleasant touch with description and character; if I must cavil it must be at the coincidence by which his characters go about armed with sharp instruments so surprisingly and unusually sharp.

The Week's Worst English: Just to show that I am not to be over-whelmed by authority, however weighty, I will demand of Mr. Chesterton what he means by the expression "much more singular".

* * *

14 April 1935
DETECTIVE AND PHYSICIAN
Re-enter Mr. Fortune

Mr. Fortune Objects. By H. C. Bailey. (Gollancz. 7s. 6d.)
The Dear Old Gentleman. By George Goodchild and Bechhofer
Roberts. (Jarrolds. 7s. 6d.)
The New Made Grave. By Hulbert Footner. (Collins: Crime Club. 7s. 6d.)

It is one of the minor trials of a reviewer's life that very often the books
he likes best are the very ones that he can find least to say about. When
an author of Mr. H. C. Bailey's calibre has been writing, over a period of
years, stories about a character so well defined as Mr. Reginald Fortune,
and has maintained a consistent standard of excellence throughout
that period, any comment is really superfluous, beyond the exhortation:
Read this!

We all know Mr. Fortune – or, if we do not, it is our misfortune,
which should be remedied without delay – and we know that beneath his
surface flippancies there are a mind and a heart sensitive to the sins and
sufferings of humanity. MR. FORTUNE OBJECTS to many things – but
chiefly to any kind of cruelty, and, above all, to cruelty practised upon
children. He takes his work seriously, both as detective and as physician,
and it is this seriousness that lends power to such stories as "The Long
Dinner" and "The Yellow Slugs", where the crimes are of a kind to
touch that inner sensitiveness most sharply. There are six tales in this
new collection, all good, all characteristic, and all, as I need not tell
Mr. Bailey's public, beautifully written.

In "THE DEAR OLD GENTLEMAN", Mr. Goodchild and Mr. Bechhofer
Roberts again offer us an old tale re-told. This time it is that most
fascinating of real-life dramas, the trial of Mrs. McLachlan for the murder
of Jessie McPherson in Glasgow in 1862. The authors have adhered very
closely to the original facts of the case and the original cast of characters;

they have, however, added a long coda of adventure and detection and offered, if not exactly a new, at any rate a more detailed solution of the problem than any previously presented. They have also brought the story up to date, and I cannot help feeling that it loses a little in the process; for when we read the report of the actual case what strikes us most forcibly is the queer, vivid spotlight that it throws upon lower middle-class life in Scotland of the sixties.

The sordid and horrible tale of the servant battered to death in that basement kitchen; of that plausible old rogue, the ancient James Fleming, drinking brandy with his son's maids and using senile familiarities with them; of his appearance in the witness-box to testify in his broad Doric to hearing "twa-three lood squeals" in the close – the whole atmosphere of the tragedy makes it really a period piece, upon which the clatter of the telephone and the purr of the motor-car break in rather incongruously. But this is a matter of taste. The authors are no doubt right in thinking that, even in Mrs. McLachlan's own statement, which, produced after her trial and conviction, cleared up so many doubtful points, the whole truth was not told; and their solution is on the whole very plausible, and very likely correct.

"THE NEW MADE GRAVE" is a rattling romantic thrill in Mr. Footner's most vigorous style; not so much a detective story as an adventure story for children of a larger growth. Rash young gentlemen who assist lovely girls to bury mysterious corpses in remote American towns must expect some alarms and excursions and some trouble with the sheriff. The characters are sympathetic, and the atmosphere of the little town well conveyed.

The Week's Worst English: Margaret Sampson's protagonists whispered against that same, dear, benevolent gentleman. – Indeed, indeed, sirs (meaning Messrs. Goodchild and Roberts), but this troubles me, that you should still think "protagonist" means "champion". It means the leading actor in a play.

21 April 1935
PLEASANT PEOPLE IN A CRIME NOVEL

Death in the Stocks. By Georgette Heyer. (Longmans. 7s. 6d.)
The Ginger Cat Mystery. By Robin Forsythe. (John Lane: Bodley Head. 7s. 6d.)

Miss Heyer's characters and dialogue are an abiding delight to me. The plot of "DEATH IN THE STOCKS" shows a great advance in plausibility upon that of "The Unfinished Clue"; but even if it did not, even if there were no plot at all, time and money would be well spent in making the acquaintance of the maddeningly inconsequent and attractive Vereker family.

I have seldom met people to whom I took so violent a fancy from the word "Go". They are charming and intelligent and perfectly infuriating to their friends; they talk interminably and enchantingly; they are exceedingly sympathetic and perpetually in some trouble or other; and they are delicately and subtly differentiated. I am not surprised that the agreeable Mr. Giles Carrington, who helps Superintendent Hannasyde with the detecting, should be deeply in love with the indiscreet Antonia; I am quite ready to be in love myself with Kenneth the painter – who achieves the difficult feat of making one believe that he really is a fine artist; while Roger, the tiresome ne'er-do-well half-brother who turns up so disconcertingly in the middle of the plot, displays the family shrewdness and the family charm in the most unexpected and disarming manner, so that one wishes him a better fate than he encounters.

The other characters are good, too – the Superintendent is a kindly soul; there is a delightful thumb-nail sketch of Carrington's father; and of course, there is that priceless woman, Murgatroyd – but it is the Verekers who carry the book upon their shoulders, and make it the pleasantest companion you could possibly want for an hour or two of humour and detection.

––––––––––

Mr. Robin Forsythe puzzles me; he writes like two men (perhaps he is).

There is the Mr. Forsythe who writes the brisk and amusing conversations between the amateur detective Anthony Vereker (no relation to the other Verekers) and Inspector Heather of Scotland Yard. There is also the dull and pompous Mr. Forsythe, who writes sentences like: "He had jocularly designated the motive that could have driven him to such an act as if to minimise its cogency as a motive", and whose characters deliver long monologues in highly artificial jargon.

Both Mr. Forsythes suffer from an inability to punctuate. But the story is lively and the plot interesting, though it involves one radical improbability which is a little difficult to accept. Curiously enough, "THE GINGER CAT MYSTERY" contains, as a kind of sideline to the main plot, the plan of a "perfect murder" so undetectable, or, at least, so unpunishable, that one wonders why it should not have been made the main theme of a story. But perhaps it would not be, in practice, as sound as it appears in theory. Some of the chief characters are introduced to us too late to capture our interest, and altogether the book is rather disappointing in form and content; but whenever the two detectives come on and talk, it wakes up and takes notice. I particularly commend an incidental definition of the difference between the thriller and the detective story: "the latter amuses people by making them think they're thinking, the thriller by doing its damnedest to prevent them thinking at all."

The Week's Worst English is Mr. Forsythe's: "Priceless clues may have vanished and our work doubled by the accident for it was an accident in a way." That is the kind of English that I can only call slop.

28 April 1935
RICH AND DAINTY FARE
Melodrama with a difference

Pins and Needles. By Edwin Greenwood. (Skeffington. 7s. 6d.)
Rope by Arrangement. By Henrietta Clandon. (Bles. 7s. 6d.)
Murder Without Weapon. By Means Davis. (Bell. 7s. 6d.)

Those hearty feeders who enjoy coarse, rich fare will relish what Mr. Greenwood calls his "melodrama" of "PINS AND NEEDLES". I am not ashamed to say that I enjoyed it very much. I will not deny the coarseness, but I must do full justice to the ripe richness of Aunt Permaine. Mr. Greenwood rather specialises in redoubtable old ladies, and this one is a fine study in squalid humour. She is very much alive and very unpleasant, and yet somehow very likable; and she is the making of the book, though that old villain Pipe, the gardener, runs her close. There are other good though disagreeable character sketches; sensitive Anglicans, especially High Anglicans, will find offence in the handling of clerical matters – particularly the episode of a confession made by an unprepared penitent to an untrained priest. The book is not "detective" in any strict sense of the word, for the criminal is made known to the reader early in the story, while the investigators try, but fail, to bring the two remarkably cold-blooded murders home to roost. The word "melodrama" perhaps does less than justice to the book's character-interest. I would not recommend it without a word of warning, but I do recommend it.

"ROPE BY ARRANGEMENT", on the other hand, is for more dainty feeders. Its merit lies in a kind of quiet tortuousness; to read it is rather like working out an intricate little string puzzle by the fireside. It is about a man who got mixed up in a murder case, and stupidly went and worked it up into a novel, and so landed himself in a great deal of suspicion among the gossips of a country town. In the course of these various narrations of the same events, so many attractive solutions are casually presented that one becomes thoroughly and pleasantly confused as to the author's intentions. The solution – if it is the solution, and even that is not certain – seems to me not quite to click as it should (I think I remember saying the same thing of Miss Clandon's earlier book, "Inquest"), but the tale makes very agreeable reading.

"MURDER WITHOUT WEAPON" is again anything but dainty, though it is perhaps less of an assault upon our sensibilities than "The Hospital

Murders" by the same author. Again the scene is laid in a hospital, and again one feels that the way in which these American doctors and nurses allow drunks and rioters to tumble in and out of the patients' rooms is a little trying. The murders take place in the family to which the hospital owes its endowments and which takes advantage of its beneficiary position to over-ride all authority: hence the murders. The murder-method is ingenious, and medical references are given to vouch for its possibility. Mr. Means Davis writes an ugly kind of English style, elliptical and pretentious. Nevertheless, he manages to get his effects, including occasional touches of rather rough humour.

The Week's Worst English Style. – "The immense inner beauty of her entreaty made him delirious with wisdom." – This is what I mean when I call Mr. Davis's style pretentious.

5 May 1935
CLASSIC AUTHORS
"The Grammarian's Funeral"

The Grammarian's Funeral. By Edward Acheson. (Hutchinson. 7s. 6d.)
Darker Grows the Valley. By Q. Patrick. (Cassell. 7s. 6d.)
The Eleventh Hour. By J. S. Fletcher. (Thornton Butterworth. 7s. 6d.)

"Many writers," says Aristotle, "having put together a good plot, fall down on the dénouement."

That is one of those shattering statements of fact (the "Poetics" is full of them) which, gathering momentum through a lapse of twenty centuries, smite the present-day author over the head like a blunt instrument. It is as true as ever it was. In all those years we have learnt nothing. The mystery writer, above all others, is faced with this frightful and perennial difficulty: how, after carrying his tale through various reversals of fortune each calculated to raise expectation to an ever-mounting pitch, to wind up his tale without anti-climax.

From this point of view we may divide mystery stories into two breeds: the straight-tailed and the curly-tailed. In the straight-tailed, the climax (consisting of the recognition of the criminal) comes some little way before the end, and is followed by a quiet explanatory coda. This is the classic method of Sherlock Holmes, and possesses the classic qualities of emotional sobriety, structural formality and intellectual order. It was contrary to the Athenian canons of good taste to end a tragedy upon the top note of hysteria; the anti-climax was deliberate; the passions released by the drama must be subdued to the control of the mind before the audience could be fitly dismissed from the theatre.

But in the curly-tailed type of story, the emotions are set above the intellect and have the last word. There must, as people say, be "a twist in the tail", a final turn given to the screw. When all, as it seems, has been discovered and explained, we must be made to gasp again. The danger of this method is, not dullness as in the straight-tailed story, but insincerity. In the effort to go one better than the best, we may lamentably achieve real, because unintentional, anti-climax; for violent emotion, if it is not sincere, is absurd.

In three books this week we see the authors energetically bent on twisting the tail. Mr. Acheson maintains a high emotional note from start to finish of "THE GRAMMARIAN'S FUNERAL", and in attempting to force his last chapters to a still higher pitch than the rest he is obliged to become a little shrill. But his twist is purely emotional; it does not affect the detective structure of the plot, and if we do not entirely accept it, it does not very much matter. And he has this excuse, that he is depicting a man of mild and unassuming character jerked out of his daily routine and driven almost to madness by finding himself the innocent suspect in a murder drama. Those about him think him crazed, and he is beginning to imagine that they may be right. This theme offers plenty of opportunity for screw-turning, and I will admit that I read the book with a great deal of excitement. The English reader's criticism will probably be that, like many American mysteries, it is just a trifle over-written.

"DARKER GROWS THE VALLEY" deals with an outbreak of killing and maiming in an American village. Both animals and children are the victims; so it is clear from the outset that here again we are in contact with the darker side of the human mind, and that the valley will grow very dark indeed before we are out of the shadow. It is not a pleasant theme, but it is well handled and the writing is good. It is only at the end, when the detective unmasks the madman, that we feel a real sense of discomfort. That is because, in his anxiety to make that discovery the high-spot of the piece, Mr. Patrick seems to transfer to his detective something of the madness and mania that permeate the rest of the story. I think this is an artistic error: the twist is too abrupt and leaves us with the sensation that a conclusion established by such violence is established as insecurely as a Ruritanian three-days' republic. A little more intellectual control would have strengthened the structure without introducing the wrong kind of anti-climax.

The late J. S. Fletcher had two themes in his books: plain detection and the daily life of country and Cathedral towns, into which he frequently introduced some kind of antiquarian interest. In his posthumous work, "THE ELEVENTH HOUR", the two themes are very happily combined. The story is about the theft of some ancient church jewels from the Cathedral Treasury and the murder of their guardian, the old verger. Nobody can describe better than Mr. Fletcher the atmosphere of the Cathedral Close. His detective is Ronald Camberwell, who has made his competent appearance in other books; but the investigation is chiefly carried on through a series of inquests and trial scenes. The story moves quietly and interestingly. Its weak point is, however, still the "eleventh hour" dénouement. The "twist" fails this time, I feel, because it is foreseen in character and conventional in presentation. It does not really startle. Between startling too much and startling too little there is the golden mean; but it is not hit once in fifty – not once in a hundred and fifty times.

* * *

12 May 1935
MURDER AMONG THE DOCTORS
AND TWO INGENIOUS PROBLEMS

The Doctors Are Doubtful. By Anthony Weymouth. (Barker. 7s. 6d.)
Crime at Guildford. By Freeman Wills Crofts. (Collins: Crime Club. 7s. 6d.)
Between Murders. By Sherry King. (Appleton-Century. 7s. 6d.)

In "THE DOCTORS ARE DOUBTFUL", very great care has obviously been taken with the elaborate mechanism of the plot, which is original and interesting.

We are presented with the spectacle of three persons, all dying mysteriously from some form of anaemia under circumstances which puzzle the doctors. It is the task of Inspector Treadgold – that nervously impulsive little detective who figured in "Frozen Death" – to unravel the complicated relationship of these three people, and to prove that the deaths were not due to coincidence and that one person and one person only had an interest in causing them all. In so doing, he nearly comes to a bloodless end himself.

I am not physiologist enough to criticise the murder-methods in detail; Mr. Weymouth has evidently taken great pains to get everything right, and I am ready to believe that it is right. It is in the mechanism of presentation that I notice some awkward jerks. If you thought that a man was being slowly murdered in a nursing home, would you leave him there on the grounds that "whoever wants to murder him can get at him as easily outside as in"? I think not. You would advise his removal to a big hospital, where it is not easy to corrupt the staff and where friends and relations are not allowed to stray about the wards at all hours of the day. Also, in a case where the murder is so clearly committed by somebody with medical knowledge, it is foolish to waste time in building up an elaborate case against somebody with special knowledge and no plausible means of access to the apparatus employed. A red herring is good – but it is necessary to provide it with a genuinely ancient and fish-like smell if the reader is to follow its false trail.

The general idea of the book is so good that it is a pity the author has not taken a little more trouble with the process called "joining his flats".

———————

Mr. Freeman Wills Crofts is, as everybody knows, one of the most honest craftsmen in existence. He leaves no flats unjoined: my only complaint against "CRIME AT GUILDFORD" is that he has at one point been a little too honest, and has joined them with a stroke so ringing and decisive as to call unnecessary attention to the stage carpenter. The story contains two problems: the problem of a murder and the problem of a robbery. That of the robbery is extremely ingenious, and I am the more ready to believe that the device employed could be brought off once, for the author's ready admission that his villains failed to bring it off twice. It was the secret of the murder that I penetrated out of due time. I was prompted to ask myself that fatal question: "If this character is not here for the purpose of committing the crime, why is it here at all?" To prevent the reader – and to prevent him by fair means – from ever asking that question is one of the mystery-monger's most exacting technical jobs. That Mr. Crofts has in this book failed to stall off the question is the one blot upon a story which is in other respects an excellent piece of construction.

———————

The American story "BETWEEN MURDERS" endeavours to evade this tiresome query by a method bold, indeed, but not original. Some readers may feel that the method is not quite fairly used; I cannot go as far as this, for, despite the camouflage, I did ask the question and I did spot the murderer. What gave the show away was an indescribable something in the tone of the writing at certain points; all things considered, I think this clue is legitimate and sufficient. But I do not greatly care about these stories in which the chief suspects are eliminated by being successively killed off; nor do I like fantastic buildings and secret doors overmuch. Thrilling as it is, I feel that Mr. King's tale is not so much constructed as piled together – and I never in my life met a more inadequate motive for multiple murder.

The Week's Worst English: "He was forced back to his room, by the matron abruptly withdrawing herself..." No; the matron used no force. What in the world has the gerund done to Mr. Weymouth that he should dismiss it from his service and entrust its duties to a totally inadequate comma?

19 May 1935
A CRIME STORY WITH A DASH OF GINGER

The Clue of the Forgotten Murder. By Carleton Kendrake. (Cassell. 7s. 6d.)
Twenty-Five Sanitary Inspectors. By Roger East. (Collins: Crime Club. 7s. 6d.)
The Ten Black Pearls. By Cecil Freeman Gregg. (Methuen. 7s. 6d.)

Mr. Kendrake is an American writer whose name is new to me; in fact, to judge by the title-page, he is a new writer. I like his vitality. Every so often I get the feeling that we English detective writers are growing rather old and staid and that even the newest and youngest of us have been born old. There is a kind of tired efficiency about our approach to a problem, as of a Government department ploughing its way through a mass of official reports.

Our American colleagues are, on the whole, free from this defect. It is true that we sometimes wonder whether they will ever grow up. We are annoyed by their outbreaks of adolescent hysteria, and by their habit of bawling and barging their way through the constitution, as though a band of fanatical revivalists were to break in upon the solemn proceedings of the Dean and Chapter. But, every now and again, a touch of this rough vigour is good for us.

"THE CLUE OF THE FORGOTTEN MURDER" starts off excellently in the Press-room at police headquarters, where the crime sleuths of various newspapers are eagerly snatching the news from under one another's noses. The reporter on "The Blade", hurrying to push his story off before his rival of "The Planet" gets wind of it, lets his paper in for the threat of a libel suit. The subsequent proceedings are highly unethical and, after the reporter has been murdered, and a prominent citizen has mysteriously died and a young woman has disappeared, we may feel that the methods of the detective are less dignified than those of Sherlock Holmes or of our dear Scotland Yard. But the dash and drive of the story cannot be disputed, nor do any of the events strike us as being exaggerated or incredible, however sadly we may shake our law-abiding heads. This is a good type of American crime story, plainly written, with an agreeable dash of ginger.

———————

Mr. Roger East has enlivened his tale with that touch of the absurd and fantastic that naturally belongs to a Ruritanian setting. He places his murder in a preposterous South American Republic and brings in a retired C. I. D. officer to cope with the situation. The offices and personnel of the derelict Ministry of Sanitation are handed over to him, with instructions to form them into a Detective Bureau. This naturally brings ex-Superintendent Simmonds into conflict with the established police force and provides many opportunities for incongruous and humorous contrast of method. If the finished result is not quite so funny as it ought to be, it is, I think, because the intrusion of real crime and death upon these pasteboard surroundings sets us face to face with an incongruity of a more fundamental kind; the blood of a human being makes an ugly splash upon the boards in the middle of a farce – the more so, when the victim is a sympathetic character. But "TWENTY-FIVE SANITARY INSPECTORS" is undoubtedly amusing, and perhaps it is merely pompous of me, at this time of day, to insist that murder should be taken seriously.

———————

Nevertheless, I will go on to say that to treat it, not merely as an amiable peccadillo but as the day's good deed, is going too far. In "THE TEN BLACK PEARLS", which is told from the criminal's point of view, and is admittedly highly exciting, Mr. Gregg expects us to feel the deepest sympathy with the gentleman who, having embraced the career of a cracksman out of pique, proceeds to commit a crime of passion and to lie and perjure his way through the courts to a happy acquittal. After which, the judge who tried him offers what can only be described as his congratulations on this fortunate outcome of an unpleasant affair. Quite apart from such a gratuitous insult to the British bench, this kind of thing is a mistake. The heroic murderer is becoming as big a sentimental bore and nuisance as the virtuous prostitute. I persist in thinking that murder is "burdensome, dangerous, and ought to be abolished"; nor, judging by its frequency in real life, does it stand in the smallest need of encouragement.

The Week's Worst English: "Now, who's fault was that?" –The fault in this instance is Mr. East's, but, believe it or not, the error is as common as green-fly in a rose-garden.

26 May 1935
PUPPETS OR PEOPLE IN STORIES OF CRIME?

Death of a Beauty Queen. By E. R. Punshon. (Gollancz. 7s. 6d.)
Dr. Tancred Begins. By G. D. H. and M. Cole. (Collins: Crime Club. 7s. 6d.)

Some years ago, as you will no doubt remember, an enterprising management presented "Hamlet" in modern dress. A good many things might be said about this, and most of them were said at the time. There was, for instance, the point of view of a good lady who sat just behind me in the stalls and, during a moving speech by the Prince of Denmark, excitedly whispered in her companion's ear: "He's got a wrist-watch!" The most favourable construction to be placed upon this remark is that it showed a keen interest in technique.

There were also the people who said the whole thing was sacrilege, and those who complained (with some justice) that the text had been severely cut about. But to me, the interesting thing about the production was this: that for the first time (and I had seen many "Hamlets") I said to myself, "But this is serious; somebody has been murdered; and a very unpleasant situation is developing in this family."

Whatever else it did, the modern setting released either the actors or myself or all of us from a whole series of conventions which had prevented us from ever before seeing "Hamlet" as a story about real people at all.

Sincerity Wanted

Now, many crime stories suffer from the same inhibiting conventions as the classical "Hamlet" productions. A person is killed, and all the characters utter the appropriate sentiments and make the gestures of passion and horror, and yet we never believe for a moment that anything of importance has happened. The utterances and gestures may be violent to the point of extravagance, as in the books of Ellery Queen; but it remains a piece of play-acting.

Some readers prefer their detective stories to be of this conventional kind; they like to enjoy the surface excitement without the inward disturbance that comes of being forced to take things seriously. But I believe the future to be with those writers who can contrive to strike the note of sincerity and to persuade us that violence really hurts.

Mr. Punshon's new book is, I think, the best thing he has done along these lines. The detection is not very elaborate, the humours of the police are subdued, the attention is concentrated on the characters and their human relationships. The result is a fine and interesting novel, where the emotional discords are resolved in a strain of genuine pathos and of what I can best call nobility. I do not mean by that, the "odour of joss-sticks and honourable high-mindedness" which sometimes passes current for nobility; I mean that the persons, particularly the father and son who play a considerable part in the story, possess that "human dignity" which does exist in the stringiest forked radish of us all and explains why, even at our most perverse, we are of more value than many sparrows. "DEATH OF A BEAUTY QUEEN" is, in fact, a very fine book, to my thinking, and I most strongly recommend it.

Mr. and Mrs. Cole have also written above their usual form in "DR. TAN-CRED BEGINS". The action takes place 25 years back, and we are promised a sequel to the story, which shall carry on the development of the characters a stage further. This accounts for a certain air of incompleteness that hangs about the solution of the mystery. The murder-method, by the way, is ingenious; I have an uneasy feeling that there might be a snag about it, but I hope the authors have experimented and found it all present and correct – it cannot be the reviewer's duty to do this every time before pronouncing judgment.

What I like about the story is that there seems to be a more settled attempt at the real novel technique than in some others of the collaborators' works, and an absence of that jauntiness of style whereby they have occasionally made the judicious grieve.

The Week's Worst English Sentence: I find there is a curious superstition going about that wherever possible the conjunctive "that" should be omitted. Like most superstitions, this notion has a measure of reason behind it; but in the following sentence of Mr. Punshon's the passion for this construction is surely carried to almost reckless lengths: "Personality is so strong and strange a thing there is nothing so insignificant we use we do not leave on it our own private stamp."

2 June 1935
STRAIGHTFORWARD AND SOUND
Variety in three stories

Three Witnesses. By Sydney Fowler. (Thornton Butterworth. 7s. 6d.)
The Green Tunnel. By Cecil Champain Lowis. (Lovat Dickson. 7s. 6d.)
The Gaol Gates Are Open. By David Hume. (Collins. 7s. 6d.)

"THREE WITNESSES" is good, straight detection about a worthy and prudent but rather likeable young man called Roger, whose still younger brother Cyril is – in the words of the blurb – "a rotter and up at Oxford".

(This is a sinister phrase to any but Cantab ears; and when we learn that Cyril "pulled stroke in the University boat", was seldom sober when not actually in training, and was, moreover, "knocking with some energy at the gates of vice", we begin to understand what is wrong with Oxford rowing.)

The family business is being managed by a gentleman called Rowton, and when Roger comes of age, Rowton tells him that things are in a bad way, and that it will be advisable to sell out. Roger, however, suspects that this advice is not disinterested, and holds on, to the disgust of Cyril, who wants the cash – in order, no doubt, to tip the porter at the gates of vice. They quarrel in Rowton's office, and, immediately afterwards, Cyril is found at the foot of a staircase, with a broken neck and a bullet in his back (so there may be a chance for Oxford next year, after all). Since there are three witnesses to prove that Roger and nobody else was immediately behind Cyril on the staircase, things look black for Roger. A good legal fight is put up for him in the magistrate's court, and the solution of the problem is agreeable in its sheer simplicity; though the final discovery is brought about without very much finesse. The psychology is sound, and the general handling pleasantly straightforward. The writing might be more careful here and there.

"THE GREEN TUNNEL" is good, straight romance. A taxi-driver accidentally runs a man down and is afraid to confess. His desperate struggles to free himself from suspicion involve a number of other people in the mess, particularly the dead man's wife and a young ex-officer who keeps a poultry farm. These two romantic idiots, having fallen in love with one another, naturally suspect one another, (I cannot understand why people in books are so eager to think the worst of those they love), and the awkwardness is made worse by the interference of the florid young woman whom the dead man has been making up to. Here are all the elements of an engaging light comedy, and excellent light comedy it is, until the taxi-driver, whose confused state of mind is very well drawn, realises the trouble he is causing and clears up the situation by turning the whole thing into a tragedy. There is no actual mystery or detection about the story, but it is prettily handled and makes pleasant reading.

"THE GAOL GATES ARE OPEN" is good, straight roughage and toughage. Here we have an immensely heroic young detective and an immensely wicked villain, who romp after one another through a crooks' playground, in which the fine flowers of forgery, arson, kidnapping, high explosive, trapdoor-and-secret-passage-work, assault, mayhem, and murder are all a-growing-and-a-blowing. It is admirable stuff of its high-spirited kind; and Mr. Hume, who knows his underworld inside out, manages to lend an air of verisimilitude to his unconvincing but thrilling narrative. He tells it all slap through from beginning to end as a rattling adventure, without too much complication; and that is what we want in this kind of tale.

The Week's Worst English. - Among many candidates, we must give pride of place to a dear old friend. "He (solicitor for the defence) disregarded ... the way in which his question was received by his legal protagonists." The legal gentlemen who "received" the question in the way recorded were the magistrate and counsel for the prosecution. Can Mr. Fowler possibly think that "protagonist" means "antagonist"? Once again: *the protagonist is the leading actor in a play,* and there is only one of him at a time.

9 June 1935
HENDON POLICE COLLEGE IN A NOVEL

Hendon's First Case. By John Rhode. (Collins: Crime Club. 7s. 6d.)
Wheels in the Forest. By John Newton Chance. (Gollancz. 7s. 6d.)
Death Treads. By Cecil M. Wills. (Heritage. 7s. 6d.)

What are we to do with our detectives as the ineluctable years advance upon them? Are they to remain the Peter Pans of fiction, unwithered by age and unstaled by custom in the infinite variety of their case-hardening experience? Or shall they, suffering the vicissitudes of love and sorrow like other men, grow old along with us, till detective, author and reader totter querulously into the grave together? Or shall we ruthlessly hurl them over the Reichenbach Falls (at the risk, to be sure, of having to haul them painfully up again later) and let younger rivals step into their shoes? The difficulty of the first course is precisely that custom does tend to stale everybody concerned, particularly the author. The second presents awkwardnesses of its own: where, for example, the hero has been initially presented as a person immune to all human passions, or has been inconsiderately married off at the end of his first adventure, so that his subsequent emotional development is confined to the anxieties attendant upon a growing family and the prospects of promotion in the police force. (Scandalous post-matrimonial complications are, for some reason, practically unknown among the detectives of fiction.) The third course brings us up against the reader who, however good the new wine may be, stubbornly grumbles that the old is better. It is all very difficult.

The title of Mr. John Rhode's new book made me think for a moment – even when I had realised that "Hendon" was not a new detective, but the Police College of that place – that he was preparing to take Course Three with Dr. Priestley (excluded by age and settled habit from Course Two, and hitherto a very successful example of Course One). But this is not so; a compromise has been adopted, which works very well. Dr. Priestley and Superintendent Hanslet are still there; but they have been given a new colleague in Junior Station Inspector James Waghorn (of Cambridge and Hendon), and are thus enabled to refresh themselves by contact with a young mind. Three ways of tackling a detective problem are fruitfully contrasted: the way of experience, the way of imagination, and the way of the scientific inquirer. Mr. Rhode has taken the trouble to inform himself accurately about the Police College and all its works, and we are grateful to him for being neither (a) funny, nor (b) snobbish about Mr. Waghorn's Old School Tie. The plot is an exceedingly good one, and "HENDON'S FIRST CASE" represents Mr. Rhode at his best.

––––––––––

"WHEELS IN THE FOREST" is new wine at its headiest. Every passion in the story goes off like an explosion and blows the cork to the ceiling. Men and women roar and fight like furies. Cars dash about the New Forest with bellowing exhausts and screaming brakes. Everything dazzles and glitters like the frightful house owned by one of the characters, a nightmare of chromium and glass. The book is by a new author, and, one would say, a young author, for it has the youthful fault of confusing violence with strength. The writing is clever; but Mr. Chance should remember that if you begin and carry on fortissimo you will have neither breath nor brass to spare for your climax. Technically, the plot is not quite worth the coil that's made for it, and the detective's habit of falling ill and fading away in a crisis, though handy to prolong the suspense, has an *ad hoc* appearance. Mr. Chance should write a good book if he will master the difficult but necessary "art of sinking".

"DEATH TREADS ..." is, I think, Mr. Wills's best effort to date. The plot – about a young woman of dubious antecedents who disappears with somebody else's jewels from a house party and is found dead in a canal – is carefully put together, and the red herrings are cunningly trailed. Geoffrey Boscobell of Scotland Yard is now an inspector and is settling down nicely in this more responsible position, and the characterisation as a whole is sound, though not remarkable.

The Week's Worst English. - I suppose it is impossible to put a stop to the epidemic of "happenings" which breaks out on every page of every book like measles, and has now infected the Oxford English Dictionary; but I should like to be able to note an occasional "occurrence", "incident", or "event" – just by way of assurance that these words have not been completely swept away by the scourge. (Reference: Detective Fiction, *passim*.)

* * *

16 June 1935
THREE STORIES OF CRIME
Disappointments – and compensations

Casual Slaughters. By James Quince. (Nicholson and Watson. 7s. 6d.)
The Mystery of the Cape Cod Tavern. By Phoebe Atwood Taylor.
(Eyre and Spottiswoode. 7s. 6d.)
Death as an Extra. By Val Gielgud and Holt Marvell. (Rich and Cowan.
7s. 6d.)

This has been a week of disappointments – one agreeable, and the other
two of the usual kind. "CASUAL SLAUGHTERS" was published some
months ago, and I put off reading it, remembering that an earlier book by
the same author, "The Tin Tree", had started with some spirit, but fallen
off into foolish thrillerdom. But this is a Quince from a different tree.
True, it has the rather odd and unreal flavour characteristic of the fruit,
but for that very reason it will appeal to those who are weary of the
standard plum-and-apple.

The slaughters take place in a country parish, and the humours of
parochial life are given full play. I do not for one moment believe that the
dear old rector would really send out the members of his Church Council,
two by two, like apostles, to undertake detective work, even with the laud-
able object of promoting co-operation and neighbourly feeling among
them; but I do not mind this, because the whole story is conceived in a
mildly leg-pulling spirit. Nothing could be more authentic than the rival-
ries that arise over the Flower Show and the Whist Drive, the horror of
the Council on realising that they, and not the incumbent, are nowadays
financially responsible for the upkeep of the churchyard, and the attitude
of the villagers to the local doctors, to superstitions and to unusual
kinds of vegetation (of course, evergreen oaks would always be known
as "them furriners", however long established and familiar – what else
could you expect?).

"THE MYSTERY OF THE CAPE COD TAVERN" is another tale about Asey Mayo, a detective for whose personality and New England dialect I have a great affection and esteem. The characterisation and general atmosphere are excellent, as they usually are in Miss Taylor's novels, and if the official police are unbelievably brutal and stupid, that is a thing to which we are accustomed in American fiction. At a pinch, too, I would put up with the surprising number of hidey-holes and secret passages in the house where the murder takes place. But I definitely refuse to believe in an eight-day clock – still less in a whole houseful of eight-day clocks – which, if not wound precisely at 9 a.m. on a Monday morning, will run down and stop at 9.2 a.m. [*sic*] Life with such clocks would not be worth living. America is notoriously a land of hustle, but in this old-fashioned country I have never known an eight-day clock that did not allow its forgetful owner a margin of at least 12 hours for rewinding. The plot could have got along quite well without calling for this staggering act of faith; and if anyone tells me that he has a clock which behaves like the Cape Cod clocks, I will remind him of what Aristotle says about the probable and the possible.

In "Death at Broadcasting House", Messrs. Gielgud and Marvell opened up a promising vein of entertainment by taking us behind the scenes at the B.B.C. They have now tried to apply the same formula to the film studio. But we are weary of murders in film studios, and particularly weary of the victim who is shot dead in mid-scene just as the blank ammunition is being fired off. Perhaps realising this, the authors of "DEATH AS AN EXTRA" have sought to enliven the story by introducing – for a motive preposterously inadequate – a bunch of the most tedious American gangsters who ever bumped their victims off in season and out of season. The leading idiot in this silly crew is said to be a brilliant chess player, and is always producing an ivory chessman from his pocket and fiddling with it. Seeing that the loss of a single pawn ruins the set, one feels that this is but a foolish habit, consistent with his all-round inefficiency as a villain. A man with a tidy mind would buy a proper pocket set with a case to it; he would also refrain from littering the place with unnecessary corpses.

The book is a disappointing return from the unconventional to an old and outworn convention.

23 June 1935
CRIME WRITERS GO ABROAD
Ruritania, Germany and France

Death of a Queen. By C. St. John Sprigg. (Nelson. 7s. 6d.)
The Death-Riders. By Cornelius Cofyn. (Gollancz. 7s. 6d.)
The Spy Paramount. By E. Phillips Oppenheim. (Hodder and Stoughton. 7s. 6d.)
Richardson Goes Abroad. By Sir Basil Thomson. (Eldon Press. 7s. 6d.)
Motive for Murder. By Aceituna and Joy Griffin. (Sampson Low. 7s. 6d.)

Where shall we go for our holidays? A trip abroad? Very good; but according to our authors this week, we shall have difficulty in finding any European excursion free from alarms.

Iconia, for example – that remote little country tucked away in the Ruritanian quarter of the Balkans – preserving its decayed monarchical institutions under the rule of an autocratic old Queen – where the cows lie down in the main street of the capital, and the palace washing is hung in the Grand Courtyard; there, surely, things will be peaceful. But no; the Queen has received threatening letters; strange intrigues disturb the Court; murder is done; and the English journalist who goes out to investigate matters very nearly pays with his life for being too clever.

Mr. Sprigg strikes exactly the right note for this kind of extravaganza; with enough gentle humour to make the absurdities of his one-horse kingdom entertaining, and enough romantic glamour to keep the murders in key. In the end he ingeniously effects a bloodless revolution without any marching about of comic-opera soldiers, praise be! My one grouse is that his journalist was rather slow to spot the means by which the criminal who brought about the "DEATH OF A QUEEN" establishes his alibi.

On Mr. Cofyn's evidence, I cannot recommend a trip either to Germany or to the West Coast of Scotland. "THE DEATH-RIDERS" are an extra ferocious Nazi organisation, who are plotting to put a torch to the powder-magazine of Europe; they are much given to floggings, assassinations, and other atrocities. A virtuous young Scot steals their secret plan of campaign and carries it off home.

All this first part is well written and full of thrills; and though the tone of its references to the German people and their present governors is ill calculated to promote international good feeling, the description of the escape from Germany carries conviction with it. But once the secret document is in Scotland, the story goes to pieces. Britons and Germans pursue each other all over the place, capturing and recapturing this confounded piece of paper, which everybody (of course) carries about handy for snatching, instead of despatching it to a safe place under care of the post office. This, like the First Player's speech, "is too long"; throughout the last quarter of the book, the characters walk into trap after trap, apparently for the express purpose of spinning out what, if it had ended a hundred pages earlier, would have been a good thriller of the better class.

———————

By way of contrast, I cannot too highly recommend the methods of Mr. Oppenheim's hero, "THE SPY PARAMOUNT". "Men do not carry papers nowadays," says this admirable man; "it is too dangerous". So we are relieved of "the papers"; but not, of course, of international intrigue or the powder-magazine of Europe. The free-lance American spy intrigues in the most mysterious manner in Italy, Germany, France, and England; and such are the authority of his manner and the suavity of his deportment, that we are not surprised to learn that "Fawley is the only man in Europe to-day who can save us from war." It is comforting to know that Mr. Fawley does save Europe, and, what is more, establish peace in perpetuity. He is modest about it. "I just had the idea," he says; "the sheer simplicity of it will amaze everyone." And so it will.

———————

"RICHARDSON GOES ABROAD" with a less tremendous purpose; he

merely goes to Paris to investigate the murder of a minor official of the British Embassy. Attempts are being made to invest the murder with a political significance, so our old friends Inspector Richardson and Sergeant Cooper of the C. I. D. are sent out to find the murderer and establish the real motive. It would have been better if the publisher had not made a pretty picture of the motive on the jacket, as this rather destroys the suspense. The atmosphere of French petty officialdom, both political and police, is amusingly done, and the detective work is as sound as one would naturally expect from an authority like Sir Basil Thomson.

There never was a more obvious "MOTIVE FOR MURDER" than in the book of that name; but the heroine, having been brought up in a country parsonage where they read no detective stories, was too innocent to spot it. This is a naïve little tale about the charming young heiress and the fraudulent guardian, and it seems to have got mixed up with a Guide-Book to Sicily.

So there you are, ladies and gentlemen: strangling in the Balkans; atrocities in Berlin; world-wrecking armaments in the Alps; throat-cuttings in Paris; and poison and assaults in Sicily. Let us take our tickets and make the Grand Tour.

28 July 1935
CRIME WRITERS AT THE TURNING POINT

The White Priory Murders. By Carter Dickson. (Heinemann. 7s. 6d.)
Thanks to Murder. By Joseph Krumgold. (Gollancz. 7s. 6d.)
Keep Away from Water. By Alice Campbell. (Collins: Crime Club. 7s. 6d.)

The detective story is passing, in these days, through an extraordinarily interesting stage of development. It has succeeded in establishing for itself a standard of technical achievement which is recognised by a considerable body of writers, critics, and readers. It is now, for example, generally accepted that the author should play fair, avoid coincidence, tuck in his loose ends, and get his poisons from the chemist instead of distilling them out of his own fantasy. A technique is not perfected all in a moment; it has taken some hard work to reach this point, and we are to be congratulated on having got so far. But now comes the moment when, having made our rules and got them by heart, we can begin to experiment and play about with them. And this will bring us face to face with a whole set of new problems, most of which will turn out to be questions of balance and treatment.

———————

Of this week's trio of writers, I place Mr. Dickson first, because he has succeeded best in keeping the equilibrium between his plot and his writing. "THE WHITE PRIORY MURDERS" is built up on the fine old theme of the lonely corpse surrounded by an area of snow, virgin except for the tracks of the person who discovers the body. We all know that (excluding suicide and the universally despised secret passage) this problem admits of only three legitimate solutions: the time was wrong, the place was wrong, or the corpse was not alone. Mr. Dickson has handled this classical material very capably, using scrupulous fairness in deduction and concealing the identity of his criminal with considerable cunning. His group of characters contains a number of oddities, but the oddities are both interesting and believable; and he uses his skill in suggesting queerness, both of psychology and atmosphere, for the legitimate double purpose of distracting attention from the material clues and preparing our minds to accept his solution. Our fat and eccentric friend, Sir Henry Merrivale, comes in to do the final detection; but his is not the only sympathetic portrait in a collection of careful character-sketches.

———————

Mr. Joseph Krumgold, dealing with a bunch of feather-headed and imperfectly sober people in a block of flats in New York, has written a rather absurd and charming love-story. Now, the difficulty about love-stories (as Racine recognised and said, a good many years ago) is that love is a very bad hand at playing second fiddle to other interests. In his eagerness to show us the quaint and delicate mutual reactions of Mr. Michael Vestry and Miss Nora Godell, the author keeps on forgetting his plot, and when he remembers it, he pushes it along hurriedly and with a bad grace. It would not matter at all if he had left the plot a little thin and sketchy; many good detective tales have survived that treatment. What he has done is to be rough and careless with it, so that the final s olution (if he means it for a solution) is completely unconvincing. He has chosen a story far too elaborate to be cleared up in an incoherent jumble of explanation at the end: something simpler and more human would better have carried his pleasantly humorous psychology. And he should have trusted to that humour, and not have indulged in a facetious rough-and-tumble suggestive of the sillier kind of film. "THANKS TO MURDER" is well worth reading – but not as detective fiction.

Miss Alice Campbell, in "KEEP AWAY FROM WATER", has made the complementary mistake of choosing a highly ingenious plot and writing it up in the undistinguished manner of the *roman-feuilleton*. I am not chemist enough to know whether the murder-method would work, but we will suppose that it would, and examine only the method of presentation. Now, here is the *roman-feuilleton* manner at its mid-Victorian flattest:–

> Gilcrest vouchsafed no response, but Sarah fancied a shade of scornful annoyance contracted his features. Harry, from the glint of merriment in his eye, evidently perceived it, for, nothing abashed, he abandoned the topic and asked point-blank …

Here, among the clichés, we can drowse on till kingdom come, scarcely opening an eye in wonder at the contracting shade.

And here we have it at its high peak of turgid excitement:–

> Her bound, bruised body was caught up in a fierce embrace, a man's arms with hard muscles strained her close while a man's kisses, equally hard and frantic, rained upon her face, her mouth.

Hungry, inescapable kisses submerging her whole being – kisses she had dreamed about; kisses which if she died of them now would send her into the other world transported with rapture.

If anybody dies of these transports it is likely to be the exasperated reader. There is more passion in Mr. Vestry's little finger than in the whole of Sarah's "bound, bruised body". Plot is not everything; style is not everything; only by combining them can we get a detective story that is also good literature.

4 August 1935
LIVELY READING IN THREE STORIES OF CRIME

A Girl Died Laughing. By Viola Paradise. (Heinemann. 7s. 6d.)
Fate Laughs. By Herbert Adams. (Collins: Crime Club. 7s. 6d.)
Blue Water Murder. By Philip Atkey. (Cassell. 7s. 6d.)

To say of a man that he is "a good actor" means to-day, in everyday life, exactly what it used to mean on the stage: one, namely, who is able to assume other personalities, all different from one another and from his own. On the stage, of course, it now tends to mean the precise opposite: a gentleman able to infuse his own charming and unmistakable personality into every part allotted to him. But the detective story, in its delightful old-fashioned way, clings to the earlier conception of the actor's art.

If a character in a detective story is or has been an actor, we are intended to understand by that that he can (oddly enough) act almost any-thing, and will do so before the end of the book. The murder-game seems indeed to hold out unlimited opportunity to those comedians who, under modern stage conditions, are hampered by their own versatility; it will be a sad day for crime-novelists when the character-actor follows the ptero-dactyl into extinction, and they have to rely entirely upon amateur talent.

Three plots this week turn upon impersonation. A young archaeologist was actually standing outside the door of an apartment in an American house when "A GIRL DIED LAUGHING", and he heard the laughter stop. This put him in an awkward position to start with – especially as he seemed to know rather too much about the young woman. Presently it became clear that somebody was impersonating him in order to make his position still more awkward. Fortunately, there was a bright young bell-hop with a knack of exact observation; and still more fortunately there was Assistant District Attorney Alby, who was an agreeable and sensible man, very unlike the bullying kind of official to whom we have become accustomed in American crime-stories.

Miss Paradise has given us a well written and entertaining book, with some excellent hidden clues and good character work. The explanations at the end are, perhaps, a trifle too hurried for comfort, and the versatility of the criminal may be thought excessive, but, having once begun, one will certainly not stop reading.

The most striking thing about "FATE LAUGHS" is the extreme slow-wittedness of the hero; but the poor young man was doubtless affected by the remarkable series of incidents and coincidences in which he was involved. It might happen to anybody, I suppose, to encounter his own double in a railway carriage and, being on his uppers, to agree (for a consideration) to impersonate the double for an hour or so. But the successive shocks of losing his heart to a lady and immediately falling heir to a large fortune must have had a stunning effect on our hero's brain; otherwise, when he learned that the husband of his double's former fiancée had been murdered during the hour of the impersonation, he ought surely to have realised, before page 220, that there might be a connection between the one thing and the other.

However, Mr. Adams has filled the interval with many surprising adventures, and the end is not as we think, because something we could not have known crops up on page 246 to disconcert us. This is not fair; but it all makes lively reading enough.

"BLUE WATER MURDER" is about an absconding financier and the various people who track him down to a lonely island in the Mediterranean in the hope of murdering him and seizing his hoard of stolen cash. The nice young hero's intentions are just as murderous as those of the rest, but he falls in love with the beautiful girl, and somebody else does all the murdering, so we see that he is a nice young man, really; and in any case, he only wanted, like Hamlet, to avenge his father. There are speedboats and seaplanes, yachts, plots, shots, hidden treasure, anonymous letters, an impersonation, and an abduction, with touches of smuggling and two love-affairs: so what more could anyone possibly want to enliven a summer holiday?

11 August 1935
MURDER AT THE OPERA
Spirited stories

Murder in Time. By Lillian Day and Norman Lederer. (Cassell. 7s. 6d.)
The House of Wraith. By Edward J. Millward. (Harrap. 7s. 6d.)
Blood On the Heather. By Stephen Chalmers. (World's Work. 8s. 6d.)

It is sometimes reasonably argued that no novelist ought also to be a reviewer, because of the difficulty of discounting personal prejudice. So let me admit at once that I started with a strong prejudice against "MURDER IN TIME". Opening it casually about the middle I came upon this passage: "'That's the name she used, Lord Wimsey, and I thought she was kidding. I suppose it's in the book.' ... 'Certainly.'" Now, upon my soul and honour, it is *not* in "the book"; and, apart from the maternal susceptibilities of the novelist, even the reviewer might be excused for thinking that anybody who could read a book of 448 pages without discovering the name of the protagonist (what fun to see that word in its right place for once!) was lacking in the observation so necessary to the detective writer.

Honesty, however, compels me to say that Miss Day and Mr. Lederer have written a good and lively story – and you may add or subtract anything you like for discount with respect to that statement. The murder is that of a conductor who is shot dead in the middle of a performance of "Götter-dämmerung" in New York. The authors know their cosmopolitan musical world and know their Wagner, and handle all this rather stubborn material with great vivacity. Their central clue is perhaps a little lightly indicated for those who do not know these things; but I confess I do not see how they could very well have been fairer without giving the show away. Later on the police rather play into the hands of the journalist-detective by a lack of thoroughness which would shock the soul of Chief Inspector French – but one must make a few concessions to dramatic necessity. The book is a spirited piece of work, and you should, I think, enjoy it – all the more if you know a little about music, a little about Jews, and a few words of German.

———

"THE HOUSE OF WRAITH" also gets high marks for entertainment. It begins as detection and wobbles a little unconvincingly into thrillerdom halfway through; but it is well written, and has the touch of romantic atmosphere which was so agreeable in Mr. Millward's earlier book, "The Copper Bottle". The corpse is found in a grave – not so original a resting-place as the characters seem to think; for about half a dozen detective stories within the last year or so have presented us with corpses in other people's graves. The most enjoyable thing in the book is the corpse's diary, with its jolly little thumb-nail sketches, all concealing clues. There is hidden treasure for those who have a passion for such things and a streak of heroic sentiment for those who like to end upon a note of gentle melancholy.

———

Judging by internal evidence, Mr. Stephen Chalmers is an American. It was, therefore, a little rash of him to stage his thriller in Scotland, where the intricacies of the criminal law will trip up anybody who is not to the manner born. Here my experience as a novelist tempers my severity as a reviewer, for I have fallen down at least twice in this strange country myself – once about accessories after the fact and once about wills. So it is with the utmost sympathy that I must point out that in Scotland there is no such thing as a coroner's inquest; that a solicitor (Scotticé: Writer to the Signet) is not, either in England or in Scotland, a "light of the British bar"; and that a Pinkerton man could not induce the "Glasgow office of the C. I. D.". (if that were its name) to act over the heads of the Argyllshire constabulary in the peremptory manner indicated. So that, despite Mr. Chalmers's gallant, and not too discreditable, struggles with the Doric, we can only award "BLOOD ON THE HEATHER" a medal for valour, and only enjoy the thrills if we deem them to have occurred in Nephelococcygia.

18 August 1935
CONFUSION AND CRIME
Trials of a woman detective

The Communist's Corpse. By Richard Wormser. (Gollancz. 7s. 6d.)
A Killer and His Star. By H. M. Stephenson. (Hutchinson. 7s. 6d.)

"THE COMMUNIST'S CORPSE" is rather a confusing book in more ways than one. It must be very confusing to be an amateur detective in New York, because you seem to have to fight the police at the same time as the criminal. Particularly if you happen to belong to the wrong political party, you run the risk of instant arrest the moment you appear on the scene of the murder; and it is very cramping to a detective's style to be continually in and out of gaol in the course of the investigation. Nor can you rely on a judge to protect you or a lawyer to defend you – not even if you pay him graft; because, if he is not taking graft from somebody else to get you put away, he is probably being blackmailed to the same end, so that your only chance is to bring political pressure to bear on him. This fogs the atmosphere for the British reader.

Secondly, Mr. Wormser, with some originality, has chosen for his detective a woman journalist, six-foot-one in height, of Communistic politics, and always down to her last nickel. He handles this unfortunate young woman with a touch of rather sordid pathos, making her courageous, humorous in a rough kind of way, generous and sadly hampered by her unusual height in what the popular Press calls her "love-life". But I think he over-estimates the entertainment to be derived from seeing even so un-gainly a female involved in rough-and-tumble fights, and having her shabby clothes torn off her back, and tearing the trousers off people smaller than herself. Besides, too much rough-and-tumble muddles the plot and takes the reader's attention off the clues.

Add to this that all the sympathetic characters live in conditions of disorder, not to say dirt; that they drink more than is good for them; and that none of them (to use the author's words) is "fussy whom he sleeps with", and it will be seen that the story appeals rather to those of strong stomach and advanced taste than to those who like a "nice book". On the other hand, the writing is vigorous, the characters lifelike, and the action brisk; though such was the dust raised by the numerous conflicts that I cannot pretend to have seen clearly whether all the loose ends of the plot were properly tied.

––––––––––

Mr. Wormser is, at any rate, much better worth reading than Mr. Stephen-son, who has brought platitudinous dullness to the pitch of a fine art. Light dies before his uncreating word. When he has brought on a couple of characters to express their elementary psychology in dialogue, he is still afraid the reader will not understand unless he dots the i's and crosses the t's. So he buttonholes him to explain that "whatever his faults, the man had courage – plenty of it", or that "the gallant colonel was a capital fellow, but lacking in perception". He even apostrophises his own puppets, thus:–

> Poor Netty! you were not born under a favourable star. Clever –
> but without any real gifts ... Insincere *poseuse* and confirmed little
> liar, do you really think you will resist for long a seducer who has
> twice your brains, five times your knowledge of the world, and ten

times your honesty of purpose? ... Your silly blasphemies ... your
silly loose talk ... you are going to pay for these things, Netty – and
a very heavy price.

At any rate, one knows where one is with "A KILLER AND HIS
STAR". The Killer has a windy, badly brewed philosophy about stars, and
this philosophy inspires and supports him in the commission of a singularly clumsy and uninteresting murder. His star, however, is a lucky one,
for, by the perjury of a good woman, the remarkable amiability of the jury,
and the author's ruthlessness in killing off all the witnesses who might
have been useful to the police, the Killer escapes hanging. But, oh, my stars!

* * *

THE COLLECTED CRIME REVIEWS

of

DOROTHY L. SAYERS

———

1937

———

30 May 1937
FAMOUS SCOTTISH TRIALS

Mainly Murder. By William Roughead. (Cassell. 10s. 6d.)

Connoisseurs in murder will probably agree that Mr. Roughead is far and away the best showman that ever stood before the door of a Chamber of Horrors. In a brief introductory speech, before conducting the public to view his latest collection, he explains the method which has put him at the head of his mournful profession.

In my reading of other writers' studies in murder I had noted that there were two disparate methods employed: the solid, dry, and technical manner of the serious inquirer, whose aim was educative and his style severe; and the brightly written, unreliable accounts of the irresponsible relator, concerned only to tell a rousing tale with scant regard to accuracy. It occurred to me that to combine the exactitude of the one with the readableness of the other, and, as in the matter of Mr. Stiggins's moral pocket-handkerchiefs, to blend amusement with instruction, might give some fresh value to the criminological essay.

To this admirable method he has consistently adhered for just over thirty years (reckoning from his biography of Pritchard the Poisoner, published in 1906); and in a period during which the reporting of fact has become steadily "brighter" and the writing of criminological fiction steadily (thank Heaven) more accurate, he has maintained his masterly pre-eminence in combining the best qualities of both schools. How little he has varied from the standard he originally set himself may be judged from the present volume, which contains three reprints from his "Twelve Scots Trials", published in 1913 and now unhappily out of print, for comparison with his study of the trial of John McGuigan, which took place as recently as 1935. In all the papers we find the same clarity of presentation, the same sense of dramatic values, and the same astringent style which, unlike that of some of his imitators, never oversteps the narrow bound between humour and offence.

A Modern Case

The most modern of the cases stands first in the book, and in many ways deserves this pride of place. A young man and a young woman were walking one evening in the "Cuddles Strip", near Perth, when, from the woods near-by, came two shots from a shot-gun, the second of which killed the young man, without injuring the girl who was standing close beside him. As the girl was bending over the body, a stranger made his appearance, as though from nowhere. She asked him to stand by the body while she ran for help; instead of this, he assaulted her and then disappeared.

Eventually, after ten days, the stranger was identified, by means of as neat a piece of detective proof as ever graced a crime-novel, with John McGuigan, a casual labourer, who had thoughtlessly used a burgled handkerchief to tie the girl's wrists. This inattention to detail brought about his undoing.

He was convicted of the burglary and the assault, but the charge of murder was held to be not proven. There were two shots, so that the shooting could scarcely have been an accident. One would have supposed that acquittal of the murder should logically have implied acquittal of the other charges also. But the jury may have been influenced by the long-winded and old-fashioned Scots indictment, which ends in a manner shocking to the English mind with the words "and you have been previously convicted of dishonest appropriation of property and of crime inferring personal violence" (i.e. assaults on women).

One of the most important witnesses in the matter of the gun failed to come forward until McGuigan had been identified through the handkerchief; saying that he did not speak earlier because he "thought the police would get him". The publicity of a coroner's inquest might have produced this witness earlier; but there is no coroner's inquest in Scotland.

"Crowner's Quest"

In view of the present movement to abolish "crowner's quest", it is interesting to note its influence on another Scottish trial in this collection, dating back to the late seventeenth century. Sir James Stanfield, a cloth manufacturer in East Lothian, was one morning found dead under highly suspicious circumstances. His family hastened "in hugger-mugger to inter him", but next day "the Englishmen in the manufactory, *who were acquainted with the Crowner Laws*, made a mutiny anent the burial." As a result, the body was exhumed and the dead man's son convicted of murder; a picturesque episode being the bleeding of the corpse at the murderer's touch, this being the last recorded instance of such a criminological miracle.

Another case abounding in colourful incident is that of the murder of Mr. Millie, the damask weaver, by his employee, John Henderson, at Whinny Park, near Cupar, in 1830. The murderer contrived to keep the horrid secret of his master's disappearance for over a month, writing himself an ingenious letter of instructions from the deceased, which opened convincingly, "John, You will begin your work with a rose and sprig pattern ..." He fell down, however, on a discrepancy in the date of a forged deposit receipt and, after being at the trouble to transfer the corpse from one grave to another, was nevertheless hanged and anatomised for his pains.

Murder of a Seaman

Other items in this excellent book are the murder of a seaman by the midshipman, Thomas Whyte, at Leith Pier in 1814, involving an interesting discussion of how far lethal violence can be justified in the carrying-out of naval discipline; the forcible abduction and marriage in 1702 of Mistress Pleasant Rawlins, with much fine period detail; the curious and doubtful case of the murder of Keith of Northfield in 1766; and further studies of such old favourites as Madeleine Smith, Katharine Nairn, and Dr. Cross, the Irish poisoner. Mr. Roughead is perhaps more successful in dealing with the men than with the women; but it may be safely said that there is no criminous pie which is not improved by the tart flavour of his observations and pinched into handsomer shape by his expert and investigating finger.

* * *

THE COLLECTED CRIME REVIEWS

of

DOROTHY L. SAYERS

―――――

1949

―――――

6 February 1949
CONAN DOYLE: CRUSADER

The Life of Sir Arthur Conan Doyle. By John Dickson Carr. (Murray. 18s.)

It cannot be helped. For all the world, and probably for all time, the fame of Conan Doyle must stand coupled with the name of Sherlock Holmes. That Doyle resented this, that he came to loathe Holmes, that he pushed him over the Reichenbach Falls in the vain hope of getting rid of him, is sad but true, and is only superficially inconsistent with Mr. Dickson Carr's assertion that, in a very real sense, "Sherlock Holmes was Conan Doyle."

Even without Doyle's own convincing detective work in the Edalji and Slater cases, we should know that any character so vital as this must have been vitalised from within, not founded on external observation only. But the creator is the whole of his creation and more; he cannot be identified with any one part of it. And if, while he is intent on exploring and expressing some new part of his creative personality, he is badgered into returning to that earlier thing which he has for the time being happily written out of his system, spontaneity is hampered, zest destroyed, and delight turned into weariness.

One cannot but regret that Doyle's enjoyment of his greatest creation was thus poisoned for him, because he was a man who liked to throw himself with generous enthusiasm into whatever he undertook. His story, from its struggling and impecunious beginnings to its wealthy and honoured close, is the adventure of an eager, chivalrous and courageous nature, accepting life in all its manifestations with an enormous gusto. It was this gusto which roared out superabundantly in "Professor Challenger", and which caused such historical novels as "Micah Clarke" and "The White Company" to be taken (greatly to his annoyance) as ebullient cloak-and-sword romances, rather than as the sober period evocations which he intended them to be.

However conscientiously he steeped himself in his source-material, he could never be dry-as-dust; what "got across" was not the accidents of study but his own substantial vitality. That is why his most triumphant success in this sort is the "Brigadier Gerard" series, where the bravura which he found in his French original, answering as it did to an irrepressible Irish buoyancy in his own nature, was admirably balanced and controlled by that pawky Scottish strain in him which he lent to Dr. Watson. For he was Watson also – though not so exclusively Watson as Sidney Paget's illustrations might persuade us to suppose; he possessed in himself a downrightness and sincerity, a simplicity of affection, an adherence to such plain outmoded virtues as loyalty, conjugal fidelity and courtesy to women, which not only lend a candid dignity to his personal life but can charm us even today in the little domestic piece called "A Duet with an Occasional Chorus".

There are many things about Doyle which we had half forgotten: his heroic war-work in South Africa, with the Longman Hospital; the tact as well as the energy which he used in defending this country against foreign criticism; the shrewdness with which he foresaw the development of modern warfare, and the vigour with which he urged military and naval preparedness upon complacent governments.

He organised the first Volunteer Reserve Company of the 1914-18 War, devoting himself to the task with the same energy with which he had, at one time or another, embarked on theatrical enterprises, embraced the new cult of the automobile, and introduced ski-ing into Switzerland. His purse and his help were always at the service of anyone who was in trouble; and in the end he wore himself to death in his eagerness to preach consolation to a bereaved world.

Mr. John Dickson Carr has made a good use of the abundant material – much of it hitherto inedited – which the Doyle family have placed at his disposal. His biography is admirably complete, and clearly and well arranged. It suffers somewhat from a determined brightness of style, reminiscent of a radio feature-programme, whereby every episode is remorselessly dramatised, every chapter begins with a tableau and a flash-back, and rhetorical questions abound. But we may bear with these surface defects for the sake of the accuracy, sympathy and balanced judgment with which he has handled his subject.

* * *

BOOK TITLES REVIEWED LISTED BY AUTHOR

AUTHOR	BOOK TITLE	REVIEW DATE
Edward Acheson	*The Grammarian's Funeral*	5 May 1935
Herbert Adams	*The Secret of Bogey House*	6 August 1933
	John Brand's Will	10 September 1933
	The Knife	24 June 194
	The Body in the Bunker	24 February 1935
	Fate Laughs	4 August 1935
Eric Aldhouse	*The Crime at the Quay Inn*	30 December 1934
Luke Allan	*Murder at the Club*	19 November 1933
	Scotland Yard Takes a Holiday	4 November 1934
H. Warner Allen	*Mr. Clerihew, Wine Merchant*	29 October 1933
Margery Allingham	*Death of a Ghost*	18 March 1934
Anthony Armstrong and Herbert Shaw		
	Ten Minute Alibi	10 June 1934
H. Ashbrook	*The Murder of Sigurd Sharon*	2 September 1934
Kenneth Ashley	*Death of a Curate*	6 August 1933
Charles Ashton	*Murder in Make-Up*	20 January 1935
Philip Atkey	*Blue Water Murder*	4 August 1935
H. C. Bailey	*Mr. Fortune Wonders*	26 November 1933
	Shadow on the Wall	6 May 1934
	Mr. Fortune Objects	14 April 1935
Nigel Barnaby	*The Secret of Matchams*	2 December 1934
Charles Barry	*Death in Darkness*	25 June 1933
	The Wrong Murder Mystery	17 December 1933
Mark Beckett	*The Murder at the Flower Show*	28 January 1934
Francis Beeding	*The One Sane Man*	14 January 1934
Garstin Begbie	*Murder Mask*	27 May 1934

John Bentley	*The Berg Case*	1 July 1934
Anthony Berkeley	*Jumping Jenny*	23 July 1933
	Panic Party	3 June 1934
(After) Tristan Bernard (By Virginia and Frank Vernon)		
	The Diary of a Murderer	16 December 1934
Harold Best	*The Flaming Hut Murder*	6 August 1933
Mary D. Bickel	*The Trial of Linda Stuart*	27 January 1935
Leonard Blackledge	*Behind the Evidence*	3 March 1935
Nicholas Blake	*A Question of Proof*	10 March 1935
Adam Bliss	*The Campden Ruby Murder*	14 January 1933
Ben Bolt	*The Snapshot Mystery*	31 December 1933
	A Shot in the Night	29 April 1934
Jean Bommart	*The Chinese Fish*	17 March 1935
Louis F. Booth	*The Bank Vault Mystery*	23 July 1933
Lawrence R. Bourne	*Stark Naked*	6 May 1934
Nicholas Brady	*Week-end Murder*	29 October 1933
	Ebenezer Investigates	4 March 1934
Ernest Bramah	*The Bravo of London*	3 June 1934
John G. Brandon	*The One-Minute Murder*	9 December 1934
Alan Brock	*Further Evidence*	5 August 1934
	After the Fact	24 February 1935
Collin Brooks	*Frame-Up*	27 January 1935
Edwy Searles Brooks	*The Strange Case of the Antlered Man*	24 March 1935
Richard Blake Brown	*The Blank Cheque*	17 June 1934
Douglas G. Browne	*The Cotfold Conundrums*	3 December 193'
	The "Looking-Glass' Murders	10 February 1935
Miles Burton	*Death at the Cross-Roads*	10 December 1933
	The Charabanc Mystery	4 March 1934
	The Devereux Court Mystery	17 March 1935
Christopher Bush	*The Case of the Three Strange Faces*	27 August 1933
	The Case of the 100% Alibis	11 March 1934
	The Case of the Dead Shepherd	9 September 1934

Alice Campbell	*Desire to Kill*	22 July 1934
	Keep Away from Water	28 July 1935
Colin Campbell	*Murder Up the Glen*	24 December 1933
	Murder on the Moors	30 September 1934
John Dickson Carr	*The Mad Hatter Mystery*	24 September 1933
	The Eight of Swords	25 March 1934
	The Blind Barber	11 November 1934
	Death-Watch	31 March 1935
	The Life of Sir Arthur Conan Doyle	6 February 1949
Joseph B. Carr	*Death Whispers*	13 August 1933
	The Man with Bated Breath	3 February 1935

John Carter and Graham Pollard

	An Enquiry into the Nature of	1 July 1934
	Certain Nineteenth Century Pamphlets	
Robert J. Casey	*Hot Ice*	3 September 1933
Olive Cecil	*The Pepper-Pot Problem*	9 July 1933
John Newton Chance	*Wheels in the Forest*	9 June 1935
Stephen Chalmers	*Blood on the Heather*	11 August 1935
G. K. Chesterton	*The Scandal of Father Brown*	7 April 1935
Nellise Child	*Murder Comes Home*	30 July 1933
	The Diamond Ransom Murders	16 December 1934
Agatha Christie	*Lord Edgware Dies*	3 September 1933
	Murder on the Orient Express	7 January 1934
	Why Didn't They Ask Evans?	9 September 1934
	Three Act Tragedy	6 January 1935
Henrietta Clandon	*Inquest*	25 June 1933
	Rope by Arrangement	28 April 1935

Colin Clements and Florence Ryerson

	Sleep No More	16 July 1933
Irvin S. Cobb	*Murder Day by Day*	8 April 1934
Cornelius Cofyn	*The Death-Riders*	23 June 1935
G. D. H. & M. Cole	*The Affair at Aliquid*	17 September 1933
	End of an Ancient Mariner	31 December 1933
	Death in the Quarry	13 May 1934
	Big Business Murder	6 January 1935
	Dr. Tancred Begins	26 May 1935

J. J. Connington	*The Ha-Ha Case*	30 September 1934
Ex-Superintendent G. W. Cornish		
	Cornish of the "Yard":	13 January 1935
	His Reminiscences and Cases	
Joan Cowdroy	*Disappearance*	28 January 1934
John Creasey	*First Came a Murder*	30 December 1934
Freeman Wills Crofts	*12:30 From Croydon*	25 February 1934
	Murder on Southampton Water	26 August 1934
	Crime at Guildford	12 May 1935
John Crozier	*Murder in Public*	23 September 1934

Moray Dalton	*The Belfry Murder*	12 November 1933
T. L. Davidson	*The Murder in the Laboratory*	6 August 1933
Means Davis	*The Hospital Murders*	29 April 1934
	Murder Without Weapon	28 April 1935
G. Davison	*A Killer at Scotland Yard*	15 October 1933
Lillian Day and Norbert Lederer		
	Murder in Time	11 August 1935
H. L. Deakin and Grace M. White		
	The Square Mark	6 August 1933
Roger Denbie	*The Time-Table Murder*	8 April 1934
	Death Cruises South	28 October 1934
Carter Dickson	*The Bowstring Murders*	19 August 1934
	The Plague Court Murders	17 March 1935
	The White Priory Murders	28 July 1935
Peter Dingwall	*The Poison Duel*	18 February 1934
Maurice B. Dix	*Twisted Evidence*	10 September 1933
	The Fleetwood Mansions Mystery	1 July 1934
Winifred Duke	*Skin for Skin*	24 February 1935
Charles J. Dutton	*The Circle of Death*	12 November 1933

Roger East	*Murder Rehearsal*	2 July 1933
	Candidate for Lilies	28 January 1934
	Twenty-Five Sanitary Inspectors	19 May 1935

Mignon G. Eberhart	*The White Cockatoo*	16 July 1933
	Death in the Fog	29 April 1934
	Murder of My Patient	11 November 1934
Herbert B. Ehrmann	*The Untried Case: Sacco and Vanzetti and the Morelli Gang*	13 January 1935
Firth Erskine	*Naked Murder*	3 March 1935
Francis Everton	*Insoluble*	11 March 1934
Gerald Fairlie	*Copper at Sea*	15 April 1934
Sidney Fairway	*The Yellow Viper*	6 August 1933
J. Jefferson Farjeon	*Dead Man's Heath*	3 September 1933
	Old Man Mystery	31 December 1933
	The Windmill Mystery	25 February 1934
	Sinister Inn	15 July 1934
	Fancy Dress Ball	23 September 1934
David Farrer	*A Career for the Gentleman*	13 May 1934
John Ferguson	*Night in Glengyle*	8 October 1933
	The Grouse Moor Mystery	14 October 1934
A. Fielding	*The Cautley Conundrum*	11 February 1934
	The Paper Chase	9 December 1934
J. S. Fletcher	*The Mantle of Ishmael*	16 July 1933
	Murder of the Only Witness	13 August 1933
	Murder of the Only Witness	20 May 1934
	The Eleventh Hour	5 May 1935
Brian Flynn	*The Horn*	17 June 1934
	The Case of the Purple Calf	9 December 1934
Hulbert Footner	*The Almost Perfect Murder*	16 July 1933
	Murder Runs in the Family	22 April 1934
	The New Made Grave	14 April 1935
Robin Forsythe	*The Ginger Cat Mystery*	21 April 1935
Sydney Fowler	*Three Witnesses*	2 June 1935
R. Austin Freeman	*Dr. Thorndyke Intervenes*	22 October 1933
	For the Defence: Dr. Thorndyke	28 October 1934

* * *

David Frome	*The Eel-Pie Mystery*	29 October 1933
	That's Your Man, Inspector	25 March 1934
	Arsenic in Richmond	7 October 1934
	The Body in the Turl	10 March 1935
Erle Stanley Gardner	*The Case of the Sulky Girl*	22 April 1934
	The Case of the Lucky Legs	19 August 1934
	The Case of the Howling Dog	20 January 1935
Newton Gayle	*Death Follows a Formula*	10 February 1935
Val Gielgud and Holt Marvell		
	Death at Broadcasting House	4 February 1934
	Death as an Extra	16 June 1935
Anthony Gilbert	*Death in Fancy Dress*	2 July 1933
	The Musical Comedy Crime	8 October 1933
	An Old Lady Dies	20 May 1934
	The Man in Button Boots	18 November 1934
Elizabeth Gill	*Crime de Luxe*	25 June 1933
George Goodchild and C. E. Bechhofer Roberts		
	The Jury Disagree	18 November 1934
	The Dear Old Gentleman	14 April 1935
John Goodwin	*The King's Elm Mystery*	8 July 1934
William Gore	*There's Death in the Churchyard*	17 June 1934
Lord Gorell	*Red Lilac*	7 April 1935
Bruce Graeme	*Epilogue*	26 November 1933
	An International Affair	20 May 1934
Edwin Greenwood	*Skin and Bone*	21 October 1934
	Pins and Needles	28 April 1935
Cecil Freeman Gregg	*Inspector Higgins Sees It Through*	6 May 1934
	The Execution of Diamond Deutsch	4 November 1934
	The Ten Black Pearls	19 May 1935
Jackson Gregory	*The Second Case of Mr. Paul Savoy*	27 August 1933
Francis D. Grierson	*The Monkhurst Murder*	9 July 1933
	The Empty House	12 November 1933
	Murder at Lancaster Gate	16 September 1934
Aceituna and Joy Griffin		
	Motive for Murder	23 June 1935

Elaine Hamilton	*The Silent Bell*	10 December 1933
J. F. W. Hannay	*When the Wicked Man*	14 October 1934
Frances Noyes Hart	*The Crooked Lane*	21 October 1934
William C. Harvey	*Death's Treasure Hunt*	17 December 1933
Jane-Eliza Hasted	*Our Mr. Richards*	10 September 1933
M. Doriel Hay	*Murder Underground*	27 May 1934
Harold Heslop	*The Crime of Peter Ropner*	4 February 1934
Georgette Heyer	*The Unfinished Clue*	1 April 1934
	Death in the Stocks	21 April 1935
T. F. W. Hickey	*The Corpse in the Church*	6 August 1933
Henry Holt	*Calling All Cars*	12 August 1934
Sidney Horler	*Harlequin of Death*	10 September 1933
Holloway Horn	*The Purple Claw*	10 March 1935
Richard Hull	*The Murder of My Aunt*	9 September 1934
David Hume	*The Gaol Gates Are Open*	2 June 1935
Theodore Hyde	*After the Execution*	2 December 1934
T. C. H. Jacobs	*Sinister Quest*	15 July 1934
Cora Jarrett	*Pattern in Black and Red*	25 November 1934
Edgar Jepson	*The Grinning Avenger*	18 February 1934
Dorothy Johnson	*Death of a Spinster*	6 August 1933
Harry Stephen Keeler	*The Travelling Skull*	12 August 1934
Carleton Kendrake	*The Clue of the Forgotten Murder*	19 May 1935
Milward Kennedy	*Corpse in Cold Storage*	8 April 1934
	Poison in the Parish	31 March 1935
Richard Keverne	*Artifex Intervenes*	20 May 1934
	He Laughed at Murder	30 December 1934
Michael Keyes	*Murder Cruise*	2 September 1934
Maurice G. Kiddy	*The Jade Hat-Pin*	27 August 1933
Thomas Kindon	*Murder in the Moor*	6 August 1933

C. Daly King	*Obelists En Route*	4 February 1934
	Obelists Fly High	17 February 1935
Rufus King	*Murder by Latitude*	6 August 1933
Sherry King	*Between Murders*	12 May 1935
Charles Kingston	*Poison in Kensington*	5 August 1934
Laurence Kirk	*Whispering Tongues*	3 June 1934
C. H. B. Kitchin	*Crime at Christmas*	14 October 1934
Ronald A. Knox	*The Body in the Silo*	25 June 1933
	Still Dead	13 May 1934
Joseph Krumgold	*Thanks to Murder*	28 July 1935
Sefton Kyle	*The Life He Stole*	2 September 1934

Alexander Laing	*The Cadaver of Gideon Wyck*	26 August 1934
Adele Leaman	*The Green Bag*	6 August 1933
Maurice Leblanc	*The Return of Arsène Lupin*	9 July 1933
Norbert Lederer and Lillian Day		
	Murder in Time	11 August 1935
A. B. Leonard	*The Judson Murder Case*	19 November 1933
William Le Queux	*The White Glove*	9 July 1933
Armstrong Livingston	*Murder is Easy*	17 September 1933
Vernon Loder	*Murder from Three Angles*	8 April 1934
E. C. R. Lorac	*Death on the Oxford Road*	17 September 1933
	The Organ Speaks	3 February 1935
Cecil Champain Lowis	*The Green Tunnel*	2 June 1935

Victor MacClure	*The Clue of the Dead Goldfish*	24 December 1933
	Death on the Set	21 October 1934
Angus MacVicar	*Death by the Mistletoe*	12 August 1934
David Magarshack	*Big Ben Strikes Eleven*	15 April 1934
	Death Cuts a Caper	27 January 1935
Barbara Malim	*Death by Misadventure*	11 February 1934
Antony Marsden	*Death Strikes from the Rear*	28 October 1934

Holt Marvell and Val Gielgud

	Death at Broadcasting House	4 February 1934
	Death as an Extra	16 June 1935
Walter S. Masterman	*The Baddington Horror*	25 February 1934
	The Perjured Alibi	24 March 1935
Paul McGuire	*Death Fugue*	22 October 1933
	Daylight Murder	9 December 1934
Catherine Meadows	*Henbane*	7 October 1934
Alan Melville	*Quick Curtain*	2 December 1934
Anne Meredith	*Portrait of a Murderer*	29 October 1933
A. Merritt	*Burn, Witch, Burn!*	22 July 1934
Laurence W. Meynell	*Watch the Wall*	31 December 1933
Edward J. Millward	*The House of Wraith*	11 August 1935
Gladys Mitchell	*Death at the Opera*	1 April 1934
Dermot Morrah	*The Mummy Case*	6 August 1933
D. Erskine Muir	*Five to Five*	16 September 1934
Isabel Briggs Myers	*Give Me Death*	25 November 1934

Elizabeth Nisot — *Shortly Before Midnight* — 21 January 1934

E. Phillips Oppenheim	*The Gallows of Chance*	28 January 1934
	The Strange Boarders of Palace Crescent	20 January 1935
	The Spy Paramount	23 June 1935
Nigel Orde-Powlett	*The Cast to Death*	6 August 1933
	Driven Death	6 August 1933

S. Hart Page	*The Resurrection Murder Case*	19 November 1933
Stuart Palmer	*Murder on the Blackboard*	11 March 1934
	The Puzzle of the Silver Persian	3 February 1935
Viola Paradise	*A Girl Died Laughing*	4 August 1935
Q. Patrick	*S. S. Murder*	19 November 1933
	Death in the Dove-Cot	27 May 1934
	Darker Grows the Valley	5 May 1935

Barry Perowne	*Raffles After Dark*	15 October 1933
Margaret Peterson	*Death in Goblin Waters*	29 July 1934
R. Philmore	*Journey Downstairs*	24 June 1934
Mary Plum	*The Broken Vase Mystery*	5 November 1933
T. Arthur Plummer	*Creaking Gallows*	4 March 1934
Graham Pollard and John Carter		
	An Enquiry into the Nature of Certain Nineteenth Century Pamphlets	1 July 1934
E. J. Pond	*The Ince Murder Case*	12 August 1934
Evadne Price	*The Haunted Light*	13 August 1933
Milton Propper	*The Divorce Court Murder*	7 October 1934
E. R. Punshon	*Proof Counter-Proof*	6 August 1933
	The Cottage Murder	6 August 1933
	Information Received	20 August 1933
	Death Among the Sun Bathers	25 March 1934
	The Cross-Word Mystery	27 May 1934
	Mystery Villa	4 November 1934
	Death of a Beauty Queen	26 May 1935
Ellery Queen	*The American Gun Mystery*	2 July 1933
	The Siamese Twin Mystery	10 December 1933
	The Ellery Queen Omnibus	7 January 1934
	The Chinese Orange Mystery	1 July 1934
	The Adventures of Ellery Queen	3 March 1935
	The Spanish Cape Mystery	7 April 1935
James Quince	*Casual Slaughters*	16 June 1935
Arthur J. Rees	*Aldringham's Last Chance*	1 October 1933
John Rhode	*The Robthorne Mystery*	7 January 1934
	Poison for One	10 June 1934
	Shot at Dawn	11 November 1934
	The Corpse in the Car	17 February 1935
	Hendon's First Case	9 June 1935
Mary Roberts Rinehart	*The Album*	1 October 1933
Clifton Robbins	*Smash and Grab*	1 April 1934

C. E. Bechhofer Roberts and George Goodchild
	The Jury Disagree	18 November 1934
	The Dear Old Gentleman	14 April 1935
Raymond Robins	*Murder at Bayside*	18 February 1934
Lewis Robinson	*The Manuscript Murder*	22 October 1933
Anthony Rolls	*Family Matters*	11 February 1934
	Scarweather	28 October 1934
James Ronald	*Cross Marks the Spot*	20 August 1933
William Roughead	*Mainly Murder*	30 May 1937
Barnaby Ross	*Drury Lane's Last Case*	3 December 1933
Charles Rushton	*The Murder Market*	23 December 1934

Florence Ryerson and Colin Clements
	Sleep No More	16 July 1933
Clive Ryland	*The Murders at the Manor*	23 July 1933
	Murder on the Cliff	19 August 1934

David Sharp	*Marriage and Murder*	7 January 1934

Herbert Shaw and Anthony Armstrong
	Ten Minute Alibi	10 June 1934
"Simon"	*Murder Among Friends*	17 December 1933
	Death on the Swim	29 July 1934
Johnston Smith	*Murder in the Square*	9 July 1933
J. M. Spender	*The Charge is Murder*	22 July 1934
C. St. John Sprigg	*The Perfect Alibi*	8 July 1934
	Death of an Airman	25 November 1934
	Death of a Queen	23 June 1935
H. M. Stephenson	*A Killer and His Star*	18 August 1935
Burton E. Stevenson	*The Mystery of Villa Aurelia*	20 August 1933
Rex Stout	*Fer-de-Lance*	31 March 1935
John Stephen Strange	*The Chinese Jar Mystery*	18 March 1934
Kaye Sunderland	*Late Harvest*	10 September 1933
William Sutherland	*Behind the Headlines*	24 September 1933
	Death Rides the Air Line	24 June 1934

Beryl Symons	*Strange Witness*	29 April 1934

Phoebe Atwood (P. A.) Taylor
	The Mystery of the Cape Cod Players	15 July 1934
	The Mystery of the Cape Cod Tavern	16 June 1935

Darwin L. Teilhet	*The Talking Sparrow Murders*	10 June 1934
N. A. Temple Ellis	*The Inconsistent Villains*	6 June 1933
	Three Went In	30 September 1934
Alan Thomas	*Death of the Home Secretary*	5 November 1933
Sir Basil Thomson	*The Kidnapper*	17 December 1933
	Richardson Scores Again!	10 June 1934
	Inspector Richardson, C. I. D.	21 October 1934
	Richardson Goes Abroad	23 June 1935
J. V. Turner	*Death Joins the Party*	10 February 1935

John W. Vandercook	*Murder in Trinidad*	18 March 1934
S. S. Van Dine	*The Dragon Murder Case*	21 January 1934
	The Casino Murder Case	18 November 1934
Gerald Verner	*Sinister House*	15 July 1934

Virginia and Frank Vernon (After Tristan Bernard)
	The Diary of a Murderer	16 December 1934

E. Charles Vivian	*Girl in the Dark*	15 October 1933
	Shadow on the House	21 January 1934
	Seventeen Cards	13 January 1935

Henry Wade	*Policeman's Lot*	30 July 1933
	Mist on the Saltings	5 November 1933
	Constable Guard Thyself!	29 July 1934
H. Russell Wakefield	*Hearken to the Evidence*	5 November 1933
R. A. J. Walling	*Follow the Blue Car*	30 July 1933
	Eight to Nine	19 August 1934
	The Five Suspects	23 December 1934
J. H. Wallis	*The Capital City Mystery*	10 September 1933
	The Mystery of Vaucluse	4 March 1934
Percy Walsh	*The Clueless Trail*	1 October 1933

Colin Ward	*House-Party Murder*	26 November 1933
F. A. M. Webster	*Gathering Storm*	24 December 1933
Anthony Weymouth	*Frozen Death*	5 August 1934
	The Doctors Are Doubtful	12 May 1935
Ethel Lina White	*Wax*	24 March 1935

Grace M. White and H. L. Deakin

	The Square Mark	6 August 1933
David Whitelaw	*The Roof*	23 July 1933
Hilda Willett	*Mystery on the Centre Court*	9 July 1933
Valentine Williams	*The Clock Ticks On*	8 October 1933
	The Portcullis Room	22 April 1934
	Masks Off at Midnight	23 September 1934
Cecil M. Wills	*Author in Distress*	15 April 1934
	Death at the Pelican	16 September 1934
	The Chamois Murder	17 February 1935
	Death Treads ...	9 June 1935
R. C. Woodthorpe	*The Public School Murder*	6 August 1933
	A Dagger in Fleet Street	14 January 1934
	Silence of a Purple Shirt	29 July 1934
	Death in a Little Town	13 January 1935
Richard Wormser	*The Communist's Corpse*	18 August 1935

Sydney Fowler Wright (See Sydney Fowler)

	Three Witnesses	2 June 1935
Anthony Wynne	*The Case of the Gold Coins*	3 December 1933
	Death of a Banker	8 July 1934
	The Toll-House Murder	6 January 1935

THE DOROTHY L. SAYERS SOCIETY

The Dorothy L. Sayers Society was formed in 1976. It promotes the study of the life and work of Dorothy L. Sayers (1893–1957), who was a writer, scholar, poet, playwright and lay theologian. The Society encourages the performance of Sayers' plays and the publication of texts by and about her work and life. The Society also maintains an extensive archive, preserving original material, providing information and assistance for researchers and devotees.

The Society organises events to celebrate the life and work of DLS throughout each year and encourages the study and discussion of Sayers' works. Central to the Society are its members and their enduring enthusiasm for Sayers. Members come from all walks of life and from across the globe. It is a truly international society.

The Society holds an annual convention and publishes its proceedings, along with its journal, *Sidelights on Sayers*, as well as a bi-monthly *Bulletin*, occasional papers and other texts.

The Society is a registered charity and provides support for early career actors, young musicians and bell ringers. In 2016, the Society introduced The Norah Lambourne Design Award in collaboration with the Royal Opera House for apprentices involved in stage design.

The Society welcomes everyone with an interest in Dorothy L. Sayers and her works.

Further information on the Dorothy L. Sayers Society can be found at **http://www.sayers.org.uk** or by writing to:

Gimsons, King's Chase, Witham, Essex CM8 1AX UK

ABOUT MARTIN EDWARDS

Martin Edwards is the author of eighteen novels, including seven *Lake District Mysteries*, the most recent of which is *The Dungeon House*. His other publications include *The Golden Age of Murder*, a ground-breaking study of detective fiction between the world wars, which has won the Edgar, Agatha, Macavity, and H. R. F. Keating awards. He has edited more than thirty anthologies of crime fiction and fact, has won the CWA Short Story Dagger and the CWA Margery Allingham Prize, and is series consultant for the British Library's *Crime Classics*. In 2015, he was elected eighth President of the Detection Club, an office previously held by G. K. Chesterton, Agatha Christie, and Dorothy L. Sayers.

THE PUBLISHER

Tippermuir Books Ltd. (*Est.*2009)
is an independent publishing company
based in Perth, Scotland.

OTHER TITLES BY TIPPERMUIR BOOKS:

Spanish Thermopylae (2009)
Battleground Perthshire (2009)
Perth: Street by Street (2012)
Born in Perthshire (2012)
In Spain with Orwell (2013)
Trust (2014)
Perth: As Others Saw Us (2014)
Love All (2015)
A Chocolate Soldier (2016)
The Early Photographers of Perthshire (2016)

FORTHCOMING:

The Fair Maid of Perth: the Perth Edition (2017)
Walking with Ghosts (2017)
Perth: Not So Fair a City (2017)

All titles are available from bookshops and online booksellers.
They can also be purchased directly at
www.tippermuirbooks.co.uk

Tippermuir Books Ltd. can be contacted at
tippermuirbooks@blueyonder.co.uk